Praise for Shirlee McCoy
and her novels

"Thrills abound in this compelling story."
—*RT Book Reviews* on *Die Before Nightfall*

"Shirlee McCoy's *Stranger in the Shadows*
is a sharp and intense mystery."
—*RT Book Reviews*

"With its dangerous edge,
The Protector's Promise is an
extremely suspenseful, touching story."
—*RT Book Reviews*

"Plenty of suspense, a fine mystery
and sympathetic main characters,
as well as intriguing secondary ones,
make this a page-turning read."
—*RT Book Review* on *Lone Defender*

SHIRLEE McCOY
Valley of Shadows

Stranger in the Shadows

Love Inspired

Recycling programs for this product may not exist in your area.

 LOVE INSPIRED BOOKS

ISBN-13: 978-0-373-65153-5

VALLEY OF SHADOWS AND STRANGER IN THE SHADOWS
Copyright © 2012 by Harlequin Books S.A.

The publisher acknowledges the copyright holder of the individual works as follows:

VALLEY OF SHADOWS
Copyright © 2007 by Shirlee McCoy

STRANGER IN THE SHADOWS
Copyright © 2007 by Shirlee McCoy

www.LoveInspiredBooks.com

Printed in U.S.A.

CONTENTS

Books by Shirlee McCoy

Love Inspired Suspense

Die Before Nightfall
Even in the Darkness
When Silence Falls
Little Girl Lost
Valley of Shadows
Stranger in the Shadows
Missing Persons
Lakeview Protector
*The Guardian's Mission
*The Protector's Promise
Cold Case Murder
*The Defender's Duty
†Running for Cover
Deadly Vows
†Running Scared
†Running Blind
Out of Time
†Lone Defender
†Private Eye Protector
The Lawman's Legacy
†Undercover Bodyguard

Love Inspired Single Title

Still Waters

*The Sinclair Brothers
†Heroes for Hire

SHIRLEE McCOY

has always loved making up stories. As a child, she day-dreamed elaborate tales in which she was the heroine—gutsy, strong and invincible. Though she soon grew out of her superhero fantasies, her love for storytelling never diminished. She knew early that she wanted to write inspirational fiction, and she began writing her first novel when she was a teenager. Still, it wasn't until her third son was born that she truly began pursuing her dream of being published. Three years later, she sold her first book. Now a busy mother of five, Shirlee is a homeschool mom by day and an inspirational author by night. She and her husband and children live in the Pacific Northwest and share their house with a dog, two cats and a bird. You can visit her website, www.shirleemccoy.com, or email her at shirlee@shirleemccoy.com.

VALLEY OF SHADOWS

This is what the Lord says: "Stand at the crossroads and look; ask for the ancient paths, ask where the good way is, and walk in it."
—*Jeremiah* 6:16

To Jude—musician, budding scientist,
young man of God. May the path God has set for
you be clear, may your faith be strong and may you
always know just how much I love you and just
how proud I am to be your mother.

To Jeannine Case. Piano teacher extraordinaire.
Thank you for all the years of hard work
and dedication you've given to your craft.
May every day, every moment be filled with joy
and every memory one to cherish.

To Ms. Dawn of Docksiders Gymnastics
in Millersville, Maryland, who gives children
wings and teaches them to fly.
What you do really does matter.

And to Melissa Endlich. Editor.
Cheerleader. Conference buddy. I promise
I'm not going to say one more word about redheads
or knights or even accountants! Maybe.

Chapter One

The warm September day had turned chilly with sunset, the brisk air heavy with approaching rain. Miranda Sheldon shivered as she stepped outside of her three-story town house, goose bumps rising on her bare arms as clammy coolness seeped through her cotton T-shirt. A jacket would have been a good idea, but she'd been in a hurry to escape the house. Grabbing one had been the last thing on her mind and, as much as she knew she'd probably regret it, she wouldn't return for one now. Not when her sister Lauren was there.

And not when memories filled every corner, sorrow every silent room.

Instead, she moved quickly, setting a rapid pace, hoping it would warm her as nothing else had in the past few days. People milled around her as she hurried down the busy Essex street. Many she recognized as patrons of the small bakery she owned. A few called out to her, some offering quiet condolences before moving on to whatever they'd planned for Friday night. Their words echoed in her ears, whispered through her head and lodged in her throat, nearly choking her with their potency. Comfort, sympathy. She wanted neither. What she wanted was to rewind the clock, to change the past, to make different choices that would lead to different outcomes.

But, of course, she couldn't do any of those things. All she could do was grieve and move on with a life that seemed empty and void.

Two blocks down and around a corner, the neighborhood grew quiet, the sounds of traffic and voices muted, the busy Maryland town hushed. Miranda hesitated at the top of a cul-de-sac, the darkness not able to hide the truth of where her walk had taken her. Not just any street. Not just any place. This was where she'd spent the better part of two days. A place where she'd greeted those who'd come to share her sorrow. A place that she'd be happy to walk away from and never see again.

Earlier, the lawn of the huge Greek revival had gleamed brilliant emerald in the sunlight. Now, it was a blanket of shifting shadows, the half-bare trees that lined the driveway skeletal. Light glowed from the lower level of the building, but the remainder of the house was dark, the tall windows eerie in the moonlight. At night, more than any other time, Green's Funeral Home looked like what it was—a place for the dead.

Miranda shivered, but moved forward anyway, knowing that she couldn't turn back now. She hadn't planned to come, but she was here and maybe it was for the best. If someone was still working at the funeral home, she might get a chance to say a final goodbye. A *private* goodbye. It was the last opportunity she'd have before the burial. She couldn't pass it up.

The foyer of the building was brightly lit and visible

through the panes of glass on either side of the door. Miranda knocked, then twisted the knob. It was locked as she'd expected, the funeral home empty. She should go home, finish the baking she was doing for the funeral and check over the list of things that had to be ready before tomorrow. That was the practical thing to do. But with her nephew Justin gone, practical didn't seem quite as important as it once had been. Nor did home seem the comfortable place she'd thought it to be. Maybe once Lauren returned to her work and travels, Miranda could return to the quiet life she'd built for herself.

Maybe, but she didn't think so. Her life had changed irrevocably—it would never be the same.

She clenched her jaw against a sob and stepped around the side of the building. The darkness was complete there, but the past two days had given Miranda plenty of time to become familiar with the grounds. Here, where the shadows were deepest, stone benches sat in shrub-lined alcoves. She sought one out and lowered herself onto it, ignoring the cold that seeped through her jeans. The night enfolded her, the muffled sounds of traffic a backdrop to her thoughts.

She rested her elbows on her knees and lowered her head into her hands, wanting to pray, but not sure what to pray for. Peace? Acceptance? Forgiveness? The words wouldn't form, her thoughts refusing to coalesce. How could she pray when she didn't know what to ask for? And how could she know what to ask for when she couldn't even begin to imagine tomorrow, let alone a week, month or year from now? She'd spent the past ten years planning her schedule around Justin. With him gone, the future stretched out in front of her, a blank slate—empty and more frightening than she wanted to admit.

Eventually, Miranda would find a way to let go of the past and move on to the future, find a way to build a life that didn't include her nephew's special needs and unique gifts. But not tonight. Tonight she'd do nothing at all. Not plan. Not think. Not worry about the empty years stretching out in front of her.

Minutes ticked by, the soft sounds of the night filling her ears, the sweet scent of grass and leaves tickling her nose. Her arms were chilled, her body shivering with cold, but she didn't want to leave her quiet refuge. Not yet. Instead, she sat in silence, listening to the melody of night creatures mixed with the soft hum of faraway traffic.

At first the low rumble blended with all the other sounds, the rough purr no different than those of the other cars and trucks that passed by. But soon it grew louder and the noisy intrusion drew Miranda's attention.

She cocked her head, listening. The sound seemed to come from behind the building, but there was no parking lot there, just a wide expanse of grass and a gently sloping yard that led to a far-off road. Grass crunched beneath tires, the quiet rumble of the engine becoming a low roar. Then there was silence so sudden and complete Miranda's breathing sounded harsh and loud in comparison. She forced herself to take a slow, deep breath, exhaling quietly as she waited to hear more. When the silence continued, she was sure she'd been mistaken, that a car hadn't been in the backyard at all, that what she'd heard had come from another direction altogether.

A door slammed, the sound so close Miranda

jumped, biting back a shriek and scrambling to her feet. Voices whispered into the darkness, the tones masculine, gruff and definitely coming from behind the building. Whatever was going on, it wasn't any of Miranda's business. The best thing she could do was head back to the front of the funeral home and leave. But something pulled her toward the back corner, some strange urging that wouldn't let her walk away. Her heart hammered against her ribs. Fast. Hard. Insistent. Telling her what she already knew—that she should be walking away from, not toward, the voices.

But it was too late. She could already make out the words, already hear what was being said.

"...crematory is a better idea."

"Takes too long. Cleaning crew will be here at midnight. We'll bring him out to the cemetery."

"It's closed. If someone sees us there and calls the cops—"

"You've got a funeral tomorrow morning, right?"

"Yeah, but—"

"So who's going to think anything of you being at the cemetery? No one. That's who. We'll just drop our friend in the newly dug grave, throw in some dirt. Tomorrow the casket goes in on top of him and, *voilà,* our problems are solved."

"I don't like it. Someone sees us out there messing around with a grave—"

"Who's going to see? The gate is locked. No one goes there after dark."

"Like I said, I don't like it. This whole business stinks like—"

"Yeah, so let's get a move on and get the key to the cemetery gate so we can get it over with."

"Fine. Sure. Get it over with. Stay here with Morran. I'll go in and get the key."

"You think I'm staying out here alone with him? No way. Now, come on. We don't have all night."

The men fell silent, their words hanging in the air, wrapping around Miranda and pulling her into something she was sure she didn't want to be part of. She needed to move away. Quietly, cautiously. Then, once she was safe, call the police.

But she couldn't. Not when she might be the only witness to a horrific crime. She crept toward the corner of the building, holding her breath, afraid the smallest sound would alert the men. Pale moonlight illuminated the backyard and an SUV parked there. Three men moved toward the funeral home, weaving a bit as they went, their shoulders pressed close together, their heads bent. They might have been college boys home from a night of partying but for the hostility that emanated from them.

And Miranda knew her fear was warranted. Knew something horrible was going on. Something violent. Something potentially deadly. Her breath hitched, her eyes straining to see more details, to take in every nuance of the picture. If she got out of this…*when* she got out of this, she wanted to have plenty to tell the police, but the rising moon shone behind the men, casting their faces into shadow. Whoever they were, whatever they planned remained hidden.

A key scraped against a lock and a door creaked open, dim light spilling out onto the faces of the men. Miranda blinked, biting back a gasp as she caught her first clear sight of them. Two she recognized. Liam Jefferson and Randy Simmons were regulars at Miranda's bakery. Both were well known in the community, one a police officer, the other the director of the funeral home. Miranda couldn't imagine either being involved in anything illegal. At least she wouldn't have been able to imagine it before tonight.

Now she had no doubt as to their true nature. Not when the third man stood between them, blindfolded, his mouth duct taped, his arms pulled tight behind his back. Was this the *friend* Liam and Randy planned to cover with dirt? She'd thought she was hearing details of a crime being hidden, a murder already committed. The truth was so much more horrible than that.

Or it would be if she didn't stop it.

No way could she run and leave the man to die. She'd wait until Liam and Randy went into the building, call the police, and then try to get close enough to read the license plate on the SUV.

As the men disappeared into the funeral home, Miranda dug through her purse, searching for her cell phone, her damp palm sliding over keys, a packet of tissue, a bottle of aspirin.

The phone wasn't there.

In her mind's eye she could see it, sitting on the kitchen counter, charging. Completely useless.

"Stupid. Stupid, stupid, stupid. Of all the nights to leave it at home." Her whispered words sounded harsh, her breath uneven. She'd write the license plate number down, then run to a neighboring house, pray someone was home and would let her use a phone.

The plan had barely formed when the door creaked open again. Randy stepped outside first, his gravely words carrying on the night air. "I don't know about this, Lee. It doesn't feel right."

Liam stepped out next, tugging the blindfolded man, then shoving him ahead a few steps while he turned to close the door. "It doesn't have to feel right. It just has to be done."

"But—"

"But nothing. Morran is scum. Getting rid of him will be doing the world a favor."

"And saving our behinds."

"Yeah, well that's the whole point, isn't it? Now get him in the car."

Randy seemed to stiffen at the harsh tone, but obeyed, reaching out for his prisoner's arm. He never had a chance to grab it. In a flash of movement the blindfolded man lashed out with a foot, knocking him to the ground.

Miranda gasped, jerked back, then froze as Liam swung toward her. His eyes probed the shadows where she stood, his gaze sweeping the corner of the building. She wanted to run, but knew any movement would have him swooping down on her. Her heart hammered double-time as she waited for discovery. But Liam turned away, stepping back toward the man who stood still as stone, giving no indication that he had moved. Miranda wanted to call out, to warn him, but thick, cottony fear trapped her words. Liam took a step closer and the man pivoted, slamming a foot into his stomach.

Now both Liam and Randy were down, but they wouldn't be for long. Already, they were struggling up. It wouldn't take much time for them to subdue their bound and blindfolded prisoner, to drag him away. To kill him.

Miranda glanced around, looking for help, for inspiration, for some way to undo what was being done. Her gaze lit on a large planter that sat near the wall of the funeral home. As weapons went, it wasn't much.

But it was all she had.

Praying for strength and for the element of surprise, Miranda moved toward it.

Chapter Two

Hawke Morran had no intention of dying. Not tonight anyway. He had payback to deliver and he wasn't heading to the great beyond until he did so. If he hadn't been gagged, he would have told his captors as much, but Jefferson hadn't taken chances. Not only was Hawke gagged and trussed, he was blindfolded. Unfortunately for Jefferson, he hadn't killed Hawke when he'd had the chance. It was a mistake he'd soon regret.

Hawke had managed to knock both men off their feet, but the rustle of movement and huff of their breathing told him they'd soon be back up. He stood still, waiting, knowing he might have only one chance to bring them down for good.

If he failed, he'd be buried alive.

He didn't plan to fail.

Rage fueled him, muting the pain that sliced through his skull, warming muscles already demanding a fight. Jefferson's overweight buddy attacked from the left, his wheezing breath speaking of too many cigarettes and too little exercise. Hawke turned toward him, ducking low and then coming up hard, slamming his head into the man's gut and hearing with satisfaction the crack of a rib.

Agony pierced his skull, the hit he'd taken earlier allowing him no time to celebrate his victory. Nor did Jefferson allow time for Hawke to regain his balance. He came fast and quiet, but not quietly enough. Hawke spun on the balls of his feet, slashing Jefferson's knee with his foot. The pop and scream of anguish that followed did little to satisfy Hawke's rage. He wanted more. He wanted his hands free, wanted to wrap them around Jefferson's neck until the man confessed every detail of the plan to set him up.

"Watch out!" A feminine voice cut through the haze of Hawke's pain and fury, the sound so surprising he swung toward it. It was a bad move. He knew it immediately. Years of survival in a world where one wrong move meant death had taught him how swift and final the consequences of such mistakes could be.

He pivoted back toward the attack he knew was coming, the world tilting, the pain in his skull breaking into shooting flames that seared his brain. Something flew by his face, a crack and thud following so quickly he wasn't sure he'd really heard them. Then silence. Thick. Heavy. Filled with a million possibilities. None of them good.

Footsteps rustled through grass, slow, cautious. Not the full-on attack Hawke expected. The air around him shifted, the scent of apples and cinnamon wafting toward him, mellow, sweet and completely unexpected.

He tensed, waited.

Fingers brushed his arm. Gentle, trembling, hesitant. "Are you okay?"

He nodded, gritting his teeth at the stars shooting through his head.

"Okay. Wait here. I'm going to find a phone. Call the police." The voice was breathless and shaky, the fingers that brushed against his forearm starting to slip away.

He managed to grab them, holding tight when she would have pulled away. Whoever she was, whatever she'd come here for, she'd gotten herself into a mess of trouble. Leaving and calling the police wouldn't change that.

"You want me to untie you first." It wasn't a question, but Hawke nodded anyway. He'd been determined to escape before. Now, he was desperate to. If he didn't, he wouldn't be the only one lying at the bottom of another man's grave.

The woman's fingers danced over the tape that bound his wrists, pulling gently as if she were afraid of hurting him.

Come on, lady. Hurry up. He wanted to shout the words, convey by his tone just how desperate their situation was, but the tape over his mouth kept him mute, and he was forced to stand silent while she worked. Sweat beaded his brow, the dizzying pain in his head making him nauseous, but he wouldn't give in to it. There was too much at stake.

Finally the tape loosened and he twisted his wrists, breaking through what was left of his bonds. The blindfold was next. Then the tape that covered his mouth.

He swung around, caught sight of the woman who'd freed him.

Soft. That was his first impression. Soft hair, soft full lips and soft eyes that widened as she took in his appearance. It was a reaction Hawke was used to and he ignored it, turning to search for his enemies. They were both on the ground. The heavier man lay in a heap, quiet groans issuing from between puffy lips. Jefferson was sprawled a few feet away from his buddy, a gun an arm's length away and bits of a clay pot scattered around him. "Looks like it's time to add flower pots to the list of deadly weapons."

"Deadly? I hope I didn't kill him." The woman's voice was as soft as her appearance, her hair swinging forward as she leaned toward Jefferson.

Hawke put a hand on her arm, stopping her before she could check for his pulse. "He's not dead."

But Hawke was tempted to finish him off. He might have if the woman hadn't been watching him with wide, frightened eyes, or if his own moral code hadn't altered drastically in the past year. An eye for an eye had once been his motto. Lately, that had changed. He hadn't quite figured out what it had changed to, but killing Jefferson was no longer an option.

Somewhere in the distance, a siren blared to life, the sound spurring Hawke's sluggish brain to action. "We need to get out of here."

He moved forward, grabbed the gun that lay by Jefferson, checked the safety. He could feel the woman's gaze, her fear and coiled tension.

"What are you doing?" she whispered, her voice shaky.

"Making sure we have protection."

"Protection? From what? Neither of them look like they're getting up anytime soon."

"It's not them I'm worried about."

"Then who?"

"I'll explain everything later. Right now, we need to get out of here."

"You're right. We need to call for help." She started away, moving toward the side of the building.

Hawke lunged forward, grabbing her arm. "Not yet."

She tried to pull back, but he didn't release his hold, just tugged her toward the SUV.

"Let me go." The panic in her voice might have made him hesitate if he weren't so sure hesitation would mean death.

"I can't."

"Sure you can." She jerked against his hold, her face a pale oval in the moonlight. "Just open your fingers and let me walk away."

"If you leave here without me there's a good possibility you won't live to see tomorrow. I don't want that on my conscience." He didn't give her a chance to argue, just pulled open the door of the SUV and glanced inside.

As he'd expected the keys were in the ignition. Another mistake Jefferson was going to regret making. "Get in."

"I'm not—"

"I said, *get in.*" He half lifted, half shoved her into the car.

"Hey! What are you doing?"

"Scoot over." Hawke ignored the woman's protest, sliding into the car and giving her no choice but to move into the passenger seat.

She scrambled for the door, and he snagged her shirt, holding her in place with one hand and firing up the engine with the other. Even with the windows closed, the sound of sirens was audible and growing louder. Hawke pressed down on the gas, gunning the engine and sending the SUV shooting up the slope of a hill toward a distant road. If he was lucky, he'd make it there and be able to hide the SUV in heavy Friday-night traffic. Unfortunately, he'd never had much luck. Maybe, though, for the sake of the woman who'd saved him, God might grant him his fair share tonight.

"Stop the car! Let me out!" The passenger door flew open, and Hawke just managed to grab the woman's hand before she could jump from the vehicle.

"Do you want to get yourself killed?" His roar froze her in place. Or maybe it was the sight of the ground speeding by that kept her from pulling from his hold and leaping out.

Hawke slowed the SUV, afraid his seatbelt-less passenger would fly out on the next bounce. "Close the door."

"I'd rather you stop the car so I can get out." Her voice shook and her hand trembled violently as she tugged against his hold, but there was no mistaking her determination.

She didn't know him, didn't know the situation and probably assumed the worst. If he'd had time to explain, he would have, but he didn't. Not with death following so close behind them.

He released her hand, pulled the gun from the waistband of his jeans and pointed it toward the already terrified woman, ruthlessly shoving aside every shred of compassion he felt for her. "I said, close the door."

She hesitated and he wondered if she'd take a chance and jump. Finally, she reached for the handle and pulled the door closed, her body tense and trembling.

"Where are you taking me?"

"Somewhere safe."

"Where exactly is that?"

"I'll let you know when I figure it out." Hawke winced as the SUV bumped over a curb, its tires sliding onto smooth pavement. Traffic was lighter than he'd expected, and he merged onto the road, picking up speed and hoping that would be enough to discourage his passenger from trying to jump out again. Being distracted didn't figure into his escape plan. Then again, escaping with a woman who looked like she belonged in a cozy home with a couple of kids playing at her feet wasn't part of his plan, either.

So he'd have to make a new plan. Fast.

But first, he needed to get to a safe place.

Miranda fisted her hand around her purse and tried to control her breathing. If she hyperventilated and passed out there'd be no chance of escape. The man beside her still held the gun pointed in her direction. Though his gaze was fixed on the road, Miranda was sure he was aware of every move she made. A few minutes ago he'd seemed a helpless victim who needed saving. Now she wasn't so sure.

Something flashed in the periphery of her vision, and she glanced in the side mirror, catching sight of blue and white lights in the distance. Hope made her heart leap and her pulse race.

Please let them be coming for us.

But even as she mumbled the prayer, her dark-haired kidnapper took the beltway ramp, speeding into traffic with barely a glance at oncoming vehicles. Miranda gasped, releasing her purse so that she could hold on to the seat. The lights had disappeared from view, but the car's speed and swift lane changes should attract more police attention.

If it didn't get Miranda and her kidnapper killed first.

As if he sensed her thoughts, the man eased up on the gas and pulled into the slow lane, dashing Miranda's hope of rescue. Tense with worry, sick with dread, she prayed desperately for some way out, her gaze scanning the cars that passed, her mind scrambling for a plan. Any plan.

"If you let me out here, I won't press charges."

"Charges?"

"Kidnapping is a serious crime."

"Kidnapping? Is that what you call this?"

"What would you call it?"

"Returning a favor. You saved my life. Now I'm doing the same for you." His voice was harsh, an exotic accent adding depth and richness to the words, but doing nothing to soften the tone.

"It's hard to believe that's what you're doing when you're pointing a gun at me."

"Sorry. It seemed the only way to keep you from doing something we'd both regret." He tucked the gun back into the waistband of his jeans, his movements economical and practiced, as if he'd done the same a thousand times before.

And somehow, looking at his chiseled face and the scar that bisected it from cheekbone to chin, Miranda had a feeling he had. She slid closer to the door, wishing they were in bumper-to-bumper traffic or that she dared jump out of a car traveling sixty miles an hour. But they weren't, she didn't. She was reduced to sitting terrified as she was driven farther and farther from home.

She eyed the man, the door, the traffic speeding by.

Maybe she could attract someone's attention with a gesture or an expression. Maybe—

"Whatever you're thinking, forget it." He wasn't even looking her way, yet seemed to sense her intentions.

She stiffened, turning to face him again. "I'm not thinking anything."

"Sure you are. You're thinking about opening the door and jumping for it. Or maybe attracting someone's attention." He shrugged. "It's what I'd do if I were in your position."

"And if I were in *your* position, I'd stop the car and let my prisoner out." She tried to put confidence in her voice, tried to sound less scared than she felt.

"You're not a prisoner."

"Then what am I?"

"The newest member of the witness protection program."

Miranda blinked, not sure she'd heard right. "Are you with the FBI?"

He hesitated and Miranda had the feeling he was trying to decide how much of the truth to tell her. When he finally answered, his tone was much more gentle than it had been before. "No, but I plan to be just as effective in keeping you safe."

"I don't need you to keep me safe. I need you to let me go."

"Then it would have been better if you'd walked away and left me to deal with Jefferson on my own."

"He was trying to kill you."

"And now he's going to try to kill us both." His tone was grim, his jaw tight, and Miranda had no doubt he believed what he was saying.

She just wasn't sure she did. "Why?"

"Because I'm a threat and because you were in the wrong place at the wrong time and were foolish enough to let him know it."

"What else was I suppose to do? Let him kill you?"

"Let whatever was to happen, happen."

"I couldn't."

"Then maybe you'll understand why I can't let you go." His tone was softer than Miranda would have expected from such a hard-looking man and she studied his profile, wishing she could read more in his face.

"Who are you?" The question popped out, though Miranda wasn't sure what answer she hoped for—a name, an occupation, some clue as to who she was dealing with.

"Hawke Morran." He answered the question without actually answering it. The name doing nothing to explain who Hawke was or why Liam had been trying to kill him.

"Who are you to Liam?"

"Liam? You know Jefferson?" The gentleness was gone, replaced by a harshness that made Miranda cringe.

"Everyone in Essex knows him."

"I'm not interested in everyone. I'm interested in you. You say you know him. Does *he* know *you?* Your name? Where you live?"

Did he? Miranda was sure he knew her name, and there was no doubt he knew where she worked, he visited the bakery several times a week. It would be easy enough to get her address. "Probably."

Hawke muttered something in a language Miranda didn't recognize, the words unintelligible, the frustration behind them obvious.

Her own frustration rose, joining the fear that

pounded frantically through her blood. She'd done what she thought was right. Now, she'd pay for it. That seemed to be a pattern in her life. "I own a business in Essex. Lots of people know me. Liam just happens to be one of them."

"He also just happens to be a murderer."

Miranda didn't need the reminder. She'd seen Liam in action; watched him pull a gun on a bound and blindfolded man, had seen the cold determination in his eyes as he'd caught sight of her. She had known then that she was seconds from death. "We need to go to the police and tell them what happened before Liam hurts someone else."

"No."

"What do you mean, no?"

"Exactly what I said. I've got a phony criminal record. The police won't believe anything I have to say. You're with me. It stands to reason they won't believe you, either." He glanced her way, his gaze searing into hers before he turned his attention back to the road.

"Why—"

"We'll discuss it all later." His tone was curt and dismissive, the kind that brooked no argument.

And Miranda didn't want to argue. She wanted to let things play out the way they would. Just as she had so many times before. With her sister. Her mother. Her father. Boyfriends. It always seemed so much easier to go with the flow than to fight against the tide. This time, though, the tide was dragging her out into dangerous waters and she had a feeling that if she didn't fight it she'd be pulled under. "Later isn't good enough. I want answers now."

He shrugged, but didn't speak as he steered the SUV onto an off-ramp.

The neighborhood he drove through was battered, the houses 1970s cookie cutters, every street lined with pickup trucks and scrap-metal cars. Miranda knew the area—a tough, crime-ridden neighborhood on the edge of D.C. When Hawke pulled into a driveway, she put her hand on the door, ready to yank it open and flee, but he grabbed her arm, his hand a steel band trapping her in place.

His breath fanned her cheek as he leaned close. "We're getting out my side, walking around to the back of the house, getting a new ride and you're not going to do anything foolish. Time isn't on our side and I don't want to waste any of it chasing after you. All right?"

The memory of the gun he'd tucked into his waistband spurred Miranda to do as he said, her heart pounding a sickening beat as Hawke tugged her across the front seat and out the door.

The moon shone bright and yellow in the navy sky and the crisp air chilled Miranda's clammy skin as Hawke hurried her around the side of a house.

An old garage stood at the back of the property and he punched numbers into a security pad on the door, then tugged Miranda to a dark sedan inside.

"Get in." His words were gruff, his hand gentle as he pressed it against her shoulder, urging her to do as he'd commanded.

The car door slammed with a finality that stilled the breath in Miranda's lungs. She shouldn't be allowing this. Crime prevention experts said it all the time— never get in a car with your attacker. Never let him take you away from the scene.

And here she was, doing exactly that.

But Hawke wasn't an attacker. He was a man who'd almost been killed. A man she'd saved. Now he claimed to be saving her. She wasn't sure if she believed him. All she knew was that eventually there'd be a chance to escape. She could only pray that when it came, she'd know for sure whether or not she should take it.

Chapter Three

Hawke's head throbbed with every movement, every sound reverberating through his brain. He ignored the pain, determined to put as much distance between his new ride and the SUV as possible. It wasn't just his life on the line this time. He had his passenger to worry about, as well.

Who was she? What had brought her to the funeral home so late at night? Not the hope of scoring drugs. Hawke was almost sure of that, though he'd been sure of things before and been proven wrong.

He risked a quick glance in her direction, gritting his teeth at the renewed throbbing in his head. The woman's arms were crossed at her waist, her eyes trained straight ahead. She looked scared, not high on drugs. "What's your name?"

His words must have startled her. She jerked, her arm brushing against his side, her breath leaving on a quick, raspy gasp. "Miranda. Sheldon."

"Miranda." The name rolled off his tongue as if he'd said it a thousand times before. "What were you doing at a funeral home so late at night?"

"I was taking a walk." There was more to it than that. Hawke was sure of it, though he couldn't blame her for denying him answers.

"And while you were walking you saved my life."

"Would you rather I had walked away and let you die?"

"Other people would have."

"I'm not other people. I'm me."

"And who is that, Miranda Sheldon? Besides a woman caught up in something she didn't ask for?"

"Just your everyday, average American." Her words were quiet, barely audible above the rumbling of the car and the slushing agony in his skull, but Hawke heard.

He glanced at Miranda again. The softness he'd noticed when he'd first seen her was only magnified in the close confines of the car. Smooth skin. Shiny hair that fell to her shoulders. Lips and face unadorned. Short unpainted nails. No rings. No jewelry of any kind. Apples. Cinnamon. A sweetness that was obvious even while she was afraid for her life. "There is nothing average or everyday about a woman who'd risk her own life for someone else."

She didn't respond and he knew he should be glad. He needed to plan his next move, not carry on a conversation. He rubbed the back of his neck, ignoring the blood that seeped from his head and coated his fingers. To formulate a plan he'd need more information and he knew just where to get it.

He yanked open the glove compartment and pulled out the cell phone he kept there, pushing speed dial to connect with the one number stored on it. The phone rang once before it was picked up.

"Stone, here." Noah Stone's voice was tight and

gruff, and Hawke knew that the call had been expected. A former DEA agent, Noah was one of the few people who knew Hawke was in the States and what he was doing there. Of those privy to Hawke's mission, Noah was the only one he trusted.

"It's Hawke."

"I thought you might be calling."

"So you've already heard?"

"That you murdered the agent you were working with and stole fifty thousand dollars cash? Who hasn't?"

"I didn't steal fifty thousand dollars."

"That leaves the question of murder open."

"Smithfield was dead when I got to the rendezvous." Lying in a pool of his own blood, his head split open.

"Murdered with a machete that had your fingerprints all over it."

"It should. It's mine. I left it in Thailand nine months ago." And yet it was here. He'd seen it with his own eyes—the flat blade and carved-bone handle worn from years of use in the jungles of Mae Hong Son. He'd been leaning down to examine it when he'd been hit from behind.

Which could only mean one thing. Someone in Thailand had set this up, had probably been planning it from the day the DEA had called Hawke in and offered him a job.

Hot anger speared through him, frustration making him want to hurl the phone out the car's window. He tightened his hand around it and growled into the phone. "Look, Stone, if you don't believe that I'm innocent we've got nothing more to say to each other."

"I'm on your side in this, Hawke, but I'm standing alone. Whoever set you up did it perfectly. The fingerprints on the weapon have every cop in the contiguous United States looking for you."

"What about the DEA?"

Noah's hesitation spoke volumes. The Drug Enforcement Agency might have hired Hawke to bring down one of the most notorious drug dealers on the East Coast, but they didn't trust him.

"So, they think I'm guilty."

"They're reserving judgment."

"Until?"

"Until they talk to you and your accomplice."

Hawke gritted his teeth, shot a look at Miranda. She was eyeing the phone as if a knight in shining armor might be on the other end of the line, ready to ride to her rescue. Unfortunately, Hawke was the only one riding anywhere and he was no knight. "Accomplice? You going to tell me who that is?"

"A woman. Apparently, the two of you have been seeing each other for several months. According to your coworkers at Green's factory, you spent more time with her than with anyone else."

"Green works fast."

"If he didn't, he would have been out of business and in jail years ago."

It was true. One of the East Coast's most successful drug traffickers, Harold Green was, by most people's accounts, an upstanding citizen of Essex, Maryland. A churchgoer, city council member and business owner, he hid his true nature beneath a facade of respectability. The DEA had hired Hawke to infiltrate Green's organization and to bring him down. He'd have succeeded if he hadn't been betrayed.

Fury threatened to take hold, but he tamped it down.

Losing control meant losing. And Hawke had no intention of doing that. "What else?"

"Word is, you were apprehended by a Maryland cop. Your accomplice took him by surprise, knocking him out, and you both escaped."

"Any news of a second man involved in that?"

"No. Just Liam Jefferson. Why? Was someone else there?"

"Yeah. The director of one of Green's funeral homes. Simmons. Randy."

"Do you think we should be looking for another body?"

"Yeah, but I don't think you'll find one. Green is nothing if not thorough. He won't leave any loose ends."

"Including you."

"Including me." Or Miranda, but Hawke didn't add the thought.

There was another moment of hesitation. "You know you need to turn yourself in."

"Do I?"

"What other option do you have?"

"I can get back home, find out who set me up and get the evidence I need to prove it."

"I take it you have an idea how this should be done?"

"You've got connections on both sides of the law. If I can make it down to your area, can you get me out of the country?"

"I've got some people that owe me favors. I'll call them in. See what I can do."

Hawke had hoped Noah would agree, but hadn't been certain. Relief loosened his grip on the phone, eased some of the pounding pain in his head. "How long will it take?"

"Give me an hour."

"Thanks."

"We're friends. I trust you. Just don't let your need for revenge keep you from doing what's right."

"You're telling me not to kill the person who set me up." A few years ago, he might have. Hawke had changed since then. Stone was part of the reason for that, though Hawke doubted he knew it.

"Taking the law into your hands won't solve anything, and it'll only make more trouble for you."

"This isn't just about me anymore, Stone." He glanced at Miranda, saw that she was watching with wide, dark eyes. "You've been pulled into it. So has the woman who's with me. I won't risk either of you for revenge. I give you my word on that."

"One hour, then." Noah disconnected and Hawke tossed the phone into Miranda's lap.

Now that he had the means to get her out of harms way, he'd make sure she had reason to cooperate. Flying halfway around the world with someone determined to escape was low on Hawke's lists of ways to keep from being noticed.

She stared down at the phone, but didn't reach for it, her hands fisted at her side, her jaw set.

"Is there someone you want to call? Someone who might be worried?"

"Yes."

"Then call." And if news was spreading as fast as Noah claimed, Miranda would hear just how much trouble she was in from someone she trusted.

Call? Miranda was sure Hawke would pull the phone from her hands as she lifted it, but he looked relaxed. Much more relaxed than he'd been before his phone call. He'd mentioned leaving the country. Maybe he planned to drop her off and let her return home. Miranda refused to contemplate anything else. She dialed, pressing the phone to her ear, her heart thrumming a frantic beat. Please, Lauren, pick up. For once be there for me.

"Hello?" Lauren's voice filled the line, high-pitched and breathless.

"Lauren, it's me. I—"

"Miranda! Thank goodness! Where are you?"

Miranda glanced at a road sign, almost gave her sister the exit number, but hesitated. There was an edge of hysteria in Lauren's voice, a breathless quality to it that didn't fit. It wasn't like her to be overly concerned with anyone but herself. That she was so upset could only mean bad news. "What's wrong, Lauren?"

"Wrong? You attack a police officer and you're asking me what's wrong?"

Miranda went cold at her words, her back rigid with mounting tension. "How did you hear about that?"

"How do you think I heard about it? The police are here. They don't take kindly to having one of their own knocked unconscious."

"I didn't have a choice. Liam—"

"Don't say anything else, sis." Her brother Max cut in, his voice such a welcome relief Miranda's eyes burned with threatening tears.

"Max. I thought your plane wasn't coming in until the morning."

"I took an earlier flight. It's a good thing I did. You're in a lot of trouble, kid."

"I didn't do anything wrong, Max. This is all some kind of misunderstanding. I—"

"We'll talk when you get home. The line is being

monitored by the police. I don't want you to say anything else until we're face to face."

"I don't have anything to hide." But her palms were sweaty, her breath hitching with fear.

"You need to come home, Randa. Max and I are here for you. We'll support you. No matter what. Max has found you a great lawyer. The best. I've already paid a retainer fee. It's the least I could do." Lauren's words caught on a sob. "After all, this is my fault. The past few years…all your time spent caring for Justin. I should have known you needed more than that."

"Your fault? What are you talking about? I went for a walk and—"

"Don't say anything." Max nearly shouted the words, his panic scaring Miranda more than all Lauren's sobs could. Older than her by fifteen years, Max had been more father than brother to Miranda, a calm steadying influence in a chaotic, unstable home.

"Tell me what's happening. Tell me what you think I did." Miranda's panic rose with Max's.

"*I* don't think you did anything. It's the police who are accusing you." Max bit out the words, his anger preferable to panic. "According to them, you've been dating a felon. The two of you plotted to steal fifty-thousand dollars from a DEA agent. The agent was found dead an hour ago."

Miranda's gaze leaped to Hawke. He'd said nothing about a murdered DEA agent. But then, he hadn't said much about anything.

"Miranda? Are you still there?" Max's words pulled her from her thoughts and she took a deep breath, trying to force a calm to her voice that she didn't feel.

"I'm here. I haven't been dating anyone, haven't stolen anything. I haven't done anything wrong. I've got plenty of friends who will verify that. All my time has been spent with Justin. You know that."

"It isn't about what I know or what I believe or even what you tell me is going on. It's about proof. And right now the police have witnesses willing to testify that they saw you and their suspect together on more than one occasion."

"What witnesses? What are you talking about?"

"Coworkers and friends. Add to that Sergeant Jefferson's testimony—"

Miranda stiffened, her muscles so taut she thought they might shatter. "About what?"

"About seeing you and the suspect together at your bakery."

"That's a lie!"

"Yeah? Well right now, it's his word against yours. He's a police officer and here. You're on the run with some guy who's got a record a mile long. Who do you think seems more believable?"

"Max—"

"Tell me where you are, Miranda. I'll come get you and we'll work things out. I promise." His tone was persuasive, the same one he'd used so often to try to convince Lauren to do the right thing. He'd never had to convince Miranda.

Even now, she wanted to respond, to tell him what he wanted to hear, but the words died on her tongue, her mind shouting a warning that she couldn't ignore. Liam had already told his side of the story. The police believed him, Miranda's family seemed to believe him and, as much as *she'd* like to believe that people would step forward to defend her, Miranda knew the truth was much more grim. Her friends knew too little about her life to say with any certainty how she spent her days. Taking care of Justin had required most of her time and energy. She'd had little of either left for friendship. If she returned home now, she'd be arrested.

Or worse.

And if that happened, Max would go after whoever had hurt her.

An image of Liam pointing a gun at Hawke flashed through her mind and she imagined Max on the other end of the barrel, imagined the loud crack of gunfire and her brother falling lifeless to the ground. She couldn't risk it, couldn't allow him to be pulled into danger with her.

"Miranda? Are you still there?"

"I'm here, but I can't come home yet, Max. Not until I can prove that I'm innocent."

"We'll find the proof together." The pain in his voice was palpable, stretching across the phone line and wrapping around her heart.

"I love you, Max. Thanks for being such a great big brother."

With that she hung up the phone, her pulse pounding, her mind racing, the truth of what she'd just done a hard, cold knot in her stomach. She'd cut her ties with home, turned her back on Max and put her life in the hands of a man she didn't know and wasn't sure she trusted. She could only pray she hadn't made a terrible mistake, because she was sure there would be no turning back. Only moving forward into the terrifying unknown.

Chapter Four

"Did the phone call not go the way you wanted?" Hawke broke into Miranda's thoughts, his voice gravely and harsh.

"You knew it wouldn't."

"I knew that it would give you a truth you might not have accepted from me."

"What truth? That I'm wanted for accessory to murder?"

"That returning home isn't the answer to your troubles."

"And staying with you is?"

"It's better than the alternative."

"Which is?"

"Your body rotting in a shallow grave somewhere."

"You act like it's a done deal."

"Walk away from me and it is. Stay with me and we'll find what we need to prove our innocence. Once Liam and Green are behind bars, you can safely return to your family."

What family?

As much as Miranda loved Max, he had a life completely separate from hers, his Chicago apartment too small to offer guest quarters, his accounting firm busy enough to make vacationing nearly impossible. Lauren was the opposite, traveling the world as a runway model and only stopping to visit Justin when she couldn't put it off any longer. Or that's what she'd done before. Now that her son was gone, Lauren would probably never return to Maryland. Which meant Miranda would be returning to an empty house, a business and memories.

She shoved the thought aside, forcing back the sorrow that came with it. "How long will it take?"

"I don't know."

"I need to be home tomorrow." For Justin's funeral. She didn't add the last, knowing the words would mean nothing to the cold-eyed man beside her.

"Sorry, babe. That's not going to happen."

She'd known it, but she'd hoped anyway, the small part of herself that refused to believe that things were as bad as they seemed telling her that everything would be okay in the morning. A few more hours of darkness and she'd wake from the nightmare. Wasn't that what she'd told herself when she'd been a kid, the darkness pressing in around her, filled with monsters? "Then what? A few days? A week? I've got a business to run. I can't be away from it for long."

"Will your business matter if you're dead?"

There was nothing to say to that, so she remained silent, turning away from Hawke and staring out the car window.

Outside, life continued as always, people traveling home from restaurants, friends and parties, making plans for the next day as they ended this one. A week ago, Miranda had been doing the same, leaving home on Friday evening to attend a bridal shower on the eastern shore. With Lauren committed to caring for Justin until the following night, Miranda had imagined hours spent window shopping, sampling pastries from local bakeries, enjoying the simple pleasure of no responsibility for the first time in way too many months.

And in one moment of senseless tragedy it had all changed.

Even if she made it home in one piece, life would never be what it had once been. Hot tears filled Miranda's eyes, but she forced them away. Crying couldn't bring her nephew back. Nor would it change her situation. Only God could do that, and she wasn't sure He would. Watching Justin die while she prayed for him to be healed had been the hardest thing she'd ever done. In the dark hours after his death, she'd wondered if God heard her frantic pleading or if He even cared. Now, she wanted desperately to grasp her tattered faith, to believe that He would work everything out for the best.

"You're crying." The gritty texture of Hawke's voice matched the rough callus on the finger he swept down her cheek.

Her skin heated in the wake of his touch and she brushed her hand down the same path his finger had traced, wiping away tears she hadn't realized she was shedding. "No, I'm not."

"I suppose the moisture on your cheeks is nothing."

"A few tears on my cheeks doesn't mean I'm crying."

"No? Then what does it mean?"

"That I'm releasing some pent-up emotion."

Hawke chuckled, a deep rumble that was a soothing

balm against her frazzled nerves. "You're an interesting lady, Miranda."

Interesting? *Quiet, sweet, helpful,* those were the words most often used to describe her. Never interesting.

Before she had a chance to respond, Hawke's cell phone rang and he lifted it to his ear.

"What's up?" The words were his only greeting, his scowl deepening as the caller spoke. "What time? We'll be there." He dropped the phone onto the console, pulled the car onto a side road, then another and another until Miranda wasn't sure where they were or which direction they were headed. Finally, he pulled into the parking lot of a convenience store and turned to face her.

"We've got a decision to make."

"We?" He acted as if they were a team, working together toward a common goal. And maybe they were, but it didn't feel that way. Not when Hawke knew so much more about what was going on than she did. And not when he seemed so determined to keep it that way.

"We." He winced, putting a hand up to the back of his head and bringing it down again, something shiny and moist staining his fingers.

"You're bleeding." Miranda reached out, wanting to help, but Hawke's quick, hard glance froze her in place.

"I'll live." His hand fisted around the steering wheel, his knuckles white. "We have more important things to worry about. We've got six hours to make it to Lakeview, Virginia. Do you know it?"

"No."

He nodded. "We'll map it out in a minute. My friend will have transportation waiting for us there. If we're late, we may not have a second chance."

"A second chance at what?"

"Someone set me up, Miranda. Planned everything that happened tonight to make me look guilty of a crime I didn't commit. Do you believe that?"

"I don't know what I believe."

"You're honest, at least."

"And you haven't answered my question. What won't we have a second chance at?"

"Getting out of the state. Out of the country."

"Out of the country?" She tried out the words, found them bitter on her tongue. "No."

"If we stay here, we'll be caught. I've got few friends that I can turn to. No one that I'm willing to drag into this mess. My home is in Thailand. The DEA recruited me there. They hired me to come to the States and bring down a drug trafficker named Green."

"Harold Green?" He owned several businesses in Essex. A moving company, a local grocery store. The funeral home.

"Right. He's been importing drugs from Thailand for years, selling them, then laundering the money through his businesses. The DEA knows it, but finding the proof to close him down and put him away has been difficult."

"So they sent you to do it for them?"

"I was sent in deep under cover. The only people who know I'm working the case are in Thailand. Their hope is that once they pull Green in, he'll give them the names of his overseas contacts. I think someone in Thailand doesn't want that to happen. Someone working for the DEA. I plan to find out who it is. It's the only way to clear my name. And yours."

"The DEA here…"

"Thinks I murdered one of their agents."

"But—"

"Babe, we're out of time. It takes five hours to get to Lakeview. Before we get there I need to know you're with me on this."

Was she? Miranda wasn't sure she trusted her own judgement in the matter. The stakes were too high. She was too scared. "Do I have a choice?"

"I haven't decided yet." He grimaced, his jaw tight. "You saved my life. I don't want to leave you here to die because of it."

There was truth in his words, in the grim determination in his eyes as they met hers. And despite herself, despite her doubt, Miranda knew she had to go with him. If there was a way out of this, it lay in the direction Hawke was going. That, at least, she felt sure of. "I guess I'm with you on it, then."

Hawke smiled, the expression softening his face, changing it from danger to safety, from ice to warmth. "That's what I was hoping you'd say."

"So, now what?"

"Now, we head for Lakeview." He turned toward the backseat, swayed, then slumped toward Miranda, his weight pushing her back toward the door and stealing her breath.

"Hawke? Hawke!" She pushed at his chest, her heart pounding. She slid her hand up to his neck, feeling for his pulse and finding the slick warmth of blood there.

"Hawke!" She shouted in his ear, desperate for a response.

This time he groaned, shifting slightly, his chin brushing against her cheek, razor stubble scratching at her skin. She shivered, pushing at him again and finally managing to maneuver him into his seat. His head slumped forward and she could see blood pooling in the hollow of his throat.

Miranda brushed a hand against his forehead and cheek, feeling for a fever the same way she had so many times when Justin was sick. But Hawke wasn't a boy, he was a man, and he wasn't sick, he was hurt.

And Miranda had no idea how to help him.

Yes, you do. You've taken first-aid classes. You know what to do. Stop panicking and think. Check respiration and pulse. Find the wound. Stop the bleeding. Get him to a doctor.

A doctor! That's exactly what they needed. She could call 911, get an ambulance to take Hawke to the hospital while she spoke to the police and told them Hawke's story and her own. The plan seemed reasonable, good even. Except for a few small things—Hawke was wanted for murder, she was wanted as an accessory and at least one person wanted them both dead.

Miranda frowned and leaned over the seat, searching for something to staunch the flow of blood that seemed to be coming from the back of Hawke's head. She found a backpack on the floor, a map on the seat. She grabbed both, opening the first and pulling out packets of dried food, a bottle of water, a T-shirt and hat. At the bottom of the bag, she found a small plastic container. She opened it quickly, her hands shaking with adrenaline and fear. Gauze, bandages, needle, thread, several white pills packed in plastic bags, antiseptic wipes, an EpiPen—Hawke had prepared for minor medical emergencies. The only problem was, Miranda wasn't sure minor was what she was dealing with.

She pulled out the gauze, then shifted Hawke's head to the side, trying to find the wound. Her

fingers probed the flesh behind his ear, wound
through silky strands of hair. At the back of his
head, close to the base of his skull, a hard lump
oozed warm, sticky blood. She pressed the gauze
to it, wincing in sympathy, though he seemed completely unaware of her ministrations. That couldn't
be good.

"Hawke?" He didn't answer, and Miranda shook his
shoulder, praying for some reaction.

His eyes remained closed, his head a leaden weight
against her hand.

"Now what?" She whispered the question out loud,
her mind scrambling for a plan, her eyes scanning the
interior of the car. Hawke's cell phone lay on the console between them, and she grabbed it. Maybe she
could find the number of the person they were supposed to meet in Virginia.

She scrolled through the options, searching for an
outgoing call log, praying that she'd find what she was
looking for.

"What are you doing?" The words were a harsh
growl, the hand that wrapped around her wrist just
short of painful.

She gasped, her heart skipping a beat as she met
Hawke's cold gaze. "Trying to decide if I should call
for help."

He stared at her, his gaze never wavering as he
straightened in his seat, slid his free hand over the
gauze Miranda still held, and nudged her hand away
from it. "It wouldn't have been a good idea."

His tone matched his gaze—icy and unyielding,
and Miranda knew he wasn't a man who would take
betrayal lightly; that he'd demand his own justice for
any wrong done to him. She swallowed back her fear,

tugging at the fingers still wrapped around her wrist. "You were unconscious and unresponsive. You need a doctor."

"I need to catch our ride. I need to find the man who betrayed me. I do *not* need a doctor." Hawke tried to add emphasis to his words, but they came out weaker than he intended. The fact was, he probably did need a doctor, but he didn't have time for one. *They* didn't have time for one.

"You're bleeding pretty badly." Miranda leaned in close, the scent of apples and cinnamon enveloping him.

No woman had a right to smell that good.

And Hawke had no business noticing.

Unless he missed his guess, Miranda was one of those rare people who remained untarnished by the world. He, on the other hand, was more tarnished than most.

He scowled, frustrated as much by the direction of his thoughts as he was by his physical weakness. "Bleeding is a whole lot better than being dead. Which is exactly what we'd both be if you'd been foolish enough to call an ambulance."

At his harsh words, Miranda jerked back, her face pale in the dim light, her dark hair a mass of curls around her face. Hawke knew enough about fear to recognize it in her eyes. Guilt at putting it there made him want to wrap an arm around her shoulders and reassure her that everything was going to be okay.

Instead, he kept the gauze pressed to his head with one hand and grabbed the road map with the other. "Our six hours are ticking away while we sit here arguing. Put your seat belt back on and let's go."

The fear he'd seen in Miranda's eyes disappeared, replaced by stony resolve. "I may not be able to make you see a doctor, but I'm not going to let you drive. Not when you could pass out again."

She had a point, even if Hawke didn't want to admit it. His head throbbed with each heartbeat and sudden movements made him dizzy. Losing consciousness again was a real possibility no matter how hard he might fight against it. Passing out while driving could get them both killed. Then again, giving Miranda control of the car might do the same. It would be easy enough for her to drive to a police station and turn them both in. "I've driven under worse conditions."

"And tonight you don't have to. I don't see a problem. Unless you don't trust me." She was issuing a challenge, but Hawke wasn't in the mood to meet it.

"I don't trust anyone."

"That makes two of us." She opened the car door, got out. "So, I guess we'll just have to figure out how to accomplish our goals anyway."

Hawke figured he had a few options—tell her to get out and go it alone, or pull out the gun and demand she get back into the passenger seat or let her have her way.

The first appealed only in as much as he could convince himself he didn't care if Miranda lived or died. Which wasn't much. The second might have worked, but imagining the fear and horror on her face when he pointed the gun at her made Hawke hesitate, a strange and alarming development in an already frustrating night.

"I don't like losing." He ground the words out, but Miranda just smiled.

"I guess that's another thing we have in common."

With that, she shut the door and started around the side of the car, leaving Hawke wondering how a woman who didn't look capable of hurting a fly had bested him.

Chapter Five

Miranda's heart slammed in her chest as she rounded the car, Hawke's words echoing in her head. The anger on his face told her just how much he didn't like losing. Yet, here she was heading around the side of the car with every intention of doing things her way. What was she thinking? He had a gun for crying out loud.

But if he planned on using it, he already would have.

Maybe she should make a break for it, run into the convenience store and ask for help. She doubted Hawke would try to stop her. Unfortunately, the same instincts that told Miranda that Hawke wouldn't hurt her, told her that she was better off with him than without. She needed answers before she could return home. Without them, she risked putting her brother and sister in harm's way—and staying with Hawke seemed the only sure way to get those answers.

She pulled open the car door, saw that Hawke had moved into the passenger seat, and did her best to act confident and unperturbed. "Where to?"

"I'll mark the route on the map. Then we'll drive straight there. No stops for anything. We've already

lost enough time. We can't afford to waste any more."
He met her gaze, his expression unreadable, his anger
concealed as he opened the glove compartment and
pulled out a pack of highlighters.

"All right. Let's do it."

It took less than a minute for Hawke to highlight a
yellow path from their location to a small town near a
lake. When he finished, he highlighted a second route
in blue. "The yellow route is the quickest. The blue
uses the most back roads. We'll try yellow first. If
there's too much police traffic, we'll switch to blue."

"Okay." Miranda's hands were moist against the
steering wheel, the reality of what she was about to do
pulsing through her veins. Until now, she'd felt more
like a victim than an active participant in Hawke's
escape, but she could no longer deny the role she was
taking. Running from the police, aiding an accused
killer.

If they were caught...

"You're doing this because you have to, Miranda
Sheldon." Hawke's voice broke into her thoughts; his
words offering assurance before she'd even voiced her
doubts.

"Do I?" She whispered the question, not expecting
an answer.

"If you don't, we'll both die."

"That's a worse-case scenario."

"If you really believed that, you would have run into
the store and called for help instead of getting back into
the car with me."

"I need answers so that I can go home. It's the only
way to make sure my family is safe."

"You'll get the answers you need. *We'll* get them.
And once we do, you'll have no worries about those

you love." He rubbed at the back of his head, his hand coming away bloody again.

"You need to keep applying pressure to that."

"I *need* to get to Lakeview."

Miranda took the hint and started the engine, pulling out of the parking lot, following Hawke's directions back to the highway. It was late, traffic sparse, what few cars there were passing in flashes of light. Miranda should have been lulled by the darkness that stretched out before them, by the quiet hum of the car engine and by Hawke's silence.

Instead, she felt wired, her body trembling with adrenaline, everything in her begging for action. Finally, she could stand the quiet no longer. "What exactly is going to happen when we get to Lakeview? Are we taking another car? A train? A plane?"

"It would be difficult to take a train or car to Thailand." His words were so matter-of-fact they almost didn't register.

When they did, Miranda cast a quick glance in Hawke's direction, saw that he was watching her with a dark, intense gaze.

"You don't mean Thailand as in the country?"

"Do you know of another Thailand?"

"No, but I'm hoping there is one, because there is no way in the world I can go to Southeast Asia."

"Sure you can. Everything is taken care of. We'll have a passport and paperwork waiting for you."

"That's great, but I won't be needing them. I can't go. When you said out of the country I was thinking Mexico or Canada, not halfway around the world." Miranda's hands were shaking on the wheel.

"I told you that the person who betrayed me to

Green has to be in Thailand. No one here knew who I was or what I was doing."

"There must be people in Thailand who can investigate."

"I also told you, I don't trust anyone."

"You go, then. I'll stay in Lakeview."

"And what? The police know who you are. They've already issued an APB. It's only a matter of time before they find you."

"I thought…" She shook her head, knowing that she *hadn't* thought. If she had, she would have known exactly what Hawke meant when he talked about leaving the country.

"What did you think?" His words were quiet, his tone more kind than Miranda expected.

"Nothing. I guess I just hoped this would all be over by tomorrow."

"There's no way that's going to happen, babe. We've got real trouble and real trouble takes time to resolve." There was sympathy in his voice, the first he'd shown her, and Miranda's throat tightened in response.

She swallowed back tears and tried to keep her voice even. "My nephew's funeral is tomorrow. I need to be there. My sister is counting on it."

"I'm sorry for your loss. Sorry you can't be there for your sister." He shifted beside her, his palm sliding against her cheek, capturing a tear she hadn't known was falling. "But allowing yourself to get arrested will only cause your family more sorrow."

"I know." She refused to let more tears fall, refused to allow herself to lean into Hawke's touch. He was a stranger, after all. A stranger who had more hardness in him than sympathy.

"Is your nephew the reason you were at the funeral home tonight?"

"It seems silly now." She stared out the windshield, the dark night and nearly empty road stretching out before her.

"Why?"

"It's not like Justin needed me there. I just…didn't want to let him go."

"You were close?"

"I've raised him since he was two." He'd been a son to her, though saying as much would have made her feel disloyal to her sister.

"His parents are dead?"

"No. I'm not sure who his father was. My sister is a model. She traveled too much to be his caregiver."

"Your sister is a model?" He tensed, and Miranda felt her own muscles tighten.

"Yes. Why?"

"Someone the general public is familiar with?"

"She's not a supermodel, if that's what you mean, but she's been on her fair share of magazine covers. She also does runway modeling."

"So, not only do the police know who you are, but the world knows your sister. This isn't good, babe."

"The world knows Lauren, but they don't know I'm her sister." Lauren had never allowed the press any information regarding her son. In that way at least, she'd done what was best for Justin.

"It won't take long for the press to find out. Once it does, your name and face will be plastered on every news station and newspaper in the country."

"Maybe the local news, but I doubt what's happened will be of much interest anywhere else." But even as she said it, Miranda had the sinking feeling Hawke was right, that the double tragedy of losing a son and then having a sister turn felon would be enough to make Lauren headline news.

"I think you know you're wrong."

Miranda nodded, wishing she could believe otherwise. "At least Lauren doesn't have any recent pictures of me."

"Someone else will. The press always finds a way."

"They'll be hard-pressed to find anything that doesn't show me thirty pounds heavier and ten years younger." In the years since she'd been caring for Justin, Miranda had had little time to spend in activities that might have involved picture taking. Except for the occasional bridal or baby shower, the past few years had been spent at her bakery, at home or at church.

"Heavier. Younger. It won't matter. Your face is one people will notice and remember."

"I'm not that memorable."

"No?"

"No." Miranda could feel Hawke's gaze as she maneuvered the car around a slow-moving vehicle, and her cheeks heated.

"Perhaps you just don't know what people find memorable."

"And you do?"

"I've made it my business to know people." The words seemed almost a threat and Miranda wondered exactly how he used the knowledge he possessed.

"That makes one of us anyway."

"You know enough about people to stick with me. That's a start."

"I just hope I'm not making a mistake." The words slipped out and Miranda regretted them immediately. Letting Hawke know how scared she really was, letting him see how unsure she felt, could only be a mistake. And she'd made enough of those for one night. "What I mean is—"

"Exactly what you said. Don't worry, sticking with me isn't a mistake. Whether or not you'll regret it, I can't say." He spoke quietly, all gruffness gone from his voice. In its smooth timbre Miranda heard echoes of exotic worlds, hard realities and a loneliness she understood all too well.

"Hawke—" She wasn't sure what she meant to say, how she planned to finish. Before she had a chance to figure it out, the high-pitched shriek of sirens rent the air.

She jumped, her hands tightening on the steering wheel, her gaze flying to the rearview mirror. Lights flashed in the distance, brilliant against the darkness and coming fast.

"The police. They've found us." Her voice shook, her foot pressing on the gas pedal in a knee-jerk reaction that sent the car lunging forward.

"Ease up, babe. Speeding will just call attention to us." Hawke rested a hand on her shoulder, his palm warm through her T-shirt.

"Call attention to us? They're right on our tail." And getting closer every minute.

"No. They're not. They're on the way somewhere else. We just happen to be between them and where they're heading."

"You can't know that."

"No, I can't. But this car's not registered in my name. There's no way they can know I'm in it. All we have to do is slow down and pull out of their way."

"But—"

"Babe, my neck is at stake here, too. Pull over and

get out of the way before they start wondering why we're speeding ahead of them." His words were calm, but there was underlying tension to them. Not fear. Something else. Frustration. Worry. Anger.

She nodded, easing her foot off the pedal, forcing herself to pull to the shoulder as the police cars sped toward them. The sirens crested to a screaming frenzy, lights flashing their dire warning. Every muscle in Miranda's body tensed, her mind shouting that she should get out and run while she had the chance.

If Hawke was wrong, if...

In a wild, shrieking chorus, three police cruisers sped by, their lights illuminating the car, then leaving it in darkness once again. Silence settled over the night, the hushed chug of the engine a quiet backdrop to the racing beat of Miranda's heart. She knew she should pull back onto the highway, get the car moving again, but she was shaking so hard she wasn't sure she could manage it.

"They're gone now. You're safe." Hawke's voice was a whispered breath against her ear, his fingers stroking down her arm and capturing her hand, his palm warm against her clammy skin. His touch much too comforting for her peace of mind. "Everything is all right."

"No, it isn't." She took a deep breath, tugged her hand from his and pressed down on the accelerator. "I'm with a man I don't know, driving hundreds of miles from home so that I can catch a ride to a country halfway around the world. The police think I'm a murderer. Some drug dealer I've never had any contact with wants me dead. My nephew..." She shook her head, stopped herself before her sorrow could take wing. "It's *not* all right."

Hawke figured it would be better not to argue the

point. Mostly because Miranda was right. While they might be all right for now, there was no telling how long that would last. "No, but we're safe for the time being. That's something to be thankful for."

She shrugged, taking one hand off the steering wheel and rubbing at the base of her neck, the bicep in her arm firm beneath pale, silky skin. Hawke resisted the urge to brush her hand away and feel the strong line of her neck under his palm, the softness of her hair against his knuckles. That would be a mistake. One he couldn't afford to make.

"Telling me we're safe for the time being doesn't make me feel safe at all."

"Then what will?"

"Waking up to find this is all a nightmare." Her voice shook, the hollows beneath her eyes darkly shadowed. For the second time that evening and probably only the second time in a decade, Hawke felt the hard edge of guilt nudging at him, telling him he'd gotten an innocent woman into the kind of danger she might not survive.

"If I could make that happen for you, I would. But I can't."

"Then I guess I'll just have to keep driving and pray we both manage to make it through this alive."

"You may want to keep me off that request, babe. God might be more willing to answer."

She glanced in his direction, the curiosity in her eyes unmistakable, but she didn't ask what he meant. Maybe she already knew. "God doesn't play favorites. He'll watch out for us equally."

"Maybe." Hawke's head was pounding too hard for him to engage in philosophical debate. Besides, while religion wasn't his thing, he'd experienced enough of life to believe there was something more to it than what could be seen; that a power greater than his own will and strength existed. What he had yet to decide was whether or not that equated to a loving God who took a personal interest in His creations.

"Sometimes I have a hard time understanding it all. How He works. Why He answers some prayers with a yes, others with a no, but I guess what it boils down to is faith. Just believing that no matter what happens, He's there." Miranda spoke so softly Hawke barely heard the quiet words that seemed more for herself than for him.

This time he gave into temptation and slid his hand under the thick weight of her hair, his palm resting on the silky skin at the nape of her neck. "Someone like you never need worry that God won't be there."

She glanced his way, her eyes shadowed. "Like I said, neither does someone like you."

She didn't seem to expect a response and Hawke didn't give one. Instead, he let the silence of the night and the darkness beyond the windows envelop them.

Chapter Six

Home. The word danced through Miranda's mind as the first glimmer of dawn streaked the horizon. She'd wound her way through the Blue Ridge mountains, stopping only once to get gas with a credit card Hawke fished from his glove compartment. The name on it was unfamiliar and, according to Hawke, untraceable. Miranda supposed she should have found comfort in that, but the longer the night had stretched on, the more the idea of returning home appealed.

Last night, she'd been desperate to escape the empty house and Lauren. Now, she'd give anything to step into the bright yellow kitchen, listen to her sister's footsteps on the tile.

And she could.

Hawke's eyes were closed, the gun peeking out from beneath the T-shirt he wore. All it would take was one quick yank and it would be in her hands. She could use Hawke's cell phone to call the police. Then wait somewhere until they arrived. If she could have imagined a good outcome, she might have attempted it, but all she could picture was a cold jail cell and a quick brutal death.

"What are you thinking?" Hawke broke into her thoughts and Miranda jerked, hoping guilt wasn't written all over her face.

"That I want to go home."

"To your sister and brother?"

"They don't live with me."

"Then what is home to you? A house? A community?"

"Justin. But he's no longer there, so I guess my job. My routine. My life the way it was before."

"Before last night?"

"Before Justin died."

He nodded. "I think many people have times they'd like to go back to."

"Even you?"

"Even me." He didn't seem inclined to elaborate and Miranda told herself she should let the subject drop. After all, this wasn't a casual conversation between friends or an intimate discussion with a man she was dating. Hawke was a stranger, a man she didn't know and wasn't sure she trusted.

She stole a quick glance at his profile—the hard line of his jaw, the scar that bisected his cheek—and couldn't keep herself from asking the questions she knew she shouldn't. "What times do you wish you could go back to?"

His mouth curved in a half smile and he shrugged. "Right now, I'll just settle for getting back to Thailand."

"Do you have family there?"

"A brother. I haven't seen him in almost a year."

"You must be happy that you'll be seeing him soon, then."

"I won't be happy until I know he's safe."

"Do you think he's not?"

"He should be, but what should be isn't always what is. The fact that you're here with me is a perfect example of that. You should be home safe. Instead, you're running for your life." He paused, reached for the pack that sat in the backseat and rifled through it, pulling out a bottle of aspirin.

"Still have a headache?"

"If you can call a sledgehammer in your skull that, yeah." He swallowed three pills dry and recapped the bottle. "But I'll live. That's our exit. We're looking for a church outside of town."

The switch in topic was so sudden Miranda almost missed it *and* her turn. She swerved toward the exit just in time, taking the off-ramp too quickly. The car fishtailed, sliding toward the shoulder as Miranda gripped the steering wheel and tried to remember what she'd heard about reacting to a spin. Should she slam on the breaks? Jerk the steering wheel toward the spin? Away from it?

Her sleep-deprived brain couldn't hold on to a thought long enough to react and she was sure whatever she did would be wrong.

Hawke's shoulder pressed into hers, his hands clamping over Miranda's, his stubble-covered jaw rubbing against hers. "You're okay. It's okay."

The car straightened and Miranda let out the breath she hadn't realized she'd been holding. Her hands were slick on the wheel, her pulse pounding, her body shaking so hard she was sure Hawke could feel the vibration of her fear.

"No, it's not okay. *I'm* not okay." She whispered the words, not meaning for Hawke to respond, but he did, his hand cupping her shoulder, his touch warm and more comforting than it should have been.

"It will be okay and you will be, too. I promise."

"Promises are a dime a dozen." She'd heard them all before—from her mother, her father, her sister. From every man she'd ever dated. And she'd believed them all until, one after another, they'd been broken.

"Not mine. I never make a promise I don't intend to keep." The gruff assurance in his voice held a dark edge, but his hand remained gentle, his fingers brushing against the exposed skin near the neckline of Miranda's shirt, their warmth easing her shivers of fear.

For a moment, she allowed herself to believe his words, to accept his comforting touch. Only the knowledge that she'd done so before with people she'd known better and trusted more, kept her from leaning into his touch, accepting his assurance.

"'He means well' is useless unless he does well." She muttered the dark reminder, the words acid on her tongue.

"Plautus."

She glanced his way, surprised. "That's right."

"Here is one for you, then—'He who promises more than he is able to perform is false to himself; and he who does not perform what he has promised, is a traitor to his friend.'"

"George Shelley. But we're not friends."

"We will be. Besides, I am never false to myself. If I didn't believe I could get you home safely, I would take a chance and leave you here with my friend and his family."

"You could leave me here anyway."

"It would be too dangerous. For you and for them. Noah's wife is expecting a baby soon. His mind is on other things. Being distracted from a mission is the first step to death."

"Another quote?"

"Yeah. From Hawke Morran's guide to survival."

"You know a lot about survival?"

"I know *everything* about survival. If I didn't, I'd have been dead a hundred times over." His hand slipped from her shoulder and Miranda shivered— whether from the cool air that slid across her skin or from his words, she didn't know.

"It sounds like you live a dangerous life."

"Did you think otherwise?" His tone was clipped and he leaned forward, staring out into the hazy morning light, his tension filling the car, seeping into Miranda's already taut nerves.

She clenched her jaw against the tremors that raced through her and tried to keep her voice calm. "What's wrong?"

"It's quiet."

"It's six in the morning. It's supposed to be quiet."

"Not like this. Something is off."

Miranda liked the sound of that about as much as she liked trusting a man she didn't know. "What?"

"Maybe a trap. Maybe just me being overcautious. Pull over."

"What? Where?" The road was narrow, too narrow to stop the car safely even if she pulled as far over as she could.

"The cornfield. Drive into it and stop the car."

"But—"

"Are we destined to waste all our time arguing, Miranda? Or can you, just this once, do things my way without a fight?"

"I don't argue and I'm not a fighter." To prove her point, Miranda did as he suggested, the bumping thump of the car as she pulled deep into the field making her wish she'd stuck to her guns and stayed the course. She shut off the engine and turned to face Hawke, the sudden silence eerie. "There. Happy now?"

"Not yet. Let's wait a while."

"If we wait too long, we'll miss our ride."

"If we walk into a trap, we won't need a ride and all the planning my friend has done will be wasted."

"The best laid plans—"

"—of mice and men. Enough quotes. Listen to me." He leaned in, placing a hand on each of Miranda's shoulders, staring into her eyes with such grim determination she was sure she wasn't going to like what he had to say. "The church is close. Maybe three miles. We're to meet my friend there in less than an hour. I'm going to jog in. Make sure it's safe. If it is, we'll be back for you by seven-thirty. If we aren't, cut through the cornfield until you find another road. Then get out of town."

"And go where?"

"Somewhere no one can find you."

"No way. There isn't a place like that. Besides, you can't run three miles with that head injury."

"Watch me." Before Miranda could even react, Hawke opened the door and stepped out of the car.

"Wait!" She scrambled across the car seat, panic giving her wings, and grabbed his hand. "I'll come with you."

"You ever run three miles before?"

"Maybe. In high school."

"And that was how long ago? Six years? Seven?"

"Twelve. But that doesn't mean I can't do it now." The coolness of the morning wrapped around her, the corn stalks whispering secrets to the sky, to the earth, to anyone who cared to hear—life and death written into the soil that fed them and singing into the air with every swaying movement. If someone came while Hawke was gone, Miranda's blood could be spilled onto the earth as easily as Abel's had thousands of years ago, seeping into the ground and feeding the plants with only God as witness to what had happened.

She shuddered and straightened her spine, doing her best to look strong, invincible and completely unafraid.

Hawke wasn't buying it. She could see it in the half smile that softened the grim lines of his face. "Sorry, babe, but I'd have to disagree. You're not made for running."

"I'm made for whatever I put my mind to."

"That I *can* agree with, but I've got to move fast. You won't be able to keep up. Stay here. It's safer for both of us."

He took a step away, tugging at her hold on his hand. She refused to release her grip, afraid of what might happen if he disappeared and didn't come back. "I can keep up."

"You're afraid, but you don't have to be. I told you I'd make sure you were all right." He spoke quietly, moving in close, pulling her forward until her head rested against his chest. She could hear the solid beat of his heart, the quiet inhalations of each breath and, despite the warnings that screamed through her, she let her arms slip around his waist, let herself cling to the comfort he offered.

"That's going to be hard for you to do if you aren't around."

"Weren't you saying last night that God doesn't play favorites? That He'll look after us both?"

"Yes, but—"

"So believe it and stop being afraid."

She nodded her head, tried to pull back and look up into Hawke's face, but his arms tightened around her as if he were as reluctant to leave as she was to let him go. He ran a hand over her hair, smoothing the curly wayward strands Miranda knew must be tangled and knotted. "Okay now?"

She nodded again, and he released his hold, stepping away, his eyes storm-cloud gray, his expression grim. "Good. Now, get back in the car. I've got to hurry."

Miranda was about to do as Hawke suggested when the sound of an engine broke the morning silence. Her heart skipped a beat, and she grabbed for Hawke's hand again. "Someone's coming."

"We're not the only people awake this morning. There are plenty of reasons someone might be on the road." Hawke didn't sound nearly as convinced as Miranda would have liked him to be, and he turned toward the road, his free hand dropping to the gun that peeked out from under his T-shirt.

Whoever it was, whatever the vehicle, it was close now, roaring along the quiet road just out of sight. Then, as suddenly as it had started the sound ceased, the sudden silence deafening.

Miranda's breath caught in her throat, her heart slamming so hard she thought it would burst from her chest.

Hawke turned his head, met her gaze, mouthing a command for her to hide.

She nodded, but couldn't bring herself to leave. Hawke was armed, but injured. There was no way she planned to hide while he fought off their faceless enemy, no matter how scared she was.

Leaves crackled and something scuffled just out of sight. Miranda jumped, nearly falling backward as a dark figure stepped into view.

The gun was in Hawke's hand so quickly, Miranda didn't even see him move. She gasped, backing up then moving closer. Not sure if she wanted to tell him to stop, or encourage him to shoot.

"I wouldn't come any closer." He growled the words, the menace in them unmistakable and enough to stop the approaching figure.

"I guess I've found the right party." If the speaker was surprised by the gun or worried by it he didn't let it show.

"Not by a long shot, so why don't you go back the way you came and forget you ever saw us?" Hawke took a step forward and Miranda shadowed him, squinting to see the person they were approaching.

"Because a friend asked for my help and I agreed to give it. He's counting on me. So are you, I think." He took a step closer and Miranda could make out shaggy light brown hair and even features. He didn't look intimidating, though she was sure that didn't mean much.

"Stay where you are and tell me your story. Fast."

"I'm a friend of Noah's. His pastor, actually. He couldn't make it to meet you, so he sent me."

"Couldn't make it?"

"He was waylaid by some unhappy federal agents. I've been driving up and down this road for an hour, hoping I'd catch you before you made it to the church. Lakeview is crawling with agents and state cops. They haven't made it as far as Grace Christian, but it's just a matter of time before they do. Better that we meet here. If they find you at the church, they'll know Noah sent you there. I don't think either of us want that."

"I'd rather not be found at all." Hawke lowered the gun, locking the safety again. He didn't sense danger from the man standing before him and he trusted his instincts much more than he trusted a stranger's words.

"Then we'd better get you out of town fast."

"Just like that you agree to help a suspected felon?" Despite his gut instinct about the man, Hawke wasn't sure he was buying the story.

"Just like that I agreed to help a friend help a friend."

"Why?"

"Because Noah is a man of strong convictions. I trust him. When his wife called me from her veterinary clinic and explained what was going on, I knew I had to help. I'm Ben Avery, by the way." He held out a hand, completely ignoring the gun Hawke still held.

"A pastor."

"Yes."

"You look military to me." Hawke could spot one a mile away and this guy reeked special forces, his stance relaxed, but alert, his balance ready for a quick shift to attack if need be.

"*Was* military. That was a long time ago."

The fact that he admitted it said something about the man. People lied when they had something to hide. The truth was a luxury reserved for the innocent. He nodded, slid the gun out of sight. "Okay. What's the plan?"

"Noah wanted to have a pilot friend fly you out to California, but the feds are nosing around everyone he knows and we can't risk it. I've called in a favor. A missionary brush pilot who retired a few years back. He's got a plane and a license and can fly you out west. There will be someone waiting at the airport with your passports and identification."

Hawke shook his head, fingering the scar that bisected his cheek. "Passports and identification or not, this'll be hard to hide from airport security."

"Not with the right tools." Ben smiled. "Disguise is something I know a little about. Stay here. I'll get my stuff."

Hawke grabbed Ben's arm as he turned away, felt hard muscles beneath flannel. The guy might be ex-military, but he was still trained and ready to fight.

"If you double-cross me...." He let the words trail off, let the threat hang in the air.

"I've got nothing to gain from it and everything to lose. I've made a life in Lakeview. A good one. I'm not going to risk it by alerting the feds to the fact that I'm aiding a felon. Now, let's get this done. You've got to be at an airstrip outside of Charlottesville in three hours. From there you head to California as honeymooners." He shot a glance in Miranda's direction and shrugged. "It was the easiest cover we could come up with. Now, are we ready to go?"

Hawke hesitated. Trust or not? It's what everything in his life eventually boiled down to. He stared into Ben's eyes, trying to find truth or falsehood there. All he saw was compassion and the strange knowledge he'd often seen in Noah Stone's eyes, a knowledge that seemed a reflection of much more than human understanding and that seemed to beg Hawke to believe in things he'd refused for much too long.

He dropped Ben's arm and stepped back. "Go get

what you need and let's get moving before someone else finds us here."

Ben smiled, the tension in his jaw and shoulders the only hint of what he was feeling, then stepped back into the shadows, disappearing as quickly as he had come and leaving Hawke with the strange feeling that things were about to change. That his life perspective was about to be challenged, that what he'd always believed might not be the truth and that what he'd sensed so many times and ignored had hooked its claws into him and was not about to let go. Good or bad. Righteous or evil. Something was tugging at his soul and Hawke wondered just how long he'd be able to ignore.

A while longer, anyway. He had a mission to fulfill. Deep thinking and soul-searching would have to wait until he completed it.

He turned to Miranda, grabbing her hand, squeezing gently. Her skin was milk-white in the morning light, the freckles on her nose and cheeks standing out in stark contrast. He'd thought her hair brown, but now he could see hints of fiery red and butterscotch yellow in its depth. Dark circles shadowed her eyes, giving her a fragile, wounded appearance. The fierce need to protect her reared up, taking Hawke by surprise. She'd saved his life and Hawke believed in repaying what was owed. Emotional involvement had never played into it before. He couldn't let it now, either. Doing so could only distract him from his goal.

"Is he telling the truth?" She whispered the words, her gaze fixed on the spot where Ben had disappeared.

"Probably."

"Probably? I don't think I like the way that sounds."

"I don't like it, either, but it's all we've got right now."

Miranda opened her mouth to respond, but crackling grass and breaking cornstalks announced Ben's return, the purposeful warning designed to keep Hawke from pulling his gun again. Obviously, the man was savvy about survival. What remained to be seen was whether or not he was as trustworthy as he claimed. Only time would tell that.

Unfortunately, Hawke and Miranda didn't have much of it left. Danger was breathing down Hawke's neck. He could feel it. If they didn't get out of Lakeview soon, they wouldn't get out at all.

And that just wasn't an option.

Hand on his gun, Hawke strode toward the approaching man.

Chapter Seven

Forty hours of flying was enough to convince Miranda that staying in one place for a lifetime wasn't entirely a bad thing. Gritty-eyed from hours of fitful sleep, skin layered with grime, she stared out the window of the 747 as the ground rose up to meet it. With a bump and thump of protest, the plane landed, the landscape speeding by in a dizzying array of colors. In a matter of minutes, she and Hawke would depart from the relative safety of the plane. Just the thought made her heart race and her breath hitch.

"Relax, sweetheart." Hawke's arm slipped around her shoulder, his lips pressing into her hair. "We've been looking forward to this trip for months. You should be excited, not terrified."

The words were a subtle warning and Miranda tried to respond, pushing back strands of stick-straight hair and smiling.

"I *am* excited." And not nearly as good an actor as Hawke. Her words sounded phony, her smile felt forced. She'd have to do better if they were going to make it out of the airport without calling attention to themselves.

"Me, too." Hawke's hand smoothed over her arm, his gaze as warm and loving as any newlywed's should be. "Two weeks alone together is exactly what we need after so many months of wedding preparations. I've missed spending time with you."

His words were meant to carry and they did. The elderly woman seated next to him sighed, smiling at Miranda. "You're a very fortunate young woman to have a such a romantic husband."

Miranda tried to return the smile, praying she'd be as convincing as Hawke had been during the long flight. "I know I am."

She leaned her head against his shoulder, felt the taut muscles and coiled strength beneath the jacket he wore. Brown contacts had turned his smoky eyes dark, and a plasticky substance disguised his scar. With his hair down, his cheeks were less prominent, his face less granite and more smooth-planed. He looked model-handsome, clean-cut and nothing like the hardened criminal he could have passed for when they'd first met. Perfect husband material. Just like he was supposed to be.

Miranda's appearance had changed, too. Her curly hair was covered by a black wig that looked so natural she was sure it was made of real hair, her lips tinged with red, her freckles covered with makeup and her cheekbones hollowed with blush. She looked older, more worldly; the kind of woman who'd marry the kind of man Hawke looked to be.

It was no wonder the elderly woman believed their story.

She just hoped the people at customs would. Unlike

the other airports they'd passed through, this one was sure to have been alerted to Hawke and Miranda's possible arrival. It wouldn't take much to give them away.

Passengers rose to grab bags and belongings, and Hawke squeezed Miranda's shoulder as if he could offer her the confidence she lacked. "This is it. Ready for the adventure?" There was warmth and humor in his voice, but his eyes flashed with impatience. No doubt he was anxious to get on with things.

Miranda, on the other hand, was not. She nodded anyway, praying that God would get them through this airport the same way He had the others they'd been through—quick, easy, no hassle. "Of course. Let's do it."

Hawke's half smile eased some of the impatience from his eyes, but Miranda still had the impression of banked fires, ready to burst to life if given the opportunity. He grabbed her hand, pulling her into the aisle behind him, the elderly woman chatting with him as they exited the plane.

It all seemed so normal, Miranda could almost believe she and Hawke were no longer in danger. Almost.

Somehow she managed to say goodbye to the older woman, exchanging a brief hug and well-wishes. Then she followed Hawke into the airport, watched as he collected the suitcase filled with clothes that Ben's friend had provided, allowed herself to be tugged toward customs. All around her the building teemed with life, bursting at the seams and ready to embrace all who came. Smiles. Everywhere. Dark eyes, dark hair, white teeth flashing in tanned faces. Hawke's home and a world away from anything Miranda had ever experienced.

In other circumstances she might have enjoyed

the newness, but now she could only feel terror and a deep-seated emptiness, her heart heavy with what she'd lost and what she might still lose. To never see Lauren again, never see Max, her friends, her church, seemed a distinct possibility. She had the sudden urge to confess all to the first English-speaking authority she met, to beg for help. Someone, somewhere should be able to convince the DEA that she and Hawke were innocent.

As if he sensed her thoughts, Hawke released his grip on her hand and wound his arm around her waist, tugging her close to his side. His leather jacket was cool against her cheek, the scent of earth and sun clinging to it despite the hours they'd spent on airplanes and in airports. "Now's not the time to panic, babe. We're almost home free. There will be people watching for us and they're trained to notice body language. Try to relax and look like you're enjoying yourself."

"I've never been much of an actress." All the drama and acting ability had been passed from her mother to her sister, leaving Miranda with an even-keeled temperament and little ability to fake emotions she didn't feel. Or hide those she did.

"You better learn quick, then, because we're about a hundred yards from an agent."

"Where?" Miranda's heart nearly leaped from her chest, and she stumbled, with only Hawke's strong hold keeping her from falling flat on her face.

"Standing on the other side of customs. Leaning against the wall. Don't even think about looking for him. You've got eyes only for me. We're newlyweds, remember?" His voice was a soft caress as his hand came up to cup her cheek, his eyes staring into hers as if she were the most beautiful woman he'd ever seen.

If she hadn't known the truth of their situation, if she'd been simply an observer watching as she and Hawke approached customs, she'd be convinced that the man beside her was completely besotted.

She nodded, trying desperately to get into character. Unfortunately, every man she'd ever cared about had been a liar, a cheat or both, and the only emotion she could dredge up was fear. "Do you think he's noticed us?"

"Not yet, but if you keep looking like a deer in the headlights it'll only be a matter of time before he does."

"I told you I'm not a good actress."

"Then I guess I'll have to compensate." Before she knew what he'd planned, Hawke whirled her into his arms and kissed her. The contact was brief, a quick press of his lips to hers. Something that should have been nothing, but felt like much more. Electricity. Chemistry. All the things she would have wanted if they were a real couple on a real honeymoon.

Her cheeks heated and she had to resist the urge to press her fingers to her lips.

Hawke seemed unfazed by the contact, his arm wrapping around her waist once again, his focus on the customs official who was waving them forward. "Hand me your passport, babe."

She pulled it from her purse, trying to still the fine tremors that raced through her, trying to calm the wild racing of her heart.

Hawke handed the man both passports, smiling down at Miranda as the documents were checked and stamped.

"Do you have anything to claim?" The official's words were deeply accented, his eyes dark brown and blank—he asked the question a thousand times a day and probably expected nothing out of the ordinary.

"No." Hawke's own accent had slipped away, replaced by a Texas drawl that made Miranda wince. Obviously, he had no formal training in voice disguise, but the customs official didn't seem bothered by it. He stamped the passports, waving Hawke and Miranda through and turning his attention to the next person in line.

One down. One more to go.

Miranda was sure she felt eyes spearing into her as she and Hawke sauntered away. The tension in Hawke's arm told her he felt it, too, and she met his gaze, saw the warning there.

Please, God, don't let us get stopped now.

The prayer chanted through her mind, her feet moving by rote, one plodding step at a time. Her body felt disconnected from the fear that thrummed along her nerves. Shouldn't adrenaline be pumping through her, adding a burst of energy to her flagging reserves? She was sure it should, but there was nothing. Not even a little oomph to help her move more quickly.

"You okay, darlin'?" Hawke spoke loudly, his drawl attracting attention from half a dozen people.

"Just tired." She hoped that was the response he was looking for.

"You sure? 'Cause you're lookin' a little green around the gills. If you need to use the little girl's room it's right down this hall." If the situation hadn't been so serious, the implications of his words so frightening, Miranda might have laughed at his suddenly overdone acting.

As it was, she was sure she was turning the greenish hue he'd mentioned, fear pulsing through her as she realized what Hawke must be trying to tell her—they'd been spotted. "I *am* feeling a little queasy. You know what a bad traveler I am."

"You'll feel better once we get settled in." He steered her toward a corridor as he spoke, his hand hard against her waist. "Looks like the restroom is right down this hall. Come on."

He pulled her into a narrow corridor marked with restroom and pay-phone signs, led her a few steps into the dimly lit hall, then dropped his hold on their suitcase, his arm slipping from her waist, his hand claiming hers. "Run!"

Before she could catch her breath, think things through, decide what Hawke's plan was, they were racing down the hall toward what looked like an emergency exit, slamming into it, forcing it open. A high-pitched shriek split the air, the sound of screams and footfall echoing into the corridor. Chaos followed them into bright sunlight and buzzing traffic, honking horns and thick, humid air. Miranda could barely breathe, whether from fear or from the moisture hanging so heavy around her, she didn't know. Her heart slammed in time with her pounding feet, her breath gasping from searing lungs.

And they ran on, past startled street vendors and waving taxi drivers, turning one corner after another, moving from affluence to squalor, from suits to rags, running on and on until Miranda was sure her heart would burst with the effort.

She stumbled, her foot catching on cracked pavement, and skidded onto her knees, pain slicing through her as Hawke yanked her back upright, barely breaking his stride.

"Come on, babe. You said you could run three miles.

Prove it." He growled the words, his grip on her hand painfully tight.

"I didn't think I'd have to do it at this fast a pace." She panted the words out, her anger at Hawke and at her weakness, at the situation making her grit her teeth and move faster.

"We do what we have to do to survive." He yanked her down a dank alley, slowing his pace from a dead run to a jog. Still, Miranda couldn't catch her breath, couldn't get her heartbeat to slow. Of all the ways to die, this would be the last she'd ever imagine for herself—collapsing from heart failure in a back alley in Southeast Asia.

Things slithered and scurried in the dark shadows, the sounds carrying above Miranda's gasps and the pounding of shoes against pavement. Snakes, rats, huge spiders, Miranda imagined any and all lurking just out of sight. None were quite as bad as what she imagined might be coming behind her. Men. With guns. Men who wanted her dead.

The thought alone was enough to keep her going.

Finally, Hawke stopped, glancing behind and ahead before approaching a run-down apartment building. "This is it."

"Home?"

"Of a sort."

"You don't think the DEA will be waiting for you here?"

"They don't know about it. Come on. We can get supplies and call for a ride." He tugged her up crumbling cement steps and into the dark lobby of the building. The water-stained red carpet must have once been lush and thick, but now looked dingy and old, the mildewy scent that emanated from it thick enough to make Miranda's eyes water.

She coughed, her empty stomach rebelling, her vision swimming, the dim light fading.

"Hey, you okay?" Hawke's hands rested on her shoulders, holding her steady, his eyes staring into hers, anchoring her even more than his firm grip.

"Fine."

He didn't move, his gaze searching hers as if he might find another answer within the depth of her eyes.

The intensity of his stare lodged in Miranda's stomach and she pulled away from his hands. In the two days they'd spent traveling, she'd learned little about her companion, their conversations limited by the public nature of their transportation. She'd wondered, though, who he was, what had made him decide to take the job the DEA had offered, whether or not he was telling her the whole truth about what was going on. In the end, she'd found no answers, only a still-quiet voice that told her Hawke was her best hope for survival.

She fidgeted under his stare, brushing at the faded denim of her jeans and tugging at one long, dark lock of her phony hair. "Aren't we going to your place?"

"Only if you can make it up four flights of stairs."

"I've made it this far. I can make it a little farther."

"Good." He started up, and Miranda followed behind, the scuffed wood railing and paint-peeling walls closing in on her as she hurried up one flight after another. At any moment she expected to hear sounds of pursuit, a door slamming open, footfall, gunshots. But besides her own gasping breath and the pad of her shoes and Hawke's, the building seemed empty.

By the time they reached the fourth-floor landing, she was ready to collapse, her wobbly knees and shaking legs making her wish she'd kept up the exercise program she'd started at the beginning of the year. Next year she'd do better. If she survived that long.

Hawke grabbed her hand, pulling her to a stop. "Wait here. I'm going to check things out."

"What things?" Miranda's heart skipped a beat at the look in his eyes. "You think someone is waiting for us?"

"If I did, we wouldn't be here, but I'm still going to check." Hawke could tell by the look on Miranda's face that she didn't like the idea of waiting around while he did recon, but he planned to do it anyway. Anything else would be a foolish risk. He'd come too far to get caught now.

She shifted from foot to foot, the dark wig she wore framing a face that was gaunt with fear and fatigue. Despite that, despite her obvious stress, her skin was flawless, her cheeks pink with exertion. Her lips…

He stopped the thought cold. Kissing her in the airport had seemed a good idea. Until he'd done it. Now he was doing his best to forget the touch of her lips against his. Thinking about the softness of her mouth was *not* the way to do that.

"Stay here." There was more force to his words than necessary, anger at what he'd done making his voice harsh.

If she noticed, Miranda didn't seem to care. Her hand fisted around his wrist. "We can go together."

"And risk getting caught together? You stay here. I'll come back for you if it's clear."

"And if you don't?"

"Then you need to find your way to Mae Hong Son." It's where his home was, the only place he ever felt truly safe. If she made it there, his team would take care of her. *If.* Miranda knew nothing about Thailand, nothing about who she could trust and who she couldn't. Without him, she'd be lost.

So, he'd just have make sure she didn't have to be without him.

Her compassion for a stranger had gotten her into this mess. His determination would get her out of it.

He hoped.

Hawke grimaced, raking his hair back from his forehead. The pounding pain in his head had faded hours ago; the dull ache that replaced it was more tolerable. Adrenaline hummed through his veins, stealing exhaustion. Here on his home turf, he knew the rules, knew how to play the game. All he had to do was stay one step ahead of his enemies. And that's exactly what he planned to do.

"Do what I say and stay here." He threw the words over his shoulder as he pushed open the door that led to the fourth-floor hallway. There were apartments on either side of the long, narrow space. All had been abandoned years ago, their doors yawning open into debris-littered rooms. Even here in one of the more derelict sections of Bangkok, money could be made from renting out the space. Hawke had no desire to do so. The occupied apartments on the lower levels were for those who had no other place to go. Women mostly. Though a few men were there, as well. Displaced, homeless, but all with families who depended on them. Hawke had given them a place to stay. In return, they kept an eye on the property. If there'd been trouble here, one of the occupants would have posted a lookout and warned him before he arrived. Still, it didn't pay to take chances and he approached the one closed door on the floor with caution, his fingers itching to wrap around the gun he'd had to leave in the States.

The door was locked just as he he'd left it nine months ago. He used his key, shoving the door open with one hand, his body pressed close to the wall. No barrage of bullets followed, no whisper of sound or pinprick of warning along his nerves. He waited anyway, his body still as death, everything inside him straining for out-of-place sounds, shifting shadows. Five minutes passed. Then seven. When nothing moved, he went in low, his gaze scanning the room. No furniture. No closets. Nowhere for someone to hide. Just the way he'd planned it.

He moved around a corner and into the empty kitchen and found no sign that his safe house had been discovered. He hadn't expected it to be. He'd told no one about the place. Not his brother and not any of his men. Betrayal could come from the most trusted ally. Even family. He'd learned that lesson too late to save his parents and sister. It was one he would never forget.

He shook aside thoughts of the past, refusing to allow distraction. One moment of hesitation, one second of inattention could cost a man his life. Another well-learned lesson. One he'd been lucky to survive.

Lucky?

The question whispered through his mind as it had so many times since the day six years ago when Noah Stone had saved his life. The jungles of Mae Hong Son weren't a place where men ran into each other. Yet somehow Noah had found Hawke lying nearly dead in the summer overgrowth.

The past again. It seemed to haunt him these last few days. Perhaps it was Miranda, her quiet resolve and obvious normality reminding Hawke of all he'd lost. Or perhaps it was his own need for something more than the life he'd made that had him dwelling on the times better forgotten. Whatever the case, he couldn't afford the distraction.

He grabbed the doorknob to the only bedroom in the apartment. Locked. Just as he'd left it. He used a second key to unlock the door. He pulled it open, his gaze dropping. A thin white thread stretched across the doorway a foot above the floor.

Hawke smiled, relaxing for the first time in days.

Unlike the rest of the apartment, this room was furnished with a bed, a desk, a computer, a dresser and a chair. To the left, a door opened into the apartment's only bathroom. To the right, a closed door concealed the supplies Hawke needed. He moved quickly, unlocking the closet door and the metal safe within it, pulling out the gun and ammo he kept there, a handful of cash and coins and a cell phone. He'd call Simon, make sure his younger brother was staying out of trouble, then call one of his men to arrange transportation.

He pushed speed dial, pulling on a shoulder harness while the phone rang. "Come on, Si, pick up." Hawke muttered the words as he strode back across the room, a sense of urgency feeding his steps. Miranda was waiting. Hopefully in exactly the place he'd left her.

The phone continued to ring, no answering machine and no answer, until Hawke finally hung up. There was something wrong. Really wrong.

A sound carried on the still air, a whisper of movement just out of sight. Hawke eased up against the wall, the gun in his hand a familiar friend, adrenaline coursing through him as it had so often in the past ten years.

This was his life. What he had become. What it seemed he would always be. A man one mistake away from death.

Another sound followed the first, a brush of fabric against the wall or the soft sigh of someone's breath. Hawke stayed put, letting the intruder come to him, listening to the air, feeling the slight disturbance of another's presence even before he saw the dark shape rounding the corner.

And then he didn't wait any longer. He lunged.

Chapter Eight

Miranda would have screamed if she'd had time, but she didn't. One minute she was creeping through a seemingly empty apartment, the next she was tackled, a full-body collision that would have sent her sprawling if a hand hadn't clamped around her waist, yanking her upright.

"Are you crazy?" Hawke's shout penetrated her terror and Miranda's legs went weak with relief.

"You didn't come back. I thought you'd passed out." Or been injured. Or worse.

"I told you to stay where you were." Hawke's eyes blazed with fury, a muscle in his jaw twitching.

"You didn't tell me how long to wait." Her own anger reared up. "If you had, I wouldn't have had to come looking."

"You could have gotten yourself *killed*." He released his hold on her waist, waved a gun near her face. "This isn't a toy. We're not playing a game. Mistakes like you just made cost lives. Do you understand?"

Miranda's eyes were riveted to the gun, her throat so tight she couldn't speak. She nodded instead, the movement jerky. Death had never been something to fear, though now, in the face of what might have happened, Miranda desperately wanted to avoid it.

"Good, because I didn't come into this mission planning to lose you. From now on you stay where I leave you. I can't spend the next few days worrying that every noise I hear might be you. Hesitation kills. I can't afford to hesitate." His voice softened as he spoke, the muscles in his jaw relaxing.

He traced a line down her jaw, lifting her chin and peering into her eyes. "Come sit down on the bed. You look like you're about to keel over."

Miranda didn't argue as he urged her down onto a soft comforter. Her legs were weak, her mind empty. "I'm sorry. I guess I wasn't thinking."

"Sure you were. You were thinking about me. Next time, think about yourself." He shoved the gun into the holster he now wore, pulled his hair back at the nape of his neck, grabbed clothes from a dresser and a backpack from a closet, his movements methodical and easy, as if he'd performed them a thousand times before.

"Are we going somewhere?"

"*I'm* going somewhere. You're staying here until I get back."

"I don't think I like that idea."

"Babe, there hasn't been an idea of mine yet that you have." He shot her a crooked grin, pulled a cell phone from his pocket. "I'm going to call my brother and arrange a ride for us. Then I've got some business to attend to in Bangkok. The safest place for you is here."

Miranda wanted to argue, but doing so would only be a waste of time. The sooner Hawke left and came back, the sooner they could find the person who'd set him up and Miranda could return home. "All right."

He cocked an eyebrow, leaned a shoulder against the wall and watched Miranda through dark eyes. "All right? Will it be that simple this time?"

"I'm too tired to do anymore running."

He straightened, crossed the room, his hand brushing over the wig Miranda still wore and coming to rest on the back of her neck, the warmth of it spreading through her and making her feel safer than she had in hours. "It's been a long few days, but this will all be over soon."

"It's been a long week and I'm not sure it will ever be over."

"It'll be over. What remains to be seen is how it will end." His hand slipped away and he punched a button on the phone, raised it to his ear, his gaze never leaving Miranda.

Her cheeks heated, her heart doing a strange dance that had nothing at all to do with fear. She rose, pacing across the room and away from Hawke's too-intense stare.

"Something is wrong." He growled the words and Miranda jumped turning to face him.

"What?"

"My brother isn't answering."

"Maybe he's at work and can't pick up."

"He works for our export company. He can do just about whatever he wants. They've got him. I'm sure of it." He slammed the phone down onto the dresser, muttering under his breath as he yanked out more clothes and thrust them into the backpack.

"Maybe—"

"There is no maybe, babe. My brother's cell phone

is always with him and always on. The phone I used is one I keep for emergencies. There's no way he wouldn't pick up when he saw the number on his caller ID."

"Who would take him? Green is still in the States."

"And the people he works with are here. So is the person who set me up. They think that by taking my brother they'll get me, but all they've done is sign their death certificates."

Miranda winced at the force of his words, at the violence she saw in his eyes. She'd known he could be a dangerous man, but had pushed the knowledge to the back of her mind, trying her best to convince herself that he was just like her—an innocent person drawn into something he'd never expected and hadn't asked for.

But innocence didn't look like Hawke. Or act like him.

And right now she'd be willing to believe him capable of almost anything.

She took a step toward the door, knowing how anger worked. Her father's rages had spilled out onto anyone in the vicinity. Her high school boyfriend's anger over lost basketball games, poor grades and parents, had bled into their relationship until it nearly destroyed her. Even Lauren could wound without thought when life didn't go her way. Yeah, Miranda knew *exactly* how rage worked and she had no intention of letting Hawke take his frustration out on her.

She took another step back, cleared her throat. "I'll just wait in the other room until you're done."

He stilled, his hand pausing over the open backpack as he met her gaze. "I'm scaring you."

"No, you're..." She shrugged. "Not much."

"Not much is still too much." He took a deep breath,

released it, his shoulders relaxing, his fisted hands opening, the rage slowly fading from his eyes. "My brother is all the family I have left. The thought of something happening to him makes me see red."

"I understand."

"Maybe you do. It seems we've both suffered loss in our lives." He crossed the space between them, cupped her cheeks in his hands as he stared down into her eyes. "But that's not an excuse for scaring you. I'm sorry."

"Sorry? That's not a word I've heard very often from the men in my life." She meant it as a joke, something to lighten the mood, but the truth of her statement must have been in her tone.

"Then I guess you haven't had the right men in your life."

"The right men? I didn't know there were such things." She pulled away from his touch, her skin burning where his hands had been.

"There are. My friend Noah is one. His pastor is another."

"Them and not you?"

"No. Not me. But I am the right man to get you out of this mess." His half smile was self-depreciating. "I've got to go."

He stepped out of the room and Miranda followed, worry a hard, cold knot in her stomach. She wanted to beg Hawke to stay or take her with him. More than that, she wanted to close her eyes, open them again and find that everything that had happened was nothing but a bad dream. "How long will you be gone?"

"I don't know."

"Then how will I know how long to wait?"

"You'll wait an eternity if that's what it takes."

"That's not practical."

"I don't care about practical. I care about your safety. Go wandering around this neighborhood by yourself and anything could happen. Even if it didn't, it wouldn't be long before one of the DEA's informants spotted you. If the DEA finds you, it's all over."

"Right now that doesn't seem like such a bad thing."

"It will be, babe. Someone in the DEA's office has been feeding information to drug dealers in the States. Including my name. He knows I'm here to find him. He can't afford to let that happen."

"But if you don't come back—"

"I'll come back."

"But if you don't—"

He pressed a finger against her lips, stopping her words. "Stop worrying. It'll be easy enough for me to stay hidden. Make yourself at home while I'm gone. There are clothes in the dresser. You might be able to find something that works. I wish I had food, but I cleaned everything out before I left. I'll try to grab something before I come back."

"Don't worry about it. I'm fine." She'd rather he come back sooner and skip the food. Besides, she was too nervous to eat.

"A successful mission is one in which every detail is worried about." He pulled open the door, stepped out into the hall. "I'll lock it. Don't open it for anyone."

"I won't."

"If someone knocks, ignore it. Don't get close to the door, don't make any noise. Not even a hint there's someone here."

"All right." The idea of being left behind sounded worse by the minute.

"Worse-case scenario, someone breaks down the door—"

"What?!"

"If that happens, lock the bedroom door and go out the window. There's a fire escape there."

"Hawke, I *really* don't like this idea."

"It's the best one we've got." He chucked her under her chin, stepped out into the hall. "You'll be fine."

"What about you?"

"I'll be fine, too." He didn't give her time to argue further, just closed the door with a firm click.

Miranda resisted the urge to pull it back open and watch him walk away. It wouldn't do any good and would only put off the inevitable moment when she'd be truly alone. She turned the lock and paced across the room, glancing at her watch as she did so. It was eleven o'clock in Maryland, but that didn't tell her what time it was here. What was the time difference? Ten hours? Twelve? Did it matter? She was stuck where she was until Hawke got back.

If he got back.

There was a very real possibility he wouldn't and as much as she didn't want to think about it, Miranda had to be prepared. She paced back to the door, checking the lock again, pressing her ear against the wood listening for something she hoped not to hear. All she heard was silence. She should have been relieved, but she couldn't shake the worry and dread that filled her.

"Pull yourself together and *do* something!" She muttered the command, forcing herself away from her post by the door. She'd search the bedroom, see what she could find. Maybe there were weapons, maps, tools and information she could use if Hawke didn't return. If there were, she'd find them.

Then she'd wait and pray she didn't have to use them.

Chapter Nine

Hawke didn't believe in lying and he hadn't lied to Miranda. Doing so would have been a betrayal of the strict moral code his parents had raised him with. His mother and father had both been religious people. Though there'd been no church, no Bibles to be read or studied when he was growing up, his parents had believed in God and in a cosmic balance of justice and mercy. To them, the Ten Commandments were not an arbitrary set of rules but a code of conduct to be lived by. Hawke did his best to honor their memory by doing so, though his own personal code had taken precedence more times than he was comfortable admitting.

Today had been one of those times. While he hadn't lied to Miranda, he hadn't told her the truth, either. He had no business to see to in Bangkok. None that the law would approve of anyway. But telling Miranda that he planned to blackmail a man to get the information he needed hadn't seemed like the wisest thing to do. She was worried enough without him adding more to the mix. Worse, she couldn't be counted on to stay where he'd left her. Leaving out information was the one way he could think of to keep her in place. The less she knew, the less likely she'd be to follow and intervene.

It shouldn't have bothered him, but it did. Much as he wanted to pretend that following the letter of the law made him innocent of wrongdoing, he knew the truth—a lie of omission was as serious a sin as any other. Yet, he'd done it over and over again in the past ten years. And he'd done worse.

So, why was this one small omission bothering him so much? Maybe because he was beginning to think the events of the last few days were payback. If God really did care about His creation, if He really did have a vested interested in humanity, He might just have decided it was time to balance the scales a little, give Hawke back what he'd been dishing out for the past decade—justice. Or maybe it was because the thought of lying to Miranda, of hurting her in any way, left him feeling cold.

Both were foolish thoughts, but neither would let him go as he wound his way through back alleys, skirted an upscale neighborhood and made his way to a busy tourist district. Street vendors lined the sidewalk, their stainless-steel carts reflecting watery sunlight and bright colors. The scent of sweet pastry and sticky rice made Hawke's stomach growl and his mouth water, but he'd left Miranda back at the apartment with no food. He wouldn't eat until she did.

Pay phones were easy to find on the busy thoroughfare and Hawke stepped into a booth, leaving the door open and facing the street. He was less conspicuous that way, and less vulnerable. Roaring traffic and a swarming crowd of tourists created a sea of motion that made blending in easy. All Hawke had to do was act like everyone else—and that was something he'd perfected over the years.

He pulled a baht from his pocket, slid it into the coin slot, knowing he was leaving fingerprints and not caring. The DEA and Royal Thai police already knew he was in Bangkok. Trying to hide the fact was a waste of energy. He dialed Pot o' Gold Exports first, listening as the phone rang once and a recorded message filled the line. *Closed pending DEA investigation.* Hawke slammed the phone down as hot, dark anger welled up inside him—the knowledge that the message had been left for him but would be heard by clients filled him with rage. Despite his reputation for skirting the law and pursuing justice with a vengeance, Hawke had made sure the family business remained untainted, its reputation reflecting the ethical dealings of his stepfather. Now it seemed that reputation would fall victim to the same faceless enemy that had tried to have Hawke killed.

Frustration spurred him on as he picked up the phone again and dialed another number. This time to his house in Mae Hong Son. The line would be tapped, but it didn't matter. His conversation would add a little excitement to someone's boring day but would offer anyone listening nothing more than that.

"Sawatdee khrap." The greeting came quickly. The soft, masculine voice was one Hawke recognized immediately.

"Sawatdee khrap, Apirak."

"You're back." The Thai words sounded almost foreign after so many months of speaking and hearing only English, but they were as much Hawke's language as the ones he had learned from his stepfather.

He slipped into the pattern and rhythm of Thai without conscious thought.

"Do you know why?"

"Trouble in the States. Trouble here." Apirak Koysayodin spit the words out, his normally smooth baritone laced with temper. Hawke's second in command and the only person besides Noah and Simon that Hawke trusted, Apirak was a master of understatements, not given to panic and loyal to a fault. If he said there was trouble, it had to be big.

"What kind of trouble is there here?"

"That hotheaded kid brother of yours got himself in deep with the DEA."

"How deep?" Hawke knew his brother could act without thinking, but couldn't imagine him being foolish enough to mess with a government agency.

"Deep enough to get carted off to jail. A couple of agents came here to question us. The one who hired you and a couple of other people. They were talking about stolen money and a murdered agent. Simon didn't take kindly to the accusations they made against you."

"What'd he do?"

"Took a swing at one of them. Gave the guy a bloody nose. He's lucky he didn't get himself shot."

"That doesn't sound like Simon."

"The agent he took a swing at had just accused the entire family of being in the Wa's pocket. The implication that your family was murdered because they double-crossed the Wa sent him over the edge."

Hawke bit back harsh words and calmed his suddenly ragged breathing. A militia group based in Myanmar, the Wa supported their guerilla efforts through drug trade. When Patrick Morran refused to ship drugs through his export business and went to the authorities with the names of men who were more willing, he, his wife and his daughter were executed by a man who had been a friend for as many years as Patrick had been in business. Hawke had been in the States obtaining an MBA. Simon had been visiting friends. Because of that, they'd lived. "The DEA knows the truth about what happened. They were taunting him for a reason."

"And he gave them a good reason to cart him off to jail. With Simon out of the picture, they probably figured you'd be easier to control, maybe even be willing to turn yourself in."

Hawke snorted. "If that's what they hope to accomplish they've made an error in judgment. I'm even more determined to stay out of their hands."

"It's more of an error in judgment than you think, Hawke." Apirak's voice warned of more bad news.

"What else?"

"Simon has disappeared."

"Disappeared?" Everything inside Hawke stilled, his nerves so alive he could hear drips of water from gutters above the street, feel the rain moving in over the city, see every speck of light and dark, each ant and roach that wove its way between cracks in the sidewalk.

"Supposedly he escaped, but I don't believe it." Which meant Simon hadn't gone to his own safe house, hadn't used the phone he had for emergencies, had made no effort at all to make contact. Apirak didn't need to say it for Hawke to know it was true. The emergency plans they'd formulated years before were meant for times such as these. If Simon wasn't using them, it was because he wasn't able to.

Hawke's jaw was tight with worry and anger. He'd

lost most of his family. He wouldn't lose Simon, too. "How long has he been gone?"

"They brought him in yesterday morning. He disappeared sometime last night."

"Any word on the street?"

"Nothing solid. Our normal informants are very quiet on this one."

"Keep listening."

"Of course." There was a second of hesitation, then Apirak spoke again. "Is the woman with you?"

"She's in a safe place." His response was vague. The less information those listening in on the conversation got, the happier Hawke would be.

"Hopefully out of sight. There have been news stories here. The tale of a mysterious and wealthy entrepreneur on the run with the sister of an American model is just too good for the press to pass up."

"I'd figured it would be."

"Just be sure you're not spotted."

"We already have been, but I'm still free."

"Make sure you keep it that way."

"I'll be in touch." Hawke hung up before Apirak could say anymore, his shoulders tight with warning. The DEA had had plenty of time to trace the call. They'd be here soon, and he had no intention of waiting around to greet them.

Hawke had been gone three hours twenty minutes and fifteen seconds. Sixteen. Seventeen.

"Just keep counting. That's doing a whole lot of good." Miranda muttered the words out loud as she raked a hand through damp hair. In the time Hawke had been gone, she'd managed to go through every dresser drawer, the entire contents of the closet—where she found a T-shirt that fell to her thighs and jeans that perched precariously on her hips—take a shower, change clothes and scare herself silly. What she hadn't done was come up with a plan of action.

She rubbed at the ache behind her eyes and surveyed the items she'd collected. A pile of weapons lay on the bed—guns, knives and something she was sure was a machete. Wooden clubs attached by a short chain and another long wooden pole of some sort looked like martial arts weapons, though Miranda had no idea what they'd be used for. A box of ammunition was on the floor, deadly looking stuff that made her cringe. Beside it sat a small canister that she did recognize— pepper spray. At least she assumed it was pepper spray. She couldn't read the label. For all she knew it was something much more toxic. The sad fact was she had enough weapons to hold off an army, but she didn't know how to use most of them.

Who was she kidding? Even if she did know how to use them, she wasn't sure she'd be able to. Just the thought of shooting someone made her light-headed. Stabbing someone was even more appalling—the feel of a blade slicing through human flesh something she refused to even imagine.

She supposed she could try one of the more exotic-looking weapons. The chained wooden clubs seemed promising. She'd knocked Liam out and he'd survived. She could do the same to anyone who broke in. All she had to do was swing the clubs around a few times.

And brandish them uselessly while the enemy closed in.

"Face it. You're hopelessly ill prepared for this kind of thing." Miranda paced to the bedroom door, thought about opening it and changed her mind. Somehow having it closed and locked made her feel marginally safer. Which wasn't nearly safe enough. She imagined someone breaking down the door, rushing toward the room where she was hiding. Worse, imagined Hawke bloodied and dying, unable to return. Unable to ask for help.

"What am I supposed to do? Wait all day? All night? Wait a week?" The words were a prayer, one she could only hope God would answer in a way that she could understand rather than in the puzzling bits and pieces He most often seemed to use.

A stab of guilt went through her at the thought. The puzzles were hers, not God's. Even when the answers seemed clear, Miranda tended to doubt them. She'd spent five months deciding to break up with her high school boyfriend even though every one of her friends had been worried and was urging her to do so. Two years later, a year after becoming a Christian, she'd dated a man she'd met at the college bookstore. For six months she'd wondered at the strange feeling she had that the relationship wasn't what it seemed. It had taken running into Stan and his wife to show Miranda just how wrong the relationship was.

She'd even hesitated when it came to taking on responsibility for Justin, sure that she should finish her education first. Over and over again, God had brought people into her life, men and women with autistic children. Yet Miranda had refused to see them for what they were—clear direction and assurance that the course she was hesitating to take was the right one.

Only when Lauren had asked her to visit a facility where she planned to enroll Justin, did Miranda finally commit to God's plan. It had almost been too late, the paperwork all but signed.

Miranda didn't want to make the same mistake again. This time she wanted things to be different, wanted to listen to the soundless voice that spoke to her soul.

And right now, it was saying stay. Give Hawke more time. Trust that he'd return. More, trust that God was with her. That *He* was in control.

"Okay." Miranda whispered the words as she shoved aside the weapons she'd spread out on the bed and flopped down on the comforter. Her muscles were tight, her mind still racing, but she forced back the panic and listened to the silence. Deep. Placid. Devoid of danger.

For now she was safe.

That would just have to be enough.

Chapter Ten

"I've got it." David Sanchat shoved back from his desk and stood, his sallow skin pale, his dark eyes meeting Hawke's then shooting away. It hadn't been hard to find the man—Hawke had been keeping tabs on him for years and knew he'd taken a job as a professor at a university, knew he'd moved into a suburb just outside of Bangkok. It had been even less difficult to convince Sanchat to help. Having information that could destroy a man tended to make him very cooperative.

And the cooperation of a computer genius was exactly what Hawke needed.

He strode over to the computer screen, read the list of agents and the information about their locations. It was what he'd been hoping for—Jack McKenzie's address there for the taking. "Print it out for me."

"You know they're going to trace this back to me, right? A guy can't hack into the DEA's mainframe without getting caught." David's voice shook, his forehead beaded with sweat.

"That's not my problem."

"I could lose my job."

"Still not my problem."

"You're a cold son of—"

"And you paid for your party years acting as a courier for the Wa. Which do you think is worse?"

"What I did twelve years ago shouldn't matter. I'm a professor. A family man. A good citizen. And have been for a long time."

"The past can't be changed. The good we do can never pay for the sins we've committed. I think you know that." Hawke grabbed the printout from David's hand.

"This isn't about what I know or don't know. It's about you taking the law into your own hands. If the law wanted me, I would have been in jail a long time ago."

"I'm not taking the law into my own hands. I'm just helping it along. I believe in justice and that we all pay for our crimes eventually. This is your time to pay."

"Justice would mean *both* of us going to jail for the rest of our lives. Hacking into a U.S. government computer system—"

"You hacked into something that's open to DEA employees. Just a directory of names and contact information. Nothing top secret."

"That won't matter to the DEA. I'll lose everything for this." David collapsed into his computer chair, leaned his head against his hands. "Don't you think I regret what I did? I was young and stupid. My father was a diplomat. I traveled all over the world with him. Passing information from one place to another seemed like an easy way to make a few bucks."

"Your morality came too late for some. People die

every day from drug overdoses or at the hands of the men who paid you."

"If I could change what I did, I would. I can't, so all that's left is to live the best life I can now." The words were spoken quietly and Hawke believed them. As much as he despised what Sanchat had done, he knew Sanchat's involvement with the Wa had ended years ago. Since then, the college professor had stayed out of trouble, devoting himself to his job and his family.

"When they come to question you, tell them I forced you to do this for me. Whatever else you choose to tell them is for you to decide."

"Listen, do you need anything else? Money? A ride?"

The questions caught Hawke by surprise and he hesitated with his hand on the office door. "Aren't you already in enough trouble?"

"Yeah, so I guess a little more isn't going to hurt."

"In for a penny, in for a pound?"

"Something like that."

"I've got everything I need."

"There'll be security guards near the front entrance of the building. You'll be better off going up to the roof and down the fire escape."

Hawke nodded and stepped out into the corridor, the quiet university closing in around him as he moved toward the stairwell, the need to hurry thrumming through him. He'd been away from the apartment for six hours. The time it had taken for Sanchat to access the DEA directory would only be worth it if Miranda was still waiting for him when he returned. He hoped she was. Sticking around Bangkok wasn't part of his plan. Neither was losing the woman who'd saved his life. If push came to shove, he'd comb the city until he found Miranda, but every minute he spent doing that was a minute his brother was in the enemy's hands.

It took only minutes to access the roof and descend to the street below. He moved along the sidewalk with purpose, but didn't rush, not wanting to call attention to himself. Bangkok never slept and the sounds of its nightlife drifted on humid night air, a pulsing beat that Hawke was all too familiar with. In years past, he'd traveled Bangkok's underworld, searching out those dealing in drugs and human flesh. Much of the money that passed hands there eventually made its way into the Wa's coffers. One name, one location, one exchange of money for drugs at a time, Hawke had provided information to the authorities that had chopped off the Wa's tail time and time again. The problem was, like many cold-blooded lizards, the Wa's tail just kept growing back.

And eventually Hawke realized that he was banging his head against a brick wall, that revenge would never be his for the taking, that justice would be meted out, just not by his hands or his power, that he was wasting his time, wasting his life on a futile effort that might lead his brother into the same cesspool of human depravity Hawke had been wading through.

He'd hoped living outside of Thailand would open doors to something different. That perhaps breaking his ties with his mother country was what was needed to end the journey he'd started after his family's murder. He'd wanted a new life. New goals. A fresh start.

Now, all he wanted was to find his brother and clear his name.

And keep Miranda safe.

An image flashed through his mind—dark hair, pale

skin, freckles. Eyes the deep green of spring, new life and promises. As much as Hawke might be due to pay for some of the wrong he'd done, Miranda deserved to be home safe. He had every intention of getting her there.

The apartment building was straight ahead, a few windows illuminated. Most dark. Hawke entered silently, climbing the stairs two at a time, a sense of urgency spurring him on.

The apartment door was closed and locked, the lights in each room turned off. Hawke strode down the hall, scanning the floor for signs of light spilling from beneath the bedroom door. There were none. He used his key to unlock the door, pulling it open as he formulated a plan to find Miranda if she'd left.

He stepped into the room, flicked on the light, and froze, his mouth curving as he caught sight of the woman who'd been so much on his mind the last few hours. She lay sleeping, hair curling wildly around her face, her body drowning in a black T-shirt and baggy cargo-style jeans. Weapons were piled on the bed around her—knives, the unloaded guns he kept in the closet, pepper spray, ammo. A nunchaku was clutched in her hand as if she'd thought holding it while she slept would keep danger at bay.

Hawke strode across the room, touched her shoulder. "Miranda?"

She came up fast, the nunchaku still in her hand, her pulse beating wildly in the hollow of her throat. "You're back."

"Did you think I wouldn't return?"

"I was beginning to wonder." Her cheeks were pink from sleep, her eyes misty green. The circles under them looked darker than when Hawke had left, as if sleep had only made her more tired.

He brushed a lock of hair from her cheek, felt the silky softness of it. "I told you I'd be back."

"Yeah, I just wasn't sure I believed you." Her lips curved, but there was no smile in her eyes.

"You can always believe me, babe." He pulled the nunchaku from her hands, his tense muscles relaxing for the first time in hours. "Were you planning to use this as a weapon?"

"Only if I needed to."

"The gun might have been a better idea."

"I don't know how to use one." To Hawke's surprise, her voice broke on the words and she turned away, her shoulders stiff, something broken and lonely in her stance.

He reached for her hand, tugging her back toward him and wrapping his arms around her waist. "Are you okay?"

"I've been scared to death."

"You were safe here." He stroked her back, inhaling the sent of shampoo and soap. She'd taken a shower, but apples and cinnamon still seemed to hover in the air around her. Memory or reality, Hawke didn't know.

Her hands trembled as she slipped them under his pack and leaned back to look into his face. "I know. It was *you* I was scared for."

The sincerity in her eyes, the worry there, melted into Hawke's heart, touching something he hadn't allowed anyone near for a very long time.

He knew he should step back, put distance between them, but found himself pulling her closer instead. She fit perfectly, her head just under his chin, her hair soft against the skin of his throat. He wanted to stay there forever, absorbing the sweet artlessness of her embrace.

But they didn't have forever. Just moments, ticking by one after another while his brother remained in the hands of men who would stop at nothing to achieve their goals.

He loosened his hold, his hands lingering at the small of Miranda's back. "You didn't need to worry about me. I've been taking care of myself for a long time."

She shrugged, her hands fisted in his shirt, her knuckles warm through the material. "I'll try to remember that next time."

He wanted to tell her there wouldn't be a next time, but couldn't. They had a long journey ahead of them. Ten hours to Chiang Mai. Then on from there to Mae Hong Son. Anything could happen and probably would. His arms tightened around Miranda for a fraction of a second before he forced himself to step back. "We need to get moving. We've got a long way to go tonight."

"Where are we headed?" She stared up into his eyes, searching for something Hawke doubted she'd find. Honor, trustworthiness. Things he'd never been able to find in himself. At least not in the past ten years.

"Chiang Mai."

"I've never heard of it."

"It's north of here. About ten hours by road." He grabbed a machete from the bed, picked up a can of pepper spray. Anything to keep his hands busy, his mind off what it felt like to hold Miranda in his arms— as if she belonged there, as if they'd been together a lifetime rather than a few short days.

She picked up the Uzi Hawke had confiscated from

a drug runner across the border in Myanmar, holding it gingerly as if afraid it might go off in her hands.

"It's not loaded, babe."

"I wasn't sure. I don't have much experience with weapons. All I know is that you have a lot of them."

"I've collected them from some men who didn't need them anymore."

"That sounds….sinister."

"Most of them went to jail. Drug runners. Couriers. Men and women determined to spread the drug trade to every neighborhood and community in the world."

"That's what you do, then? Go after drug dealers?"

"What I do is run an export company in Bangkok. It's a family business. One my brother and I inherited after my father died. We buy handcrafted goods from the hill tribes up north and send them all over the world."

"Then how—"

"The story about how the rest of this came about is too long to tell now."

She opened her mouth, shut it again and shook her head. "Okay. I won't ask. It's none of my business anyway. Let's go."

She started away, but Hawke grabbed her arm, tugging her back around to face him. "I never said it wasn't your business. You deserve answers. I just can't give them now. We've got a long way to go and we've got a lot of people who'd like to stop us before we get there."

"That's an easy excuse, Hawke. I've been pulled into a situation I didn't ask to be in. I don't understand half of what or who is involved. I don't like not being in control. I don't like not having my life in my own hands."

"And I don't like talking about my past. It's not something that's easy to share." He bit out the words, not wanting to give her even that, but knowing she deserved at least some of the truth.

"I guess that's something I *do* understand."

With that, she strode from the room. This time, Hawke let her go. There was nothing he could say, nothing he *should* say. Despite the heartache she'd suffered, Miranda had spent her life cut off from the uglier side of humanity. She didn't understand the darkness that Hawke walked through every day.

Or maybe she did. One way or another, he didn't want to taint her with the shadows that lived in his soul. That meant keeping his distance and that's exactly what he intended to do.

He put away the last of the weapons, grabbed more money from the safe in the closet, then left the room, closing and locking it behind him.

Miranda was waiting by the front door to the apartment, looking more like a child playing dress up than a grown woman. The hem of the T-shirt she'd borrowed fell to her thighs and the cuffs of the jeans bagged around her ankles. The whole outfit was way too long and cumbersome for the journey, but there was nothing Hawke could do about it now.

"Ready?"

"As I'll ever be. What will we do once we get to Chiang Mai?" Her eyes had flecks of gold and brown and seemed to change color as her emotion changed. First mossy green with fatigue. Then bright green with frustration. Now hazel with uncertainty.

"Have a little talk with my boss. First, though, we've got to get some food and a ride."

"I'm not hungry. Let's just go."

"Hungry or not, you need to eat." He pulled off his pack, grabbing fruit that he'd purchased from a vendor several hours before. "I've got bananas and rambutan. Which do you want?"

"I've only ever heard of the first, so I guess I'll have that."

"Live a little. Try something new." He peeled the round, spiny red fruit as they walked down stairs to the second floor, handing her the slick white meat inside.

Miranda took the fruit Hawke offered her, the slippery flesh silky in her hands. It had the sweetness of a grape and a texture slightly thicker than one. Her stomach rumbled in thanksgiving as she took another bite. "It's good."

"I thought you'd like it. Eat another." Hawke handed her a second peeled fruit, then used a key to unlock the door at the second floor landing, grabbing her hand and pulling her inside.

Unlike the rest of the building, this area was well kept, the walls freshly painted, the carpet thick and new looking. A garlicky aroma filled the air, making Miranda's already rumbling stomach growl in acknowledgment.

She pressed a hand against the sudden, gnawing ache of hunger and hurried behind Hawke. He bypassed the first and second apartment doors, rapping hard on the third. It opened immediately, a small, wizened man staring out at them.

"Sawatdee khrap. Sabaaidee rue khrap?" His raspy words were accompanied by a wide grin.

"Koon Aran, Sawatdee khrap." Hawke spoke quietly, his tone fluid and musical, his hand still wrapped around Miranda's. She had the urge to lean her head against his shoulder and close her eyes for just a

moment. She'd been sick with worry and fear for hours. Now, with Hawke back, his words flowing in a gentle cadence around her, she wanted to cave in, close off and forget for just a while the trouble she was in.

"Whoa! You're fading, babe." Hawke dragged her up against his side, his gaze smoky with concern and some other emotion Miranda couldn't name.

The older man looked alarmed and shouted something into the apartment before hurrying inside.

"I'm okay. Just daydreaming. What's going on?"

"*Koon* Aran has agreed to let us rent his motorcycle for a few days. He's gone to get it."

"From inside his apartment?"

"The people who live here have very little. What they have they can't afford to lose." As he spoke an elderly woman appeared carrying two bowls, a white porcelain spoon sticking up from each.

She spoke quietly, handing one bowl to Hawke and placing the other in Miranda's hands.

"She says to eat."

"What is it?" Miranda glanced down into the bowl, the scent of spring onions wafting from the steamy contents. Wide noodles, small chunks of meat and bits of onion floated in light brown broth.

"*Lat Na.* Rice noodles in broth with chicken." Hawke didn't waste any time digging in to his, and Miranda realized he must be as hungry as she was. Had he eaten while he was gone? Or had he gone hungry the way Miranda had?

He lifted a brow, gestured toward her bowl of noodles. "Eat."

She did as he suggested, the warmth of the soup sliding straight into her energy-starved body. "It's good."

"New things aren't always bad." His lips curved, his hard features softening.

Despite her anxiety, Miranda's own lips curved in response. She might still be in danger, might still be running for her life, but at least she wasn't alone. The relief of having Hawke back with her would have been comforting if she weren't so sure that what was coming next was going to be worse than what she'd already experienced. "I still think I'd rather be home."

"You will be."

"When?"

"Soon."

Miranda might have asked exactly what he meant by soon, but the elderly man appeared in the threshold of the door, a black motorcycle rolling along beside him.

Hawke pulled a wad of cash from his pocket, handed it and their empty bowls over. Then he turned and met Miranda's gaze. "Ready?"

No, but the only other choice was to stay behind and there was no way Miranda was going to do that. "Yes. Let's go."

He grabbed her hand again, his fingers curving around hers, his calloused palm rasping against her skin. She shivered at the contact, the warmth that spread through her at Hawke's touch something she hadn't expected and didn't want.

"Cold?" His words whispered against her ear and she shook her head, afraid if she spoke he'd hear what she was feeling.

"All right then. Let's go." He squeezed her hand then let it go, rolling the bike down the hall.

Miranda hurried after him. In just a few minutes they'd be on the way to Chiang Mai, heading toward the answers they needed so desperately. Miranda wanted to believe they'd find them, that Hawke had been right when he'd said she'd be home soon. But something told her that her journey through Thailand had just begun and that things would get much worse before they got better.

If they got better.

As she stepped out into the balmy night, she could only pray that they would.

Chapter Eleven

Miranda had ridden on the back of a motorcycle before, but never on a dark, empty road in a foreign land; never when she was running from the police and being chased by a killer. Helmetless, she clung to Hawke's back as the bright lights of the city faded into the distance and the heavily populated suburbs gave way to open, empty land. Rain was in the air. She could feel it in the moisture that clung to her skin and turned her wild, whipping hair into a sodden, slapping mass of curls. Soon the sky would open up, pouring gallons of rain down on their heads, but even then they couldn't afford to stop. There was too much at stake. Their lives. Their freedom. The life of Hawke's brother. She knew it. Hawke knew it. No discussion was needed on the subject. They'd drive until they needed gas. Then they'd drive some more.

Mile after mile, minute after minute passed, the first sixty not bad, the second more uncomfortable. By the third, Miranda was shivering with cold, the thin cotton T-shirt she wore no buffer against the chilly night air. The scent of wet earth, rotting plants and asphalt filled her lungs and clogged her throat. She coughed, but couldn't dislodge the moist fetid air.

"You okay?" Hawke shouted the words above the roar of the engine, his words breaking the monotony of the ride for the first time since they'd left Bangkok.

"Yes."

"You're shivering."

"It's a little cold, but I'll be fine."

To her surprise, the bike slowed, easing to the side of the road, and then stopping, the engine dying, the sudden silence deafening.

Hawke shifted, his shadowy form angling toward her. "A little cold? You're shaking like a leaf."

He rubbed her arms, his hands sliding against cotton and flesh, generating heat Miranda desperately needed.

"Better?"

"Yes."

"Hop off the bike." Miranda did as he suggested, watching as Hawke did the same. He pulled off his jacket, wrapped it around her shoulders. "Put that on."

"You need it more than I do. I've at least got someone blocking the wind."

"Don't worry. Being prepared for trouble may not make life's journey less bumpy, but it makes those bumps more comfortable. Always be prepared."

"Another Hawke Morran quote?"

"A Patrick Morran quote. My stepfather loved to mix his own wisdom with that of history's great sages." He pulled off his pack, grabbed a lightweight jacket out of it, and shrugged it on.

"It sounds like he was a neat guy."

"He was. Why don't we stretch our legs? Have some water?"

"I've got another five hours in me before I need a

good stretch." That wasn't quite the truth, but there was no way Miranda planned to be the reason they had to take a break.

"You're a trooper, babe." There was a smile in his voice. "But even the toughest soldier has to stop sometimes." He zipped the jacket she'd put on, and pulled the collar up around her neck, his scent enveloping her—masculine and strong.

"I may be tired of riding on the back of this motorcycle, but not tired enough to risk our lives or your brother's to take a break."

"Have you always been like this, Miranda Sheldon?" His hands framed her face, his eyes gleaming in the darkness.

Miranda's face heated beneath his touch, her mind suddenly blank. "Like what?"

"Practical. Determined."

"No." She used to be a dreamer, her head filled with fairy tales, but that had changed. One too many broken promises. One too many shattered dreams. "I've had to learn to be. My nephew was autistic. Practicality and determination went a long way in creating a good life for Justin."

"And love. I bet you showered your nephew with love." His hands slipped from her face, and he tugged her a few steps away from the motorcycle, darkness pressing in around them. Somehow it freed the words that Miranda hadn't been able to say. Not to Lauren. Not to Max. Not to friends. Barely to herself. "Yes, but in the end, I failed him. The night he died, I was going to a bridal shower, leaving him with my sister for the night."

"Leaving him with his mother."

"*I* was his mother. I should never have left them together. Lauren is self-absorbed. She couldn't be expected to care for someone with Justin's needs."

"What happened?"

"Justin wandered outside while Lauren was on the phone. He was hit by a drunk driver just a block from our house. I know he was looking for me." Her voice broke, and she stopped, tears clogging her throat and seeping from her eyes.

"You can't know that." Hawke wrapped his arms around her, pulling Miranda's head to his chest, his hand stroking her hair.

"Maybe not, but I believe it." She let herself relax, the beat of his heart, the quiet inhalations of his breathing steady and sure and as familiar as her own. How that could be, she didn't know. They were different in every way, his past so far removed from her's that they were like creatures from different planets. She was quiet, bookish, boring. He was energy, action, barely concealed violence. Yet she couldn't deny the thread that stretched between them, pulling them closer with every moment spent together.

The thought made her uncomfortable and she stepped out of his embrace. "We need to get going again."

"We do, but not before I tell you this." He shifted, leaning close and staring into her eyes. His face was a stone sculpture, cold and hard with only a hint of human warmth beneath it. "I've learned in life, babe, that we can't change yesterday. Believing you could have done something to prevent your nephew's death is a waste of energy. Instead, you should remember all the love you gave him while he was alive and know you did the best you could for him."

"That isn't easy to do."

"No, but in the end it's the only way we can keep from being destroyed." He sounded like he knew what he was talking about and Miranda strained to see more of his expression in the dim light. All she saw were hard angles, harsh planes and secrets; the kind of man that, if she saw him on the street she'd avoid. Yet, here they were a team. Together for however long it took to find the person who'd set Hawke up. Maybe coincidence had brought them together. Or maybe God had. If so, there was a reason for it. One Miranda could only hope she'd eventually understand.

"Hawke—"

"You were right, we do need to go." He led her back to the motorcycle and climbed on, his tense muscles telling her more than words just how closed the conversation was.

It was for the best. Building more of a connection with Hawke could only be a mistake. Once this was over, he'd go his way. She'd go hers. It was as inevitable as getting back on the motorcycle and heading toward whatever trouble awaited them in Chiang Mai.

Miranda sighed, climbing on the bike behind Hawke, wrapping her arms around his waist, her eyes trained on the asphalt stretching out before them, beckoning them to answers or to death. Miranda shuddered and for just a moment Hawke's hand covered hers, his fingers pressing gently in silent support.

And the thread that stretched between them wound itself just a little tighter around her heart.

Golden fingers crept across the horizon as Hawke pulled the motorcycle into an alley and parked it. The buildings on either side were three stories high, their whitewashed brick facades stark in the hazy purplish

light. Cars and motorcycles zipped past the mouth of
the alley, rickety pickup trucks and rumbling buses
interspersed between them. The humid air was thick
with the scent of garlic, spices and a sweet flowery
scent that Miranda didn't recognize.

This was Chiang Mai.

Miranda didn't know if she should be relieved that
they'd finally arrived at their destination or terrified
of what would come next.

Hawke climbed off the bike and offered a hand to
Miranda. If he was tired, it didn't show. There were no
shadows beneath his eyes, no hollowness to his face.
Black stubble covered his jaw and his eyes were eerily
light against his tan skin. "That last hour was rough.
You did good, babe."

"All I did was hold on."

"That's a whole lot better than the alternative." He
smiled, extending a hand and pulling Miranda off the
motorcycle. "Unfortunately, we're not done yet. We've
got three blocks to go before we're where we need to
be."

"Your boss's house?"

"Yes. He lives in a compound in town. It shouldn't
be hard to get there. Provided he doesn't already know
we're coming."

His words did what arriving in Chiang Mai hadn't,
shooting adrenaline into Miranda's blood and giving
her the energy she needed to move. "And if he does?"

"Then we'll know it soon enough. Come on." He
led her to the mouth of the alley and onto a street alive
with early-morning traffic. A vendor moved up the
sidewalk pushing a silver cart, a wide-brimmed straw
hat hiding his face, his flip-flops slapping against the
concrete as he walked. A woman swept the pavement

in front of a store, the fan-shape broom swooshing with each brush and sway. It seemed a peaceful, ordinary morning, but that didn't mean trouble wasn't lurking around the next corner.

"Do you think they're out here looking for us?" She whispered the question, afraid that speaking too loudly would upset the balance and send the world tumbling back into terror.

"The DEA or friends of the man who set me up?"

"Either. Both."

"There's a chance, but I'm banking on them heading to Mae Hong Son instead."

"What's in Mae Hong Son?"

"I have a home there. Men who work for me. Resources available to me. It would make sense for me to go there." He pulled her around a corner and down a side street, his stride long and confident, as if he had no fear at all that they'd be spotted.

"What do you plan to do when we get to your boss's house?" *If* they got there. Miranda still wasn't sure they would.

"Nothing much. I just want to have a little chat with him." The grim tone warned Miranda that there might be a lot more to Hawke's plan than he was letting on.

"What if *he* doesn't want to have a chat with *you?*"

"Did I say I was going to give him a choice?" Hawke shot a look in her direction, his eyes steel-gray and cold.

"Not unless I have to."

"I don't like the sound of that." Miranda grabbed the sleeve of Hawke's jacket and stopped. "If you do something to him, we'll be in even more trouble than we're already in."

"Babe, we can't possibly be in any more trouble.

Besides, Jack McKenzie and I have known each other for years. He'll tell me what I want to know."

"I don't know about this."

"I do."

"Wouldn't it be better if you called your boss instead? Just asked him the questions over the phone."

"It would be better if you were quiet for a while. This isn't a touristy part of town and your English is going to call attention to us."

"Sorry."

"Don't be sorry, babe. Just be quiet." He grinned and squeezed her hand.

Miranda's heart skipped a beat, but she couldn't quite return the smile. For all Hawke knew, there were a hundred men waiting for them at his boss's house, ready to arrest them. Or kill them.

"We're here," Hawke whispered close to her ear, his words barely vibrating in the air.

Here was a thick white wall topped with shards of glass that glistened in the early-morning sun. Blades of yellow grass clung to the base of the wall, scraggly and unsure.

"Ever ride a horse?"

Hawke's question took Miranda by surprise and for a moment she could think of no answer. Finally, she nodded. "A few times."

"Good. Hand me the jacket."

Miranda shrugged out of Hawke's jacket and passed it to him, watching with growing worry as he tossed it onto the top of the fence. Surely he didn't plan for them to scale the fence. If he did, he was going to be disappointed in Miranda's climbing abilities. She'd spent her childhood reading books, not climbing trees and jumping fences.

"You first. I'll follow." Hawke gestured to the wall, and Miranda took a step back.

"I'm not very good at this sort of thing."

"Sure you are. I'll give you a leg up. Just mount the fence like you would a horse. Then lower yourself down the other side."

"There isn't a horse alive as tall as that fence. It must be ten feet high."

"Eight." His eyes dared her as he cupped his hands together and waited.

She took a deep breath, nodded her head. "All right, let's do it."

Hawke smiled again, a crooked grin that hooked Miranda's heart and tugged hard. She looked away, not wanting him to see the heat staining her cheeks; not wanting to contemplate the reasons *why* heat was staining her cheeks.

If Hawke noticed her discomfort, he didn't comment. Instead, he grabbed her foot, supporting the arch in his hands. "Make sure you go over the jacket. The glass shards will tear your hands to pieces if you don't."

Miranda nodded, though torn hands were the least of her worries. If she wasn't careful, she'd go over on her head and break her neck. She just prayed she'd manage to land on her feet.

Hawke straightened, boosting Miranda in a quick, effortless movement that had her sailing upward at an alarming rate. She grabbed the top of the fence, spiky glass digging into her skin despite the thick leather of the jacket. A quick pivot, a swing of her leg and she was over, dangling by her hands, her feet scratching against stucco as she tried to convince herself to drop.

A thump and bang warned her that Hawke was on his way over, but still she couldn't release her grip.

"Are you planning to hang there all day?" Hawke's gruff voice whispered down at her. She looked up, saw him perched on the fence, balancing on the balls of his feet and looking completely at ease.

"Is there anything you can't do?" She panted the words out, her arms burning from the effort it took to hold her weight.

"I can't jump eight feet to the ground and I can't drop from this spot until you do."

He had a point. Even if he hadn't, Miranda's fingers were slipping from the leather. She closed her eyes, released her hold and dropped, tumbling onto her backside in the fragrant grass and moist earth.

Seconds later, Hawke landed next to her, dropping down in a crouch, his eyes searching her face.

"Good job, babe. You okay?" His lips touched her ear as he spoke, the warmth of it shivering along her nerves.

"Right as rain." Even if she was trembling from head to toe. She hadn't broken her neck and that was definitely something to be thankful for.

Hawke stared her down for a moment, then stood, pulling her to her feet. "Good. Come on. McKenzie's house is number 1492."

"What if he's not home?"

"Then we go in and take a look around."

"That's illegal."

"So is selling information to drug dealers. So is murder."

"Do you really think he's responsible?"

"I don't know, but I plan to find out."

"Hawke—"

"You need to stop worrying so much. It's bad for your health."

"So is stress and I've been under a tremendous amount of that ever since I met you."

"Then we'll have to make sure to do something relaxing and fun when this is over." He didn't say *if* it was over, but Miranda was thinking it as Hawke tugged her to the edge of a stucco-sided house. "Here's what I want you to do. Walk around to the front of this house and take a look at the number."

"Me?"

"I'd do it, but you're much more innocuous looking."

He was right, and Miranda wasn't even going to try to convince him otherwise. No one would look at her and see a threat. Hawke, on the other hand, was six foot two of pure trouble.

She took a deep breath, prayed she wouldn't be spotted and stepped around the side of the house.

Chapter Twelve

Early morning light washed the world in dull color as Miranda moved across the front yard, the flowers, trees and buildings taking on a sepia tone. Sodden grass squished beneath her feet, the scent of wet earth pungent and full. The community lay silent and sleeping, doors closed, shades drawn, unsuspecting, unaware. All Miranda had to do was get the house number and get back to Hawke's side. Easy.

Except she couldn't see a house number. Not on the door. Not on the mailbox. Not anywhere obvious.

"It's got to be somewhere." She muttered the words, her heart pumping so fast and so loud, she was sure it would wake the entire neighborhood.

"Can I help you, miss?" a deep voice called from somewhere behind her, and Miranda spun to face the speaker, hoping she didn't look as terrified as she felt.

The man was tall, skinny and wearing a crisp brown uniform, a hat and a belt with a radio and some kind of club hanging from it. A guard. Miranda's blood froze in her veins, her mind blank. Every word, every thought jumbled in her head, refusing to coalesce into coherent words.

"Miss?" He stepped closer, his smile turning to a frown, his hand dropping to the radio he carried. "Is everything okay?"

"Everything is fine. I'm just out for a walk. It's such a beautiful morning." If her smile looked as forced as it felt the dark-eyed, clean-shaven young man would know in an instant that something was wrong. She needed to relax, pretend she belonged.

But she didn't belong and she couldn't relax and she *still* didn't know what to say.

"You are a friend of *Koon* Miller?" He motioned toward the house, the sharp edge to his gaze a warning that things might be about to go very badly.

Miranda scrambled for an answer. Yes was what her head insisted she say. No was what her gut wanted her to respond. "No. I'm a friend of..." What had Hawke said his boss's name was? "Mr. McKenzie. I couldn't sleep, so I thought I'd go for a walk, but now I'm turned around and can't seem to find his house. They all look the same." And they did—white stucco, orange shutters, wide driveways and manicured lawns.

The guard seemed to relax at her words and he smiled. "Ah. I see. You came last night in the van?"

"No, yesterday afternoon. I'm in from the States." *Please let that be the right answer.*

The young man nodded. "It's easy to get confused when you first arrive. *Koon* McKenzie's house is just five houses up on this side of the street." He gestured to the left. "You will be staying a while?"

"Yes."

"Good. There's much to see here. You've been to Thailand before?"

"No, this is my first trip." Miranda wanted desperately to make an excuse and hurry away, but didn't dare.

"Go see the elephants then. All visitors like the elephants."

"I will." *Pretend you have all day. Pretend you have nothing to hide.* The words chanted through her mind, her heart pounding so hard and fast, she thought it would explode from her chest.

"Good. My shift is ending. If you go for a walk tomorrow morning, look for me. I'm Klahan."

"M— Margaret."

He smiled again, flashing white teeth and offering a bow. Miranda followed his example, then waved as the guard walked away, her heart still slamming against her ribs, her pulse racing.

She needed to find Hawke and get out fast, but forced herself to walk toward McKenzie's house until the guard disappeared around the corner. Only then did she do what she so desperately wanted to—racing through a side yard, heading back toward the fence. Her feet slipped in wet grass and mud and she flew backward, her arms scrambling for purchase. Hard hands wrapped around her waist, pulling her upright and preventing her from taking a seat on the grass again.

Hawke.

Miranda knew it even before he whispered in her ear. "This is becoming a habit."

"Me falling, you helping me or me getting us into trouble?" she whispered back, her shaky words sounding louder than she intended.

"You forgot one—you getting us *out* of trouble. I

thought I might have to come take care of things, but you handled the situation well."

"Don't be too sure of that. I think we need to get out of here while we still can." She started toward the fence, but Hawke pulled her up short.

"We can't leave until McKenzie and I have a little talk. Besides, the guard bought your story. You even managed to get the location of McKenzie's house out of him."

"Hawke, I really think we should leave."

"We've got no choice but to stick it out. McKenzie is either guilty, or has some idea of who is. He can give us the name and location of the people who knew I was in the States. Without those, we may as well head back to Maryland and turn ourselves in."

Miranda wasn't sure that was a bad idea, but as much as she'd like to believe going home was the answer, she knew they'd face just as much danger there. Maybe more. Once in police custody, they'd have no way of defending themselves against whatever threat Green and his men offered.

She kept her mouth shut and followed Hawke through one backyard after another. His footsteps were silent, his movements lithe and fluid. He barely seemed to disturb the air. Miranda, on the other hand, stepped on every stick and every loose stone, brushed against bushes and low-hanging leaves, and made enough noise to alert anyone who might be listening that she was trespassing. The way she saw it, if their success was based on the ability to reach McKenzie's house silently, she was blowing their chances big-time.

"This is it." Hawke paused at the corner of a house that looked like every other house in the community.

"You're sure this is the fifth house?"

"Positive."

"What now?"

He gestured toward the back door. "See the shoes?"

She did. Yellow flip-flops sat neatly on a cement slab outside the closed back door. "Yes."

"They're not McKenzie's. They're his maid's."

"Which means?"

"Maids in communities like this visit each other for coffee or tea in the morning before their employers wake up. They always use the back door. All we have to do is knock and wait. We'll be in before McKenzie gets out of bed."

"Are you crazy? We can't just knock on the door and then push our way in." She grabbed Hawke's arm, but he kept moving toward the door, Miranda's dragging heels not slowing him in the least.

"Sure we can. It might not be the best plan, but it's the only one we've got. And—" he paused, patting his side and the gun that was strapped there "—if it doesn't work, I've got backup."

"What if the maid doesn't open the door?"

"She'll open the door."

"What if—"

He knocked. Two soft raps on the door, as if he knew exactly how a maid might gain her friend's attention. He must have. The door opened, a woman's voice audible before the interior of the room was visible. It halted abruptly, a small dark-haired woman, standing in the threshold, her mouth open, her eyes wide.

Hawke moved past her, speaking in Thai, the gun suddenly in his hand.

"Hawke—"

"She knows I'm not going to hurt her. She just needs to cooperate." He said something else in Thai, his gentle tone contrasting sharply with the gun he still held.

The woman nodded, speaking quickly and gesturing toward a doorway that led farther into the house.

"What's she saying?" Miranda's heart slammed against her ribs, her stomach knotted with anxiety. They shouldn't be here. They should have turned themselves in, not come halfway around the world for answers.

"McKenzie is home. Stay here and make sure the maid doesn't leave. I'm going to find him."

Arguing would only waste time and Miranda was desperate to be done and gone. She nodded, trying to smile at the Thai woman, but only managing a grimace.

"I won't be long." Hawke spoke as he stepped out of the room and disappeared from sight.

Miranda stood in taut silence, her ears straining to hear evidence that Hawke had found McKenzie, her gaze on the maid who shuffled around the bright kitchen as if this were any other day, as if a man with a gun hadn't just gone looking for her boss.

"You want tea?" The Thai woman gestured to a pot on the stove.

"No, thank you."

"Food?"

"No. I'm fine." Discussing food and drinks while Hawke was stalking through the house with a gun seemed bizarre, and Miranda wondered what Hawke had said to the woman that had her offering hospitality rather than hysteria.

"You sit down then."

A loud thud sounded from somewhere above their heads, the crash making both women jump. Another crash followed the first and Miranda grabbed the other woman's hand. "We've got to see what's going on."

"No. We stay here."

"We're going." She gritted her teeth and pulled the smaller woman across the room and through the doorway. Silence had returned and that worried Miranda more than the thud and crash she'd heard.

"Where is Mr. McKenzie?" She asked the question as she hurried across a long, white-walled living room.

"Upstairs getting ready for work. But we stay down here. We don't interrupt."

Miranda ignored the protest and started up the stairs, still clutching the maid's arm. If Hawke was in control of the situation, she'd go back down to the kitchen. If he wasn't...

What?

What could she possibly do? She didn't have a weapon, didn't have a plan. All she had was adrenaline speeding through her body and fear burning at the back of her throat. Maybe she could get her hands on the gun, or grab a vase or lamp from somewhere in the room. Though she doubted hitting McKenzie over the head with either would be an option. She'd need the element of surprise for that and between her huffing breaths and the maid's high-pitched protest, Miranda felt pretty sure she'd lost that.

The upstairs hallway was empty, three closed doors beckoning. "Which room is McKenzie's?"

Before the maid had a chance to reply, a scuffling sound carried from the room at the far end of the hall, the door banged open and a man stumbled out. Medium height and build with unremarkable features, dressed in a dark suit and understated tie, he looked about as dangerous as a butterfly.

Miranda stepped back anyway, her pulse racing as she searched the dark recesses beyond the door for Hawke. She didn't have long to wait. He moved into sight, his gun down by his side, a scowl darkening his face. "Didn't I tell you to wait downstairs?"

"I heard banging. I thought you might need help."

His scowl deepened, pulling at the corners of his mouth and creasing his forehead, his eyes the brooding gray of February sky. "Everything is under control. Jack was just telling me where my brother is."

"I was just telling you that your brother escaped while he was being transported to Bangkwang prison. If I knew where he was, he'd be back in custody." Jack McKenzie's voice was as unassuming as his face, his demeanor relaxed and unperturbed, as if he'd been expecting them and was glad they'd finally arrived.

Miranda edged back toward the staircase, sure she'd hear the sounds of slamming doors and pounding feet. If McKenzie had been expecting them, it was only a matter of time before his backup arrived.

"Hawke, I think we should leave." Her voice sounded thick and rough, the taste of fear bitter on her tongue.

"Not until I get my answers." Hawke's gaze never left McKenzie.

"I've given you the only answer I have, Morran." McKenzie's gaze shifted to Miranda, his sharp focus disconcerting. "You must be Miranda Sheldon. A lot of people in the States are worried about you. I'm glad to see you're all right."

"I'd be better if you'd tell Hawke what he wants to know, so we can leave and you can get on with your day."

"There's no need for you to rush away. We have

plenty of time for discussion—my ride to work won't be here for another twenty minutes."

"Only if that discussion has to do with who set me up and what you're going to do about it." Hawke bit the words out.

"It will." Jack lips curved in a smile that didn't reach his eyes.

"You know something." Hawke shoved his gun into his shoulder holster and leaned against the doorframe. "Why don't you stop playing games and tell me what?"

"No games, Morran. I don't know where your brother is and I don't know who set you up, but I believe someone did. We've been this close to Green several times in the past few years. He always slips through our fingers. We've suspected for a while that someone has been leaking information to him. Now we know it for sure. There were only a few men who knew you were working for us. It has to be one of them."

"Or you."

"You don't think it's me anymore than I think you killed a man in cold blood to steal fifty thousand dollars. Though, I've got to admit, I'd have preferred it to be you rather than any of my men."

"Thanks."

Jack shrugged. "None of us want to believe someone we trust would betray us or the ideals and principles we represent. I'm sure you felt the same way when Sang Lao bought one of your people last year and that young girl was taken right out from under your nose."

Hawke's lips tightened, and he nodded. Obviously, he knew exactly what Jack was referring to.

Miranda wished she did. She'd thought Jack and Hawke would be adversaries, facing each other from opposite sides. Instead, it seemed they had some trust for one another. That could only be good. She prayed that Jack would tell them everything was okay, that the DEA knew Hawke was innocent and was working hard to find the guilty party, but as the two men stared tight-jawed at one another, she had the sinking feeling that wasn't going to happen.

Finally, Hawke spoke, not moving from his post by the door. Though he seemed relaxed, Miranda sensed his coiled tension. "What are your plans, McKenzie? Obviously you have one, or we wouldn't be standing here discussing things."

"I plan to fix some leaky plumbing and I think you're just the man to help me."

"I'm no plumber, McKenzie. All I want is my brother, and the proof I need to get back to my life."

"I'd say our goals are the same. We can accomplish more together than we can alone."

"And I'd say we had this conversation twelve months ago when you told me I was just the man to help you bring down Harold Green. All that's gotten me in a truckload of trouble. I'm thinking this time, I'll stick to helping myself."

"What about Miranda? If you go down. She goes down, too."

"I don't plan to go down." Hawke smiled, a feral showing of teeth that held no humor.

"But someone has to."

"Then let's play this my way. *You* help *me*. Then we'll talk about what I can do for you."

Miranda was sure that Jack would refuse, that he'd tell Hawke that things were going to be done his way or no way at all. Instead, he nodded. "Fair enough. What do you need me to do?"

Chapter Thirteen

Hawke wasn't surprised that Jack agreed to his terms. Though they'd never actually worked together, the other man's reputation was well-known, his fierce commitment to putting a stop to the drugs being trafficked out of Thailand making him a formidable adversary to those who made money off illegal narcotics. As much as Hawke had suspected Jack of being the leak, he'd been relieved to find it wasn't true.

"I want the names of everyone who knew I was working for you."

"It's a short list. Five of us made the decision to bring you in on the Green case." Jack spouted off four names. None were familiar to Hawke, though that was about to change.

"Are you investigating any of them?"

"We've investigated everyone in the Chiang Mai office over the past year. There's nothing that indicates anyone has been taking payoffs. They're all living within their means, none have extra money in their bank accounts."

"That doesn't mean much."

"It means we don't have just cause to pull anyone in for questioning. It also means you're the perfect scapegoat. You've skirted the law too many times, Hawke. It finally caught up with you. Our man knew he could warn Green of the sting we'd set up and throw you to the wolves afterward. He probably assumed there'd be no one willing to believe your story."

"He assumed I'd be too dead to tell it. I'll need names, addresses and work schedules for all four of those men."

"Breaking and entering is against the law."

"That's never stopped me before."

"You know that if you get caught I had nothing to do with this."

"And if I find the leak and the evidence we need to prove it?"

"Then we'll pretend the breaking and entering didn't happen and you can either go back to your life here or return to the States a free man." He flashed a cold, hard smile. "The way I see it, if someone in my office is leaking information to Green, it's a good possibility that person is in the Wa's pocket. Breaking a few laws is a small price to pay for finding out who it is."

"Maybe you and I are more alike than I thought."

"We're more alike than you could ever know." The words were grim, belying Jack's bland expression. He pulled a folded paper from his jacket pocket, handed it to Hawke. "I've written down names and addresses. All four men are working today."

"You're very prepared considering you didn't know I was coming."

"Who said I didn't know?" Jack drummed his fingers against his arms, his gaze conveying what Hawke had only begun to suspect.

"You had this all planned before I went to the States. This was your real goal." Anger reared up, hot and searing, but Hawke tamped it down. There would be time later to discuss McKenzie's methods.

"My goal was to take Green down. I'd be lying if I said I wasn't hoping we'd also find our leak."

"Didn't you care that you put Hawke in a dangerous situation? That he could have been killed?" Miranda spoke quietly, her eyes the color of mountains in the mist, jungle foliage, lush fields.

The color of home.

Hawke's heart clenched, closing against the thought and the longing that went with it. He'd given up the dream long ago, had accepted well before he'd met Miranda that there would never be soft arms and warm smiles to go home to.

"I've known Hawke for years, Ms. Sheldon. I had every confidence he could take care of himself." Jack's smooth baritone and ingratiating smile grated on Hawke's nerves, but it was the way the man's gaze traveled Miranda's body, touching on her face, lingering on her lips, that made him want to knock his head off.

He bit back the urge. Barely.

"Jack believes the end justifies the means."

"And you don't, Morran?"

Did he? A year ago, he would have readily agreed. But not anymore. He'd changed. Softened. Become more aware of something much deeper and truer than himself. Though if he were honest, he'd admit that the change had been taking place for much longer than a year. He'd been changing since the day Noah Stone had carried him half-dead from the jungle. Hawke wasn't sure he was happy about it and was even less sure there was anything he could do about it.

"One more thing." Jack spoke quietly, his gaze hard. "There's already a cell in the Bangkok Hilton with your name on it. I'm the only reason you're not in it yet. If I so much as *think* I made a mistake in trusting you, I'll pull you in so fast your head will spin. You'll spend the rest of your life rotting in Bangkwang prison and I won't feel one bit of guilt over it."

"And if I find out you really are the leak, you won't have to worry about spending time in Bangkwang."

"As long as we understand each other." Jack's shoulder's relaxed. "I think you should leave the woman with me."

"The *woman* isn't being left anywhere." Miranda stiffened, her gaze jumping from Jack to Hawke and back again.

"You've been through a lot this past week, Ms. Sheldon. Having all this happen on the heels of your nephew's death must have exhausted you." His words were warm as melted butter.

Hawke gritted his teeth to keep from saying something rude. It was no business of his if Jack wanted to play nice to a beautiful woman. Except that Miranda wasn't just any woman. She was Miranda. Hawke had to resist the desire to smash his fist into Jack's smiling face.

"I'm fine, Mr. McKenzie." Miranda didn't return Jack's smile. Her gaze was solemn. The new hollows beneath her cheekbones and the sprinkling of freckles against her ashen skin made Hawke want to pull her toward him, wrap an arm around her waist and stake a claim he had no right to.

"And I want you to stay that way." Jack pressed his point. "If you stay here, I can guarantee your safety."

"Like you guaranteed my brother's?" Hawke couldn't stop the sarcasm that seeped into his words anymore than he could have stopped the tide from rolling in.

"Everything that happened to your brother was outside my jurisdiction."

"That's bull. You sent men to question him. Your agency handed him over to the police."

"And that's where our responsibility for him ended. Beside, Ms. Sheldon is in a different situation. She's not going to be taken anywhere. She can stay here."

"While you're at work? Anything could happen."

"Why would it? No one knows she's here. Even if someone found out, there are guards stationed at the gate. They won't let anyone get in."

"They let us in." Miranda interrupted the argument, her words quiet, but firm.

"Ms. Sheldon, I don't think you understand how much danger Hawke will be in once he steps outside this complex."

"I don't think *you* understand how much danger we've already been in. Partly because of you." She sounded weary and Hawke decided it was time to end the argument.

"She's coming with me." He took Miranda's hand and started moving toward the steps, but Jack grabbed his arm.

"You can't do your job if you're worrying about her."

"Which is why I'm not leaving her here. I'll be in touch as soon as I know something." He turned his back on the other man, shrugging away from his hold.

Though Hawke knew he wanted to, Jack didn't

argue any further, just followed them down the stairs and to the back door. "I'm the second pickup of the day. The van starts at Laurence's apartment. You'll want to go there first."

"You going to tell anyone I was here?"

"The news will get out one way or another." Jack cut a look toward his maid who'd been listening wide-eyed for much too long. "It's best if it comes from me."

"What are you going to tell them?"

"That you came in with a gun, looking for information about your brother and claiming you were set up."

"The truth is always the best cover."

"You and I really are alike, Morran." Jack pulled the back door open. "Good luck and Godspeed."

"I'll need both."

"You'll find your quarry. You always do."

He was right and this time would be no different. Not with the stakes so high. Simon's life and Miranda's hung in the balance. Failing the mission would mean failing them. "If you hear any news of my brother, call my compound in Mai Hong Son. I'll check in there periodically."

"Will do."

Hawke felt Jack's hard stare as he and Miranda moved away from the house, but he didn't look back. There was a lot of ground to cover before this journey ended. Looking back would only slow things down.

"Where to now?" The weariness in Miranda's voice remained, the deep circles beneath her eyes speaking of sleepless nights and fear.

"I'm heading to an apartment complex a few miles from here. I'm thinking that maybe you *should* stay here." A few hours alone in Jack's house might be preferable to dragging an obviously exhausted woman through the streets of Chiang Mai.

She blinked, shook her head. "I don't agree."

"When have you ever?" He smiled, caressed the smooth skin of her hand. "You'll be safe here for a few hours and that's all the time this will take me. You can rest, get ready for whatever happens next."

"While you're off fighting bad guys? I don't think so." The worry in her voice, in her eyes would have been humorous if Hawke hadn't been so touched by it.

He'd learned to take care of himself early. The death of his biological father, a marine who'd served in Vietnam, forced his mother to take on long hours of work to support Hawke. By the time Patrick Morran came into the picture, Hawke was ten years old going on twenty—responsible, hardworking and determined. No one had felt the need to worry about him. Since his parents' death, few had bothered.

And now he was staring into the eyes of a woman who had every right to be worried about herself, every reason to be moaning at her fate.

Instead all her energy, all her worry seemed to be for him.

"You don't need to worry about me, babe." He held her chin in his hand, her skin soft and smooth beneath his palm. "I've been doing this sort of thing for a long time. I'll be fine."

"And I'll be with you to make sure you are."

"Miranda—"

"I'm safer with you than alone. You know it. So do I. If you leave me behind, I'll just come looking for you. Now, come on. We're wasting time. I want to get this done."

"If you come with me, you do what I say."

"I always do."

"I can name at least two times when you didn't. Both could have gotten you killed."

"I thought you needed my help."

"I didn't. And even if I did, I wouldn't want you getting in the middle of things. No more running to my rescue, Miranda. Agreed?"

She frowned, but nodded. "Agreed."

"Then let's get out of here."

"I don't suppose we can walk out the front gate?"

"Sorry. We don't know who might be out there waiting for us to make an appearance." He hurried her toward the fence where his jacket still hung. "Ready for a leg up?"

"Ready."

"Try to drop fast this time. There will be people up and moving around by now."

"I'll do my best, boss."

Hawke smiled, brushing strands of Miranda's curly hair away from her cheeks. "I'm glad you finally understand how things work."

With that he hooked his hands around her foot and boosted her up to the top of the fence. As she disappeared over the other side, he did something he hadn't done in years. He prayed. Not for himself, but for Miranda. Surely a God like the one his parents had trusted in would be willing to listen to a selfless plea.

And maybe, just maybe, that same God would be willing to give second chances. If so, Hawke figured he needed one. The past few years had taught him how fleeting life was, speeding by so quickly that a man could be at the end of it before he ever realized he'd left the beginning.

After a decade spent chasing justice and revenge,

Hawke had chosen not to kill the man who'd ordered his parents' death. He didn't regret letting Sang Lao live. Sometimes, though, he regretted the years he'd devoted to bringing the drug kingpin down. While his high school and college friends had wives and children and had settled into the routine of family life, Hawke had settled into nothing but the knowledge of his own mortality; had gained nothing but scars and the memories that haunted him in the darkest hours of the night.

Sometimes he thought it was too late to change that. Other times, he knew he had to try. As he scaled the wall, he prayed that maybe, just maybe, God would grant him what he knew he desperately needed— peace.

Chapter Fourteen

Miranda landed on the pavement with a thud, stumbled backward and fell in a heap on the ground. Again.

"You okay?" Hawke dropped down beside her, offering a hand and pulling her to her feet.

"Sure, and though I think I've got the fall down pat, next time, I'd prefer landing on my feet."

"Let's hope there isn't a next time." Hawke put his hand on her elbow, hurrying her along the sidewalk and back the way they'd come. Chiang Mai had come to life in the time that they'd been in Jack McKenzie's house. People filled the sidewalk, some rushing to their destination, some sauntering along. Cars, motorcycles and taxis sped by. As did the strange three-wheeled vehicles Miranda had noticed in Bangkok. Three wheels. Justin would have loved it. His entire life had revolved around threes. Three sips of every drink. Three bites of every food. Three of every shirt, every pair of pants he'd owned. The thought brought hot tears and Miranda blinked them away, sure that if she let them fall, they'd never stop.

"What do you call that?" She pointed to the vehicle, forcing her mind to something other than her nephew.

"A *tuk-tuk*."

"It looks like a giant motorized tricycle."

"It is." He sounded distracted, his gaze scanning the growing crowd. "When this is over, we'll ride in one. I'll take you to the floating market, show you some of the tourist sights and some that aren't so touristy."

"*If* this is ever over." She was beginning to doubt it would be.

"It will be. Jack didn't give me those names because one of them might be the leak we're looking for. He gave them to me because he knows one is."

"Maybe, but I don't trust him. He used you."

"Yeah. And he and I are going to have a long talk about it. *After* I find the leak. But my gut says he's telling the truth."

"What if it's wrong?"

"It hasn't failed me yet." He frowned, glancing over his shoulder. "You did a pretty good job keeping up on our run yesterday. You ever run in the morning?"

"For exercise? Do I look like I do?"

"You look just like a woman should." His eyes met hers and Miranda's pulsed leaped at the admiration she saw there. "But I'm thinking now is as good a time as any to start a morning routine."

He yanked her in front of him, released his hold and gave her a gentle shove. "Go."

She ran, her feet pounding the pavement, Hawke right on her heels issuing directions in a calm, tight voice that worried her more than loud shouts would have. Someone was following them. That much was clear. Who or why remained to be seen.

Miranda fought the urge to look back over her shoulder, sure that if she saw someone coming up behind them, she'd freeze and get Hawke and herself killed.

"Come on, babe. You can move faster than this." Hawke urged her on and Miranda took off in a full-out sprint.

"Left."

She followed Hawke's command, turning left into a narrow alley and almost running headlong into a fence.

"Whoa." She skidded to a stop, her breath heaving from her lungs, her eyes scanning the trash-clogged area she stood in. "We're trapped."

"You're looking at it from the wrong perspective. We're not the ones trapped. They are."

They?

A shout sounded from somewhere close, the sound skittering along Miranda's nerves.

"Come here." Hawke grabbed her hand, pulling her to several trash cans overflowing with garbage. "Get behind these and don't come out."

She hurried to do as he said, squatting down behind the garbage, nearly gagging as the smell hit her nose. Rotted food littered the ground near her feet and a dead rat stared at her through flat, black eyes, maggots crawling through its fur in white wiggling masses. She looked away, her stomach rebelling at the sight, the stench and her fear.

Another shout followed the first, this time accompanied by pounding feet and muttered words. It sounded like an army was entering the alley. Miranda's pulse raced, adrenaline pouring through her so that she wanted to leap from her hiding place and run for safety.

Please, get us out of this in one piece, Lord.

The prayer had barely formed when silence descended. Thick and filled with malice, it surrounded

Miranda, taunting her, daring her to peek out from behind her hiding place. She bit her lip, her muscles rigid, her breath stalling in her throat. A soft sound drifted on the rank air, a shuffling footstep that made the hair on the back of Miranda's neck stand on end.

Her hands fisted, her fingernails digging into her palm. The sound came again, this time closer, and Miranda was sure someone was standing on the other side of the trash cans. She didn't dare move. Didn't dare breathe. Just slowly lifted her gaze, prepared for whatever she might see. *Whoever* she might see. No one was there. Not even a hint of a shadow drifted across her vision.

Seconds stretched into minutes. Minutes into eternity. Perhaps they'd gone to search another area. Or maybe they were waiting for Miranda or Hawke to make the first move.

A hoarse cry broke the silence, the sound so loud and so close, Miranda jumped. There was a crash, another shout, a thud. Muffled grunts. Muttered words. Something slammed into the trash can, releasing an avalanche of papers and garbage.

And then it was over.

Nothing moved, the air in the alley so still and thick Miranda was sure she would suffocate.

"Come on out." Hawke's voice broke the silence, the relief of it sweeping through Miranda in waves. She scrambled to her feet, her gaze searching for Hawke.

He stood at the far end of the alley, a man's body at his feet. Another lay a few yards away. A third slumped against a pile of garbage, blood seeping from his mouth and dripping onto the grimy pavement.

"Are they dead?" Miranda whispered the question, not really sure she wanted to hear his response.

"No, but they will be if they don't give me some answers." His eyes were icy with rage, his jaw set, each word a staccato beat that jabbed into the air.

"You're not really going to kill them." It was a protest more than a question.

"No? Watch me." He reached down, dragged the man up by his shirtfront and said something in Thai.

The man shook his head, speaking in quick, frantic gasps.

Hawke smiled, the expression so filled with malice Miranda took a step back. He spoke again, releasing the man's shirt and grabbing his neck.

"Hawke! No!" Miranda raced forward, horror at what she was seeing overriding fear, common sense and the self-preservation that had kept her still and quiet behind the rotting garbage and rat carcass.

"Stay there, Miranda." Hawke didn't raise his voice, his focus never straying from the man whose life he held in his hand, but his words were a steel-edged blade that might cut quickly and ruthlessly if she didn't obey.

A little more pressure and the man's air supply would be cut off, his tan skin already growing dusky and bluish, would darken. A lot more pressure and his trachea would be crushed, all hope of survival disappearing with his air supply. But there was no way it would come to that. No way Hawke would push things that far.

Would he?

Miranda didn't want to believe it could happen, but the image danced through her mind, sickening and real, the moment like a nightmare, her words sticking in her throat, her feet glued to the ground, indecisiveness holding her in place. She'd seen Hawke's rage, but he'd always maintained control. That didn't mean he couldn't or wouldn't lose it.

Trust him.

The thought came out of nowhere, so foreign Miranda wanted to ignore it. Trusting men wasn't what she did. Not anymore. She didn't plan to change that anytime soon. Especially not when the man was someone she barely knew. Yet somehow trusting Hawke at this moment, in this instance, seemed right; believing that he wouldn't coldheartedly murder a man seemed more possible than believing he would.

She stayed put, watching with a sort of numb detachment as the man Hawke held twisted and struggled in his grip, his skin growing a shade darker, his eyes bulging in terror. Finally, just as Miranda was sure he'd pass out, he spoke, the words rasping out in a waterfall of unintelligible sound.

Hawke must have understood. He smiled again, his eyes that of a predator, cold, hard and completely focused as he dropped the man to the ground in a puddle of coughing, choking humanity. Hawke spoke in harsh, angry tones and the man nodded, scrambling away, rushing from the alley.

Only then did Hawke turn his attention back to Miranda. His eyes gleamed cold and unforgiving, but his voice was calm, almost cajoling. "Come on, babe. We've got to hurry."

He held out a hand and Miranda moved toward him, her legs shaking so hard she was afraid they'd give out. "What did he tell you?"

"Not as much as I'd hoped he would. A drug dealer named Mahang Sharee hired him to bring me in. Apparently, Sharee has my brother and wants to negotiate a trade."

"Attacking us in an alley is a funny way to open up negotiations."

"Yeah, it is that, isn't it? They would have killed me and brought my body in if they could have managed it. Offering my brother in trade was plan B."

"In trade for what?"

"Me. I turn myself over. My brother goes free."

"Not really."

"No," he spoke quietly, his hand on her shoulder in unconscious support. "And they know I know it. They also know I'll do whatever it takes to have at least a chance of gaining Simon's freedom."

"What now?"

"We find Sharee."

"Do you have any idea where he is?"

"Last time I heard, he was over the border in Myanmar."

"That's pretty vague."

"Yeah, but I'm not worried. His man will pass along my message. In a few hours, I'll be hearing from him."

"And hopefully he'll lead you to Simon."

"Right."

"But what does Sharee have to do with what happened in Maryland? We're half a world away from Liam and Green."

"Half a world away from Green, but not from the Wa and that's who pays the bills for both men."

"The Wa?"

They reached the motorcycle and Hawke got on, gesturing for Miranda to climb on after him. "They're a militia group based in Myanmar and make their money selling opium. Sharee is a big part of that. The DEA has been trying to bring him down for years, but every time they get close he disappears, or their informants do."

"Just like with Harold Green."

"Just like with him." Hawke squeezed her hand.

"So, the same agent leaking information to one is also leaking it to the other."

"We're thinking alike, babe. And I'd say Green and Sharee aren't the only ones who are paying for inside information. Our guy has got to be making a lot of money. The question is, what is he doing with it?"

"Putting it in a Swiss bank account?"

"Maybe."

"Where else could it be?"

"Used for something that Jack hasn't found yet."

"Like?"

"I don't know, but I plan to find out. Let's go check out some houses. A man's loyalties can be found in his personal space."

With that they roared out of the alley and into traffic, the motorcycle speeding past vehicles, exhaust fumes stinging Miranda's lungs. She clutched Hawke's waist, buried her head in the back of his shirt, trying to quiet the wild throbbing of her pulse and praying that Hawke was right, that they'd find the information they needed. That soon she'd be on her way home, heading back to the silent town house and her little business, to the life that had seemed enough until Justin's death, but that now stretched out before her, devoid of purpose.

No, that wasn't quite right. Her life wasn't devoid of purpose, it was devoid of the certainty she'd had. In the years that she'd been Justin's primary caregiver, she'd been so sure of her place here on earth. Now that he was gone, she didn't know what direction her life would take, wasn't even sure how she could know if the direction she chose was the one God wanted for her.

She was determined to figure it out, though. Determined to do it right this time, to not hesitate when God put a task before her, to trust that He would guide her and keep her from making the same foolish mistakes she'd made in the past.

Of course, all her determination wouldn't mean a thing if she didn't make it out of Thailand alive. She prayed that she would, that she'd have another chance to mend fences with her sister, to create a stronger relationship with her brother, to live life to its fullest. No fear. No timidity. No shying away from what she knew was right.

Hawke took a sharp corner, the motorcycle tilting, the world tilting with it, colors and sounds so bright and vivid, Miranda closed her eyes and pressed closer to Hawke's back, inhaling his masculine scent. Her fingers dug into his side, her heart beating in time with his, her prayer for herself becoming a prayer for him, that he, too, would find purpose in the wild, crazy world he lived in. That God would touch his heart, heal his hurts and bring him safely through whatever trouble was to come.

That He'd bring them both through it.

Together.

The word floated through her head, stuck fast in her heart, making her feel less alone than she had in a long, long time.

And that, Miranda thought, was not a good thing.

Chapter Fifteen

Breaking into houses was easier than Miranda could have imagined. Still, she wasn't sure if she should be impressed or appalled that Hawke was so good at it. They entered the first apartment through the front door, sauntering through a lobby, into an elevator and onto the correct floor as if they belonged there. Hawke knocked twice, waited a few minutes and then set to work on the lock. Within minutes, he had the door open.

"There's no security system that I can see. Let's go."

"What if there's one that you can't see?"

"Then we're in trouble." He tugged her into the apartment, and closed the door behind them. They were standing in a beige living room. The carpet, walls and furniture all varying shades of light brown. A few pictures decorated the wall, but even they lacked color, the watery pastel prints commanding little attention.

"I don't think this is our guy." She whispered the words, though the house felt empty.

"No? Why not?"

"He's got no imagination and no drive. Look how bland this room is."

"Maybe it's that way because his time and creative energy is being used somewhere else."

"How can we know?"

"We search."

"For...?"

"For something that looks important."

An hour later, they'd found nothing more exciting than an application for a dating service and Miranda was more convinced than ever that the man who lived in the apartment wasn't the leak.

"I think we're wasting time." She shot a glance at Hawke who was sifting through a canister of flour, his dark hands coated in white powder.

He brushed them off, replaced the canister lid. "You've got good instincts, babe. Let's get out of here."

The next apartment was occupied, the woman who answered the door a fortysomething American with bleached-blond hair and a bright smile. "Yes?"

"Mrs. Austin?"

"Yes?"

"I'm Agent Randolph and this is Agent Johnson. We work with your husband."

"Is something wrong?"

"Not at all. We conduct a drug awareness program at the orphanage just outside of Chiang Mai. Do you know it?"

"I do. My friends and I visit there once a month."

"That must be why your husband said you might have something to contribute." Hawke smiled, his voice warm and friendly. He looked nothing like the man who'd nearly choked someone in an alley just a short time ago.

"Contribute?"

"We're collecting used books and toys to take over there later today."

"He must have forgotten to mention it, but I'm sure I've got some things here you can have. Come on in. I'll only be a minute." She opened the door wide, gestured for them to enter. "Would you like something to drink? Tea? Water? Coffee?"

"We're fine, and you don't need to trouble yourself looking for donations. We can come again in two weeks when we're scheduled to go back to the orphanage." Hawke smiled again, shooting a warning in Miranda's direction, his lies so smooth and convincing it was hard to believe he hadn't practiced them.

"Oh, no. You're here and I've got fifteen minutes before I need to leave for my women's club meeting. Let me just run and have a look." She disappeared down the hall, and Hawke moved quickly, crossing the room, scanning a bookshelf that stood against the wall, picking up a framed photo. Then another.

"Do you—"

He shook his head sharply, stepping away from the shelf as Mrs. Austin returned, her arms filled with books. "My kids don't read these anymore. I'd love for you to take them."

"Thank you. Do you mind if I use your restroom before we leave?"

"Go right ahead. It's down the hall and to the left."

"Thanks. And maybe I'll take you up on the offer of a drink if it's not too much bother."

"Of course. What can I get for you?"

"Water will be fine. How about you, Ms. Johnson?" There was a message in Hawke's eyes, but Miranda couldn't read it. Did he want her to accept? Refuse?

"Sure, a glass of water would be great." She managed to get the words out, saw the approval in Hawke's gaze and knew she was on the right track.

If this were a movie, she'd create a distraction so Hawke could search the rest of the house. But what kind of distraction? A fainting spell? A fire?

Maybe simple conversation was the best bet.

"Let me help you." She stood, following Mrs. Austin into her bright, airy kitchen. The dust motes dancing in the sunlight that streamed through the tall windows, the yellow walls and the crayon-art decoration on the refrigerator all reminded Miranda of home. "You have a lovely home."

"Thank you. It's not really what I'd hoped for when we got here. I'd been thinking we'd get a single family home, but they didn't have any available. How about you?"

"I'm in an apartment here, too."

"Have you been here long?"

"No. I just arrived."

"I thought so. My husband mentioned that a new agent was arriving soon. How do you like it so far?"

"Thailand seems like a wonderful place to work." She hoped Mrs. Austin wouldn't press for more, because she knew nothing about the kind of day to day work that went into being a DEA agent.

"It's a great country. Though I've got to say, I'm looking forward to returning home." She handed Miranda a glass of ice water.

"When will that be?" Miranda took a sip of water, hoping she could keep the conversation focused on the other woman.

"Another year. Maybe two. We were going to return

to Michigan this year, but my husband thought staying here for another year would help us financially."

Miranda's pulse accelerated at the mention of finances. If Hawke had been in the room, he would have known what to say, but he wasn't and Miranda struggled to come up with something that would keep the conversation moving in the same direction. "That sounds like a smart move."

"I guess so. We've got two kids to put through college, so I can't argue that it's not, but I miss home. My parents, sister and brother, their kids. I'd be happy to be back there with them again." She shrugged, smiled. "But you didn't come here to hear my life story."

"It's okay. I understand."

"Do you have a large family?"

"Not really, but what I have I already miss." That, at least, was the truth.

"Are we ready, Johnson?" Hawke strode into the room, the books in his hands, and accepted the glass of water Mrs. Austin held out to him.

"Yes." More than ready.

"Thank you for your donation, Mrs. Austin."

They said their goodbyes, stepped out into the hall, and walked away as the door clicked shut behind them.

Miranda almost sagged with relief. "I hope the next place is empty. I'm not good at pretending to be someone I'm not."

"I don't think we're going to have to worry about it." Hawke stepped past the elevator and pushed open a door that led to the stairwell, pulling Miranda inside.

"What do you mean?"

"The picture on the bookshelf was interesting."

"The family photo?"

"Yeah. But it wasn't the family that caught my attention. It was the background. It looked like it was taken in Russia. I found a photo album in their bedroom. One of those scrapbooks women like to keep. Labeled real nice. There were pictures of a trip the Austins took to Chechnya before they were married."

"You were in their bedroom?"

"Did you really think I was visiting the little boy's room, babe?"

"No. You just work fast. Do you think the trip to Chechnya has relevance?"

"I think someone very close to the Austins must live there."

"That's not surprising. Lots of people in the States have relatives in other countries."

"True, but I've got a feeling about this."

"What kind of feeling?"

"The kind that tells me Austin might have a place to send tens of thousands of dollars a year. The kind that tells me we'd better wait for his wife to leave and take a closer look at the apartment."

"I hope you're wrong. She seems so nice and they've got two kids"

"Life would be a lot simpler if the bad guys were easy to spot. Most of the time, though, they're just average people on the surface. Only further examination can ever reveal the truth."

"I hope further examination proves Austin is innocent. If he isn't, the entire family will be devastated."

"Bad choices lead to bad consequences. Not only for the one who makes them. We've got to accept that and do what we've set out to do. If that means bringing a nice woman's husband to justice, so be it." Hawke cracked the stairwell door open. "Mrs. Austin said she had a meeting. Let's see if she leaves on time."

It didn't take long. Fifteen minutes later, Miranda followed Hawke back into the Austin's apartment.

"You search the living room. I'll take the bedroom." Hawke disappeared down the hall and Miranda went to work. She had no idea what they were looking for, but she searched anyway, rifling through books, leafing through opened mail that lay in a pile on an end table. There was nothing suspicious, nothing unusual.

"I don't see anything in here." As she spoke, a sound came from the corridor beyond the closed apartment door. Miranda's heart leaped and she hurried toward the bedroom and Hawke.

He was kneeling in front of a bureau, looking at a piece of paper, but rose to his feet as Miranda entered the room. "What's up?"

"There's someone out in the hall."

"Probably someone returning to his apartment." As he said it, he grabbed what looked like a packet of letters and some old photographs from the drawer. "But we'd better take the back way out just in case."

"Back way? What back way?" Miranda was almost afraid to hear Hawke's answer.

"Right here." He unlocked a window, opened it, shoved out a screen and gestured Miranda over. "Come on."

Miranda peered out the window, saw a wrought-iron fire escape. "Wonderful."

"It could be worse."

A loud crash sounded from down the hall, and Miranda jumped, her eyes meeting Hawke's.

"Go!" He growled the words and Miranda obeyed, clamoring through the open window and onto the fire escape, her hands slippery on the cold metal, her body humming with adrenaline.

She didn't hear Hawke following her and didn't waste time looking to see if he was. Whoever was coming in the apartment wasn't being subtle about it and Miranda had no intention of sticking around to find out why. She raced down the fire escape, ran around the corner of the building and kept going, not sure where she was headed, only knowing she had to get away.

Chapter Sixteen

"Slow down, babe. People are starting to notice us."
Hawke grabbed Miranda's arm and forced her to walk,
shortening his own stride to match hers.

"Are they behind us?" Miranda's voice shook, but
she looked almost calm, the pulse beating rapidly in
the hollow of her throat the only indication of the terror
she was feeling.

"If they are, they're staying back." He glanced over
his shoulder as he spoke, but saw only the crowd of
tourists and business people rushing to their destina-
tions.

"But they could be there."

"They could be."

"I was hoping you'd disagree."

"Sorry, babe. I call it like I see it."

"You found something in the apartment, didn't you?
Something that's convinced you Austin is the leak."

"Yeah, I did." He smiled, but the hair on the back of
his neck was standing on end, alarm bells screaming
that their pursuers were close.

"Come on. This way." He yanked Miranda into an

alley, running now, keeping a few steps behind her, knowing that his body was poor protection from a bullet.

"Here!" He yanked her into a small fabric shop, the Indian proprietor taking in his and Miranda's appearance.

"Can I help you?" His English was precise and clear, his unhappiness obvious.

Hawke ignored him, moving through the store quickly, then into a back room, the man following along and complaining the entire time. A back door led out into another alley, and Hawke hurried Miranda into it. "Just a little farther. We're close to where I left the motorcycle."

"How close?" Miranda panted the words, her breath heaving with exertion as they ran full-out, her shorter legs moving twice as fast to keep up the pace.

"Really close."

"Did we lose them?"

"No. We just bought a couple minutes. Here we are." He nudged Miranda down a side street teaming with tourists and lined with vendors selling brightly colored hats, silk fans and fruit. Hawke wound his way through the crowd, his hand on Miranda's shoulder, his muscles tight, his skin prickling with awareness. Danger wasn't far behind them. He knew it. He could only hope the crowd would keep it at bay long enough to get Miranda to safety.

The street where he'd left the motorcycle was quiet, only a few locals and tourists wandering from shop to shop. Hawke hurried Miranda to the motorcycle, everything inside him saying they needed to get out of Chiang Mai *now*.

"Where are we going?"

"Home."

"Mine or yours?"

"Mine."

"In Bangkok?"

"Mae Hong Son."

"Where is that?"

"You ask a lot of questions, babe."

"Maybe if you gave more answers I wouldn't have to." She climbed onto the motorcycle behind him, her hands wrapped around his waist, small and warm and more familiar than they should have been after only a few days. It seemed they'd known each other much longer than that; a bond had formed between them, one that spanned more than a few dozen hours, a few shared moments and a common goal.

Hawke shook his head, denying the thought. There could never be a bond between people as completely different as he and Miranda.

He turned the ignition, starting the motorcycle just as two men rounded the corner of the street, their gazes scanning the area and settling on Hawke and Miranda. A flash of metal warned Hawke seconds before the pavement exploded just feet away from the motorcycle.

Miranda screamed, her fingers digging into his sides as Hawke gunned the engine and headed toward the approaching gunmen.

"Are you crazy? You're going to get killed!" Miranda shouted the words, hoping to penetrate whatever crazed fog Hawke was in.

"Keep your head down and hold on." His shouted reply did nothing to ease the horror that squeezed the air from her lungs, and cut off another scream.

She could see the men clearly—their tan complexions, their dark, cold eyes, the grim determined expressions on their faces.

Their guns.

They took aim. Fired. A bullet whizzed by. Another slammed into the sidewalk. Someone screamed, the sound echoed by another and another. People dove for cover, hiding behind cars, diving onto the pavement, protecting themselves in whatever way they could.

But Hawke didn't seem concerned about protection. He just kept going, driving straight toward the shooters, determined to run them down, accelerating so that wind tore at Miranda's hair and stung her eyes, nearly blinding her. Tears streamed down her cheeks but she couldn't close her eyes, couldn't force herself to look away from the horrifying tableau.

The men dove for cover as Hawke raced toward them, their guns firing, the bullets going wild. Miranda was sure that at any moment Hawke would slump forward, blood streaming from a bullet wound, the motorcycle crashing onto the pavement and skidding to a stop. She expected to feel the impact of a bullet tearing through her own flesh, and wondered if it would throw her off the cycle. If she would even be alive to find out.

Then they were rounding a corner, putting a building between themselves and the gunmen, and the sound of screams, of gunfire, of panic disappeared under the chugging rumble of the motorcycle.

Shock kept her silent. That was the only explanation Miranda could think of for not saying what she was thinking—that Hawke Morran had almost gotten himself killed. Minutes passed as buildings and shops gave way to houses and thick grassland. Terraced rice fields gleamed in the sunlight, attended by women wearing sarongs and straw hats. Dark clouds darkened the horizon, giving the world a sinister atmosphere despite the bright sun shining in a brilliant blue sky.

Everything seemed sinister. The man using water buffalo to plow a field. The thatched huts that stood on spindly legs above thick green foliage. The women walking along the side of the road, baskets held close to their bellies or perched on their heads. All had the potential for hidden danger. Another attack could come from any direction at any time and Hawke might very well run right into it again.

Miranda's heart beat faster, her body shaking with fear she no longer seemed able to control. A few scattered buildings dotted the landscape, signs jutting up from paved parking lots filled with buses and cars. Hawke pulled into one, stopping the motorcycle next to a gas pump and filling the tank.

Miranda could feel his gaze as he worked. She knew he was studying her but she didn't meet his eyes.

"You're still shaking." He pulled her off the bike and wrapped his arms around her, pressing her head against his chest as he murmured something in Thai, his voice so warm, so filled with concern, she wanted to dive into it, eke out all the comfort it offered.

"I've never been so scared in my life."

"But it's over now and you're safe." His hands smoothed down her hair and rested on her waist, his fingers tracing patterns on her back.

"I'm safe, but you almost got yourself shot trying to run those men down. For what? Revenge? Would it have been worth it if you ended up dead on the street?"

"Is that what you think? That I was trying to run them down?" His arms dropped away and he took a step back, all the concern, all the warmth gone from his voice.

"Weren't you?"

"Is that the kind of man you think I am? One that would risk your life to carry out a vendetta?" His eyes were storm-cloud gray, his expression shuttered.

Did she? Over the past few days Hawke had never done anything to jeopardize Miranda's safety. At times when he might have abandoned her, he'd stuck close, slowing down to accommodate her even when that meant risking his own safety. "Not my life. Yours. And I just thought that in the heat of the moment—"

"In the *heat of the moment* you thought I would trade your safety for revenge? That's supposed to make me feel better?" He spit the words out, disgust curling his lip and hardening his jaw.

"But you rode right toward them. You could have just turned and driven away." Her words were a lame attempt to justify what she'd believed, but even as she spoke them she knew they had no weight, no meaning.

"And have you shot in the back while we rode away? I took them by surprise. They were expecting retreat. I attacked. It was enough to get us to safety." He climbed back on the motorcycle as he spoke, his shoulders stiff, his tone harsh.

"I—"

"Get back on the bike. We've got hours to go before we make Mae Hong Son."

"Hawke—"

"Get on the bike." He bit out each word, anger making his scar stand out stark white against his dark skin, his gaze so cold and implacable that Miranda knew the conversation was over.

She climbed on behind Hawke, putting her hands

on his waist. He tensed beneath her touch, his muscles unyielding as he started the engine.

Miranda was sure he'd pull back out onto the road, but he drove toward one of the many vendors set up in the open stalls instead and called to a young woman selling wide-brimmed straw hats. She hurried over, carrying a hat and a scarf made of red Thai silk. They bantered back and forth for a moment before Hawke exchanged a few coins for the hat. As soon as the woman walked away, he turned in his seat and faced Miranda with an expression devoid of emotion. "You're getting a sunburn."

"I'll be okay."

He ignored her comment, turning his attention to the hat, pulling the silk over its crown and pushing it through slats in the straw on either side. When he was finished, he placed it on Miranda's head, tying the silk snugly beneath her chin.

"Thank you."

He nodded, turning away without comment.

His anger had been understandable. His kindness nearly broke Miranda's heart.

As they pulled out onto the road, she felt a loss she couldn't explain, her stomach sick with the knowledge that she'd hurt a man who'd been doing everything he could to protect her. She wanted to apologize, but the roar of the motorcycle and her own guilt kept her from speaking. What could she possibly say that could make things better? How could she possibly explain her thoughts?

She didn't know, so she remained silent as the miles passed and the distant clouds moved closer.

Chapter Seventeen

They drove into the downpour, a heavy sheet of rain slapping Miranda's shoulders and pinging off the pavement. Where everything had been dry, there was now half an inch of water, the fields and road swimming in it. Miranda thought Hawke would press on, driving through the sudden onslaught.

Instead he pulled the motorcycle to the side of the road. "Those trees will provide some cover. Let's go."

He got off the motorcycle, motioned for Miranda to do the same, then started across the field, heading toward two distant trees whose thick fronds provided a canopy of sorts. Leaves and branches weren't going to do much good—Miranda was already soaking wet—but pointing it out would be a waste of time, so she followed Hawke, the world reduced to slashing rain and green grass, gray skies and splashing puddles. Ankle-deep water sloshed against her legs as she walked, seeping into her shoes, socks and jeans until she felt waterlogged, her legs heavy, her body moving in slow motion. The idea of stopping where she was and sitting in the wet grass while the rain poured down appealed a lot more than continuing toward the trees.

She kept going anyway, her feet sinking into mud and muck, her nose filling with the loamy scent of wet earth, creatures scurrying in front of her, bugs, rodents and birds taking flight as she moved toward them.

Finally, she made it to the trees, ducking under low-hanging leaves and into a relatively dry patch of earth and grass. Hawke had the motorcycle parked near the trunk, and was crouching in front of his pack, rummaging through it.

He looked up as Miranda entered the shelter, his silvery eyes unreadable. "As soon as the rain stops, we'll get back on the road."

"How long do you think that will be?"

He shrugged, turning his attention back to the pack. "Fifteen minutes. An hour. More. It's hard to say during the rainy season."

"I'll pray it's less time rather than more."

Hawke didn't comment, just pulled a packet of papers and photos from under his shirt, wiped the moisture from them and wrapped them in a plastic bag he'd pulled from his pack. When he was finished, he closed the pack and held it out to Miranda. "Use this as a pillow and rest for a while. We've got another five hours of driving ahead of us and I don't want to have to stop again unless we have to."

The words were curt and Miranda took them for what they were—a not-so-subtle hint to stop talking. She wanted to ignore them, wanted to keep trying to fill the hollow silence, but knew being quiet would be the smarter choice. Her words had done enough damage for one day.

She grabbed the pack, laid it on the grass and

dropped down beside it, the ground surprisingly soft beneath her as she stretched out on her side. The patter of rain above, the splash of it beyond the leaves became a quiet lullaby, the humid air a blanket. Miranda's eyes drifted closed, but she forced them open, afraid to sleep; afraid of what she'd wake to.

"Let yourself go for a while, Miranda. I'll make sure you're safe."

She jumped at the sound of Hawke's voice, saw that he had moved closer and was sitting with his arms crossed in front of his chest, his damp hair falling across his cheeks.

Miranda couldn't see his expression, but sensed a softening in him. If she were going to apologize now was the time to do it. "I'm sorry I hurt you. I wasn't thinking clearly."

"It's hard to think with bullets flying by your head."

"You managed it."

"I'm used to it."

"So you do this kind of thing a lot?"

"Not if I can help it, but tracking down drug dealers often puts a person in situations he'd rather avoid."

"How long have you been working with the DEA?"

"Nine months. But I've been hunting down drug traders for ten years."

"That's a long time."

"A lifetime." He raked his hair back, tying it with a strip of leather he pulled from his pocket. His profile was strong, stark, devoid of softness, but his hand was gentle as he placed it over Miranda's mouth. "Now be quiet and sleep. We've got a long day ahead of us."

She tugged his hand away from her mouth, holding it as she studied his face, his scar, his long fingers and broad palms, everything about him completely familiar and absolutely foreign. "I really am sorry. I should have known you wouldn't put yourself in danger without good reason."

He shook his head, smiling a little. "Will you spend the rest of our time together worrying more about me than you do about yourself?"

"Trust me, I'm worried about myself."

"Yet it didn't even occur to you that turning the bike around and riding away from the shooters could easily have gotten you killed."

"Given enough time I probably would have thought about that."

"Maybe, but I doubt it." He skimmed the knuckles of his free hand down her cheek. "You've asked a lot of questions. Now, I have one for you."

"What is it?"

"The first night we met, you smelled like apples and cinnamon, so sweet and intoxicating I was sure I must be imagining it. Was it some exotic perfume designed just for you?"

"I'd been baking a pie. It's what I do. Bake things." She was stammering, her face heating.

"Bake things?"

"I own a bakery in Essex. Or I did. Now that Justin is gone…"

"What?"

"I opened it mostly for him. To give him a place other than the house where he could feel comfortable. We spent a lot of time there together. I'm not sure I want to keep working in a place that holds so many memories."

"Good memories?"

"Mostly. Some not so good."

"It was hard raising your nephew."

"No. Raising him wasn't hard. What was hard was knowing Justin was locked inside himself and that there was no key to open his mind and let him out."

"You were his key, I think."

"No. I wanted to be, but even I couldn't manage that. I use to pray all the time that he'd be cured, that some miracle drug would be found and Justin would become the child he use to be."

"But he is now. After death, a person is freed from disease, from heartache, from pain. Isn't that what you believe?" He watched her, his stillness and intensity making Miranda wonder what it was he was seeking.

"Yes. It's part of what I believe, anyway."

"What's the other part?"

"That dying means eternity spent with God."

"For some."

"For anyone who believes. It's about faith. Relationships. Love."

"Perhaps that's the part I've been missing."

"Belief?"

"No. I believe there is a God. How could I not? Relationship and love are what I haven't quite figured out."

"And faith?"

"I'm learning." He stretched, pulled his cell phone from his pocket. "Let's see if this works. It's past time I contacted Jack. And I should be hearing from Sharee soon, too. News of my brother will be welcome."

Miranda nodded, settling back onto the ground, her skin chilled from the wet clothes she wore.

Hawke's quiet words were barely audible, his face turned away. Miranda let her mind wander, her thoughts drifting on the pattering hum of rain. Thoughts that only seemed able to go in one direction—Hawke.

Miranda had known atheists. She'd known agnostics. She'd never known a man who believed in God but had no faith in Him. Who understood the existence of the creator but didn't have a relationship with Him.

But, then, she'd never known a man like Hawke.

Her own father had professed to be a Christian, his pilgrimages to Christmas and Easter services fulfilling whatever need he had to live that faith. Every man she'd ever dated had been the same, professing Christianity only when it suited him.

Hawke was different. Whatever he believed, he lived. Whatever road he took, he stayed on it until he reached the end. He wouldn't sit on fences, waffle between ideals or change his mind with his moods. He was constant, steady, someone who could always be counted on to know the truth and live it.

She closed her eyes, praying for Hawke as the rain continued to fall and her mind finally gave in to sleep.

"We've got to get moving." The words drifted into Miranda's dreams, pulling her from sleep.

She jerked upright, her heart racing, stars dancing in front of her eyes at the quickness of the motion.

"Slow down, babe." Hawke put a hand on her shoulder, holding her steady.

"I'm ready."

"Just sit for a second. Here." He took a banana and a bottle of water from his pack and handed to her. "Eat."

"What about you?"

"I already had something."

Miranda took a bite of banana, swallowed some water and stood. "Now I really am ready."

"Finish the banana, then we'll go."

"Are you always so bossy?"

"Are you always so combative?" He smiled as he said it, pulling the water from Miranda's hands and taking a drink from it before passing the bottle back to her.

"Only when I'm with you."

"Then I guess we bring out the best in each other."

Miranda laughed and took another bite of banana. "If this is my best, I'd hate to see what my worst is. How long did I sleep?"

"Two hours. Longer than I would have liked, but we both needed the rest."

"Were you able to reach Jack?"

"Yeah. He gave me some information about Austin. Most of it I'd already guessed. He was adopted from Russia when he was six. According to birth records his parents were from Chechnya."

"What about the photos?"

"I described them, but there's not much Jack can take from that. He's going to do some research. See if he can find any connection between Austin's paternal or maternal family and the militia groups in Chechnya."

"What are you thinking?"

"I'm thinking that if Austin is the one selling information, he's using his earnings to fund one of the groups fighting for power in the country where he was born."

Hawke grabbed the pack, stood and extended a hand to Miranda. "We've got to get moving. I want to reach Mae Hong Son before nightfall. We'll both be safer there."

"Don't worry, I'm as anxious to get there as you are."

"Good. Because if something happens to me, if

we get separated, I want you to find your way there. People in town know me. They'll be able to get you to my home. That's the only place where you'll be safe."

"What's going on? Why are you telling me this?"

"Because things are about to get a whole lot worse than they've been. Mae Hong Son is close to Myanmar. Myanmar is the Wa's playground. And the Wa and I go back a long way."

"Ten years."

"Yeah. I've been doing everything in my power to close them down since the day they murdered my family. And they've been doing everything in their power to keep me from succeeding. Come on, we've wasted enough time." He turned away, pushing the motorcycle out from under the trees.

Miranda raced after him, splashing through puddles, his words replaying over and over again as she climbed onto the back of the bike and they began their journey again.

Chapter Eighteen

By the time they reached the outskirts of Mae Hong Son, it was dark and Hawke could feel Miranda sagging against his back, her forehead resting on his shoulder, her hands barely holding his sides. She'd been exhausted when they left Chiang Mai. Now her fatigue seemed a living thing, weighing her down and threatening to topple them both from the motorcycle.

"You still with me?" He shouted the words over the rumble of the motor. Miranda lifted her head, her grip tightening a fraction, his words apparently dragging her from the half-sleep state he'd suspected she was in.

"Where else would I be?"

"In a dream a whole lot nicer than our reality."

"It's kind of hard to dream when you're sitting on the back of a motorcycle." Fatigue and dehydration added a raspy edge to her voice and Hawke winced in sympathy. It had been two hours since their last stop for fuel. Longer since their last drink of water. The fact that she wasn't complaining didn't mean Miranda wasn't suffering. But as much as he sympathized, Hawke couldn't make himself stop.

The stakes weren't the same as they had been in Bangkok and there was no time to waste on rest and refreshment. Sharee had upped the ante when he'd taken Simon. If the drug lord hadn't called Hawke's Mae Hong Son compound already, Hawke would find a way to send word to him. It was time to set the meeting. The sooner the better.

"Is that Mae Hong Son?" Miranda interrupted his thoughts, her words pulling him from the dark path his mind was traveling.

"Yes."

"It's beautiful."

Hawke looked at the town where he'd spent the first ten years of his life—the mountains dark shadows against the night sky, the houses and buildings a cluster of lights, the night unfolding in a hushed expectancy. There was mystery here, carried in on the mountain mist that shrouded the town in the morning and evening, gathering force from the thick jungles that surrounded the tiny place. There was, he supposed, beauty in that, though it had been years since he'd taken the time to notice it. "Yes, it is. More so during the day, though, when you can see the mountains and jungles, the water and sky."

"Then it won't just be beautiful. It will be breathtaking." She paused for a moment, her body shifting slightly as if she were trying to get a better look. "It's smaller than I thought."

"Most people say the same. Mae Hong Son is a surprise. They expect a larger town, but are never disappointed in what they find here."

"What do they find?"

"It depends on what they seek. Some find peace, a sense of oneness with nature. Others find proof of God

in His creation. Too many find easy access to heroin."
His biological father had been one of those, his death
from overdose taking him just a year after he'd married
Hawke's mother. Hawke hadn't known him enough to
mourn him. Patrick had been his father, his mentor,
his friend. He, Hawke did mourn and probably always
would.

"That's sad."

"More so for the families that are destroyed by it."

"You sound as if you know."

"My father became an addict here. It killed him."

"Is that why you're so determined to destroy the
Wa?"

"No. He chose to give his life over to his addic-
tion. My stepfather, mother and sister did not. They
were killed in cold blood as an example of what would
happen to businessmen who refused to work with the
Wa." Even now, so many years later, saying it filled
Hawke with fury. His hands tightened on the handle-
bars; his jaw clenched to keep more words from pouring out.

"I'm so sorry, Hawke."

"I am, too, but the past is just that. The present is
for the living."

"If it is, then why are you trying so hard to avenge
the murder of your family?" If anyone other than Miranda had asked the question, Hawke would have ignored it. But there was something about Miranda that
demanded answers. Even when Hawke wasn't quite
sure what those answers were.

"I didn't want revenge. I wanted justice."

"Sometimes they're the same thing."

"Maybe they are, but what happened to my family
demanded retribution." Or so he'd thought. Now, after

years of fighting drug traffickers, he wasn't so sure that retribution would accomplish anything.

"Retribution isn't for us to demand."

"But if you could demand it from the drunk driver who killed your nephew, would you?"

She was silent for a moment and Hawke wondered if his words had poured salt in the wound of her loss. He opened his mouth to apologize but she spoke before he could. "Maybe."

It was an honest answer and more than what he would have given with a loved one's death still so raw and new. "And maybe if I'd devoted myself to something else, you and I wouldn't be here tonight."

He turned down the side road that led to his compound, the lights from Mae Hong Son disappearing from view as he drove in the opposite direction of the town, the darkness suddenly complete but for headlights illuminating the road.

"I thought we were going to Mae Hong Son."

"We're there."

"The town, I mean. It's behind us."

"I live a few miles outside of it."

"How many is a few?" The weariness in her voice was obvious and Hawke wished he had a different answer.

"Twenty."

"So. A half hour more. I can do anything for a half hour." She rested her head against his back again. He could feel the smooth curve of her cheek and jaw. He imagined her moss-green eyes and freckled skin, imagined driving her through the mountains of Mae Hong Son when the sun was shining and Sharee's men weren't after them. It was a dangerous thought. One he couldn't afford. Miranda wasn't the kind of woman who'd take to riding on the back of a motorcycle. She was more the type to stand in a sunny kitchen baking pies and humming hymns. That simplicity, that wholesomeness wasn't something Hawke wanted to taint with the darkness he carried in his soul.

He forced his mind to the conversation and away from what he shouldn't even be contemplating. "You can do whatever you set your mind to for as long as you need to."

"I think you have more confidence in me than I have in myself."

"Whatever it takes, babe." He glanced in the mirror, peering into the darkness behind them, his skin suddenly tight, his nerves shooting warnings to his brain. He saw nothing but blackness, heard nothing but the rumble of the motorcycle and his own quickening heartbeat.

But something was there. He sensed it as surely as he'd sensed trouble in the seconds before he'd been knocked unconscious in Essex. If Sharee's men were going to attack this would be the place to do it. Too far from town and from Hawke's compound to have their attack interfered with, no side roads for Hawke to lose them on.

He accelerated, pushing the motorcycle to speeds that were just short of reckless. The ill-kept road, bumpy and slick from rain, was an accident waiting to happen, but only the thought of Miranda, helmetless on the back of the cycle, kept him from pushing it to top speed.

"What's wrong?" Miranda's shout barely carried above the rush of wind and roar of the motor.

"Just a feeling."

"What kind of feeling?"

"The feeling that trouble is right behind us."

She shifted and Hawke was sure she'd turned her head to try and see whatever might be there. "I think you're right."

"You see something?"

"I think so. No headlights, but something darker in the blackness." She paused. "Or maybe not. It's hard to tell."

If she thought she was seeing something, Hawke figured she was.

"Hold on tight." He pushed the motorcycle harder, the bounce of wheels on the cracked and crumbling asphalt making him worry even more for Miranda's safety.

"I think it's a car. And I think it's gaining on us." Hawke sensed her panic in the taut, clipped tone of her voice and the painful grip she had on his waist.

Far in the distance, the compound beckoned—a pinpoint of light that might have been a star, a campfire, or headlights, but that Hawke knew was home. He cut the lights on the motorcycle, the world becoming a pitch-black tomb, then coasted to a stop.

With the engine off, he could hear the rumble of another vehicle speeding toward them.

"What's going on? What are we doing?" Miranda whispered the question, as if fearing that the sound of her voice might carry to those coming after them.

"We can't outrun them on this bike, but we may be able to outsmart them on foot."

"On foot? Are you crazy? We're in the middle of nowhere."

"No. We're not." He got off the motorcycle, and tugged Miranda off beside him. "See that light?" He turned her head, so that she was looking in the direction of the compound.

"The one that looks like it's a hundred miles away?"

"That's home. Gates, guns and guards I trust with my life. All we have to do is get there." He pulled the motorcycle into knee-high grass, laying it down so that a passing car would easily miss it.

"I like the sound of that."

"Come on." He moved deeper into the grass. "It won't take them long to realize I've pulled off the road and we're on foot."

"Then we'd better run."

"Exactly." Hawke grabbed Miranda's hand, felt her fingers link with his, her muscles tense. And then they were off, racing through thick grass toward the distant light of home, the sound of pursuit growing louder behind them.

"Do you think they'll see us?" Miranda was already gasping for breath and Hawke tightened his grip on her hand, afraid if he loosened it, he'd lose her in the blackness.

"I don't know. If they have night vision, we're in trouble."

"Night vision? As in those alien-looking goggles I've seen on the military channel?"

"Yeah."

"What's the likelihood they do?"

"Not high." But higher than he would have liked. The Wa could afford to furnish the best military equipment for their men. Hawke could only hope there hadn't been enough time for the crew coming up behind them to be outfitted with state-of-the-art technology.

"Maybe you should call your guards. Have them get out here to help us."

"We won't get a signal. Too many mountains. Too many trees."

"Maybe—"

"You need to save your breath, babe. We've got a long run ahead of us."

"Okay, but listen—" she panted out the words "—if I start slowing you down, you should go on ahead. You can get the help we need and bring them back for me."

"No."

"It makes sense. I won't be able to keep this pace up for long. We both know it. I'll never forgive myself if you're hurt because of me."

"Then you'd better keep up the pace, because I'm not going to leave you behind." There were plenty of things the Wa could do with a woman like Miranda. None of them were good. None of them were even pleasant. Hawke had seen those that the Wa owned— the blank-eyed prostitutes who worked on the outskirts of the poppy fields, hardened women whose beauty had faded with their innocence. He'd also seen the dis- ease-ridden wasted bodies—the corpses of those who had no access to medical care and no one who cared enough to help them find it. Imagining Miranda among them left him with the same sick, hollow feeling the thought of losing Simon gave him.

"Hawke, I really think—"

"I really think you should do as I say. Save your breath. If you need to talk, talk to God. Ask Him for a miracle." They were going to need it, and for the second time in just a few hours, Hawke did what he'd never felt a need to do before. He prayed, hoping for help he really didn't believe he'd receive.

But somehow, as he pushed through thick foliage, Miranda panting along beside him, he had the strange sense that his prayer was being heard, that what he'd never quite been willing to accept had accepted him long ago. That all he had to do was reach out and grasp what was being offered. And more than anything, that's exactly what he wanted to do.

Chapter Nineteen

Miranda couldn't decide which terrified her more—running blind through wet trees and knee-high grass or hearing the oncoming vehicle's engine growing louder with every step. Miranda didn't just want to run from it, she wanted to fly—spread invisible wings and soar above the danger like she had in a million nightmares. But this wasn't a nightmare, it was reality. And as much as she wanted to fly, all she could do was command her feet to move faster. Faster, though, seemed an impossibility. Her legs churned in slow motion, only Hawke's firm hold on her hand keeping her moving forward.

Blackness pressed in around her, stealing her breath, the sting of branches as they hit her face and the clawing tangle of vines and thorns her only clue as to the kind of landscape they were running through. She didn't need to see to imagine what might lurk in the depths of the foliage. Snakes. Spiders. Rats. Tigers.

Men with guns, ready to kill.

How far was Hawke's house? Miranda could no longer see the tiny light he had pointed out earlier and she wondered how he could possibly know they were running toward it. She wanted to ask, but knew he'd been right when he told her to save her breath. Her lungs were already on fire, her legs burning with the effort to keep pace with Hawke. Speaking would only use precious energy.

The engine cut off, the sudden silence so complete, Miranda stumbled.

"They know we're on foot." She gasped the words, terror pouring through her in futile waves of adrenaline. Her body was too tired to respond, her resources dried out and used up long ago.

"They passed the place we left the motorcycle before they stopped. They're going to have to backtrack to find it."

"Are you sure?"

"Does it matter? We've got to run either way." His hand tightened around hers, his grip almost painful.

"It matters to me. The more time we have before they start after us, the better I'll feel."

"Then I'm sure. Now, stop talking. Sound carries a long way here."

As if in response to his words, the sound of an engine broke the stillness again, the slow, throbbing chug of it telling of a vehicle moving with care rather than speed. Hawke's pace quickened to a sprint, his hand jerking Miranda forward, her feet slipping in moist soil as she tried to keep up. He jerked her arm, keeping her from going down on her knees, but not slowing the pace.

Miranda's heart galloped, every breath seeming shallow and useless, every step a trembling torture. Just a few more minutes, just another mile and they'd be safe. She silently chanted the words to the beat of her pounding feet, but didn't believe them. She'd seen how far away Hawke's home was. Getting there would take more than a few steps and a few miles.

Sweat trickled down her forehead and into her eyes, mixing with the tears that she hadn't known were falling. Good out of bad. The Bible promised it. She believed it. But with Justin's death things had gone horribly wrong and all she saw was more trouble, more tragedy following. Where was the good that she so desperately needed to believe in? If she and Hawke were caught, there was no doubt they'd be killed, their bodies left for the beetles and vultures to devour.

Could there be any good in that?

Miranda didn't think so, but then, she couldn't picture the full tapestry of her life as God did, couldn't see the totality of His plan. If she could, maybe she'd understand all that had happened, all that was still happening, a little better.

Please, Lord. Get us out of this. I know You can. I want to believe You will.

She imagined the prayer drifting toward the sky, catching on the thick canopy of leaves above her and remaining there. But God wasn't in the sky, the heavens, someplace far above where she and Hawke raced through the jungle. He was here. In her mind, her soul, her heart. And in the quieting of her panic, she felt His silent reassurance. Whatever happened, God was in control of it. She'd just have to trust that His plan didn't include her body lying forgotten on the floor of the Mae Hong Son jungle.

The engine sounds stopped again, the silence an ominous warning. Miranda didn't dare speak, didn't dare ask Hawke how much distance they'd put between themselves and their pursuers, afraid her words would carry back to the men who followed.

Small drips of water landed on her shoulders and rolled down the neck of her borrowed T-shirt, each drop coming faster than the next. Rain. Despite the thick canopy of leaves, it poured down, making the ground even more slick than it had been.

Hawke slowed to a jog, pulling Miranda close to his side, his breath whispering near her ear. "They've found the motorcycle. The rain will slow us down, but it will slow them down, too, and make it harder for them to follow our tracks. We'll move slower, so we can keep as quiet as possible."

Thank you, God. Thank you, God. Miranda didn't speak the thanks out loud. Nor did she respond to Hawke's comment. The dark world was silent but for her harsh breathing and the roaring slash of rain falling through the trees. Whoever was coming after them was doing it silently, and Miranda willed her breathing to slow, her lungs to fill, afraid the gasping noise she made would draw their enemy toward them.

It seemed a lifetime passed while the downpour continued, the trudging half jog Hawke led them in more painful with every moment. Miranda's clothes were soaked, her hat catching on branches and trees. She wanted to tear it off and leave it lying in a soggy heap of straw and silk on the ground, but was afraid to leave behind evidence that she and Hawke had been there.

"We're close." Hawke leaned in again, wrapping his arm around Miranda's shoulders. "When we step out of the trees, we'll be on top of a hill. We've got to make it to the bottom, then up another hill. All of it clear. There's no cover. No place for us to hide."

"Let's go." Miranda started forward, afraid if she

thought too much about what he'd said, she'd be frozen with terror and unable to do what had to be done.

"Wait." He pulled her back against his chest, then let out a low, haunting whistle that reminded Miranda of a mourning dove's call.

Seconds later, a higher-pitched whistle sounded above the pouring rain. Distant, but clear, it could only be a signal of some sort.

"That's it. Apirak knows we're coming. Let's go." His arm dropped from her shoulder, his hand claimed hers and they were running again, racing through trees and out into an open field, rain still pouring, the sound of breaking branches and a muffled shout coming from somewhere behind them.

"Faster!" Hawke's shouted command spurred Miranda on, her feet slapping against waterlogged grass, a scream lodged in her throat. She wanted to let it loose, shout loud enough to wake whatever creatures had made beds for themselves in the thick grass and decaying leaves, but bit her lip to keep from doing what she knew she'd regret, the salty taste of her own blood a horrifying reminder of what would happen if Sharee's men found them.

The world tilted beneath her, the steep slope and slick ground forcing her to move faster than was safe. She tripped, her foot catching on something hard. Hawke's grip tightened, but even he couldn't stop her fall this time. She tumbled head over heels, the crash and crack of grass and branches a cacophony of noise that must have been audible for miles. Her body sliding in muck and puddles until she landed with a thud and splash in what felt like a small stream of rushing water.

Stunned, she lay still, starring up at the night sky,

the sound of distant shouts and crashing footfall barely registering.

"Babe! You okay?" Hawke knelt beside her, black against the indigo sky.

"Yeah. Fine." But neither of them would be for long if she didn't get up and get moving.

"Are you sure?"

"Does it really matter? I can hear Sharee's men. They're getting closer. Let's get out of here." She started to rise and Hawke grabbed her hand, tugging her upright and dragging her into a run.

"See the blackness at the top of this rise? That's the fence that surrounds my compound. There will be men at the top, watching our progress. Men out here, too, probably coming up behind Sharee's men." He was barely breathing hard, and Miranda couldn't even force one word past her straining lungs.

She glanced up, nearly groaning when she saw the steep slope in front of them, her legs churning, her feet moving, but her body protesting every movement. "I don't see any lights."

"They've been turned out to keep us from being backlit while we're coming up the rise. We're already moving targets. We don't want to be well-lit moving targets. Come on, you've got more speed in you." He raced on and she had no choice but to join his frantic run up the steep hill, her legs burning, her lungs straining, stars dancing in front of her eyes.

Someone shouted, the Thai words unintelligible to Miranda, but Hawke must have understood. He pushed her down to the ground, throwing his body over hers as a barrage of bullets slammed into the earth a few feet away.

More gunfire followed, this time coming from

somewhere in front of Miranda and Hawke's position. "My men are covering us. Let's move."

Hawke stood in a smooth movement, bringing Miranda with him as bullets continued to fly, the sound deafening. There was no time to discuss a plan, no time to think things through, just a swerving chaotic run upward toward darkness and a house Hawke insisted was there.

Then, as quickly as it had begun, the gunfire ended, the silence ringing in Miranda's ears. Dark shadows swarmed toward her from all sides, tall and deeper black against the night. At first Miranda thought they were a figment of her imagination brought on by her oxygen-starved brain. Then the shadows took on more solid form, men carrying guns, their faces shrouded by the night, and Miranda realized how real they were.

"Hawke…" His name came out a high-pitched squeak carried on her panting breath.

"Don't worry. They're my people." He didn't stop running, though Miranda sensed a change in him, his tight grip on her hand easing a little. Together, they crested the rise of the hill and Miranda blinked. A clear expanse of grass stretched toward a tall fence. Beyond that, a house soared up toward the sky, its steep roof and rounded turrets reminding her of the Gothic mansions she'd seen on the covers of her mother's old romance novels.

"This way." Hawke urged her along the line of the fence then around a corner. A large gate slid open as they approached and Hawke hurried Miranda into the compound, the shadowy figures who'd surrounded them following along. A soft slide of sound and a clang of metal announced that the gate had closed, but Hawke didn't pause in his run, just continued up a long drive and onto a wide porch. There was still no light, but the front door of the house swung open before they reached it.

Hawke pushed Miranda in through the doorway, his gentle shove nearly toppling her. He moved in behind her, the quiet thud of the closing door followed quickly by blinding light.

As Miranda's eyes adjusted, she realized the hallway she stood in was filled with people. Six or seven men and women dressed in black and carrying the kind of weapons Miranda had only ever seen in movies, stared at her through dark almond eyes.

She tried to smile, but she was shaking too hard, her overworked muscles threatening to give out. Hawke said something in Thai and the men and women dispersed, some of them leaving the house, a few walking up stairs that led to the second floor. Finally, only one man was left, a small-built Thai man with a well-worn face and a short, compact body.

"Miranda, this is my business partner, Apirak. Apirak, Miranda Sheldon." Hawke made the introductions, his stormy eyes scanning Miranda's face, her soaked and mud-spattered clothes.

"Nice to meet you." Miranda held out her hand to Apirak and was surprised when he ignored the gesture and bowed instead.

She followed his example, dropping her head, and bowing from the waist. It was a mistake. As she straightened, the world spun, twisting and turning around her in a sickening array of colors. She swayed, knocking into a picture on the wall.

"Hey, careful there." Hawke's warm, callused palm gripped hers, his other hand resting on her shoulder and holding her steady.

"Sorry."

"For what? You just ran ten miles. I'd say you've got nothing to be sorry for."

"You go sit down. I'll bring some tea." Apirak's voice had a soothing melodic quality, his offer of tea making Miranda feel as if she'd stepped from a nightmare into normality.

"Orange juice would be better, Apirak, and some crackers. Also, see if we can find some dry clothes Miranda can use."

"Will do. It's good to have you back, Hawke." The Thai man gave Hawke a quick salute and disappeared down the hall.

"We'll go in the living room and wait there." Hawke started toward an open door, and Miranda tried to follow, but her legs refused to move.

"That sounds great, but I don't think I can move." The words came out half laugh, half sob, all the terror and anxiety of the past few hours welling up and spilling out in barely contained hysteria.

Hawke's expression softened, his eyes going from icy silver to warm gray. "Then I guess it's good you don't have to."

Before Miranda realized what he was going to do, he scooped her into his arms and strode through the open doorway.

Chapter Twenty

"Put me down. You'll break your back." Miranda wiggled against his hold, but Hawke ignored her struggles. She'd been serious when she'd said she couldn't move. He'd seen it in her eyes, could feel it now in her trembling muscles. They'd run close to ten miles at a breakneck speed. If she weren't exhausted he'd be surprised.

"You don't weigh enough to strain my back, let alone break it." He set her down on the sofa, water dripping from her hair and clothes onto the soft brown leather. "We need towels."

"Why? I'm kind of getting used to being soaking wet." Her teeth were chattering, her skin was ashen, but she smiled, the curve of her lips tugging at Hawke's heart in a way not much had in recent years.

"Yeah, well, I'm not going to let you catch pneumonia on my watch. Stay here. I'll grab some towels and be back in a minute."

"I'll come with you." Her eyes were dark with fatigue and worry as she started to rise.

He pushed her back down onto the couch, feeling

the narrow width of her shoulder, the spastic tremors of overworked muscles. "You'll stay here and rest. Apirak is bringing juice. I want you to drink it all."

She blinked and Hawke was sure there were tears in her eyes. He wanted to sit beside her, throw an arm around her shoulder, let her know that they really were okay, but there were things that needed to be done. Sitting would accomplish none of them.

He strode from the room, calling for his housekeeper and not at all surprised when Doom stepped from the office across the hall, her lined face filled with concern.

"The *farang* is okay?" She spoke in Thai and Hawke responded in the same.

"She needs a hot shower, something to eat and some sleep. Can you make up the room at the top of the stairs?"

"I will. Have you heard anything of Simon?" The fear in her voice was obvious. Doom had been hired to help Hawke's mother the year Simon was born. She'd been working for the Morrans ever since.

"Sharee has him."

"No." She shook her head, tears filling her eyes and spilling down her cheeks.

Hawke took her hand. "Simon is tough. He'll be fine until I get to him."

"Let us pray you are right." She hurried up the stairs and Hawke followed, grabbing towels from the linen closet, then returning to the living room, a timer ticking in his head, counting down seconds and minutes. He had to get in touch with Sharee, arrange a meeting, get Simon back.

Miranda was where he'd left her, shivering on the couch, a glass in her hand, juice sloshing over the edges. Apirak leaned against the wall, his dark eyes meeting Hawke's.

"A call just came in on the office line. When you get Ms. Sheldon settled, we need to talk."

Hawke nodded, took the glass from Miranda's hand and placed it on the table before wrapping a towel around her shoulders. "My housekeeper will be down in a minute. She'll show you to your room."

"Where will you be?" Her eyes were mossy green and deeply shadowed, her dirt-stained face surrounded by heavy strands of dark hair.

"In my office. Apirak and I need to plan Simon's rescue."

"Good. Let's do it." She stood, swayed, managed to stay upright.

"Babe, you need to sleep."

"So do you." Her chin jutted, her eyes flashed, the stubbornness that had brought her through the rain and jungle not diminished by exhaustion.

"I will, but not yet."

"I don't want to—"

"You ready, miss? Your room is prepared and I have found some dry clothes you can change into." Doom peered in the open doorway, her face still streaked with tears.

Hawke knew there was no way Miranda would refuse her.

He was right. She hesitated, then nodded. "Sure. Thank you. You're going to be here when I'm done, right?" The question was directed at Hawke. He nodded, ushering her to the door as he spoke.

"I'll be here."

"And you'll let me know what the plans are? You won't go anywhere without me?"

"I'll let you know." But he would be going without her. The next part of the mission was too dangerous, Miranda too fragile to risk taking her with him.

"You'd better. I'm just as much a part of this as you. And I have almost as much at stake."

"Almost? We could both lose our lives." Hawke followed her into the hall, surprised at the reluctance he felt at letting her out of his sight. He'd been hypervigilant about background checks since he'd been betrayed to the Wa last year and a young girl had been kidnapped from the compound. The men and women who worked for him were loyal to him and to the cause they fought for. Because of them, dozens of DEA and police raids had been carried out in the past year alone. Hawke had no reason to question Miranda's safety here. And still he felt reluctant to let her go.

"Yes, but my brother is safe in Essex. At least, I hope he is."

"If Green tries to harm your family, the police will get suspicious. He can't take the chance of a deeper investigation."

"I guess not." But she still looked worried, lines of fatigue and anxiety creasing her smooth brow.

Doom stepped in, sliding an arm around Miranda's waist and urging her to the stairs. "Come. You'll feel better when you're dry and rested."

Hawke resisted the urge to follow. Instead he stayed where he was, watching their retreating figures until the door to the room near the top of the stairs closed on them.

When he turned back toward the living room, Apirak was standing in the doorway. "You care for that woman."

It wasn't a question, but Hawke gave an answer anyway. "She saved my life."

"And so you dragged her halfway around the world with you."

"It was that or leave her to die at Green's hands."

"I don't know that being here is any safer."

True. But at least here she wasn't alone. Hawke didn't say as much. "What was the phone call about?"

"McKenzie called. He said you were right. Austin's maternal grandfather was killed by Russian troops eight years ago. There are rumors that he was the leader of one of the resistance armies. There is no concrete evidence, but McKenzie thinks it's interesting that that same army has grown fifty fold in the years since Austin was transferred here. They've got the best weapons. The best training. Before they were a ragtag group with more rhetoric than fight. Now they're a force to be reckoned with."

"Does he think he can get proof that Austin is funding the group?"

"He's working on it now. He's also keeping the search for you under his own control. The police here in Mae Hong Son will lay low until he tells them different."

"He's taking a risk with his career. If I go down, he'll go down with me."

"Maybe, but if he can pull this off and find the leak in his office, he'll be a hero."

Hawke nodded. "What else?"

"Austin is acting as if nothing is wrong. He reported your interview with his wife and is insisting on a full-out manhunt."

"Did he mention that anything was missing from his apartment?"

"No. Is there?"

"Yeah. I found letters and photos. The letters are written in a language I'm not familiar with, but I think they might be of interest to McKenzie."

"It seems odd for Austin not to mention them. There must be a reason for it."

"I'd say he doesn't realize McKenzie and I are working together and he thinks Sharee will take me out before I can figure out what the letters say."

"He's underestimated you, then." Apirak motioned toward the office. "We've sent Sharee's men running. We'd better get ready for his next move."

"It'll be a trade. Simon in exchange for me and the documents I took." Hawke moved into the large room behind his friend, the teak furniture, rich leather and wood floors both familiar and strange after so many months away.

"And Miss Sheldon. They'll want her, too."

"Too bad. I don't plan on bringing her with me."

"If we want to convince Sharee that he's got us on the run, you're going to have to act like you're willing to cooperate."

"When have I ever cooperated with drug dealers?" Hawke shrugged out of his T-shirt, grabbed another from the closet and pulled it on.

"You've never had good reason to. Now, they've got your brother. They'll think you will be willing to do just about anything to get him back."

"And I am. But that doesn't include risking an innocent woman's life."

The phone on the desk rang, cutting off further argument. Hawke picked it up, knowing before he heard the voice who'd be on the other end of the line. "Morran."

"You've got something I want." Sharee spoke in the guttural dialect of his hill tribespeople, his words hissing out like a serpent's warning.

"And you have someone I want. Where is my brother?"

"Alive. For now."

"Let me speak to him."

There was a moment of silence, then Simon's voice filled the line. "Took you long enough, bro."

Some of Hawke's tension drained away and he smiled. "If you hadn't gotten yourself into trouble, I wouldn't have had to come at all."

"For once, it wasn't me who started the trouble."

"I know. Things got out of control in the States."

"So much for starting a new life, eh?" There was a strain in Simon's voice that Hawke didn't like. It hinted at injury.

"Are you okay?"

"I'll be better once I get out of here."

"It won't be l—"

"Now you see that your brother is okay," Sharee interrupted. "Are you ready to listen?"

"Go ahead."

"You bring the pictures and letters you took from Austin and meet me at the village a half mile north of Wat Mueng Sai. You know it?"

"Yes."

"Bring the woman with you."

"No deal."

"Bring the woman or your brother will die." Sharee disconnected before Hawke could respond.

"How did your brother sound?" Apirak sat near the door, his shoulders tense. Like Doom, he'd been working for the Morrans for years and had become part of the family.

"Ornery as ever."

"That's good, then."

"Yes. Now I just have to make sure he stays that way."

"What's the plan?"

"We can't go in force. That's what Sharee will be expecting." Hawke crossed the room, pulled a rolled-up map from a shelf and spread it out on his desk.

"What do you suggest?"

"I'm thinking Sharee doesn't dare kill me until he makes sure I have the documents he's after."

"Agreed."

"So, we send out some of our guys and one of our ladies. While they're making slow progress toward the Myanmar border, you and I will move quickly. We get in the village, dispatch Sharee and his men, and find out if Simon is there."

"And if he isn't?"

"We get someone to tell us where he is. One way or another, we're taking control of the situation."

"I like the sound of that." Apirak's eyes gleamed in anticipation.

"Let's map out the quickest route. I want to be out of here fast."

"I'll map it. You go brief the team. Then you need to do what you told Miss Sheldon and rest." Apirak took a seat at the desk and grabbed a highlighter. "The sooner we get going. The happier I'll be."

"You and me both."

It took only minutes to get his men together, go over the plan and send them off to gather weapons and supplies. It took him even less time to ready himself. He'd done this many times before, though never with so much at risk. Infiltrating drug labs, gathering names, dates and other data to pass on to the police or DEA had been part of Hawke's life for a decade. At any other time, the idea of catching one of Thailand's most elusive drug cartels would have filled him with purpose. Now, his sole focus was on finding Simon and getting him home alive.

"Hawke?" Miranda hovered outside the open door to his office. Dressed in a snug black T-shirt and black cargo pants, her face freshly scrubbed, her hair pulled back from her pale, bruised face, she looked exhausted and much more lovely than she should have after all she'd been through.

"I thought you were sleeping."

"And I thought you weren't going anywhere." She gestured toward the backpack on his shoulders and the gun belt he'd strapped to his hips.

"I said I'd be in my office. I was. Now, I'm going to find my brother."

"And I'm supposed to stay here?"

"It's the only way to keep you safe."

"I've been safe with you."

Her trust in him pulled at Hawke, the intangible bond that seemed to draw him to her growing stronger. He stepped away, not trusting himself to keep from pulling her into his arms, inhaling the sweet scent that clung to her. "I've got to move fast, babe. You're not up to it."

If she'd argued, Hawke might have found a reason to separate himself and his emotions from Miranda, but she only nodded, leaning her shoulder against the doorjamb, her gaze filled with sadness and worry. "I know. I've just got this feeling that if we get separated, we'll never find each other again." She flushed, her cheeks a deep pink. "What I mean is—"

"No need to explain, babe. We started this as a team, and we'll end it as one. This part, though, I've got to do myself." He moved past her, stepping into the hallway, the need to be on the road warring with the desire to keep Miranda close.

"How long will you be gone?"

"Anywhere from a few hours to a few days."

"Days?"

"If it takes that long to find Simon."

"And I'm just supposed to sit around here and wait?"

"That's exactly what you're supposed to do."

"I'm not sure I like this plan."

"I'm not sure you've got any say in it."

Miranda opened her mouth, closed it and then shook her head, laughing, the sound peeling through the hallway and wrapping around Hawke's heart. He smiled, wishing he had more time to stand in the hall watching laughter play across her face. "What's so funny?"

"You and me. We've had this conversation too many times to count."

"That we have."

"I don't think we've agreed on anything since we met."

"We've only known each other a few days. There's still time."

"A few days. It seems like a lifetime." She'd stopped laughing, but her eyes still sparkled and Hawke wondered what it would be like to know her under different circumstances, at a time when danger didn't lurk at every corner.

"Has knowing me been that bad?" He meant to

tease, but his words came out much more serious than he intended.

"Not bad. Just…familiar. Like you're an old friend I've suddenly reconnected with." She smiled, shrugged. "That's silly, I know."

"Is it? I've been thinking something similar." He cupped her neck in his hands, feeling the quiet thrum of her pulse beneath his fingers. "Listen, babe, no matter how long I'm gone, I want you to stay here. I don't want anything to happen to you while I'm out searching for my brother."

"I'll stay here as long as I know *you're* safe."

"I will be. This assignment is no different than any other I've been on. I've always managed to come through in one piece."

"Yeah? Well, that scar you're sporting says you've come pretty close to *not* coming out in one piece."

"God had other plans for me the day this happened." Hawke fingered the ridge of skin, remembering the day he'd almost been killed by men loyal to the Wa. Noah Stone had saved his life. Or at least that's what Hawke had chosen to believe. Now he felt different. It was too hard to believe that coincidence had brought first Noah and then Miranda into his life at just exactly the right time to save him. "He had other plans for me the day I met you, too."

He leaned forward, placed a gentle kiss on her lips, reveling in the soft warmth of her skin, the flowery scent of the shampoo she'd used. But this was dangerous territory—the kiss he'd meant to be nothing more than a thank-you, threatened to become something more. Hawke forced himself to step away. "I've got to go."

Miranda nodded, her cheeks flushed. "I'll stay here. And I'll be praying for you."

In years past, Hawke would have scoffed at the words. But things had changed. He'd changed. "I'll be praying for you, too, babe."

And he would. God had laid a foundation on Hawke's heart years ago when his mother and stepfather had taught him the truth of the Creator's love and sacrifice for humanity. Hawke had chosen to ignore their teachings, his anger and need for revenge overriding the quiet voice inside that yearned for peace.

He wouldn't ignore it any longer. God had saved him twice. Hawke could no longer turn his back on that. As he walked away, he gave his future to the one he finally believed held it in His hands.

Chapter Twenty-One

The sun rose over Mae Hong Son in silent streaks of gold and glittering mist. Miranda watched from her bedroom window on the second-story floor, following the first faint glimmers of light as they spread across the domed mountains and the shadowy valley below. Hawke and Apirak had left hours ago and were now somewhere deep in the tangled jungles beyond the compound. Painted in greens and grays, the world seemed a place of both beauty and danger. A place where a man or woman could easily be lost. A place where bodies could lie unnoticed while scavengers tore the flesh from their bones and stole their identities.

Miranda shivered, the image not one she wanted to dwell on. As mysterious and dangerous as the misty jungle seemed to her, she knew Hawke and his men were at home there, that they'd moved through it, explored it for most of their lives. They'd be okay. She prayed they would be, anyway.

And she prayed they'd return quickly. Imagination was a poor companion. One that had haunted the restless sleep she'd fallen into. Nightmare figures had skulked just out of sight, their long shadows dancing across thick beds of leaves. Faceless bodies lying in dreadful stillness had created a path that stretched as far as her dream-self could see. She'd woken an hour after she'd fallen asleep and had been awake ever since, the silent house seeming to wait with her as dawn slowly arrived.

It was probably for the best that Hawke hadn't been able to tell her when he'd return. If she had expectations about how long his mission would take, she'd be watching the clock, worrying about every extra second it took for him to return.

Who was she trying to kid?

She *was* watching the clock. She *was* worrying. More and more as the seconds stretched into minutes, the minutes into hours. "Please, Lord, get them all back safely. Help Hawke find his brother quickly. Keep all of them from injury and harm."

She whispered the prayer, her voice sounding strangely out of place in the quiet house. The moment, her plea, reminding her of the time she'd spent at the hospital standing vigil over Justin's failing body. Then she'd been alone, too, Lauren gone home to sleep, convinced that Justin was too far gone to need her. Miranda hadn't been able to leave him, though, and she'd sat through the dark, quiet night, listening to muted hospital sounds and the constant beep of machinery until night had turned to day and day to night again.

How long she'd stand here, staring out into the morning, remained to be seen. Obviously, doing so wouldn't do Hawke or his men any good. It would only lead to more worry and tension, but Miranda couldn't seem to leave her vigil, her mind jumping from thought to thought, her heart beating a ragged, unhappy rhythm.

"Miss?" A soft knock sounded on the door and Miranda turned to see Hawke's housekeeper stepping across the threshold. "Will you have some breakfast?" Her English was flawless, her accent just slightly thicker than Hawke's.

"No, thank you."

"You must eat something. I'll make you coffee and toast. Maybe some fruit. You like pineapple?"

"Yes, but…" Miranda let the protest die. She didn't have the energy or the will to argue. "That's fine. Thank you."

"Shall I bring it up for you?" The woman's dark eyes were filled with the same worry Miranda was feeling. That, rather than any desire to leave the room, made her step toward the door.

"I'll come down."

"We will have coffee together while we wait." She smiled, her lined face creasing. "I am Doom."

"I'm Miranda." They stepped out into the hallway together and moved down the steps.

"You met Hawke in the United States."

"Yes." Though she wouldn't exactly call what had happened a meeting. They'd been thrown together, had stayed together, and now not having him nearby left her anxious and antsy.

"He's a good man, but it is time he stopped fighting his battle and settled down. It is what his mother would have wanted for him. I think it is what he wants for himself."

"Is that why he was in the United States?"

"Yes, he had hopes of expanding the export company he and his brother own. Eventually bring Simon to the States. Thailand is dangerous for the Morrans, now. So many people do not appreciate the work they do."

"Exporting goods?"

Doom cast her a curious look. "That's the business Mr. Morran started. The boys have done quite well with it, but it's not what has gained them enemies." She gestured Miranda into a bright kitchen and pulled out a chair at the round teak table there. "Sit here."

"Then what *has* gained them enemies? His work against drug dealers?"

"Yes. Hawke has invested time and money in that pursuit. This compound, the people that work for him here are all part of that. Hawke has built a business much different than the one his stepfather began. Its sole purpose is to fight against the Wa. You know the Wa?"

"Hawke mentioned them."

"A bad group." Doom shook her head as she placed a plate of toast and fruit in front of Miranda. "They control many exporters to one extent or another, paying money to have their heroin shipped out of the country. Mr. Morran, he wanted nothing to do with that. When the Wa approached, he went to the police and turned in the local man who was working for them. A few nights later he, his wife and daughter were dead."

Miranda's stomach clenched and she pushed the toast away. "That's terrible."

"It was a very terrible time. Simon was only thirteen, staying with a friend for the night. That was what saved him."

"And Hawke?"

"Away at school in the States, getting his master's degree. He flew back from college as soon as he heard

and has been here ever since, going after every drug
dealer, every courier." Doom shook her head again.
"That's what his life has been about. I think he is ready
for something different."

"Then we need to pray he gets an opportunity to
have it."

"Pray. Yes. That's something I've been doing every
day since I came to work for the Morrans."

A sound from the front of the house interrupted the
conversation. An opening door, footfall, loud voices.
Miranda jumped up from the chair, racing into the hallway after Doom.

What she saw there brought her skidding to a halt,
her heart stuck in her throat. Five men dressed in black
stood near the door, guns in their hands, their faces set
in hard, angry lines. A sixth man stood in the middle
of the group, his brightly colored shirt and small build
setting him apart from the others.

The door flew open again and Hawke strode in,
Apirak close behind him. Both men had guns in their
hands and dark scowls on their faces. Hawke's eyes
glowed light gray and cold, his focus on the brightly
dressed man. He said something in Thai, the words
more growl than language. The man jumped, turning to face Hawke, words pouring from his mouth in
a quick, breathless stream.

For a moment Hawke said nothing, just stared at
the man with the same hard look. Then he nodded,
gesturing with a hand and stepping back as the black-
clad men moved in. They weren't gentle as they urged
the sixth man up the stairs, their booted feet pounding
against the floor.

In the wake of their departure, the foyer fell silent,

the tension thick. Miranda spoke into it, anxious to know what was going on. "Did you find your brother?"

Hawke's cold gaze focused on her and she resisted the urge to take a step back. "No, but we're going to."

Disappointment and sadness made her step toward him. She touched the rigid muscle of his bicep, wishing she had words that would ease the pain he must be feeling. "I'm sorry."

At her words, his expression softened and he pulled her into a tight hug. "Me, too, but I know where he is. Nothing is going to keep me from bringing him home this time."

"You know this is a trap and you're going to walk right into it." Apirak spoke English and Miranda wondered if he did it purposely to pull her into an argument she had a feeling had been going on for a while.

"What's going on?" She pulled back from Hawke's arms, trying to read the truth in his face.

"We found Sharee where he said he would be, but my brother wasn't with him. A little encouragement and he was able to tell us where he left Simon."

"Left him?"

"Austin gave him instructions to keep Simon alive until he had the documents in hand, but to not let us near each other. Simon's in a warehouse in Mae Hong Son. I'm going to get him."

"Austin will be waiting for you. And he won't be alone." Apirak spoke again, his frustration obvious.

"Sharee wasn't alone, either, and we were fine."

"Sharee is a fool. Austin is not."

"Anyone who does what he has done is a fool." Hawke dropped the pack he was carrying.

"And going up against him alone isn't foolish as well?"

"Alone?" Miranda interrupted the argument, not liking what she was hearing.

"It's the only way to make sure no one knows I'm coming. The only way to keep Simon from being killed."

"You're not the only one able to move quietly and quickly, Hawke." Apirak dropped his own pack on the floor, his jaw set.

"Which is easier to spot, my friend, one tiger lurking in the grass or two?" Hawke's tone was almost gentle and Miranda knew he understood his friend's worry. Just as she knew he didn't plan to let it stop him.

"Tigers hunt alone."

"Exactly. I'm going into the warehouse and I'm getting my brother. I want you here with Sharee until someone from the Royal Thai police comes to collect him."

"You've got five men guarding him. You do not need one more. The truth is, you know you are probably walking into a death trap and you refuse to bring any of us with you."

Hawke didn't deny it and Miranda went cold with the truth of what Apirak had said. "Hawke—"

"Call Jack, Apirak. He's on his way to Mae Hong Son. Tell him that I'm headed to the old warehouse south of town. He'll know it. If anything happens, you've got the documents. Make sure he gets them."

"You should wait for him to arrive and go together," Miranda tried again, but Hawke seemed determined to ignore her protest.

"I can't waste any more time. I've got to go." He turned to his friend. "I'm trusting you to take care of Miranda while I'm gone. However long that might be."

He was asking for more than a few hours or even a

few days. He was asking a man Miranda didn't know to protect her for as long as was necessary; to take responsibility for her life if he could no longer do it.

But her life was her responsibility and Miranda had no intention of staying safe in Hawke's compound while he walked into danger alone.

She thought about arguing with him, but knew she wouldn't change his mind. She'd let him leave and then she'd find a way to follow.

Apirak's jaw tightened, his eyes flashed, but it seemed he, too, had given up the argument. "You are a brother to me. Of course, I will do as you request."

Hawke nodded, then pushed open the door. "I'll be back as soon as I have Simon."

Miranda thought he'd walk away without another word, but his gaze swept from Doom to Apirak and finally came to rest on her. "Stay with Apirak."

"I will." For as long as it took for her to find a ride into town.

"Promise me, Miranda." His gray eyes speared into hers.

He knew. She was sure of it. He'd seen her plan written on her face or in her eyes and he wanted to keep her from following through on it.

Too bad. She wasn't promising anything. "You'd better go. Your brother needs you."

"Babe, I'm not going anywhere until I have your word you'll stay with Apirak. Every minute you refuse to give it is another minute Simon is in the hands of brutal men who have no conscience that can't be bought."

He knew her too well. Miranda couldn't imagine how that was possible after so few days of knowing each other, but he did and he'd called her bluff.

She swallowed back her protest, threw her arms around his waist, holding him tight for just a moment, feeling his warm strength and vibrant life.

And she couldn't imagine going back to a life without him in it.

"Be careful, Hawke."

"You know I will."

"Then I'll promise to stay with Apirak, but I'm not happy about it."

He tilted her chin, staring down into her face, a soft smile playing at the corners of his mouth. "You don't have to worry about me, babe. You know that faith you were talking about? I've finally found it and one way or another, I'm thinking I'll be just fine."

With that, he placed a gentle kiss on her lips and walked away.

Apirak pulled the door closed, his stiff shoulders and angry scowl telling Miranda just how unhappy he was to be left behind.

"Do you think he'll be okay?" She knew there was no answer to the question, but asked it anyway.

"I think I would be happier if I were going with him."

"We need to call Jack. Maybe he'll be able to get there with some agents."

"He won't bring any agents in with him. Too big a show of force and Simon will be killed outright. It is better for a few highly trained men to go in."

"But not one?"

"No." He shook his head. "Hawke never would have allowed any of us to go in alone. He goes himself, though, to protect his men and his brother."

"But what does any of that matter if Hawke and Simon don't have a chance?"

"They have a chance. They'd have more of one if I could be there. Come." Apirak took her arm and led her into a large office. "I need to call McKenzie."

He picked up the phone, dialing a number he must have memorized. While he spoke, Miranda paced the room, restless energy shivering along her spine and demanding she take action. Prayers flitted through her mind, barely coalescing before they took flight. There had to be something she could do besides hide away in the house waiting for Hawke and his brother to be murdered.

No, there wasn't. She'd given her word to stay close to Apirak.

To stay close to him.

Miranda's heart skipped a beat, then accelerated. She'd given her word to stay close to Hawke's friend. She hadn't given her word to stay in the compound. Should she try to get Apirak to take her to the warehouse?

Lord, I don't know what You want me to do. Please, give me some idea of what path I should take. The prayer whispered from the deepest part of her soul. Making a mistake, doing the wrong thing, could quite possibly get her and several men killed. And doing nothing might mean Hawke and Simon's death.

There had been so many times in her life when she'd hesitated, so many times when she'd missed opportunities and blessings because she was afraid to trust God's ability to steer her course.

This would not be one of those times. In her heart, she knew she had to go after Hawke. For now, that was all that mattered.

She'd waited until Apirak hung up the phone and then she set to work convincing him that her plan was a much more reasonable one than Hawke's.

Chapter Twenty-Two

Hawke felt the cool metal of the gun he'd pulled from its holster and the soft kiss of mist pressing against his skin, but only as periphery sensations. His focus was on the warehouse that sat in the midst of overgrown grass and overflowing garbage bags. Years ago, he'd played here with friends, exploring the building with both fear and exhilaration, the empty warehouse too tempting for the children to ignore. Then, as now, the building held an air of secrecy, the mist drifting over the empty parking lot and the fields that surrounded it making it seem haunted and lonely. If Simon was there, Sharee's men would be there, as well. And Hawke had no reason to doubt Sharee's word on the matter. The man was a coward. Without men and guns to back him up, he'd caved, sputtering places and names with abandon, confirming Hawke's belief that Austin had set up Simon's kidnapping and insisting Hawke's brother was still alive.

Hawke prayed the second part was as true as the first. He hadn't expected Simon to be in the village, but his disappointment had still been real. Now he was counting on finding Simon in the bowels of an abandoned warehouse. If his brother wasn't there, Hawke would keep searching, keep questioning until he found him.

For now, he'd focus on this moment, this goal.

He eased toward the building on his belly, using thick mist and shifting shadows to hide his movements, his gut screaming for him to hurry, his mind insisting he continue the slow, plodding pace. The area surrounding the warehouse offered plenty of cover. The parking lot and open fields that used to resound with activity and motion had been abandoned years ago and were now filled with debris and car carcasses.

Hawke used the refuse to his advantage, slithering behind piles of garbage and rusted vehicles until he was close enough to see inside the broken windows. He stayed there watching, waiting for any sign the warehouse was occupied. It came within minutes, a dark figure passing in front of the broken glass. A sloppy move. One that could cost a man his life. Minutes later, a guard moved around the side of the building, careless and at ease. Which meant the element of surprise was still with Hawke.

He waited until the man turned the next corner, then moved up behind him, knocking him out with the butt of his gun and catching his body before it could hit the ground. Now he moved quickly around the back of the building, his senses on high alert, his body humming with adrenaline.

The back of the warehouse was clear of guards and he moved to a window there, pulling a cutting tool from his belt and using it to remove the glass. Noise drifted from deep inside the old building, muted voices and laughter that set Hawke's teeth on edge. Sharee's men laughed while Simon suffered, but it wouldn't be for long.

Hawke eased into the dark room beyond the window, the scent of decay and the musty odor of age hitting him in the face. He ignored it, concentrating his attention on the voices and laughter, straining to hear any sound of approaching footsteps as he tried to picture the building's layout in his mind. Offices along the back wall, a hallway that led out into the open part of the warehouse and an upper level that housed a kitchen, dining area and one more office. If Hawke was keeping a hostage that would be the place he'd do it, not on the lower level where escape would be easy. There were two sets of stairs—one off the main warehouse area, the other at the end of the hallway outside the door.

Hawke eased the door open, peering out into the dark hallway. Nothing moved and the voices remained muted. Sharee's men were as foolish as their leader. He moved silently, the carpeted floor making soundless movement easy. The stairwell was empty, the darkness above suggesting that the upstairs was empty, too. Hawke took the stairs two at a time, pausing at the top, listening to the silence. From here, the voices were almost inaudible, the hollow empty feel of the upstairs hallway doing nothing to ease Hawke's alert state.

The hair on the back of his neck stood up, his nerves humming a warning. Something was wrong. As much as he believed Sharee's men to be fools, they wouldn't leave a prisoner without a guard. Either Simon wasn't here, or they were so confident he couldn't be freed, they had nothing to worry about.

Either was bad news and Hawke moved with caution, peering into the open doorway that led into the employee cafeteria. There was little left there. A few chairs, a table, layers of dust and rat droppings that showed no sign of having been walked through recently. The kitchen was the same, empty, layered in dust, the smell of old food still hanging in the air.

The office was at the end of the hall, the door closed, no sounds coming from beyond it. It wasn't locked, and Hawke knew that if Simon were inside, he wouldn't be alone. He pushed it open anyway, knowing that was his only choice.

"I thought you'd be here sooner. I guess I gave you more credit than you deserve." The voice was smooth as honey, the man who stood on the other side of the door tall, lanky, with blond hair and deep brown eyes.

Austin. Hawke recognized him from the pictures he'd seen at the apartment. "And I thought someone who worked for the DEA would have more honor than to sell secrets to the Wa."

"What is honor worth? Not much in today's market." Austin smirked. "Put your gun down, Morran. I wouldn't want your brother to get hurt after you took the time to come save him." He gestured to the left, and Hawke caught sight of his brother. Seated in a metal folding chair, his hands tied behind his back, his feet tied to the chair legs, he looked haggard, bruised and as cantankerous as ever.

"Like I said before, it took you long enough, bro." Simon's voice was raspy and he winced as he spoke, his normally tan skin pale beneath the bruises.

"I was trying to give you plenty of time to escape on your own. I didn't want your youthful self-esteem to be injured by having to have me rescue you." As he spoke, Hawke took stock of the two men who stood on either side of Simon. Both were armed and built like fighters.

"I hate to cut this touching reunion short, but you've got something I want. Hand it over now before I lose what little patience I have left."

"Let my brother go. Then the papers are yours."

"You don't hold all the cards this time, Morran. I do. Now, drop your weapon and give me the documents." Austin nodded toward one of the men, his dark eyes flashing as the man put a gun to Simon's head.

"Don't do it, bro."

The man slammed a fist into Simon's head and Hawke lunged forward, ready to do battle for his brother. The click of a gun safety froze him. The barrel of the man's gun pressed into the soft flesh beneath Simon's jaw. And Hawke had no choice but to place his gun on the floor and wait for Austin's next move.

Convincing Apirak to bring her to the warehouse had taken less effort than Miranda had imagined it would. Now they were heading toward the town of Mae Hong Son, the morning mist drifting in lazy patches across the road. The sky had darkened in the time since Hawke had left, golden dawn replaced by bleak, gray clouds. It seemed an ominous warning. Was she making a mistake? Should she have stayed in Hawke's compound? She asked herself the same questions over and over again as Apirak maneuvered through narrow streets and dim alleys. Finally, he pulled the motorcycle to a stop and climbed off. "You stay here. I'll go find Hawke and Simon."

"No way. We're supposed to stick together, and that's exactly what we're going to do." Miranda scrambled off after him, nerves making her stomach twist and churn.

"Lady, this is not a game. This is real danger. Men

with guns are going to try to kill us both if we give them a chance."

"Sounds exactly like the past few days. I'll feel right at home."

Apirak shot her a look, his dark eyes reflecting nothing of what he felt. "Hawke will have my hide if I bring you into that warehouse."

"Hawke's going to have *both* our hides for coming out here." Rain began to fall in light drops that ran down Miranda's cheeks and splattered her T-shirt. She brushed drops from her forehead and hurried to keep up with Apirak. She didn't know where the warehouse was located, knew nothing about the small town she was hurrying through and had no desire to get lost in it.

"With good reason. He's trying to keep you safe. Bringing you here isn't going to accomplish that."

"But we're doing it, so let's just get over the fact that I'm going to be in danger and get this done."

Apirak shot her another glance, this time something like amusement glowing in the depth of his gaze. "I can see why Hawke enjoys being around you."

"He doesn't enjoy it. He feels he has no choice."

"Because you saved his life. So he told me, but I don't think that's the only reason. Come on—" he grabbed her elbow and pulled her into a narrow alley "—the warehouse is just outside of town."

"Do you think Jack is already there?"

"I wish I did. He was a half hour out when we spoke."

"We could call in the police."

"Not yet. The police go running in there with guns drawn and people will die. We can't risk that one of those people will be Hawke or Simon."

"So we're going in there alone?"

"*I* am going in there alone. *You* are staying outside and staying hidden."

"But—"

"Do you have a gun?"

"No."

"Know how to use one?"

"No, but—"

"Then the only thing you can do is get in the way." They stepped out of the alley and crossed a field of knee-deep grass. In the distance, mist danced around a brick building, touching piles of trash and beat-up old clunkers that were parked nearby.

"That's it. The warehouse. We've got to move in slow and stay close to the ground. I'll find you a safe spot when we get nearer. Ready?"

"As I'll ever be." Which wasn't saying much. As far as Miranda was concerned a life of intrigue and danger was something she could do without.

"Then let's go." Apirak moved forward, hunching down so that the long grass partially hid him. Between that and the heavy mist, he became almost invisible, his silent movements causing him to blend effortlessly with his surroundings. Miranda's own movements were more awkward, her hunched, sliding shuffle producing too much noise and motion. If anyone were watching from the warehouse, they'd see her for sure.

She could only pray no one was watching.

With every step, the warehouse came into sharper focus—worn bricks, broken windows, a parking lot half full of broken-down cars—it seemed a lonely abandoned place. If people were in it, there was no evidence. No cars, no lights, nothing that would indicate occupancy.

She and Apirak approached from the front, a double-wide door and dangling faded sign indicating the entrance. They were a few hundred yards away when the door banged open. Before Miranda could react, she was on the ground, Apirak pressing her down into moist grass and earth. "Stay here. I've got to see what's happening."

He crept away before she could respond, slithering like a snake toward the building. For a moment, Miranda felt disorientated, not sure if she should do as he said, slink back the way they'd come or move forward. She levered up just a little, saw several men moving out of the building. She caught a glimpse of dark clothes and guns, and felt the same sense of determination she'd felt the night she'd met Hawke. She hadn't been able to turn her back when he was a stranger. Nor could she do it now.

Slowly, one soft slide after another, she moved toward the warehouse and the men.

Chapter Twenty-Three

Timing was everything. Hawke knew it. And so he waited, letting Austin and his men take his weapon, search him for the documents and then force him outside, his hands tied behind his back, Simon shuffling along beside him. The procession moved toward an old jeep that looked as junky as any of the other vehicles abandoned in the parking lot, the tension in the air as thick as the morning mist.

"Those documents better be in your car, Morran." Austin's face and neck were flushed with irritation and anger, but there was worry in his eyes and a sheen of sweat on his brow. Time was running out and he knew it.

"We'll find out soon enough, won't we?" Hawke kept his voice bland, not willing to be pulled into the other man's emotion. If he were going to get his brother out of this alive, he needed a cool head and quick reflexes. A little divine help wouldn't hurt, either. *Lord, I know I'm coming to You a little late in my life and I know I've made a lot of mistakes, but I finally believe what my parents told me. I finally believe You gave ev-*

*erything up for me and I'm ready and willing to give it
all up for You. If this is the end for me, I'm prepared,
but please don't let it be the end for Simon. Help me
get him out of this alive.*

He said the prayer quickly, his muscles tensing as
one of Austin's men shoved Simon into the Jeep. This
was it. The time to make his move. And it better be a
good one.

A sweep of his foot brought Austin down. A swing
of Hawke's bound wrists to his neck kept him there.
Hawke spun, lifting his arms to block the blow one
of Sharee's men was aiming his way. His wrist went
numb, but he ignored it and swung for the man's face,
hearing the satisfying crunch of bone against bone.

Someone shouted, the words not registering as
Hawke slammed his knee into another man's stomach. Simon was out of the Jeep now, head-butting a
third man. If they could get a gun, get the keys to the
Jeep, they just might have a chance.

More men poured from the warehouse. Ten, maybe
more. Hawke tried not to think of the odds stacked
against him.

"Find the keys, Simon. We need to get out of here!"
He shouted the words as he reached for Austin's fallen
gun. A volley of shots and the ground near his feet exploded. He dove for cover, rolling under the Jeep, his
gaze searching for Simon and finding him crouching
behind a pile of garbage.

"Get out of here, kid. They won't shoot me. Not until
they have what they want, but they've got no qualms
about doing away with you."

"No way, bro. If we go down, we go down together."

"Then let's both get out of here. If we can't get the
Jeep, maybe we can outrun them." It was hopeless.

Hawke knew it, but trying for freedom was better than sitting and waiting for recapture. "On the count of three." He met Simon's eyes, saw his own hopelessness and determination reflected there.

"One. T—"

Another barrage of bullets followed the first, this time coming from the behind Hawke. He glanced back, saw Jack McKenzie and three other men crouched down and moving in.

"Move, Morran. We'll cover you."

Hawke didn't wait for another invitation. He met Simon's gaze again. Nodded. And ran.

This was as close to war as Miranda ever hoped to get. From her vantage point behind a garbage can, she watched as several of Sharee's men fell to the ground. The rest dove for cover, firing shots wildly as they went. Hawke and a dark-haired young man were running toward Jack McKenzie. They wove and zigzagged, bullets flying too close for comfort as they went. Apirak had disappeared at the first sound of gunfire, slipping into mist and shadows. Miranda imagined he was slipping closer to Sharee's people, hoping to get a clearer shot.

She, on the other hand, was cowering behind garbage and praying for all she was worth. It seemed the battle went on for an eternity, gunfire being exchanged, shouts and groans and a harsh metallic scent hanging in the air. Then, as quickly as it started, it ended, the world falling silent. Not even a bird or a chirping cricket breaking the stillness.

In the silence, Miranda could hear every beat of her heart, feel the mad pulsing of her terror. She wanted to run, but had no idea who had won the battle or if it had been won at all. Had no idea which direction she should go if she decided to run. Toward the building? Away from it?

She slid down on her belly, slowly, cautiously moving backward, sure that at any moment her movement would attract attention and bullets would fly once again. Something wrapped around her ankle and Miranda jumped, barely stifling a scream as she scrambled to her knees, pivoting to face her attacker.

The dark hair, scarred face and quick-silver eyes were so familiar Miranda felt as if she'd been seeing them every day for years. She scrambled to her feet, relief coursing through her. "Hawke."

"Didn't you give your word that you'd stay with Apirak?" Hawke growled the words, his irritation obvious.

Miranda didn't care. She was so glad he was okay—that at least for now they were safe—that she lurched toward him, wrapping her arms around his waist, clinging tight, sure she would be happy to stay that way forever. "Is it over?"

"Close. Jack and his men are cleaning things up, trying to pull Sharee's men out of any holes they might be hiding in. So—" he leaned back so he could look down at her "—we were discussing the fact that you broke your word."

"Actually, I didn't. Apirak is here."

"It's true." Apirak stepped into view. "We came together."

"As if that makes it a good thing." Hawke scowled, but there was a lightness to his expression that Miranda hadn't seen before, a peace that emanated from him.

"Your brother is okay?" Miranda asked the question, though she was sure she already knew the answer.

Hawke wouldn't be so relaxed if his brother was injured or in danger.

"Simon is good." Hawke wrapped his arm around Miranda's shoulder as if he didn't want to let her out of his sight again. "There he is. With Jack." Hawke gestured to the man Miranda had seen running beside him before the battle began.

"He's young."

"Thirteen years younger than me. Come meet him." He led her toward the other men, his stride easy and unhurried, as if he had all the time in the world. Maybe he did. He was home now. Safe. And soon Miranda would be returning home, as well. The thought brought a sadness she hadn't expected to feel. She swallowed it back as she greeted Simon and Jack. Sirens sounded in the distance and a police car raced into sight, pulling into the parking lot, a marked truck following close behind it. Men leaped from the vehicles and fanned out to cuff and escort men to the waiting transportation.

This was it then. The truth would be revealed. She and Hawke would be cleared. Life would go on the way it always had. Except that Justin wouldn't be in it. And she would never be the same. Her loss, the things she'd been through, seemed carved into the very fiber of her being. She leaned against an old car, listening as the men spoke, their words flowing over her in strangely comforting waves.

Until chaos broke out again. A gunshot, a shout, a police officer falling to the ground.

"I don't want any trouble," a tall, thin American spoke, his face swollen and splattered with blood, his voice empty of emotion, a gun held to the head of the police officer who stood in front of him.

"It's too late for that, Austin." Jack spoke quietly, a

weariness in his tone that Miranda thought must come from facing someone once trusted and now proven untrustworthy.

"I've hurt no one, Jack. Not yet. And I don't plan to. Just give me some time to talk to my wife and kids. Then I'll turn myself in." As lies went, this one wasn't convincing, the words of a desperate man and nothing more.

"I think you know it doesn't work that way. Put the gun down. Killing a man won't accomplish your goals."

"But it will buy me some time." He pulled the trigger, firing past the officer as he moved backward, the shot landing several feet away. The rest seemed to happen in slow motion. Standing beside Hawke and Apirak, Jack pulled his gun. All of their focus was on Austin. Miranda's own gaze was trained in that direction, but something drew her attention, a subtle shifting in the air, a warning of danger that had her turning. A man lurched up from the tall grass, a gun drawn and pointed at the nearest target.

"Simon! Watch out!" Miranda yelled the warning, hurled herself toward the young man, pushing him out of the way.

Something slammed into her chest, throwing her backward, stealing her breath. She gasped, trying for air that wouldn't come, something hot and thick sliding down her arm. She tried to wipe it away, but couldn't move, her body weighted and pressing ever deeper into the welcoming earth.

The sound of more gunfire came as if from a distance, dull reports that danced at the edge of Miranda's conscience. Her eyes drifted closed, but she forced them open, trying to turn her head to see if Simon was okay.

"Babe!" Hawke was there, kneeling beside her, his face pale, his expression stark and raw.

"Simon..."

"Is fine. Don't talk, okay?"

"I'm fine." Or maybe not. Her vision blurred, her head swam and darkness pressed in on her. She kept her eyes open, afraid to let go, afraid of what would happen if she did.

"I said don't talk. You're bleeding. This is going to hurt." He pressed against her shoulder and the pain she hadn't felt exploded through her, stealing the light. This time, she didn't fight it.

Chapter Twenty-Four

It hurt to breathe. That was Miranda's first thought. The second came as she opened her eyes. She was alive.

"Miranda?" The voice was familiar, but not the one she must have been subconsciously hoping for. She turned her head, meeting Lauren's bright blue eyes.

"Lauren. Am I back home?" No. That didn't make sense. She was in a hospital, a television running monotonous, unintelligible tones.

"You're in Bangkok. You were flown here five days ago. I came as soon as I was called. Max is here, too. He's gone to get coffee. We've been worried sick about you. Why didn't you tell me the truth, Miranda? How could you let me think you were a criminal?" Lauren sniffed, but there were no tears in her eyes. Nor was there concern or any of the other things Miranda might have hoped for.

"I tried to tell you. You chose not to believe me." Her throat hurt and she was desperate for the water she could see sitting on the table beside her bed. She tried to reach for it, but the simple movement sent pain shooting through her shoulder and chest.

"You could have tried harder, Miranda. All those interviews I had with the press, telling them that you were just confused, that you'd been pulled in by a man more worldly than you." She shook her head, bit her too-perfect lips. "I look like a fool."

"Sorry." Miranda had no energy to say anything more, and she closed her eyes to block out the sight of her sister.

"You're not going back to sleep before Max gets back, are you? He's been beside himself with worry."

Miranda forced her eyes open again, saw that Lauren was peering down at her. "At least one of you was."

"You're not implying that I wasn't worried?"

"Of course not, Lauren."

"I know you've been through a lot, but I don't think that gives you the right to be snooty."

Miranda responded with a question she'd wanted to ask since she'd opened her eyes. "Where's Hawke?"

"Hawke? The man with the scar, you mean?"

"Hawke."

"I sent him away. Max and I thought seeing him would bring back bad memories."

"Sent him away? When?"

"Five or six times since I got here. I'm hoping this time it sticks. He's not your type, Miranda. You know that, don't you?"

"How would you know what my type is?" The question slipped out and Miranda was glad. Her pain was increasing by the minute, her throat hot and tight. She wanted to ask for a drink of water, but opted for feigning sleep instead. Better to ignore Lauren than to fight with her.

She heard a door open, knew it must be Max returning, but didn't have any desire to see even him, her pain becoming so intense, her fatigue so overwhelming, she didn't have the energy to even open her eyes.

"She woke up for a minute, but went right back under. I still think we should transfer her home now. She'll get better faster there." Lauren's words seemed muffled, her inflections oddly out of sync.

"You know she's not stable enough for that, Laur. Did you tell her I was here?"

"Yes. She seemed less than impressed."

"What do you expect? She's been through three surgeries...." His words faded away as the pain dragged Miranda back under.

When she surfaced again, the room was silent but for the quiet beep and hum of machinery. Miranda's pain crested and receded with every breath she took. She tried to open her eyes, but her lids seemed fused together, all her effort not producing even the slightest movement. Panic beat a hard fast rhythm in her chest, each beat of her heart only adding to the pain. She wanted to scream, but her vocal chords seemed paralyzed, her body refusing to respond to any of her commands. The slow beep of the machine accelerated and Miranda wondered if she'd die here, frozen in place, unable to call for help.

A warm hand pressed against her forehead, the touch so comforting tears slipped from her eyes. If she were going to die, at least she wouldn't be alone.

"No more tears, babe. My heart is already broken enough."

Hawke. Miranda tried again to open her eyes, focusing on the gentle brush of his hands against her cheek. Finally she managed it, the effort making her queasy. The room was dimly lit, the television off, Hawke's rugged face bent close to hers, the shadow of a beard covering his jaw.

"There you are. I was wondering when I'd look in those beautiful eyes again." He spoke quietly, setting a book down on the table and grabbing a cup with a straw sticking out of it. "Here. Take a sip."

She did, the icy water easing some of the burning in her throat, though it did little to ease her pain. "Thank you."

But more tears slipped out, sliding into her hair, dripping into her ears.

"Shh." Hawke wiped the tears away, his hand a butterfly kiss against her skin. "Are you in pain?"

"Yes."

"Here. Press this and the pain will be gone before you know it." He put her thumb over a small button.

Miranda didn't even ask what it was, or what it would do to her. She just wanted every breath to stop being agony.

Within minutes the pain eased to a dull ache, her tense body finally relaxing.

"There. You already look more comfortable." Hawke brushed a hand along her shoulder and down her arm, gently cupping her hand in his. "Your sister said you woke earlier. Didn't she tell you about the morphine pump?"

"She was too busy telling me what an inconvenience I've been to her. Where is she? And Max? Isn't he here, too?" Miranda's throat was burning again, an aching dryness that she couldn't ignore. "Can I have some more water?"

He nodded, held the cup while she sipped again, his eyes silvery gray and filled with emotion Miranda couldn't name. "Your family is at their hotel. I convinced them it would be for the best if they got some rest. Would you like me to call them? They're close. It won't take long for them to come."

She shook her head. "I'd like to see Max, but I can't handle Lauren right now."

"You don't have to handle anything, babe. I'll handle it for you." He spoke in smooth soothing tones designed to comfort and Miranda let herself be drawn into them, her muscles relaxing, her head easing back onto the pillow.

"How is your brother?"

"Simon is great. He's been here several times and is anxious to thank you for saving his life."

"And Austin?"

"He's recovering from several gunshot wounds. He'll live, but I'm not sure he's going to be happy about it."

"Did he confess?"

"Not at first, but once Jack threatened to hand him over to the Thai authorities, he was more willing to talk. He admitted that he'd been in the Wa's pocket for years, almost from the day he'd arrived in Thailand. That he passed on information about me to Green."

"He must have known he'd eventually get caught."

"Maybe he did. Maybe he didn't care. His cause was everything. He'd reconnected with his birth mother and her father years after he was adopted and was brought into his grandfather's militant philosophy. When his grandfather died, Austin took up his cause. A few months after he arrived in Thailand, Sharee offered him big money to be the Wa's informant. He agreed and has been sending money to Chechnya ever since."

"And Green? Liam?"

"Both have been arrested. Neither will admit to anything, but there's enough evidence to convict them."

"And Randy?"

Hawke shook his head and squeezed her hand. "He's disappeared. I don't think he'll ever be found."

"You think he's dead?"

"Yeah. I do. Liam and Green would have seen him as the weak link. Getting rid of him would have assured his silence."

"I hope you're wrong. I hope he's alive somewhere and that the police find him. I hate to think of him being murdered."

"Then don't think about it. Think about getting better." He brushed strands of hair from her cheek, his fingers lingering there.

"I guess this means the police aren't after you anymore. You're finally in the clear. I'm so glad."

"I told you before you didn't have to worry about me, but I think I'm starting to like it." He smiled and Miranda's heart filled with an emotion she didn't want to name. One she hadn't wanted to feel. But it was there, as real as the man sitting beside her, as real as the connection between them that had become stronger with each passing day, each passing moment.

"Hawke—"

He pressed a finger against her lips. "Enough talking for now. You've got to rest so you can heal."

"I've been resting for five days."

"Five days isn't nearly long enough, babe. You almost died in Mae Hong Son. They airlifted you here once you were stabilized. Performed surgery to repair your lung. Had to go back in twice more to stop internal bleeding. It's been a tough few days. Now that you're awake, things are looking up. Let's keep it that way."

"I don't remember anything about what happened." Except the pain. And Hawke. He seemed to be part of all her memories, all her thoughts, and having him here made the world seem much more right than it had when she'd opened her eyes to find Lauren. "But I know I'm glad you're here." The words slipped out and she didn't wish them back.

"And I'm glad *you're* here." Hawke leaned in, pressing a tender kiss to her lips. "I thought we were going to lose you."

"I guess I'm tougher than you thought."

"You're exactly what I thought—a sweet, strong, funny woman who cares just a little too much about everyone. Meeting you has changed me, Miranda. For the better. I want you to know that."

He was going to say goodbye. Miranda knew it and she fought unwelcome tears at the thought. She'd known from the very beginning that they were from different worlds, that they had nothing in common. "Are you leaving now?"

"Leaving? Babe, I'll stay here for the rest of my life if you want me to." He grinned, but there was a seriousness to his voice that made Miranda's heart jump.

"The rest of your life might be a long time."

"The rest of my life won't be nearly long enough if I get to spend it with you."

"Hawke—"

"I know this isn't the time to discuss it, but every time you were wheeled into surgery, I prayed that God would give me the opportunity to tell you what an important part of my life you've become."

"I feel the same."

"Then maybe when you're feeling better and finally get out of here, we can spend time doing what normal couples do—dinner, movies, walks on the beach."

"As opposed to running from drug dealers, racing through the jungle and getting shot?"

"Exactly."

"I'd like that. I'd like that a lot."

Hawke smiled again, lifting her hand, kissing her knuckles, his lips warm against her flesh, his eyes promising all the things she'd thought she'd never have. "Me, too. But first, healing. How's the pain?"

"Better. I can't even tell where I was shot." Miranda glanced down, trying to find bandages, but a blanket was pulled up to her shoulders and she could see nothing.

"A few inches below your collarbone. The bullet missed your heart, but went through your lung and out your back. The doctors say you are very lucky to be alive. I say you are very blessed."

"A week ago, I'm not sure if I would have agreed. Now, I know you're right. It was so hard to lose Justin. For a while I was sure God had turned His back on me. He didn't, though. He was there for me. And He'll keep being there. I know that now."

"I understand. I've spent ten years looking for justice only to realize that justice is for God to mete out. Not me. I've quit my job with the DEA and I'm selling my portion of the business to my brother. He plans to stay here."

"And you?"

"I'm going to Virginia. My friend Noah told me a

year ago that he had a job for me if I ever wanted one. I'll be training service dogs."

"That's wonderful."

"Yeah, it is. A new life. A new home. And something that appeals to me even more."

"What's that?" Her heart thumped a slow, thick rhythm as she looked into his eyes.

"I'll only be a few hours away from a woman I can't imagine living life without."

Miranda smiled, her eyes drifting closed, sleep wanting to steal her away again. A thought floated on the edge of dreams and she forced her eyes open, looked into Hawke's eyes. "I'm getting tired of living in Essex."

"Are you?"

"Yes. And I can open a bakery just about anywhere."

"Where are you thinking would be a good place?"

"Somewhere close to you."

Hawke's smile lit his face. He leaned toward her, gently pulling her into his arms and the emotion Miranda hadn't wanted to name welled up inside, the word for it dancing through her head and in her heart until she couldn't deny it any longer. "I love you, Hawke."

"You know what, babe? I love you, too."

Epilogue

"You really don't intend to live here?" Lauren's
voice was high pitched, her blue eyes, framed by styl-
ish glasses, scanned the small living room she and Miranda were standing in.

"Actually, I do." Miranda lifted a box from the floor,
wincing a little as the muscles in her chest and back
pulled against scar tissue.

"But it's…" Lauren looked around the little bunga-
low Miranda had purchased a week after her return
from Thailand. It had taken another few weeks to finalize the sale of her bakery to an employee who'd jumped
at the chance to own it. The town house had also been
easy to sell. Now, after a month of nervous anticipation, moving day had arrived. Unfortunately, Lauren
had felt the need to be part of it and had followed Miranda's Saturn and the moving truck and crew she'd
hired, her Mercedes crammed with boxes of Miranda's
belongings.

"It's what?" Miranda glanced around the cozy
room—the gleaming hardwood floors, the muted
yellow paint, the windows that lined the front wall and

looked out onto the blue-green water of Smith Mountain Lake.

"Small. Old."

"I think it's cute and homey."

"Which just shows how confused you are. Miranda, this is just a bad idea all around. You've fallen for a man who isn't right for you. That's bad enough. But to move hundreds of miles from home to be near him. That's insane. Obviously you still haven't recovered from your injury."

"The injury was to my lung, not my brain." Miranda pulled a pile of books out of the box and placed them on one of the built-in bookshelves that flanked the fireplace. The clock on the mantel said twelve-thirty. When she'd spoken to Hawke the previous night, she'd told him she'd be at the house by noon. He'd said he would be there to meet her. She'd counted on it. Now disappointment beat a sullen pulse behind her eyes, the headache she'd been fighting off during the five-hour drive from Maryland slamming full-force through her skull.

She pulled another pile of books from the box, shooting a look at her sister as she did so and gesturing toward the partially open front door. "Why don't you head to the airport, Lauren? You wouldn't want to miss your flight."

"I've got hours before it takes off. Besides, I've been thinking of canceling the photo shoot."

Miranda knew that wasn't the truth, but she played the game anyway. "Why?"

"Because you obviously need me here. I'd hoped that Max could leave his job for a week and come stay with you, but he just refused to take more time off."

"He refused because he'd already stayed with me

in Essex for two weeks. I wanted him to get back to his life, so I told him I'd be fine on my own. And I am." She dropped the empty box, lifted another one and froze as a short, sharp rap sounded on the door. It swung open the rest of the way, a tall, dark figure filling the doorway.

"I knew if I was a few minutes late you'd get into trouble." Hawke's gravely voice was so familiar, so welcome, tears filled Miranda's eyes.

"I'm not getting into trouble. I'm unpacking."

"And I think that was exactly what I told you not to do." He strode forward, took the box from her hands, a gentle smile softening the harsh planes and angles of his face. He'd left his hair down and it fell forward, brushing against Miranda's skin as he leaned down to capture her lips in a searing kiss.

"Excuse me, but you're not alone, you know." Lauren huffed the words and Miranda pulled back, her cheeks heating.

She might have stepped away, but Hawke hooked an arm around her waist and pulled her close. "Do you see that comfortable-looking chair over there?" He pointed to the antique rocker that the movers had brought in a half hour ago. "I want you to sit there and relax while I take care of the rest of these boxes."

"We're doing fine without you, Mr. Morran, and one more person in this room will only make it more claustrophobic. Feel free to leave and come back later after we're done." Lauren's voice was icy cold, her expression haughty.

"I invited Hawke here because I wanted him here, Lauren. And since this is my house, I think I get to decide who stays and who doesn't." Miranda leaned her aching head against Hawke's shoulder and his arm tightened around her waist.

Lauren stiffened, her back ramrod straight and her eyes slitted. "I went out of my way to help you today, Miranda. You act like you don't appreciate it."

"Of course I do, but that's beside the point. You're being rude and you know it. If you can't be more pleasant, you can leave." Miranda's heart broke as she spoke, her dreams of building a relationship with Lauren dying in the face of her sister's inability to think of anyone but herself.

"Obviously, you've decided you don't need family now that *he's* in your life."

"Hawke is the closest family I've ever had."

Lauren blinked and for a moment Miranda thought she'd soften. Then she shrugged, started across the room. "I'm sorry you feel that way. I guess I'll leave you to your *family*." She stepped outside, closing the door firmly behind her.

"Lauren—"

"Let her go, babe. One more word out of her mouth and I was going to throw her out anyway." Hawke spoke quietly.

"I know she's obnoxious, but she's my sister."

"And maybe one day she'll realize it. How two such different women could come from the same family, I don't know." Hawke brushed a hand over Miranda's hair, his fingers tangling in the strands and massaging the base of her neck. "You okay?"

"Better than I was when I arrived and saw that you weren't here."

"Sorry about that, babe. I picked up a surprise for you on my way here and it wasn't cooperating."

"A surprise?" Miranda smiled, easing away from

Hawke's arm and turning to face him, her fingers tracing the strong line of his jaw, the ridge of the scar on his cheek. "Did Simon finally decide to visit?"

"Not yet. He's planning to come out in November."

"Then what's the surprise?"

"Sit down and I'll tell you."

"Bribery?"

"Whatever works."

Miranda did as he asked, easing down onto the rocking chair and smiling up at him. "Okay. I did my part. What's the surprise?"

"It's in the car. Wait here and I'll bring it in."

He disappeared out the door and was back moments later, a wiggling, squirming bundle of fur in his arms, the big pink bow tied around its neck sliding and slipping as it moved.

"A puppy!" Miranda reached for the little fur ball, laughing as it licked her chin. "She's adorable. Oh, Hawke, thank you!"

"I thought you might like some company when I couldn't be here."

"You thought I needed a guard dog is more like it." Miranda laughed again, reaching for Hawke's hand, loving the way the solid warmth of it felt.

"Does she look like a guard dog?"

Miranda studied the puppy's brown fur and dark face, her soulful eyes and wagging tail, the pink bow and the shiny gold ring hanging from one end of it.

Shiny gold ring?

Miranda's breath caught in her throat, her hand shaking as she reached out to touch it. A marquis diamond flashed in the overhead light, reflecting all the colors of life, of hope, of dreams fulfilled.

"My friend Noah said I should wait. He said it was

too soon to ask you to marry me. But I don't want to wait, babe. Not a year. Not two years. Not somebody else's idea of what a reasonable amount of time is." He knelt down in front of her, his eyes glowing with silver fire. "I love you now. I'll love you tomorrow. I'll love you an eternity from now. So, what do you say?"

"I say your friend doesn't know what he's talking about." Miranda smiled past the tears of joy that were sliding down her cheeks. "I say yes."

* * * * *

Dear Reader,

The world is filled with scary situations. Our faith may be shaken when our prayers seem to go unanswered, or our deepest dreams are never realized. However, true faith is more than believing that God will make everything go our way. It is what Shadrach, Meshach and Abednego had when they said, "If we are thrown into the blazing furnace, the God we serve is able to save us from it…. *But even if He does not,* we will not serve your gods." Their faith did not require a miracle. Our faith should be the same. Solid in the face of whatever might come.

This is a truth Miranda Sheldon learns as she is thrust into a situation that might lead to her death. Forced to trust a man she doesn't know, she must believe that whatever happens, God will be there. Join Miranda and Hawke Morran as they journey to Mae Hong Son, Thailand, in search of evidence that will clear their names. What they find there is something neither of them expect, but both desperately need.

All His best,

Shirlee McCoy

STRANGER IN
THE SHADOWS

Send forth your light and your truth,
let them guide me; let them bring me to
your holy mountain, to the place where you dwell.
—*Psalms* 43:3

To Brenda Minton, who makes me laugh when
I want to cry. Thanks for the brainstorming sessions
and the pep talks, but mostly thanks for being you.

And to Bob and Jan Porter and Dick
and Carolyn Livesey, who are true encouragers.
Thanks for always cheering me on!

Chapter One

It came in the night, whispering into her dreams. Silent stars, hazy moonlight, a winding road. Sudden, blinding light.

Impact.

Rolling, tumbling, terror. And then silence.

Smoke danced at the edges of memory as flames writhed serpentlike through cracked glass and crumbled metal, hissing and whirling in the timeless dance of death.

Adam! She reached for his hand, wanting to pull him from the car and from the dream—whole and alive. Safe. But her questing hand met empty space and hot flame, her body flinching with the pain and the horror of it.

Sirens blared in the distance, their throbbing pulse a heartbeat ebbing and flowing with the growing flames. She turned toward the door, trying to push aside hot, bent metal, and saw a shadow beyond the shattered glass; a dark figure leaning toward the window, staring in. Dark eyes that seemed to glow in the growing flames.

Help me! She tried to scream the words, but they

caught in her throat. And the shadow remained still and silent, watching as the car burned and she burned with it.

The shrill ring of an alarm clock sounded over the roar of flames, spearing into Chloe Davidson's consciousness and pulling her from the nightmare. For a moment there was nothing but the dream. No past. No present. No truth except hot flames and searing pain. But the flames weren't real, the pain a fading memory. Reality was...what?

Chloe scrambled to anchor herself in the present before she fell back into the foggy world of unknowns she'd lived in during the weeks following the accident.

"Saturday. Lakeview, Virginia. The Morran wedding. Flowers. Decorations." She listed each item as it came to mind, grabbing towels from the tiny closet beside the bathroom door, pulling clothes from her dresser. Black pants. Pink shirt. Blooming Baskets' uniform. Her new job. Her new life. A normality she still didn't quite believe in.

The phone rang before she could get in the shower, the muted sound drawing her from the well-lit bedroom and into the dark living room beyond.

"Hello?" She pressed the receiver to her ear as she flicked on lamps and the overhead light, her heart still racing, her throbbing leg an insistent reminder of the nightmare she'd survived.

"Chloe. Opal, here."

At the sound of her friend and boss's voice, Chloe relaxed, leaning her hip against the sofa and forcing the dream and the memories to the back of her mind. "You've only been gone a day and you're already checking in?"

"Checking in? I wasn't planning to do that until tonight. This is business. We've got a problem. Jenna's gone into labor."

Opal's only other full-time employee, Jenna Monroe, was eight months pregnant and glowing with it. At least she had been when Chloe had seen her the previous day. "She's not due for another four weeks."

"Maybe not, but the baby has decided to make an appearance. You're going to have to handle the setup for the Morran wedding on your own until I can get there."

"I'll call Mary Alice—"

"Mary Alice is going to have to stay at the store. We can't afford to close for the day and between the two of you, she's the better floral designer."

"It doesn't take much to be better than me." Chloe's dry comment fell on deaf ears, Opal's voice continuing on, giving directions and listing jobs that needed to be done before the wedding guests arrived at the church.

"So, that's it. Any questions?"

"No. But you do realize I've only been working at Blooming Baskets for five days, right?"

"Are you saying you can't do this?"

"I'm saying I'll try, but I can't guarantee the results."

"No need to guarantee anything. I've already left Baltimore. I'll be in Lakeview at least an hour before the wedding. We'll finish the job together."

"If I haven't ruined everything by then."

"What's to ruin? We're talking flowers, ribbons and bows." Opal paused, and Chloe could imagine her raking a hand through salt and pepper curls, her strong face set in an impatient frown. "Look, I have faith in your ability to handle this. Why don't you try to have some, too?"

The phone clicked as Opal disconnected, and Chloe set the receiver down.

Faith? Maybe she'd had it once—in herself and her abilities, in those she cared about. But that was before the accident, before Adam's death. Before his betrayal. Before everything had changed.

Now she wasn't even sure she knew what the word meant.

It didn't take long to shower and change, to grab her keys and make her way out of her one-bedroom apartment and into the dark hallway of the aging Victorian she lived in.

Outside it was still dark, brisk fall air dancing through the grass and rustling the dying leaves of the bushes that flanked the front porch. Chloe scanned the shadowy yard, the trees that stretched spindly arms toward the heavens, the inky water of Smith Mountain Lake. There seemed a breathless quality to the morning, a watchful waiting that crawled along Chloe's nerves and made the hair on the back of her neck stand on end. A million eyes could be watching from the woods beside the house, a hundred men could be sliding silently toward the car and she'd never know it, never see it until it was too late.

Cold sweat broke out on her brow, her hand shaking as she got in the car and shoved the keys into the ignition.

"You are not going to have a panic attack about this." She hissed the words as she drove up the long driveway and turned onto the road, refusing to think about what she was doing, refusing to dwell on the darkness that pressed against the car windows. Soon dawn would come, burning away the night and her memories. For now, she'd just have to deal with both.

Forty minutes later, Chloe arrived at Grace Christian Church, the pink Blooming Baskets van she'd picked up at the shop loaded with decorations and floral arrangements. It was just before seven. The wedding was scheduled for noon. Guests would arrive a little before then. That meant she had four hours to get ready for what Opal and Jenna had called the biggest event to take place in Lakeview in a decade. And Chloe was the one setting up for it.

She would have laughed if she weren't so sure she was about to fail. Miserably.

Cold crisp air stung her cheeks as she stepped to the back of the van and pulled open the double doors. The sickeningly sweet funeral-parlor stench nearly made her gag as she dragged the first box out.

"Need a hand?"

The voice was deep, masculine and so unexpected Chloe jumped, the box of wrought iron candelabras dropping from her hands. She whirled toward the sound, but could see nothing but the deep gray shadows of trees and foliage. "Thank you, but I'm fine."

"You sure? Looks like you've got a full van there." A figure emerged from the trees, a deeper shadow among many others, but moving closer.

"I can manage." As she spoke, she dug in her jacket pocket, her fist closing around the small canister of pepper spray she carried. She didn't know who this guy was, but if he got much closer he was going to get a face full of pain.

"I'm sure you can, but Opal won't be happy if I let you. She just ordered me out of bed and over here to help. So here I am. Ready to lend a hand. Or two." His voice was amiable, his stride unhurried. Chloe released her hold on the spray.

"Opal shouldn't have bothered you, Mr…?"

"Ben Avery. And it wasn't a bother."

She knew the name, had heard plenty about the handsome widower who pastored Grace Christian Church. Opal's description of the man's single-and-available status had led Chloe to believe he was Opal's contemporary. Late fifties or early sixties.

In the dim morning light, he looked closer to thirty and not like any pastor Chloe had ever seen, his hair just a little too long, his leather jacket more biker than preacher.

"Bother or not, I'm sure you have other things to do with your time, Pastor Avery."

"I can't think of any offhand. And call me Ben. Everyone else does." He smiled, his eyes crinkling at the corners, the scent of pine needles and soap drifting on the air as he leaned forward and grabbed the box she'd dropped.

Chloe thought about arguing, but insisting she do the job herself would only waste time she didn't have. She shrugged. "Then I guess I'll accept your help and say thanks."

"You might want to hold off on the thanks until we see how many flower arrangements I manage to massacre."

"You're not the only one who may massacre a few. I know as much about flowers as the average person knows about nuclear physics."

He laughed, the sound shivering along Chloe's nerves and bringing her senses to life. "Opal did mention that you're a new hire."

"Should I ask what else she mentioned?"

"You can, but that was about all she said. That and,

'It'll be on your head, Ben Avery, if Chloe decides to quit because of the pressure she's under today.'"

"That sounds just like her. The rat."

"She is, but she's a well-meaning rat."

"Very true." Chloe pulled out another box. "And I really could use the help. This is a big job."

"Then I guess we'd better get moving. Between the two of us we should be able to get most of the setup done before Opal arrives." Ben pushed open the church door, waiting as Chloe moved more slowly across the parking lot.

"Ladies first." He gestured for her to step inside, but Chloe hesitated.

She hated the dark. Hated the thought of what might be lurking in it. The inside of the church was definitely dark, the inky blackness lit by one tiny pinpoint of light flashing from the ceiling. She knew it must be a smoke detector, but her mind spiraled into the darkness, carried her back to the accident, to the shadowy figure standing outside the window of the car, to the eyes that had seemed to glow red, searing into her soul and promising a slow, torturous death.

She swayed, her heart racing so fast she was sure she was going to pass out.

"Hey, are you okay?" Ben wrapped a hand around her arm, anchoring her in place, his warmth chasing away some of the fear that shivered through her.

"I'm fine." Of course she *wasn't* fine. Not by a long shot. But her terror was only a feeling, the danger imagined.

She took a deep breath, stepped into the room, the darkness enveloping her as the door clicked shut. Chloe forced herself to concentrate on the moment, on the soft pad of Ben's shoes as he moved across the floor, the scent of pine needles and soap that drifted on the air around him.

Finally, overhead lights flicked on, illuminating a wide hallway. Hardwood floors, creamy walls, bulletin boards filled with announcements and pictures. The homey warmth of it drew her in and welcomed her.

Chloe turned, facing Ben, seeing him clearly for the first time, her heart leaping as she looked into the most vividly blue eyes she'd ever seen. Deep sapphire, they burned into hers, glowing with life, with energy, with an interest that made Chloe step back, the box clutched close, a flimsy barrier between herself and the man who'd done what no other had in the past year— made her want to keep looking, made her want to know more, made her wish she were the woman she'd been before Adam's death.

His gaze touched her face, the scar on her neck, the mottled flesh of her hand, but he didn't comment or ask the questions so many people felt they had the right to. "The sanctuary is through here. Let's bring these in. Then I'll make some coffee before we get the rest from the van."

Chloe followed silently, surprised by her response to Ben and not happy about it. She'd made too many mistakes with Adam, had too many regrets. There wasn't room for anything else. Or anyone.

"Where do you want these?" Ben's question pulled her from her thoughts and she glanced around the large room. Rows of pews, their dark wood gleaming in the overhead light, flanked a middle aisle. A few stairs led to a pulpit and a choir loft, a small door to one side of them closed tight.

"On the first pew will be fine. I'll start there and work my way back." She avoided looking in Ben's direction as she spoke, preferring to tell herself she'd imagined the bright blue of his eyes, the warm interest there. He was a pastor, after all, and she was a woman who had no interest in men.

"Am I making you nervous?"

Startled, Chloe glanced up, found herself pulled into his gaze again.

"No." At least not much. "Why do you ask?"

"Sometimes my job makes people uncomfortable." He smiled, his sandy hair and strong, handsome face giving him a boy-next-door appearance that seemed at odds with the intensity in his eyes.

"Not me." Though *Ben* seemed to be having that effect on her.

"Good to know." He smiled again, but his gaze speared into hers and she wondered what he was seeing as he looked so deeply into her eyes. "And just so we're clear. Florists don't make *me* uncomfortable."

Despite herself, Chloe smiled. "Then I guess that means we'll both be nice and relaxed while we work."

"Not until we have some coffee. I don't know about you, but I'm not much good for anything until I've had a cup."

His words were the perfect excuse to end the conversation and move away from Ben, and Chloe started back toward the sanctuary door, anxious to refocus her thinking, recenter her thoughts. "I'll keep unloading while you make some."

Ben put a hand on her shoulder, stopping her before she could exit the room. "If the rest of the boxes are as heavy as the last one, maybe you should make the coffee and I should unload."

"I'll be fine."

"*You* will be, but I won't if Opal finds out I let you carry in a bunch of heavy boxes while I made coffee."

"Who's going to tell her?"

"I'd feel obligated to. After all, she's bound to ask how things went and I'm bound to tell the truth."

For the second time since she'd met Ben, Chloe found herself smiling at his words. Not good. Not good at all. Men were bad news. At least all the men in Chloe's life had been. The sooner she put distance between herself and Ben, the better she'd feel. "Since you put it that way, I guess I can't argue."

"Glad to hear it, because arguing isn't getting me any closer to having that cup of coffee. Come on, I'll show you to the kitchen." He strode out of the sanctuary, moving with long, purposeful strides.

Chloe followed more slowly, not sure what it was about Ben that had sparked her interest and made her want to look closer. He was a man, just like any other man she'd ever known, but there was something in his eyes—secrets, depths—that begged exploration.

Fortunately, she'd learned her lesson about men the hard way and she had no intention of learning any more. She'd just get through the wedding preparations, get through the day, then go back to her apartment and forget Ben Avery and his compelling gaze.

Chapter Two

The industrial-size kitchen had a modern feel with a touch of old-time charm, the stainless steel counters and appliances balanced by mellow gold paint, white cabinets and hardwood floor. Chloe hovered in the doorway, wary, unsure of herself in a way she hadn't been a year ago, watching as Ben plugged in a coffeemaker and pulled a can of coffee from a cupboard. He gestured her over and Chloe stepped into the room ignoring the erratic beat of her heart. "This is a nice space."

"Yeah, it is, but I can't take credit. We remodeled a couple of years ago. The church ladies decided on the setup and color scheme. Opal pretty much spearheaded the project."

"That doesn't surprise me. She's a take-charge kind of person. It's one of the things I admire about her."

"Have you known her long?" He leaned a hip against the counter, relaxed and at ease. Apparently not at all disturbed by the fact that he'd been called out of bed before dawn on a cool November day to help a woman he didn't know set up flowers for a wedding he was probably officiating.

Strange.

Interesting.

Intriguing.

Enough!

Chloe rubbed the scarred flesh on her wrist, forcing her thoughts back to the conversation. "Since I was a kid."

"You grew up in Lakeview?" His gaze was disconcerting, and Chloe resisted the urge to look away.

"No, I visited in the summer." She didn't add more. The past was something she didn't share. Especially not with strangers.

Ben seemed to take the hint, turning away and pulling sugar packets from a cupboard. "It's a good place to spend the summer. And the fall, winter and spring." He smiled. "There's cream in the fridge if you take it. I'd better get moving on those boxes."

With that he strode from the room, his movements lithe and silent, almost catlike in their grace. He might be a pastor now, but Chloe had a feeling he'd been something else before he'd felt a call to ministry. Military. Police. Firefighter. Something that required control, discipline and strength.

Not that it mattered or was any of her business.

Chloe shook her head, reaching for a coffee filter and doing her best to concentrate on the task at hand. Obviously, the nightmare had thrown her off, destroying her focus and hard-won control. She needed to get both back and she needed to do it now. Opal was counting on her. There was no way she planned to disappoint the one person in her life who had never disappointed her.

She paced across the room, staring out the window above the sink, anxiety a cold, hard knot in her chest. New beginnings. That's what she hoped for. Prayed for. But maybe she was too entrenched in the past to ever escape it. Maybe coming to Lakeview was nothing more than putting off the inevitable.

Outside, dawn bathed the churchyard in purple light and deep shadows, the effect sinister. Ominous. A thick stand of trees stood at the far end of the property, tall pines and heavy-branched oaks reaching toward the ever-brightening sky. As the coffee brewed, the rich, full scent of it filled the kitchen, bringing memories of hot summer days, lacy curtains, open windows, soft voices. Safety.

But safety and security never lasted. All Chloe could hope for was a measure of peace.

She started to turn away from the window, but something moved near the edge of the yard, a slight shifting in the darkness that caught her attention. Was that a person standing in the shadows of the trees? It was too far to see the details, the light too dim. But Chloe was sure there *was* a person there. Tall. Thin. Looking her way.

She took a step back, her pulse racing, her skin clammy and cold. This was the nightmare again. The stranger watching, waiting on the other side of the glass. Only this time Chloe wasn't trapped in a car and surrounded by flames. This time she was able to run. And that's just what she did, turning away from the window, rushing from the kitchen and slamming into a hard chest.

She flew back, her bad leg buckling, her hands searching for purchase. Her fingers sank into cool leather as strong arms wrapped around her waist and pulled her upright.

"Careful. We've got a lot to do. It's probably best if we don't kill each other before we finish." Ben's words tickled against her hair, his palms warm against her ribs. He felt solid and safe and much too comfortable.

Chloe stepped back, forcing herself to release her white-knuckled grip on his jacket. "Sorry. I didn't mean to run you down."

"You didn't even come close." His gaze swept over her, moving from her face, to her hands and back again. "Is everything okay? You look pale."

"I…" But what was she going to say? That she'd seen someone standing outside the church? That she thought it might be the same person who'd stood outside her burning car, watching while the flames grew? The same person who'd been in jail for eleven months? "Everything is fine. I'm just anxious to get started in the sanctuary."

He stared hard, as if he could see beyond her answer to the truth that she was trying to hide, the paranoia and fear that had dogged her for months. Finally, he nodded. "How about we grab the coffee and get started?"

Go back into the kitchen? Back near the window that looked out onto the yard? Maybe catch another glimpse of whoever was standing near the trees. No thanks. "You go ahead. I'll start unpacking boxes."

She hurried back toward the sanctuary, feeling the weight of Ben's gaze as she stepped through the double wide doors. She didn't look back, not wanting him to see the anxiety and frustration in her face.

She'd been so sure that moving away from D.C., leaving behind her apartment, her job, starting a new life, would free her from the anxiety that had become way too much a part of who she was. Seven days into her "new" life and she'd already sunk back into old patterns and thought processes.

Her hands trembled as she pulled chocolate-colored ribbon from a box and began decorating the first pew. Long-stemmed roses—deep red, creamy white, rusty orange—needed to be attached. She pulled a bouquet from a bucket Ben had brought in and wrestled it into place, a few petals falling near her feet as she tied a lopsided bow around the stems.

"Better be careful. Opal won't like it if the roses are bald when she gets here." Ben moved toward her, a coffee cup in each hand, sandy hair falling over his forehead.

"Hopefully, she won't notice a few missing petals."

"A few? No. A handful? Maybe." He set both cups on a pew and scooped up several silky petals. "I brought you coffee. Black. You didn't look like the sugar and cream type."

He was right, and Chloe wasn't sure she was happy about it. "What gave it away?"

"Your eyes." He didn't elaborate and Chloe didn't ask, just lifted the closest cup, inhaling the rich, sharp scent of the coffee and doing her best to avoid Ben's steady gaze.

Which annoyed her. She'd never been one to avoid trouble. Never been one to back away from a challenge. Never been. But the accident had changed her.

She took a sip of the coffee, pulled more ribbon from the box, forcing lightness to her movements and to her voice. "They say the eyes are the window to the soul. If you're seeing black coffee in mine, I'm in big trouble."

"I'm seeing a lot more than black coffee in there."

He grabbed a bouquet of roses, holding it while Chloe hooked it in place and tied a ribbon around the stems, feeling the heat of Ben's body as he leaned in close to help, wondering what it was he thought he saw in her eyes.

Or maybe not wondering. Maybe she knew. Darkness. Sorrow. Guilt. Emotions she'd tried to outrun, but that refused to be left behind.

She grabbed another ribbon, another bouquet, trying to lose herself in the rhythm of the job.

"The flowers look good. Are they Opal's design, or Jenna's?" The switch in subjects was a welcome distraction, and Chloe answered quickly.

"I'm not sure. They were designed months before I started working at Blooming Baskets."

"Do you like it there?"

"Yes." She just wasn't sure how good she was at it. Digging into the bowels of a computer hard drive to find hidden files was one thing. Unraveling yards of tulle and ribbon and handling delicate flowers was another. "But it's a lot different than what I used to do."

"What was that?"

"Computers." She kept the answer short. Giving a name to her job as a computer forensic specialist usually meant answering a million questions about her chosen career.

Former career.

"Sounds interesting."

"It was." It had also been dangerous. Much more dangerous than she ever could have imagined before Adam's death. But that was something she didn't need to be thinking about when she had a few dozen pews and an entire reception hall left to decorate.

Chloe pulled out more ribbon, started on the next

pew and wondered how long it was going to take to complete the decorations on the rest. Too long. Unless she started working a lot faster.

She moved forward, more ribbon in her hand. Ben moved with her, his sandy head bent close to hers as he helped hold the next bunch of roses in place, his presence much more of a distraction than it should have been. "Maybe we should split up. You take the pews on the other side of the aisle. I'll finish the ones over here."

"Trying to get rid of me?"

Absolutely. "I just think we'll get the job done more quickly that way."

"Maybe, but we seem to be making pretty good headway together. Two sets of hands are definitely helpful in this kind of work."

He had a point. A good one. If she had to hold the flowers *and* tie the ribbons it would probably take double the time. And time was not something she had enough of. "You're probably right. Let's keep going the way we are."

"Silently?"

Chloe glanced up into Ben's eyes, saw amusement there. "I don't mind talking while we work."

"As long as it's not about the past?"

"Something like that."

"I bet that limits conversation."

Chloe shrugged, tying the next bow, grabbing more ribbon. "There are plenty of other things to talk about."

"Like?"

"Like what Opal's going to say if she gets here and we're not done."

The deep rumble of Ben's laughter filled the air. "Point taken. I'll lay off the questions and move a little faster."

* * *

Four hours later, Chloe placed the last centerpiece on the last table in the reception hall; the low bowl with floating yellow, cream and burnt umber roses picked up the color in the standing floral arrangements that dotted the edges of the room. Roses. Lilies. A half a dozen other flowers whose names she didn't know.

"You did it! And it looks almost presentable." Opal Winchester's voice broke the silence and Chloe turned to face the woman who'd been surrogate mother to her during long-ago summers, watching as she moved across the room, her salt and pepper curls bouncing around a broad face, her sturdy figure encased in a dark suit and pink shirt.

"I didn't do it alone."

"I know. Where is that good-looking young pastor?"

"Home getting ready for the wedding. Which he's officiating after spending almost four hours helping with the floral decorations."

"Did he complain?"

"No."

"Then I don't expect you to, either." Opal slid an arm around Chloe's waist and surveyed the room. "It's beautiful, isn't it?"

"It is. You and Jenna did a great job."

"So did you and Ben." Opal cast a sly look in Chloe's direction, her dark eyes sparkling. "So, what did you think of him?"

"Who?"

"Ben Avery. As if you didn't know."

"He's helpful."

"And?"

"And he's helpful." Chloe brushed thick bangs out of her eyes and limped a few steps away from Opal, smoothing a wrinkle out of a tablecloth, determined not to give her friend any hint of how Ben had affected her. "How was your drive?"

"You're changing the subject, but I'll allow it seeing as how I'm so proud of what you've accomplished this morning. The drive was slow. I thought I'd never get here." Opal adjusted a centerpiece, straightened a bow on one of the chairs. "But I'm here and happy to announce that Jenna had a bouncing baby boy fifteen minutes ago."

"That's wonderful!"

"Isn't it? A wedding and a birth on the same day. You can't ask for much better than that. I'm going to stop by the hospital after the reception is over. Maybe slip Jenna a piece of wedding cake if Miranda and Hawke don't mind me bringing her some. Speaking of which." She paused, spearing Chloe with a look that warned of trouble. "You're going to have to attend."

"Attend?"

"The wedding."

"No way." She had no intention of staying to witness the marriage of two people she didn't know, two people who, according to both Jenna and Opal, were *meant to be together*.

Meant to be.

As if such a thing were possible. As if *meant to be* didn't always turn into goodbye.

"I understand your reluctance, Chloe, but it's expected."

"You know I never do what's expected."

"I know you never did what was expected. You're starting fresh here and in a small town like Lakeview, doing what's expected is important."

"Opal—"

"Don't make me use my mother voice." She glowered, straightening to her full five-foot-three height.

"I'm not ready for a big social event."

"Well, then you'd better get ready. The entire church was invited to the ceremony and the reception. It's a community event."

"I don't attend this church."

"But Jenna does. You'll be taking her place, offering support to the couple and representing Blooming Baskets."

"I'm sure—"

"I won't listen to any more excuses. I don't like them." The words were harsh, but Opal's expression softened, her dark eyes filled with sympathy. "It's been a year, Chloe. It's time to move on. That's why you're here. That's what you want. And it's what I want for you. So, ready or not, you're attending the wedding."

Much as Chloe wanted to argue, she couldn't deny the truth of Opal's words. She did want to leave the past behind, to focus on the present and the future. To create the kind of life she'd once thought boring and mundane but now longed for. "Okay. I'll stay. For a while."

"Good. Now, I'm going to make sure everything is perfect in the sanctuary. You grab yourself a cup of coffee and put your leg up for a while."

"I'll come with you."

"You'll do exactly what I told you to do." Opal bustled away, leaving Chloe both amused and frustrated. Opal was a force to be reckoned with. In her absence, the room felt empty, the hollow aloneness of the moment a hard knot in Chloe's chest, the beauty of the flowers, the tables, the bows and ribbons reminding her of the wedding she'd almost had.

Almost.

All her plans, all her dreams had died well before the accident. Now her dreams were much simpler and much less romantic. She wanted to forget, wanted to move on, wanted to rebuild her life. Maybe with God's help she could do that, though even here in His house, she felt He was too far away to see her troubles, too far away to care.

And that, more than the flowers and decorations and memories, made her feel truly alone.

Chapter Three

Ben Avery's attention should have been on the bride and groom, the wedding party, the guests who joked and laughed, ate and talked as the reception wound its way through hour three with no sign of slowing. Instead, his gaze was drawn again and again to Chloe Davidson. Straight black hair gleaming in the overhead light, slim figure encased in a fitted black pantsuit, she smiled and chatted as she moved through the throng, her limp barely noticeable. On the surface, she seemed at ease and relaxed, but there was a tension to her, a humming energy that hadn't ebbed since he'd first seen her unloading the van.

He watched as she approached Opal Winchester, said a few words, then started toward the door that led outside. Maybe she needed some air, a few minutes away from the crowd, some time to herself. And maybe he should leave her to it. But he'd seen sadness in her eyes and sensed a loneliness that he knew only too well.

And he was curious.

He admitted it to himself as he smiled and waved

his way across the reception hall and out the door. Already the day was waning, the sky graying as the sun began its slow descent. The air felt crisp and clean, the quiet sounds of rural life a music that Ben never tired of hearing.

He glanced around the parking lot, saw Chloe leaning against Blooming Baskets' pink van and strode toward her. "It looks like the flowers were a big success."

"Opal is pleased, anyway." Her eyes were emerald-green and striking against the kind of flawless skin that could have graced magazine covers. Only a deep scar on the side of her neck marred its perfection.

"She should be. You worked hard." He leaned a shoulder against the van, studying Chloe's face, wondering at the tension in her. Opal had told him almost nothing about the woman she'd hired a week ago. Only that Chloe was recovering from surgery and working at Blooming Baskets. There was more to the story, of course. A lot more. But Ben doubted he'd get answers from either woman.

"So did you. Thanks again for all your help." She smiled, but the sadness in her eyes remained.

"It was no problem. People in my congregation call me all the time for help." Though he had to admit he'd been surprised by Opal's early morning summons. Flowers? Definitely not his thing.

"That may be true, but being woken up before dawn and asked to do a job you're not getting paid for goes way beyond the call of duty."

"But not beyond the call of friendship."

"If that's the case, Opal is lucky to have a friend like you."

"In my experience, luck doesn't have a whole lot to do with how things work out."

"You're right about that." She straightened, brushing thick black bangs from her eyes. "Opal came into my life just when I most needed someone. I've always thought that was a God thing. Not a luck thing."

"But?"

She raised an eyebrow at his question, but answered it. "Lately it's been hard to see much of God in the things that have happened in my life."

"You've had a hard time." The scars on her neck and hand were testimony to that, the pain in her eyes echoing the physical evidence left by whatever had happened.

Chloe's gaze was focused on some distant point. Maybe the trees. Maybe the last rays of the dying sun. Maybe some dream or hope that had been lost. "Yes, but things are better now."

He was sure he heard a hint of doubt in her voice, but she didn't give him a chance to comment, just shrugged too-thin shoulders. "I'd better get back inside before Opal sends out a posse."

The words and her posture told Ben the conversation was closed. He didn't push to open it again. Much as he might be curious about Chloe, he had no right to press for answers. "I'm surprised she hasn't already. There must be at least five unmarried men she hasn't introduced you to yet."

"Is that what was going on? I was wondering why almost every person she introduced me to was male." She laughed, light and easy, her body losing some of its tension, her lips curving into a full-out grin that lit her face, glowed in her eyes.

"You should do that more often."

The laughter faded, but the smile remained. "Do what?"

"Smile."

"I've been smiling all day."

"Your lips might have been, but your heart wasn't in it."

She blinked, started to respond, but the door to the reception hall flew open, spilling light and sound out into the deepening twilight.

"There you are!" Opal's voice carried over the rumble of wedding excitement as she hurried toward them. "Things are winding down. It won't be long before Hawke and Miranda leave."

"Are you hinting that we should get back inside?"

"You know me better than that, Ben. I never hint."

It was true. In the years Ben had been pastoring Grace Christian Church, Opal had never hesitated to give her opinion or state her mind. A widow who'd lost her husband the same year Ben lost his wife, she was the one woman Ben knew who'd never tried to set him up with a friend, relative or acquaintance.

She had, however, told him over and over again that a good pastor needed a good wife. Maybe she was right, but Ben wasn't looking for one. "So, you're *telling* us we should get back inside?"

"Exactly." She smiled. "So, let's go."

There was no sense arguing. Ben didn't want to anyway. He'd come outside to make sure Chloe was okay and to satisfy his curiosity. He'd accomplished the first. The second would take a little more time. Maybe a lot more time.

That was something Ben didn't have.

Much as he loved his job, being a pastor was more than a full-time commitment. Opal's opinion about a pastor needing a wife aside, Ben had no room for anything more in his life. That was why he planned to put Chloe Davidson and her sad-eyed smile out of his mind.

Planned to.

But he knew enough about life, enough about God, to know that his plans might not be the best ones. That sometimes things he thought were too much effort, too much time, too much commitment, were exactly what God wanted. Only time would tell if Chloe was one of those things.

He pushed open the reception hall door, allowing Chloe and Opal to step in ahead of him. Light, music, laughter and chatter washed over him, the happy excitement of those in attendance wrapping around his heart and pulling him in.

"Ben!" Hawke Morran stepped toward him, dark hair pulled back from his face, his scar a pale line against tan skin.

Ben grabbed his hand and shook it. "Things went well."

"Of course they did. I was marrying Miranda. Thank you for doing the ceremony. And for everything else. Without your help we might not be here at all." The cadence to his words, the accent that tinged them, was a reminder of where he'd grown up, of the life he'd lived before he'd come to the States to work for the DEA, before he'd been set up and almost killed. Ben had met him while he was on the run, offered the help Hawke needed, and forged a friendship with him.

"There's no need to thank me. I was glad to help."

"And I'm glad to have made a friend during a very dark time." He smiled, his pale gaze focused on his wife.

"Are you returning to Thailand for your honeymoon?"

"We are. I want Miranda to experience it when she's not running for her life."

"Try to stay out of trouble this time."

"I think my days of finding trouble are over." He paused, glanced at the hoard of women who had converged on his bride. "Miranda is finally going to toss the flowers. Come on, let's get closer. My wife doesn't know it, yet, but as soon as she finishes, she's going to be kidnapped."

That sounded too good to miss and Ben followed along as Hawke moved toward the group. Miranda smiled at the women crowded in front of her, turned and tossed the bouquet. Squeals of excitement followed as the ladies jostled for position, the flowers flying over grasping hands and leaping bridesmaids before slapping into the chest of the only silent, motionless woman there.

Chloe.

Her hands grasped the flowers, pulled them in. Then, as if she realized what she was doing and didn't like it, she frowned, tossing the bouquet back into the fray. More squeals followed, more grasping and clawing for possession. Chloe remained apart from it all, watching, but not really seeming to see. Ben took a step toward her, hesitated, told himself he should let her be, then ignored his own advice and crossed the space between them.

Chapter Four

"I think that's the first time I've ever seen a woman catch the bouquet and throw it back." Ben Avery's laughter rumbled close to Chloe's ear, pulling her from thoughts she was better off not dwelling on. Hopes, dreams, promises. All shattered and broken.

She turned to face him, glad for the distraction, though she wasn't sure she should be. "I didn't *throw* it. I tossed it."

"Like it was a poisonous snake." The laughter was still in his voice and, despite the warning that shouted through her mind every time she was with Ben, Chloe smiled.

"More like it was a bouquet I had no use for." She glanced away from his steady gaze, watching as a little flower girl emerged triumphant from the crowd of wannabe brides, the bouquet clutched in her fist. "Besides, it seems to have gone to the right person."

Ben followed the direction of her gaze and nodded. "You may be right about that, but tell me, since when do flowers have to be useful? Aren't they simply meant to be enjoyed?"

"I suppose. But I'm not into frivolous things." Or things that reminded her of what she'd almost had. That was more to the point, but she wasn't going to say as much to Ben.

"Interesting."

"What?"

"You're not into frivolous things but you work in a flower shop." His gaze was back on Chloe, his eyes seeming to see much more than she wanted.

To Chloe's relief, a high-pitched shriek and excited laughter interrupted the conversation.

"Look." Ben cupped her shoulder, urging her to turn. "Hawke told me he was going to kidnap his bride. I wasn't sure he'd go through with it."

But he had, the broad-shouldered, hard-faced groom, striding toward the exit with his bride in his arms, the love between the two palpable. Chloe's chest tightened, her eyes burning. At least these two had found what they were seeking. At least one couple would have their happy ending.

For tonight anyway.

The cynical thought weaseled its way into Chloe's mind, chasing away the softer emotions she'd been feeling. She brushed back bangs that needed a trim and stepped away from Ben, ready to make her escape. "I'm going to start cleaning things up in the sanctuary."

"You most certainly are not." Opal appeared at her side, a scowl pulling at the corners of her mouth. "You're going home. I'll take care of things here."

"I'm not going to leave you to do all this alone."

"Who said I'd be alone?" As she spoke a white-haired gentleman stepped up beside Opal, his hand resting on her lower back. Opal glanced back and met his eyes, then turned to Chloe. "This is Sam. He and I go back a few years."

"A few decades, but she won't admit it." The older man smiled, his face creased into lines that reflected a happy, well-lived life. "Sam Riley. And you're Chloe. I've heard a good bit about you."

"Hopefully only good things." Sam Riley? It was a name she hadn't heard before. That, more than anything, made her wonder just what kind of relationship he had with Opal.

"Mostly good things." He winked, his tan, lined face filled with humor. "But I promise not to share any of the not-so-good things I heard if you'll convince Opal to go for a walk with me after this shindig."

"Sam Riley! That's blackmail." Opal's voice mixed with Ben's laughter, her scowl matched by his smile.

"Whatever works, doll."

"How many times do I have to tell you not to call me that?" But it was obvious she didn't really mind; obvious there was something between the two. A past. Maybe even a future.

And no one deserved that more than Opal. "If you agree to go for a walk with Sam, I'll agree to go home without an argument."

Opal speared her with a look that would have wilted her when she was a scared ten-year-old spending the night with her grandmother's neighbor. "And that's blackmail, too. I thought I'd taught you'd better than that, young lady."

"You tried."

Opal looked like she was going to argue more, then her gaze shifted from Chloe to Ben and back again. She smiled, a speculative look in her dark eyes. "Of course, I'll need the van and you'll need a ride back to the shop. Ben, you don't mind giving Chloe a ride to Blooming Baskets, do you?"

"Of course not."

"I appreciate that, Ben, but we've put you out enough." It was a desperate bid to gain control of the situation. One Chloe knew was destined to fail.

"You're not putting me out at all."

"Good." Opal smiled triumphantly. "It's all settled. We'd better get started, Sam. It's getting colder every minute and I don't plan on freezing just so you and I can go for a walk." She grabbed Sam's arm and pulled him away.

"I guess we've got our orders." Ben's hands were shoved into the pockets of his dark slacks, his profile all clean lines and chiseled angles. He would have fit just fine on the cover of *GQ*, his sandy hair rumpled, his strong features and easy smile enough to make any woman's heart jump.

Any woman except for Chloe.

Her heart-jumping, pulse-pounding days of infatuation were over. Adam's betrayal had ensured that. Still, if she'd had her camera in hand, she might have been tempted to shoot a picture, capture Ben's rugged good looks on film.

"Trying to think of a way out of this?" Ben's words drew her from her thoughts. She shook her head, her cheeks heating.

"Just wishing Opal hadn't asked you to give me a ride. Like I said, you've already done enough."

"Why don't you let me be the judge of that?" His hand closed around her elbow, the warmth of his palm sinking through the heavy fabric of her jacket as he smiled down into her eyes.

And her traitorous, hadn't-learned-its-lesson heart skipped a beat.

She wanted to pull away, but knew that would only call attention to her discomfort, so she allowed herself to be led out into the cool fall night and across the parking lot toward the trees that edged the property. Evergreens, oaks and shadows shifted and changed as Chloe and Ben moved closer. Was there someone watching? Maybe the same someone she'd seen that morning.

Chloe tensed, the blackness of the evening pressing in around her and stealing her breath. "Where's your car?"

"It's at my place. Just through these trees."

Just through the trees.

As if walking through the woods at night was nothing. As if there weren't a million hiding places in the dense foliage, a hundred dangers that could be concealed there. Chloe tried to pick up the pace, but her throbbing leg protested, her feet tangling in thick undergrowth. She tripped, stumbling forward.

Ben tightened his hold on her elbow, pulling her back and holding her steady as she regained her balance, his warmth, his strength seeping into her and easing the terror that clawed at her throat. "Careful. There are a lot of roots and tree stumps through here."

"It's hard to be careful when I can't see a thing."

"Don't worry. I can see well enough for both of us." His voice was confident, his hand firm on her arm as he strode through the darkness, and for a moment Chloe allowed herself to believe she was safe, that the nightmare she'd lived was really over.

Seconds later, they were out of the woods, crossing

a wide yard and heading toward a small ranch-style house. "Here we are. Home sweet home."

"It's cute."

"That's what people keep telling me."

"You don't think so?"

"Cute isn't my forte, but my wife, Theresa, probably would have enjoyed hearing the word over and over again. Unfortunately, she passed away a year before I finished seminary and never got a chance to see the place."

"I'm sorry."

"Me, too."

"You must miss her."

"I do. She had cystic fibrosis and was really sick at the end. I knew I had to let her go, but it was still the hardest thing I've ever done."

Chloe understood that. Despite anger and bitterness over Adam's unfaithfulness, she still mourned his loss, and desperately wished she could have saved him. She imagined that years from now she'd feel the same, grieving his death and all that might have been. "I understand."

"You've lost someone close to you?" He pulled the car door open, and gestured for her to get in, his gaze probing hers.

"My fiancé." Ex-fiancé, but Chloe didn't say as much. "He died eleven months ago."

"Then I guess you do know." He waited until she slid into the car, then shut the door and walked around to the driver's side. "Had you known each other long?"

"Three years. We were supposed to be married this past June." But things had gone horribly wrong even before the accident and they'd cancelled the wedding a month before Adam's death.

"Then today's wedding must have been tough."

Chloe shrugged, not wanting to acknowledge even to herself just how tough it had been. Dreams. Hopes. Promises. The day had been built on the fairy tale of happily-ever-after and watching it unfold had made Chloe long for what she knew was only an illusion. "Not as hard as it would have been a few months ago."

"That's the thing about time. It doesn't heal the wounds, but it does make them easier to bear." He smiled into her eyes before he started the car's engine, the curve of his lips, the electricity in his gaze, doing exactly what Chloe didn't want it to—making her heart jump and her pulse leap, whispering that if she wasn't careful she'd end up being hurt again.

Chapter Five

It was close to seven when Chloe pulled her Mustang up to the Victorian that housed her apartment. Built on a hill, it offered a view of water and mountains, sky and grassland, the wide front porch and tall, gabled windows perfect for taking in the scenery. When Opal had brought her to look at the place the previous week, Chloe had been intrigued by the exterior. Walking through the cheery one-bedroom apartment Opal's friend had been renting out, seeing its hardwood floors and Victorian trim, modern kitchen and old-fashioned claw-foot tub, had sealed the deal. She knew she wanted to live there.

Unlike so many other places she'd lived in, this one felt like home.

Tonight though, it looked sinister. The windows dark, the lonely glow of the porch light doing nothing to chase away the blackness. Her car was the only one in the long driveway and Chloe's gaze traveled the length of the house, the edges of the yard, the stands of trees and clumps of bushes, searching for signs of danger. There were none, but that didn't make her feel better. She knew just how quickly quiet could turn to chaos, safety to danger.

She also knew she couldn't stay in the car waiting for one of the other tenants to return home or for daylight to come.

She stepped out of the car, jogging toward the house, her pulse racing as something slithered in the darkness to her right. A squirrel searching for fall harvest? A deer hoping for still-green foliage?

Or something worse?

Her heart slammed against her ribs as she took the porch steps two at a time. The front door was unlocked, left that way by one of the other tenants, and Chloe shoved it open, stumbling across the threshold and into the foyer, the hair on the back of her neck standing on end, her nerves screaming a warning.

Shut the door. Turn the lock. Get in the apartment.

The lock turned under her trembling fingers, her bad leg nearly buckling as she ran up the stairs to her apartment. She shoved the key into the lock, swung the door open. Slammed it shut again.

Safe.

Her heart slowed. Her gasping terror-filled breaths eased. Everything was fine. There was nothing outside that she needed to fear. Even if there was, she was locked in the house, locked in her apartment.

A loud bang sounded from somewhere below, and Chloe jumped, her fear back and clawing up her throat.

The back door.

The realization hit as the step at the bottom of the stairs creaked, the telltale sound sending Chloe across the room. She grabbed the phone, dialed 911, her heart racing so fast it felt as though it would burst from her chest.

Blackness threatened, panic stealing her breath and

her oxygen, but Chloe refused to let it have her, forcing herself to breath deeply. To take action.

She grabbed a butcher knife from the kitchen, her gaze on the door, her eyes widening with horror as the old-fashioned glass knob began to turn.

Chloe clutched the phone in one hand and the knife in the other, praying the lock would hold and wondering if passing out might be better than facing whatever was on the other side of the door.

Ben Avery bounced a redheaded toddler on his knee, and smiled at his friend, Sheriff Jake Reed, who was cradling a dark-haired infant. "I'm thinking we may be able to go fishing again in twenty-one years."

"You're going next weekend." Tiffany Reed strode into the room, her red hair falling around her shoulders in wild waves. Three weeks after having her second child, she looked as vivacious and lovely as ever. "Jake needs a break."

"From what?" Jake stood, laid the baby in a bassinet and wrapped his arms around his wife. "This is where I want to be."

"I know that, but Ben's made two week's worth of meals for us. It's time for you to take him out to thank him."

Ben stood, the little girl in his arms giggling as he tickled her belly. "I made the meals because I wanted to. I don't need any thanks."

"Of course you don't, but you and Jake are still going fishing next weekend. Right, honey?"

Jake met Ben's eyes, shrugged and smiled. "I guess we are. What time?"

Before Ben could reply, Jake's cell phone rang. He glanced at the number. "Work. I'd better take it."

Tiffany pulled her daughter from Ben's arms, shushing the still-giggling child and carrying her from the room.

Ben made himself comfortable, settling back onto the sofa and waiting while Jake answered the phone. Whatever was happening couldn't be good if Jake was being called in.

"Reed here. Right. Give me the address." He jotted something down on a piece of paper. "Davidson?"

At the name, Ben straightened, an image of straight black hair and emerald eyes flashing through his mind.

"Okay. Keep her on the phone. I'll be there in ten." Jake hung up, grabbed a jacket from the closet.

"You said Davidson?"

"Yeah. Lady living out on the lake in the Richard's place is reporting an intruder in the house. My men are tied up at an accident outside of town, so I'm going to take the call."

"Did you get a first name?"

"Chloe."

"I'm coming with you."

Jake raised an eyebrow. "Sorry, that's not the way it works."

"It is this time. I'll stay in the squad car until you clear things, but I'm coming."

"Since I don't have time to argue or ask questions, we'll do it your way."

It took only seconds for Jake to say goodbye to his family, but those seconds seemed like a lifetime to Ben, every one of them another opportunity for whoever was in the house with Chloe to harm her. As they climbed into the cruiser and sped toward the lake, Ben could only pray that she'd be safe until he and Jake arrived.

* * *

Sirens sounded in the distance and Chloe backed toward the window that overlooked the front door, her gaze still fixed on the glass knob. It hadn't turned again, but she was expecting it to and wondering what she'd do if or when the door crashed open.

"Chloe? Are you still there?" The woman on the other end of the line sounded as scared as Chloe felt.

"Yes." She glanced out the window, saw a police cruiser pull up to the house, lights flashing, sirens blaring. "The police are here. I'm going to hang up."

"Don't—"

But Chloe was already disconnecting, tossing the phone and knife onto the couch and hurrying toward the door. The stairs creaked, footsteps pounded on wooden steps and a fist slammed against the door. "Ms. Davidson? Sheriff Jake Reed. Are you okay?"

"Fine." She pulled the door open, stepping back as a tall, hard-faced man strode in, a gun in his hand.

"Good. I'm going to escort you to my car. I want you to stay there until I'm finished in here."

"Finished?"

"Making sure whoever was here isn't still hanging around."

Still hanging around?

Chloe didn't like the sound of that and hurried down the stairs and outside, the crisp fall air making her shiver. Or maybe it was fear that had her shaking.

"I won't be long. Stay in the car until I come back out. I don't want to mistake you for the intruder."

"And I don't want to be out here alone." She might not like the idea of someone being in the house, but she liked the idea of staying outside by herself even less.

"Then it's good you don't have to be." As he spoke

a figure stepped out of the cruiser. Tall, broad-shoul-dered and moving with lithe and silent grace.

Chloe knew who it was immediately, her visceral re-sponse announcing his name, her betraying heart leap-ing in acknowledgement. "Ben, what are you doing here?"

"How about we discuss it in the cruiser?" He wrapped an arm around her waist and hurried her down the steps. Strong, solid, dependable in a way Adam had never been. The comparison didn't sit well with Chloe. Noticing how different Ben was from the man she'd once loved was something she shouldn't be doing.

"Climb in." He held the cruiser door open for her, then slid in himself, his knee nudging her leg, his arm brushing hers.

She scooted back against the door, doing her best to ignore the scent of pine needles and soap that drifted on the air, but he leaned in close, his jaw tight, his face much harder than it had seemed earlier. "Are you okay?"

"Just scared."

"Jake said someone was inside the house with you. Did he make it into your apartment?"

"No, but it looked like he was trying to get in." She shuddered, watching as the lights in the attic area of the Victorian flicked on.

"Did you see the person?"

"I saw something before I went in the house, but if it was a person, I couldn't tell. There was no way I was going to open the apartment door to take a look."

"I'm glad you didn't. That would have been a bad idea." The porch light flicked off, then on again, and

Ben pushed open the car door. "That's Jake's all clear. Ready to go back inside?"

"Of course." But she wasn't really. Sitting in the car with Ben seemed a lot safer than stepping back into the darkness.

He rounded the car, pulled open her door and offered a hand. "It'll be okay, Chloe. Whoever it was is long gone."

Chloe nodded, not trusting herself to speak, afraid anything she said would be filled with the panic and paranoia that had chased her from D.C. Nightmares. Terror. The feeling of being watched, of being stalked. She'd been plagued with all of them since being released from the hospital nine months ago. Post-traumatic stress. That's what the doctors said. That's what the police said. Given enough time, Ben and Jake would probably say the same.

She braced herself as she stepped back into the house, sure that Jake would tell her he'd found nothing, that her mind had been playing tricks on her, that nothing had happened. She was only partially right.

Jake seemed convinced that something *had* happened, but his list of evidence was slim—an unlocked back door, a smudge of dirt on the back deck that might have been a footprint, fingerprints that might have belonged to the intruder, but more likely belonged to someone who lived in the house.

"We'll get prints of the other tenants. See if I've picked up anything that doesn't belong to one of you. Can you come to the station Monday?"

"I've got to work, but I'm sure Opal will give me the time off."

"Good. In the meantime, keep the doors locked and don't take unnecessary risks. I'm thinking this is probably a kid playing a prank or hoping to find some quick cash, but you never know."

"No, you don't." Chloe shifted her weight, trying to ease the ache in her leg, trying to convince herself that the sheriff was right and that what had just happened had nothing to do with her former life.

Tried, but wasn't successful.

He must have sensed her misgivings. His gaze sharpened, going from warm blue to ice. "Is there something you're not telling me? If so it's best to get it out in the open now."

"I'm just not sure what happened tonight was random." There. It was out. For better or worse. If it made her look crazy, so be it.

"And you have a reason for thinking that?" His tone was calm, but there was an edge to his words, a hardness to his face that hadn't been there before.

"This isn't the first time I've been followed into a building. It's not the first time I've felt like I was in danger."

"It sounds like there's a lot more to the story than what happened tonight. Maybe we should finish this discussion in your apartment." He started up the stairs, giving Chloe no choice but to follow.

Which was fine.

It was better to get everything out on the table now rather than later. And Chloe was pretty sure there *would* be a later. As much as she'd hoped things would be different here, she hadn't been convinced she could leave all her troubles behind. Apparently, she'd been right.

"Do you want me to wait outside?" Ben spoke quietly as he followed her up the stairs and Chloe knew what her answer should be. Yes, wait outside. Yes, keep your distance.

Unfortunately, knowing what she should say didn't make her say it. "No. You're fine. I'm going to get some coffee started. Then we'll talk."

She stepped into the living room, limped to the kitchen, and pulled coffee and a package of cookies from the cupboard. If she had to talk about the past, she might as well have sugar in her while she did it.

"Cookie, anyone?"

The sheriff shook his head, a hint of impatience in his eyes. "You were going to tell me why you don't think tonight was a prank."

Chloe nodded, forcing her muscles to relax and her tone to remain calm. Sounding hysterical was a sure-fire way to make herself seem unbalanced. "Eleven months ago someone tried to kill me. He failed."

The words had an immediate effect. Both men straightened, leaned toward her. Intent. Focused. Concerned.

Now if they'd just stay that way through the entire story, Chloe might believe that things really were going to be different.

"Who?" Jake pulled a small notebook from his pocket, started scribbling notes in it.

"A man named Matthew Jackson."

"Do you know where he is now?"

"Federal prison serving a life sentence for murder."

"Murder?" Ben reached over and took the cookies from her hand, pulled two out of the package and handed her one.

"My fiancé was killed in the accident Jackson caused."

Jake glanced up from the notepad. "And you think that has something to do with what happened tonight?"

"I don't know. I just know that ever since the accident, things have been happening."

"Things?"

Was there a tinge of doubt in Jake's voice, a look of disbelief on his face? Or was Chloe just imagining what she'd seen so many times on the faces of so many other police officers. "Like I said, I've had the feeling that I was being followed. A couple of times I was sure someone had been in my apartment."

There was something else, too. Something that she didn't dare bring up.

"You contacted the police?"

"Yes. They investigated."

"And?"

"At first they thought I was being stalked by some of Jackson's friends. He was part of a cult that I'd helped close down a few months earlier."

"The Strangers?" Ben took another cookie from the pack.

Surprised, Chloe met his gaze, saw the interest and concern there. "Yes."

"I remember hearing about it in the news. A computer forensics specialist was investigating a cult member's death and found evidence that implicated the leader. He went to jail for money laundering, but they couldn't prove that he'd killed his follower."

"The deceased's name was Ana Benedict. She started working as an accountant for the cult's leader and was dead a few months later. Her death was ruled a suicide, but her parents didn't believe it."

"You seem to know an awful lot about it." Jake was still writing, a frown creasing his forehead.

"I worked freelance for the private investigator Ana's parents hired. They had her laptop, but there wasn't much on it. I was hired to search for deleted files and I found plenty. Ana had documented everything. The Strangers were involved in the drug trade and were laundering money through their organization. I brought the information to the FBI."

"And Jackson blamed you when the cult dispersed."

"Yes."

"You said that after the attempt on your life, you felt like you were being followed and that someone had been in your apartment. The police suspected other cult members?"

"For a while."

"And then?"

Chloe grabbed mugs and poured coffee into them. Anything to keep from facing the two men who were watching her so intently. "They decided it was all in my head."

"I see." Jake spoke quietly, but Chloe knew he didn't see at all.

She turned back around, handing a cup to each man. "Look, Sheriff Reed—"

"Call me Jake."

"Jake, there may not be evidence proving I'm being stalked, but that doesn't mean it's not happening."

"I don't think I said it wasn't." He sipped his coffee, exchanging a glance with Ben, one that excluded Chloe and conveyed a message she couldn't even begin to figure out.

"No, you didn't, but I've been told it enough times to imagine that's what you're thinking."

"What I'm thinking is that I don't know what happened in D.C. Whatever it was, it's not going to happen here." He placed his coffee cup on the counter. "I'd better head out. If you think of anything else that might be helpful, give me a call."

"I will." Chloe followed him to the door, holding it open as he stepped out and started down the stairs.

Ben held back, the concern in his eyes obvious. "Will you be okay here alone?"

"I've been living alone since I was eighteen."

"That doesn't mean you'll be okay."

"Of course I'll be okay. What other choice do I have?" She tried to smile, but knew she failed miserably.

"You could stay with Opal."

And bring whatever danger was following her into her friend's life? Chloe didn't think so. "No, I really will be fine."

Ben watched her for a moment, his gaze so intense Chloe fidgeted. Then he nodded. "All right. Keep the doors locked and be safe."

He stepped out into the hall and pulled the door shut behind him, leaving Chloe in the silent apartment.

Be safe?

She didn't even know what the word meant anymore. She sighed, grabbed a cookie from the package and collapsed onto the easy chair. Maybe she'd figure it out again. Maybe. Somehow she doubted that would be the case.

Chapter Six

"Sounds like your friend has a big problem." Jake's comment echoed what Ben had been thinking since he'd walked out of Chloe's apartment.

"Really big."

"Unless the police in D.C. are right and the stalker is all in her head."

"She seems pretty sure about what's been going on."

"Being sure of something only means we've convinced ourselves that it's true. I don't put much stock in it." Despite the gruff words, Jake sounded pensive and Ben knew he was leaning toward Chloe's version of things.

"You seemed to believe someone was at her apartment."

"I do. I'm just not convinced it has anything to do with what happened in D.C. It could just as easily have been a kid, or someone out to steal a few bucks."

"It could have been."

"But you don't think so?"

"I think there's more to the story than Chloe is telling. I think that until we have all the information, it'll be hard to know exactly what's going on."

"Agreed. I'm going to call some friends that are still on the D.C. police force and see what they have to say." He paused as he pulled into the driveway of his house. "Regardless of what they say, I'm treating this like any other investigation until I can prove it's not one."

"I didn't expect anything less."

"And I didn't expect to be as curious about you and Chloe as I am." Jake grinned, pushed open his door. "So, are you going to tell me what's going on between you two, or am I going to have to speculate?"

"I met her at the wedding today."

"And?"

"And I would have introduced the two of you if you'd been there."

"I'm almost sorry I missed it."

"Almost?"

"Tiffany isn't ready to take the baby out or leave him with a sitter yet. I'm not ready to spend my Saturday away from her."

"Who'd have thought marriage would make you into such a romantic?" Ben grinned and got out of the car. "I'd better head home. I've got to work tomorrow."

"Good avoidance technique, but I still want to know about you and Chloe."

"You've been living small-town life for too long. You're getting nosy."

"Only when it comes to my friends."

"Sorry to disappoint, but you know as much about Chloe as I do."

"I'm not interested in what you know about her. I'm wondering what you think of her."

"Right now? I think she's a nice lady who's been hurt a lot."

"Look, Ben, if you were anyone else, I'd keep my nose out of it, but you're not, so I'm going to say what's on my mind."

"Go ahead."

"Chloe does seem like a nice lady, but I know trouble when I see it. I see it when I look at her."

"And?"

"And be careful. I don't want that trouble coming after you."

"Thanks for the worry, but I'm pretty good at taking care of myself. I'll be fine."

Jake nodded, but his jaw was tight, his expression grim. "I've got a bad feeling about this. Really bad. Watch your back."

With that he walked away, stepping into his well-lit house, into the warmth of family and home, and leaving Ben to himself and his thoughts.

Thoughts that were similar to Jake's.

Trouble did seem to be closing in on Chloe. If Ben were smart, he'd keep his distance from it and from her. Unfortunately, he didn't think that was going to be possible. Something told him that Chloe was about to become a big part of his life. He might not want the complication, might not like it, but that seemed to be where God was leading him. If that were the case, Ben would just have to hold on tight and pray the ride wasn't nearly as bumpy as he thought it was going to be.

Apparently, Chloe's intruder was big news in Lakeview, and at least half a dozen customers converged on the flower shop minutes after it opened Monday morning. Opal seemed happy about all the business, but by noon Chloe was tired of the sometimes blatant, sometimes subtle questions. How many times and how many ways could a person say "I don't know" before she went absolutely insane?

Not many more than Chloe had already said.

She pulled a dozen red carnations from the refrigerated display case, grabbed some filler and headed back to the shop's front counter, doing her best to tamp down irritation as she listened to two elderly women discuss the "incident" in loud whispers.

"Here they are, Opal." She spoke a little more forcefully than necessary, hoping to interrupt the women's conversation.

It only seemed to make them think she wanted to be *part* of it.

The taller of the two smiled at Chloe. "Those are absolutely lovely, dear. I'm impressed that you could focus on picking the perfect flowers after such a harrowing experience."

"Thank you." What else could she say? "I try to keep my mind on the job."

"But aren't you terrified?" The shorter, more rotund woman shuddered, her owl-eyed gaze filled with both fear and anticipation, as if she were hoping for a juicy tidbit of information to pass along.

"Not really." At least no more than she'd been before she'd come to Lakeview. "The sheriff assured me he'd do everything he could to find the person responsible."

Though Chloe wondered if he'd be saying the same after he talked to the police in D.C. She wasn't looking forward to the conversation they were going to have when he found out about her recent hospitalization and its supposed cause.

She refused to worry about it and tried to focus on her job instead, shoving the carnations into a vase and scowling when two stems broke.

"Keep it up and I'll be out of business in no time." Opal took the flowers and vase from her hands, smiling at the women who were watching wide-eyed and interested. "I'll finish this up. Aren't you supposed to go to the police station today?"

"Yes, but it can wait."

"You know how I feel about procrastination. It only makes more work for everyone. Go punch out and head over there. Since we don't know how long it's going to take, I think you should just take the rest of the day off."

"We've had a lot of business so far, Opal. Are you sure you want to handle the rest of the afternoon alone?"

"I handled it alone for two years before I hired help. Besides, I've hired a kid from church to come in after school until Jenna gets back. Laura's her name. She's a senior trying to save money for college. It should work out well for all of us. Now, go ahead and do what needs doing. Then go have some fun."

"Fun?" Fun was puppies and kittens, laughter and friendship. Relaxation. Fun was something Chloe wasn't even sure she knew how to do anymore.

"Yes, fun. Go shopping. Get your nails done. Better yet, go to Becky's Diner and have a slice of warm apple pie with a scoop of ice cream on it. *That's* fun."

"It does sound good." But being at home sounded better. Safe behind closed doors and locked in tight.

"But you won't do it."

"I might."

"Hmph. We'll see, I guess. Now, get out of here. I've got work to do and you're distracting me."

"Destroying flowers *and* distracting you. I don't know why you keep me on."

"Because you bring in so much business. Now, shoo."

Chloe laughed as she stepped through the doorway that led to the back of the shop.

It didn't take long to punch out and gather her jacket and purse. Outside, the day was misty and cold, the thick clouds and steely sky ominous. Several cars were parked in the employee parking lot behind the building, but Chloe was the only person there. In the watery afternoon light, the stillness seemed unnatural, the quiet, sinister, and she was sure she felt the weight of someone's stare as she hurried toward her car.

She shivered, fumbling for her keys, the feeling that she was being watched so real, so powerful, that she was sure she'd be attacked at any moment. Finally, the key slid into the lock, the door opened and she scrambled in, slamming the door shut, locking it.

Against nothing. The parking lot was still empty of life. The day still and silent.

"You're being silly and paranoid." She muttered the words as she put the car into gear. "Being afraid because an intruder is in the house is one thing. Being afraid to cross a parking lot in the middle of the day is ridiculous."

But she *was* afraid.

No amount of self-talk, no amount of rationalization could change that.

She sighed, steering her vintage Mustang toward the parking lot exit. Opal was right. She needed to do something fun, something to get her mind off the tension and anxiety she'd been feeling since Saturday night, but she hadn't had time to make friends since she'd come to Lakeview and she had no intention of going anywhere or doing anything by herself. The fact was, despite what the D.C. police had told her, despite what her friends, doctors and psychologist had said, she couldn't shake the feeling that danger was following her. That the accident hadn't been the end of the violence against her. That eventually the past would catch up to her. And when it did, she just might not survive.

No, she definitely didn't want to go anywhere by herself, but she didn't want to go *with* someone, either. Look what had happened to Adam because he was with her when a murderer struck.

Hot tears stung her eyes, but she forced them away. Tears wouldn't help. Only answers could do that and Chloe didn't have any. She'd been living her life, doing what she thought was right, trying her best to be the person God wanted her to be. Then the rug had been pulled out from under her, the stability she'd worked so hard for destroyed. All her childhood fears had come to pass—death, heartache, pain, faceless monsters stalking her through the darkness. Now, it seemed that God was far away, that her life had taken a path that He wasn't on and that no matter how hard she tried to get back on course, she couldn't. As much as she wanted to believe differently, as much as she knew that God would never abandon His children, abandoned was exactly how she felt.

Abandoned and alone, her mind filled with nightmare images and dark shadows that reflected the hollow ache of her soul.

Chapter Seven

By the time she finished at the police station and returned home, it had started to rain. First a quick patter of drops, then a torrential downpour that pinged against the house's tin roof and seemed to echo Chloe's mood. Outside, the clouds had turned charcoal, bubbling up from the horizon with barely contained violence.

Chloe put her mail on the kitchen table, grabbed a glass of water and opened sliding glass doors that led to the balcony off her living room. From there she could see the stark beauty of the lake as it reflected gray clouds and bare trees. Winter would arrive soon, bringing with it colder air and a starker landscape. It would be good to capture those changes on film, to hang a few new photos on the wall. The thought brightened her mood.

It had been a long time since she'd photographed anything. In the aftermath of the accident, she hadn't had the time or the inclination. Now, with surgeries and physical therapy behind her, she did. She just hadn't had any desire to.

Except once.

An image flashed through her mind—sandy hair, vivid blue eyes, a half smile designed to melt hearts.

"Enough!" She grabbed her digital camera from the top drawer of her dresser, refusing to think about Ben and determined to do what she should have months ago—regain her life. Get back into her routines. Enjoy the hobbies she'd found so much pleasure in before the accident. Maybe she couldn't go rock climbing anymore, but she could shoot pictures. And she would.

A soft tap sounded at the front door and Chloe jumped, her heart racing. She wasn't expecting company. Anyone could be out there, waiting to finish what was started almost a year ago.

She sidled along the wall, imagining bullets piercing the door and knowing just how ridiculous she was being. "Who's there?"

"Ben Avery."

"Ben?" Surprised, relieved, Chloe pulled open the door and stepped aside so he could walk in. "What are you doing here?"

"Carrying out my orders." He smiled, rain glistening in his sandy hair and beaded on his leather jacket, the scent of fall drifting into the room with him. Fall and something else. Something masculine and strong.

Chloe took a step back. "Orders?"

"Opal and I ran into each other at the diner. She asked me to bring you this." He held out a brown paper bag, and Chloe took it, catching a whiff of apples and cinnamon.

"Apple pie?"

"And ice cream. She had Doris put that in a separate container."

"Fun in a bag?"

"I guess you could call it that."

"Those are Opal's words. Not mine. She said I should have a little fun today. I guess she wanted to make sure I did." Chloe smiled, touched by her friend's thoughtfulness, though she wasn't sure she was happy with her methods. "Thanks for bringing this over. I'm sure you had better things to do with your time."

"It seems like we had this conversation before. And I'm going to tell you the same thing now that I did then—I can't think of any." He leaned his shoulder against the wall, his vivid blue gaze steady. "Of course, bringing it here was only part of my job."

"What was the other part?"

"I'm supposed to make sure you eat it."

"Tell me you're kidding."

"I'm afraid not. She said that if you faded away to nothing she wouldn't have any reliable help at the shop."

"She's conveniently forgetting Mary Alice and the new girl she hired."

"Laura. She mentioned that she'd left her to watch the store for a few minutes and had to hurry back."

"You and Opal must have had a long conversation."

"Not too long." He didn't seem inclined to say more, and Chloe decided not to press for details. Knowing Opal, she'd said more than she should have. Eventually, she and Chloe would have to talk about that. For now, the pie smelled too good to ignore.

"Since you've been ordered to make sure I eat this, maybe we can share." She moved into the small kitchen and set her camera down, grabbing two plates from the cupboard.

"I was hoping you'd say that. I brought enough for both of us." Ben moved toward her, an easy grin curving his lips and deepening the lines near his eyes. Was he thirty? Thirty-five? Older?

She shouldn't be wondering, but was.

And that didn't make her happy.

"You knew I was going to invite you?"

"No, but I was hoping." He pulled a large plastic container from the bag, opened it up to reveal two slices of apple pie. "It's my day off. Apple pie, ice cream and interesting company seemed like a good way to spend part of it."

"What if I hadn't asked you to stay?"

"Then I would have gone home and had a couple of oatmeal cookies in front of the TV."

"No way."

"No way what?" He served the pie, scooped ice cream onto both slices.

"No way would you be sitting home in front of the television eating oatmeal cookies."

"You're right. I would have gone back to the diner and bought more pie. It's much too good to pass up. *Then* I would have gone home and watched TV." He smiled and Chloe's pulse had the nerve to leap.

"Funny, I picture you as more the outdoor type. Hiking. Camping. Boating."

"Good call, but today is too rainy for outdoor activities."

"Then I guess I'm glad I could provide you with something to do. I'm going to have to have a talk with Opal, though. She can't keep asking you to come to my rescue."

"Who says I'm rescuing you? Maybe you're rescuing me."

"From an afternoon of boredom?"

"Exactly." He smiled again and dug into the pie, his

hair falling over his forehead, his broad hands making the fork look small.

Chloe resisted the urge to pick up her camera and shoot a picture, choosing instead to fork up a mouthful of pie, the flaky crust and tart apples nearly melting in her mouth. "You're right. This *is* too good to pass up. I guess I'll have to thank Opal instead of lecturing her."

"She cares a lot about you."

"And I care a lot about her."

"You said you spent summers on the lake. Is that how you two met?"

"My grandmother rented a cottage next to Opal's property."

"Your grandmother, not your mother?"

Chloe hesitated, then shrugged. "My mother preferred to leave my upbringing to other people."

"And your grandmother filled in?"

"Not really." She scooped up another bite of pie, not willing to say any more about her childhood. "How about you? Was your family the *Father Knows Best* type?"

"It was as far from that as you can get. Absent father. Drug-addicted mother. My sister and I were in foster care by the time I was thirteen."

"I'm sorry."

"Don't be. It was the best thing that ever happened to me. My mother may not have cared much about me, but God did, and He used her neglect to get me to people who did care."

"You must have been a great kid."

He paused, his fork halfway to his mouth, his eyes so blue they seemed lit from within. "I was a little hoodlum. By the time my parents stepped in I'd been in ten foster homes, a group facility, and was about to be thrown into a juvenile detention center."

"Are you kidding?"

"Not even close to kidding. My foster parents got my case file from a social worker they knew. A few days later they came to visit me and told me I had a choice—come stay with them and straighten up my life or stay on the path I'd chosen and end up in jail or worse."

"So you decided to straighten up."

"I wish I'd made it that easy on them. The fact is, I thought Mike and Andrea were softhearted enough to be taken advantage of. I agreed to go home with them, but had no intention at all of changing my life. Fortunately, they stuck with me." He stood and put his empty plate in the sink. "I'd better get out of here. You've probably got things you need to do."

Agree. Send him on his way. Forget the story he just told and the new light it cast him in.

But Chloe had never been great at listening to advice. Even her own.

Especially not her own.

"Nothing pressing. I was just going to take some photographs."

"A florist, a computer expert *and* a photographer? What other surprises are you hiding?" Ben settled back down into his chair and Chloe could almost imagine him as a kid, sitting in one kitchen after another, searching for someone to believe in him. To love him.

"No surprises. What you see is what you get."

"Somehow I doubt that." He steepled his fingers and stared at her across the table, his gaze somber and much too knowing.

But Chloe didn't plan on sharing more about her

life, her hobbies, her past or the shadows that lived in her soul. "Doubt it all you want, but it's the truth. How about you? What surprises are you hiding?"

"The fact that I cook surprises people, but it's not something I hide."

"I wouldn't have thought a widowed pastor in a small town like this would ever have to cook. Aren't the church ladies knocking on your door begging to cook you a meal?"

"They were. That's why I had to learn to cook. By the time I'd been in town a month, I had so many cas-seroles in my refrigerator there wasn't room for any-thing else. No milk. No eggs. No vegetables or fruit. Learning to cook was a matter of self-preservation."

Chloe laughed, relaxing into the moment and the conversation. Enjoying the company. The man.

"You're laughing, but it was a serious issue." His eyes gleamed with humor as he lifted Chloe's camera. "Now it's your turn."

"My turn?"

"To tell why you got into photography."

"I moved around a lot when I was a kid. Taking pictures helped me remember where I'd been." So she would know where she didn't want to go, the kind of life she didn't want to have.

"So you do landscape photography."

"And architectural. The pictures on the wall are mine." She gestured to a black-and-white photo of the White House and a colored photo of Arlington National Cemetery.

"They're good. Mind if I take a look at the ones on your camera?"

"Only if I get a chance to sample your cooking." The

words were out before she could stop them and Chloe regretted them immediately. "What I mean is—"

"That you'd like to have dinner with me?" His eyes dared her to accept the offer.

"I don't think that would be a good idea."

"Really? Two friends sharing a meal sounds like a great idea to me."

She should refuse. Friendship with Ben wasn't a good idea. Friendship with *anyone* wasn't a good idea. "I don't want to drag you into my troubles, Ben."

"I'm not the type of person who gets dragged any-where I don't want to go." He leaned across the table, and squeezed her hand. "So, how about that dinner?"

Say no.

But once again Chloe ignored her own advice. "All right. A meal with a friend."

There was no harm in that.

She hoped.

Ben smiled and released her hand, turning his atten-tion to the camera. As she watched, his smile faded, a frown creasing his brow.

"Interesting choice of subject matter." His voice was tight, his frown deepening.

"What?" She leaned toward him, curious to see what he was looking at. It had been months since she'd used the camera. There might be photographs of Adam, of the house they'd planned to buy. Of the church where they were going to be married.

But the photo wasn't of any of those things.

Bright flowers. Dark wood. Adam lying in white silk, his face almost unrecognizable.

Ben scrolled back and the same picture appeared again. And again.

Chloe gagged, shoving away from the table and

stumbling backward, her mind rebelling at what she'd seen, her body trembling with it. Panic throbbed deep in the pit of her stomach, stealing her breath until she was gasping, struggling for air.

"Hey. It's okay." Ben's voice was soothing, his hands firm on her shoulder. "Chloe, you're fine. Take a deep breath."

"I can't." Blackness edged her vision, the shadowy nightmare coming closer with every shallow breath.

"Sure you can." His hands smoothed up her neck, cupped her cheeks, forcing her to look up and into eyes so blue, so clear, she thought she could lose herself in them. "You're a survivor. A couple photos can't take that away from you."

His words were warm, but she sensed the hard determination beneath them. He had no intention of letting the nightmare take her, and that, more than anything, eased the vise around Chloe's lungs.

"Right. You're right. I'm sorry."

"Don't apologize." His words were gruff, his hands still warm against her cheeks. "Tell me what's wrong."

"I didn't take those pictures."

He stared into her eyes for another minute, then nodded. "I'd better call Jake."

His hands dropped away and he strode to the phone, leaving her in the kitchen with the camera and the horrifying images.

Chapter Eight

"When was the last time you used the camera?" The question was the same one Jake Reed had asked fifteen times in the past ten minutes. If he were hoping for a different answer than the one she'd already given, he was going be disappointed.

Chloe's fist tightened around the coffee mug she held, but she kept her frustration in check. "I don't know. A few months before the accident."

Jake lifted the camera in gloved hands, staring at the image. "And you didn't take these photos?"

"No!" Her tone was sharper than she'd meant and she reigned in her emotions. "They're sickening."

"Sickening, but fake."

"Fake?"

"Take another look. The guy in the casket is in a different position in each photo. The 'casket' is too wide. Looks like a twin bed with pillows and white silk on top of it."

"I'll take your word for it."

"You thought it was your fiancé?"

"Yes."

"It's not. The date on the photos is September of this year. Months after your ex-fiancé's funeral. And he was your ex-fiancé, right?"

Apparently, he'd been talking to people in D.C. What else had they told him? Chloe's hands were clammy, but she looked him straight in the eye as she answered. "Yes, but I don't think that's relevant."

"What you think is relevant doesn't matter, Chloe. What matters is finding out what's going on. The only way to do that is to get all the information available. You didn't provide me with that Saturday night."

"I provided you with what I thought was important. My relationship with Adam was complicated. We were friends before we started dating and were trying to maintain that after we broke up." He'd wanted more than that, but Chloe hadn't been able to forgive.

"You broke up because he'd been seeing another woman."

Chloe's cheeks heated, but she nodded, refusing the urge to glance at Ben. "Adam was a nice guy. He collected friends like other people collect knickknacks. A lot of those friends were women. One became a little more than just a friend."

"You're leaving out a lot of details." Jake leaned back in the kitchen chair and tapped gloved fingers against the table. "Like the fact that you did freelance work for Adam's P.I. company. That the two of you had testified at a criminal trial the day he was killed."

"I'm sure the D.C. police were glad to fill you in."

"I would have been happier if you'd been the one to do it."

"Jake, you're not dealing with a suspect here." There was a subtle warning in Ben's voice.

"And I don't want to be dealing with a body, either.

Chloe needs to be open and honest. Hiding information is never a good idea."

"I wasn't hiding information. It's just hard to talk about Adam." Chloe stood and grabbed a bottle of aspirin, her hand shaking as she tried to pry open the lid.

"Here. Let me." Ben leaned in, his shoulder brushing hers, his hands gentle as he took the bottle and popped the lid. He placed two in her hand, closed her fingers over them, his palm pressing against her knuckles, the warmth of it chasing away the chill that seemed to live in her soul. "It's going to be okay."

She wasn't so sure he was right. "Maybe."

"Things *will* be okay once we find out who's after you." Jake's voice was hard, his face grim. "Can you tell me who had access to your camera."

"Anyone who visited my apartment. I usually kept it out near my workstation."

"Can you give me a list of those people?"

"Probably, but the past few months are blurry. I had surgery on my leg a month ago and the recovery was brutal. There were people in and out all the time trying to help out."

"Do the best you can. I'll also want a list of anyone who had a key to your place in D.C."

"That's a shorter list. Jordyn Winslow. James Callahan. They both worked with Adam. Morgan Gordon had the apartment next to mine. They took turns taking care of things while I was in the hospital during the months after the accident."

"Good. We'll start there." Jake pulled a pen and small notebook from his pocket, jotted the names down. "Do you know the name of the woman Adam was involved with?"

"No. He wouldn't tell me and I didn't press for the information. Maybe I really didn't want to know."

"You didn't leave a forwarding address with the police in D.C."

"There didn't seem to be any reason."

"But you did leave it with friends?"

"I left it with some of my former employers. Companies that owed me money. No one else knows where I am. I was hoping that would keep me safe. I guess I was wrong."

"Let's not jump to conclusions yet. It's possible that whoever took the photos doesn't know where you are."

"I don't believe that. I don't think you do, either."

"There's only one thing I believe. Matthew Jackson has nothing to do with what's been happening to you. The rest I plan to find out." He closed his notebook and stood. "Do you have any other cameras?"

"A Nikon."

"Is there undeveloped film in it?"

"Yes."

"Do you mind if I take that one, too?"

"Not at all." As a matter of fact, she'd rather have it out of the house than spend the next few days wondering what might be on the undeveloped film.

She limped to her room, pulled the camera from a storage box in her closet and brought it out to Jake. "Here you go. I think I used it the week before Adam and I broke up. We'd gone on a picnic to Great Falls. The day was perfect. We…" Her voice trailed off and she shook her head. "Those should be the last pictures on the roll."

"I'll develop the film, see if there's anything there that shouldn't be. In the meantime, try not to worry too much." He smiled and she was surprised by the warmth and genuine concern in his eyes.

"I appreciate it, Jake. Thanks."

"Hold off on the thanks until I figure out what's going on." He strode to the front door and pulled it open. "I'll see you this weekend, Ben."

"Saturday, 6 a.m. Unless that's too early."

"The baby has us up at five every day. Six won't be a problem."

Jake stepped out into the hall, hovering near the top of the steps as Ben turned to Chloe.

"I've got to head out, too, but before I leave, tell me something?"

"What?"

"Do you like fish?"

"Fish?" She'd expected a question about Adam, about their relationship. His death. She hadn't expected to be asked about fish.

"Yeah, fish. Trout. Catfish."

"Sure."

"Good. That's what I'll make, then."

"Make?"

"For dinner. We had a deal. I still need to fulfill my end of the bargain."

"That's not necessary, Ben." All thoughts of a quiet dinner spent with a friend were gone, replaced by cold dread. Something terrible had followed her from D.C. Something that was determined to destroy her and anyone who got near her.

"Isn't it?" He smiled, brushing her bangs out of her eyes and tucking long strands behind her ear.

Her stomach knotted and she stepped away. Surprised. Uncomfortable.

Afraid.

For herself. For Ben.

"No. It really isn't."

"You're chickening out."

"I'm not. I'm just…" Terrified that something terrible was going to happen. Scared that she'd be hurt. That Ben would be hurt.

"Just going to have dinner with a new friend. Is that so bad?"

"I don't want to get hurt again, Ben. And I don't want you to be hurt."

"How can having dinner hurt either of us? How does Saturday night around six sound?"

He was purposely ignoring the point and Chloe frowned. "You'll be fishing with Jake that day."

"Right. Fresh fish for dinner. What could be better?" He smiled, his eyes flashing with humor and inviting her to join in.

And despite herself, despite the warnings she knew she should heed, she relaxed. "You have a lot of faith in your ability to catch fish."

"No. I've got a lot of faith in my ability to track down a meal. If I don't find it in the lake, I'll get it from the grocery store."

"Won't that be cheating?"

"Only if I try to pass it off as my own." He grinned. "Your place or mine?"

"Mine." She answered without thought, and knew she wouldn't take the word back.

"Great. See you then." He stepped out into the hall, joining Jake there.

The other man nodded at Chloe, but she couldn't miss the concern in his eyes. Obviously, he was as worried about Ben's safety as she was. "I'll be in touch,

Chloe. In the meantime, don't hesitate to call if something comes up."

"I won't."

Jake hesitated, rubbing a hand against the back of his neck. "Listen, my wife is part of a quilting circle that meets at Grace Christian on Wednesday nights. Seven o'clock. They make blankets for NICU babies and little bears for kids who have to stay at Lakeview General. They'd love to have another set of hands."

"I've never quilted before." But she couldn't deny the small part of her that longed for something new, something more than flowers and bows and evenings spent alone.

"They'll teach you everything you need to know."

"I don't usually go out at night."

"Understandable, but you'll be with a large group of people. That might be better than being here alone. Think about it. Here's my home phone number. Call my wife if you've got any questions." He scribbled the number on the back page of his notebook and tore it out.

"I will, thanks."

"No problem. Now, I really do need to get out of here. You coming? Or are you planning to spend another half hour saying goodbye?" He glanced at Ben and the amusement in his eyes was unmistakable.

"Knock it off." Ben growled the words, but smiled at Chloe, waving as he and Jake started down the stairs.

Chloe closed the door on their retreating figures, shutting out the sounds of their lighthearted banter and pacing across the living room.

She'd thought the room cozy before. In the wake of Ben and Jake's departure, it seemed empty and hollow, a sad reflection of her life.

She grimaced, moving into her bedroom, flicking on the light and turning on the CD player she kept near her bed. An upbeat modern tune filled the room, the thrumming, strumming tempo of it doing nothing to lift Chloe's mood.

"Get over yourself, Chloe. Things could be worse."

She flopped onto the bed, knowing she should get up and do something. Television. A good book. Anything that would take her mind off the loneliness that she was suddenly feeling.

Her gaze caught on the Bible lying abandoned on the bedside table. Opal had given it to her when she was twelve and she'd had it ever since. Lately, though, she hadn't spent much time reading it. She picked it up, thumbing through it, skimming some of the passages Opal had highlighted in yellow. Little by little, she was drawn into what she was reading, her loneliness slowly fading away. She might feel as if God had abandoned her, but the truth was much different. Despite the trials and troubles she'd faced, she had to hold on to that certainty, had to believe that He was there, working His perfect will for her life. Had to trust that in the end everything would turn out okay.

But would it?

As much as she wanted to believe, to trust, Chloe couldn't imagine things getting better. She could only imagine them getting much, much worse.

She shook her head, closing the Bible, setting it back on the table and praying that she was wrong. That somehow everything *would* be okay. That what she imagined wasn't what would be and that eventually the nightmare would be over and she'd be able to rebuild her life.

Chapter Nine

Maybe quilting wasn't such a good idea after all.

Chloe stood in the doorway of the reception hall and eyed the people gathered there. Old and young, tall and short, thin and stout, they were a swarm of bees, humming with energy as they performed a dance that had meaning only to them.

She took a step back, pretty sure she'd made a poor decision when she'd left Blooming Baskets and headed toward Grace Christian. She'd come on a lark, another night alone at the apartment appealing to her about as much as a root canal. Now she was thinking a root canal might not be so bad.

"You must be Chloe." A tall redhead stepped from the throng, a broad smile creasing her face.

"That's right."

"I'm Tiffany Reed. My husband told me he'd invited you. I wanted to call and tell you a little more about what we're doing here, but Jake refused to give me your number. He said you might not be ready to face the Lakeview Quilters."

"He might have been right."

Tiffany laughed, the sound full and unapologetic.

"We're not as scary as we look. Come on. I'll introduce you to a few of the ladies. Then you can get started."

"I've never quilted before in my life. I barely know how to sew."

"Not a problem. We've got people doing everything from cutting squares to stuffing bears."

"I might be able to handle that."

"Of course you can. Jake tells me you're a computer forensics specialist." She started toward the group and Chloe followed, moving fast to keep up.

"I *was* one. Now I'm a florist." Though if she smashed one more of Opal's intricate bows, she might not be that for long.

"You and I have a lot in common, then. I was a computer tech before I opened my quilt shop. I'd love to hear more about your old job. Why don't you come over after work one day? We can have a cup of coffee and chat. Of course, you'd be exposed to my noisy munchkins, so..." She blushed. "Sorry, I'm speed-talking again. I've got a two-year-old and a newborn at home. When I talk to adults, I'm so excited to actually have people that understand me, I feel like I've got to get it all out at once."

"Talking fast is better than talking to yourself. Which is what I've been doing lately."

Tiffany laughed again, looping an arm through Chloe's. "You know. I think you and I are going to get along fine. Now, let's get to work before Irma Jefferson sees us chatting and cracks the whip."

"She's the group leader?"

"No, she just thinks she is."

Chloe laughed and allowed herself to be tugged deeper into the buzz of activity.

Ben typed a sentence. Deleted it. Typed another one. Deleted *it*.

Disgusted with his lack of focus, he stood and

walked to the small window that looked out over the churchyard. Fall had ripped the leaves from the tall oak that stood in the center of the lawn. Its broad branches were clearly visible in the moonlight. Beyond that, the parking lot was still half full. Wednesday night's prayer meeting was over, but there were plenty of other activities. Choir. Youth Bible study. The quilting circle.

The quilting circle where Chloe might be.

He'd thought about calling her several times during the past few days, but had decided against it. They'd have dinner Saturday night and catch up then. Anything else seemed like...

Exactly what it was. Interest.

Ben ran a hand over his hair, rubbed the tension at the back of his neck. There were fifteen single women at Grace Christian Church. All of them were nice, sweet and as uncomplicated as women could be. Which was much more complicated than Ben wanted to deal with. Friends and acquaintances had set him up with dozens of their female relatives during the past six years—daughters, nieces, cousins, aunts. Mothers. None of them had caught and held his attention the way Chloe seemed to be doing.

He wasn't quite sure how he felt about that and was even less sure that how he felt mattered. Chloe seemed to be the direction his life was heading. Whether or not that was a good thing remained to be seen.

"Busy?" Jake's deep voice pulled Ben from his thoughts and he turned to face his friend who stood in the doorway of the office.

"No. Come on in." He waited while Jake stepped across the threshold and closed the door. "I'm surprised to see you here. I thought you'd be on child-care duty."

"I got called into work. Tiffany's mom is babysitting the kids."

"Anything serious going on?"

"Kyle Davis is feuding with his neighbor again, insisting Jesse Rivers is stealing mail from his box."

"That does sound serious." Ben grinned, gestured to the chair across the desk. "Want to have a seat?"

"I've only got a minute. I just wanted to check in on Tiffany, make sure she's not overdoing it."

"Is it possible to overdo it while quilting?" Ben tried not to smile but failed. The gruff, hardened police officer who'd come to Lakeview five years before had definitely been softened by love.

Jake scowled. "Go ahead and laugh, my friend, but from my vantage point, it seems your time has come."

"Does it?" Ben lifted a pen from the desk, tapped it against his palm.

"You brought Chloe pie."

"Opal insisted."

"I've seen you refuse other insistent matchmakers."

True, and Ben didn't deny it. "Chloe's had a tough time."

"And is still having one." There was tightness to Jake's voice that Ben didn't like.

"You've got more information?"

"I spoke to someone else on the D.C. police force. He was willing to tell me a little more than just what's in the records."

"Like what?"

"Chloe was diagnosed with post-traumatic stress disorder a couple of months after the accident."

"And?"

"The complaints she filed were vague—things being moved around in her apartment, someone following her. She reported her laptop stolen. Then found it in the trunk of her car."

"So, they assumed she was making it up?"

"No. Both men I spoke to have worked with Chloe in the past. Her skills in computer forensics have helped close some difficult cases. Both said she was professional, intelligent, easy to work with. Neither thinks she was making things up."

"Then what do they think?"

"That losing her fiancé in an accident that was meant to take her life left her…unbalanced."

"She doesn't seem unbalanced to me. Just scared."

"I told the guy I was talking to today the same thing. He disagrees. The brake line on Chloe's car had been cut. She was driving. After the accident she told several people that she wished she'd died instead of Adam." Jake raked a hand through his hair, ran it down over his jaw. "Look, I don't know if this is something I should be sharing, but I can trust you to keep it quiet and you might have better luck getting more information about it from Chloe than I will."

"What?"

"Chloe attempted suicide two weeks before she left D.C."

Ben stilled at the words, his fist tightening around the pen he held. "No way."

"She refused to admit it, but paramedics found an empty bottle of antidepressants in her trash can. The prescription was filled less than a week before."

"Chloe called for help?"

"No. A friend called to see how Chloe was feeling and thought she sounded odd. She called an ambulance. That saved Chloe's life."

"Was the friend Opal?"

"I didn't ask, but it's possible. Chloe left D.C. less than two weeks later. Didn't bother leaving a forwarding address or telling the police that she was going. According to the guy I talked to today, Chloe insisted someone had tried to murder her. Investigation revealed nothing. No sign of forced entry into the apartment. No fingerprints but Chloe's."

"And your thoughts on this?"

"The same as they were before—I think there are missing pieces to the puzzle. I think something is going on that we don't understand. I also think I could be wrong, that maybe I'm misreading Chloe and she really does have some deep-seated problems."

Ben nodded. "I can see that."

"But you don't agree?"

"No. I don't. Chloe doesn't seem depressed enough to try and end her life."

"Maybe she isn't anymore."

"That kind of depression doesn't just go away, Jake." He dropped the pen back onto the table, rolled his shoulders trying to ease the tension in his neck. "What's the next step?"

"One of us needs to ask Chloe what happened that night."

"You're the police officer."

"I can't see upsetting the woman and that's probably what my blunt questions would do."

"You're not that bad."

"Sure I am. Even my wife says so. Speaking of which." He smiled, frustration and worry draining from his face. "I've got a redhead to track down before I go home."

"I'll walk with you, see if Chloe showed up at the quilting circle."

"Call me once you two talk."

Once they talked? Ben doubted there'd be much

talking going on once he asked Chloe if she'd attempted suicide. No matter how he tried to couch the question, he was pretty sure it wouldn't be taken well.

They stepped into the reception hall, the buzz of activity and enthusiasm washing over Ben. He loved watching the women and men as they worked, the busy, almost frantic pace they set like an intricately choreographed dance to the music of chattering voices and laughter.

"There's my wife." Jake's soft smile and quick, eager steps as he moved toward Tiffany brought back memories of Ben's own happiness with Theresa, his own eagerness to be with her.

Now, he had no one to rush to. No one waiting for his return home. No one to ask about his day. He'd had seven years to get used to that, but sometimes it still bothered him. Sometimes he still felt the aching pain of loss and loneliness.

He shook aside the thoughts, not willing to dwell on what he didn't have. The key to happiness and contentment, he'd found, was in dwelling on what he *did* have. A home. Friends. A job he loved.

He scanned the room, searching for Chloe's coal-black hair and slim figure, not sure he'd be able to spot her in the crowd if she were there. A few men were interspersed among the women, mostly widowers, though some were young teenagers or college students. One or two die-hard bachelors were in the mix as well, looking for someone new to set their sights on. Ben searched their faces, wondering if Brian McMath were there. If he was, he'd probably hightail it to the only single woman in attendance who didn't know his reputation.

It took only a few seconds to spot the doctor, his

buttoned-up white dress shirt and dark tie setting him apart from the rest of the crowd. Standing at the stuffing table, shoving filler into a quilted bear, Brian looked like a fish out of water. The woman beside him looked more comfortable, her faded jeans and dark sweater more in keeping with what the rest of the group was wearing.

Chloe.

Both surprised and pleased to see her there, Ben strode toward the two. "Hi, Brian. Chloe. Mind if I join you?"

"Actually, we were discussing some medical issues that Chloe would probably prefer to keep private." McMath's dismissal was curt.

Ben ignored it.

"Sounds fascinating." He smiled at Chloe and she returned the gesture, her lips curving, her eyes begging for intervention.

"Not even close. Here." She handed him a flat bear patchworked in various yellow prints. "You can stuff Cheers. He's starting to feel left out."

"Cheers?"

"He's bright enough to cheer anyone up."

"Did you name yours, too?" He gestured toward the purple-toned bear she held.

"Of course. This one is Hugs."

"Because he'd make any kid want to hug him?"

"You catch on quick, Ben." This time her smile was real.

"I hate to break the news to you two, but they're stuffed bears. They don't require names."

Chloe met Ben's eyes and her smile widened. "Of course they do. That's the whole point of having a stuffed animal. You give it a name. Pretend it's your friend."

"Must be a girl thing." Brian grumbled and grabbed another handful of filler.

"I don't know about that. I can remember having a stuffed bear when I was maybe five. I called him Brown Bear." He'd given it to his sister when she was a toddler and she'd recently passed it to her one-year-old.

"Brown Bear. Very creative, Ben. My toys were more educational. Puzzles. Word games. Those kinds of things. How about you, Chloe? I'm sure a computer forensic expert…"

"I'm a florist, Brian."

"But you *were* an expert in computer forensics. I'm sure the kind of intelligence it takes to do that sort of work starts in early childhood."

"Actually, I didn't have many toys when I was a kid. Just a stuffed turtle that Opal gave me. A floppy green and brown one that was perfect for cuddling."

"And you named him, of course." Ben shoved a handful of stuffing into the yellow bear, wondering if the bright, relaxed woman next to him was really the tragically broken woman the D.C. police had painted her to be.

"Of course. I called him Speedy."

"That's a strange name for a turtle." Brian frowned, tossed the green bear he was stuffing onto the table where another group was stitching closed openings. "But let's talk about something that is more grown-up. Like those scars. There are ways to correct some of the damage, Chloe."

"I'm sure there are, but I'm not interested." Chloe finished stuffing the bear she was working on and grabbed the last one off the table, slashes of color staining her cheeks.

"Surely a woman as beautiful as you—"

"Knows her own mind." Ben spoke firmly, hoping to put an end to Brian's pushiness.

"Like I said when you joined us, the conversation is confidential. Something between patient and doctor."

"You're right, Brian. I think that's exactly what I'll do. Discuss things with my doctor." Chloe finished filling the last bear and set it on the to-be-stitched table, her smile sweet as pecan pie, but not quite hiding the bite to her words.

"I'm sure you haven't had time to find one yet."

"My surgeon recommended someone. I've got an appointment for next week."

"I see. Who with?"

"I think that's probably confidential, Brian." Ben smiled at the doctor, then gestured to the empty table. "It looks like we've finished the last bear. How about joining me for a cup of coffee, Chloe?"

Chloe's brow creased, a frown pulling at the edges of her mouth. Ben thought she'd refuse. Then she glanced at Brian and nodded. "Sure. It was nice talking to you, Brian."

"Maybe we'll see each other next week."

"Maybe."

"I'll see you Sunday, Brian."

The doctor's nod was curt, his shoulders stiff as he moved away.

"I guess we should go get that coffee." Chloe sounded tired, the dark shadows under her eyes speaking of too many sleepless nights.

"You don't seem too enthusiastic."

"It's been a long day."

"Opal's working you too hard?"

"You know that isn't even close to the truth."

"I do." He led her into the office, gestured for her to have a seat. "So maybe she's not working you hard enough."

"Boredom *can* make the day long, but I wasn't bored today. We're almost too busy this week what with half of Lakeview coming in to hear about what happened Saturday night."

"So if it's not boredom maybe there were too many thorns on the roses. Too many petals in your hair."

She smiled, shook her head. "Too many nightmares last night."

"I'd like to say that was going to be my next guess, but it wasn't." He poured coffee from the carafe on the coffeemaker and handed her a cup. "Want to tell me about them?"

"Not really." She smiled again, lowering her gaze and tracing a circle on the desk with her finger. "You and Jake walked into the reception hall together."

"He stopped by to see his wife."

"He had news, though. About me, right?"

"He did say he'd spoken to D.C. police again."

"And?" She met his gaze, her eyes shadowed, whatever she was thinking well-hidden.

He could beat around the bush or he could lay it all out on the table. The latter was more his style and Ben couldn't think of a good reason to change it now. Much as he might want to avoid the issue, he wasn't going to hide the truth. "The guy he spoke to today said you tried to commit suicide."

"I knew that would come up eventually."

"Yet you didn't mention it to Jake."

"And give him reason to doubt me? I lived with that

for almost eleven months. I didn't want to live it here, too." She brushed her bangs off her forehead, her eyes flashing emerald green fire.

"Like Jake told you before, he can't help you if he doesn't have all the necessary information."

"He knows everything I do."

"Everything except whether or not you actually were attempting suicide."

"If I'd been trying to kill myself, I wouldn't have picked up the phone and had a conversation with Opal." Her words were blunt, her gaze direct, but there was a forced quality to both, as if she were trying to convince herself of the very things she wanted him to believe.

"I believe you."

"Do you? Because lately I'm not even sure I believe myself." She stood abruptly. "I've really got to go. Like I said, it's been a long day."

Ben stood, too, putting a hand on Chloe's arm and holding her in place when she would have walked out the door. Her skin was pale, her mouth drawn in a tight line, the moisture in her eyes tempting Ben to wrap her in a hug that he knew she wouldn't appreciate. "Whatever is going on, Chloe, you don't have to face it alone."

"I appreciate the thought, but all the platitudes in the world can't change the fact that I *am* facing it alone."

"I don't believe in placating people. I believe in telling the truth."

"What truth? That you and Jake are going to help me? That God is looking out for me? I've trusted the police before. I've trusted God. But it hasn't done me any good. The nightmare is still chasing me. Eventually, it's going to catch up." There was no anger in her voice, just a weariness that Ben knew all too well. "I really do need to go."

He nodded, reluctantly letting his hand slide from her arm. "Your apartment is only five minutes from here. If anything happens and you need help fast, give me a call." He grabbed a sheet of paper from his desk and scribbled his home and cell phone number on it.

"Thanks."

"I'll be praying for you, Chloe."

"Thanks for that, too. I guess I'll see you Saturday?"

"I wouldn't miss it."

She nodded and stepped out of the office.

Ben pulled the door closed, wishing he could do more than offer words and friendship, wishing she would accept more. But he couldn't, she wouldn't, and he knew the best thing he could do for both of them was pray.

Lord, I don't know why my life has intersected with Chloe's. I don't know what Your purpose is for us, but I know there is one. I pray that Your will be done in both our lives and that in Your infinite mercy You will give Chloe the faith she needs to overcome whatever obstacles and challenges she faces.

The prayer was simple, the peace that washed over Ben a familiar friend. He took a seat behind his desk, tapping a pen against his palm, the glimmer of an idea forming. He smiled, grabbed the phone and dialed.

Chapter Ten

Chloe paced the length of her living room for the fifth time, the walls pressing in on her, the darkness beyond the window preventing her from doing what she wanted to do—leave.

Exhaustion dragged her down, but the bone-deep ache in her thigh wouldn't allow her to sink into sleep. The skin on her neck felt tight, the bands of scars uncomfortably stiff. She wanted to blame both on her work at Blooming Baskets, but being on her feet for a few hours a day wasn't the cause. Neither was bending over flower arrangements. Anxiety. Tension. Fear. They haunted her days and filled her nights with dreams that stayed in her mind long after she woke.

She moved toward the computer that sat on the desk against one wall of the living room. Maybe she should e-mail a few friends, catch up with them. Make a few phone calls. See how everyone was, but that would mean explaining all that had happened in the past month. Explaining that she'd left town because she hadn't attempted suicide. Explaining that someone wanted her dead.

The story sounded far-fetched even to her.

She grimaced, stalked into her bedroom and picked up her Bible before returning to the living room and pushing open the balcony door. The full moon cast bluish light across the yard and reflected off the lake, painting the world in shades of gray. If she'd had her camera, she would have taken a picture, but she didn't and instead she tried to soak it all in, memorize it, pack it away in her mind so that she could take it with her if she was forced to run again.

The phone rang, the sound drifting out onto the balcony and offering a welcome distraction.

She hurried to pick it up. "Hello?"

"Chloe? It's Ben." The warmth of his voice washed over her, and she sank down into the recliner, relaxing for the first time in what seemed like hours.

"Hi. What's up?"

"I was just out for a ride and thought I'd give you a call."

"Opal must have put you up to it."

"No, but she did give me your number."

"I bet you didn't have to twist her arm for it."

"Not even a little."

Chloe smiled, enjoying the conversation more than she knew was good for her. "So, if Opal didn't put you up to calling me, who did?"

"Me. I had a thought after you left the church the other night and I wanted to share it with you."

"I'm all ears."

"It'll be hard to explain over the phone. What would you say to going for a ride with me?"

"Now?"

"You're not busy. I'm not busy. What better time than now?"

Chloe glanced toward the still-open balcony door and the darkness beyond. "I don't usually go out at night. The darkness hides too much."

She spoke without thinking, her cheeks heating as she realized what she'd said. "What I meant was—"

"No need to explain. Let's do it another time."

"You haven't even said what *it* is."

"And ruin the surprise?"

"I'm not much for surprises." Most of the ones she'd had weren't good.

He chuckled, the warmth of it seeping through the phone line and tugging at Chloe's heart. "I had a feeling you were going to tell me you didn't like surprises. So, here's the thing, I have a friend who's a veterinarian. She's got a litter of puppies she needs to find homes for."

"Puppies?"

"Puppies. As in little yapping bundles of fur."

"Should I ask what this has to do with me?"

"I thought you might like some company at night. A puppy seemed perfect."

"I've never had a dog. I wouldn't know the first thing about taking care of one." Though she had to admit, the idea held a certain appeal. The past few nights had been long, filled with odd noises and sinister shadows, nightmares and memories. A distraction might be just what she needed.

"There's a first time for everything, Chloe." There was a smile in Ben's voice and Chloe's lips curved in response.

"My landlady might not allow pets."

"The Andersons across the hall from you have one. They've brought it to a couple of church picnics."

"The little mop they dress in a sweater doesn't qualify as a pet."

His laughter rumbled out again. "Tell you what, why don't you think about it? You can give me a call, or we can talk about it when we get together for dinner."

She should definitely think about it. Rushing into something like a puppy could only lead to trouble and regret, and she had enough of both of those to last a lifetime.

She didn't *want* to think about it, though, because saying no would mean spending another night alone in the apartment. Another night jumping at every sound, wondering about every shadow. "Is the offer still open for tonight?"

"Sure."

"Then I think I'll take you up on it."

"Great. I'll be there in five."

Five minutes was just enough time for Chloe to check her copy of the rental agreement she'd signed, pull on shoes, pop two aspirin and waffle back and forth on the puppy idea a dozen times.

By the time Ben knocked, she'd driven herself crazy with indecision. Over a dog. But she couldn't deny the excitement she felt. The sense of fun and adventure that had been missing from her life for far too long and now welled up inside as she pulled the door open. "Five minutes on the dot."

"I'm a stickler for being on time. Ready?" His easy smile was as familiar as an old friend's and just as welcome.

"Indecisive." She limped over and grabbed her purse off the couch, pulled on a jacket.

"Then it's good you don't have to decide anything tonight." Despite his smile, Ben seemed more subdued than usual, his normally abundant charm overshadowed by something dark and sad.

"Is everything okay?"

"Yes." But it wasn't. Fatigue had darkened his eyes from sapphire to navy. Tension bracketed his mouth. "We'd better get going. Tori said she'd be at the clinic until eight-thirty. I don't want to keep her longer than that."

Chloe nodded, stepping out into the hallway and moving down the steps toward the front door, knowing she shouldn't ask the questions that were clamoring through her mind, but unable to stop herself. "Were you working today?"

"Friday's the day I do visitations. We've got several housebound members of the congregation and a few in the hospital." He paused, ran a hand over his hair. "I also conducted a funeral for a two-year-old boy."

"Just a baby. That's terrible."

He nodded, his jaw tight. "It's hard enough to say goodbye to someone who has lived a long, full life. Saying goodbye to a child who has barely begun to live is devastating."

"I can't even imagine what that must be like for the parents."

"Me, neither." He pushed open the front door, his movements stiff. "Talking to people who are so devastated, so desperate to know why the tragedy happened, how God could have allowed it, is tough, because there are no answers. We live in a fallen sinful world. Tragedy is part of that. We know that God loves us, that He wants what's best for us. That makes accepting things like a child's death even more difficult."

He ran a hand over his face, then stepped out onto the porch. "Maybe tonight isn't such a good night for this, after all. I came to cheer you up, not drag you down into the pit with me."

Chloe hesitated, then put her hand on his arm, feeling the rigid tension of the muscles beneath his sleeve. "I was already in the pit before you arrived. Since we're both in it together, we may as well hang out. Who knows? Maybe we'll manage to hoist each other out."

Ben stared down at her, his eyes dark, the angles of his face harsher in the porch light. He looked harder, tougher, much more like the teen he'd said he'd been than the man he'd become.

Finally, he shrugged. "Then let's go look at puppies."

He started down the porch steps and Chloe followed, the coolness of the evening seeping through the long-sleeved blouse and lightweight jacket she wore. She shivered, stumbling down the first step, her bad leg buckling.

Ben grabbed her arm before she could fall the rest of the way. "Whoa! Careful. If you fall and break your leg, Opal will have my hide."

"And my surgeon will have *mine*." She limped down the last two steps, pausing at the bottom to let the aching pain in her thigh ease. "She spent a lot of hours putting it back together. She won't be happy if I undo all that work."

"Then we definitely need to make sure it doesn't get broken again."

"I don't think we have to worry about it too much. I've got enough rods and screws in it to set off a metal detector."

"Sounds pretty indestructible, but let's not take any

chances." He put a hand under her elbow and led her to his sedan, his slow pace matching her limping stride.

Even with Ben beside her, Chloe felt fear creeping close, breathing a dire warning in her ear. Something was out here with them. Something dark and evil. Something ready to strike. Ready to kill.

She glanced around the yard, searching for signs of danger. There was nothing there. At least nothing she could see.

As if he sensed it, too, Ben stilled, his body tense. "Something seems off."

"Off?"

"Yeah. Off. And it's crawling up my spine and shouting a warning in my ear." He glanced around the yard, the hardness Chloe had seen while he stood on the porch even more pronounced.

"Come on." He hurried her toward the car, pulled open the door. "Get in."

Chloe did as he asked, sliding into the sedan and expecting him to do the same.

"Lock the door. I want to take a look around." He pushed the door closed, but Chloe caught it before it could snap shut, pushing it open once again.

"Look around? For what?"

"For whatever it is that's out here with us."

"Ben, I don't think that's a good idea. Let's go inside and call the police."

"Use my cell phone to call. It's in the glove compartment. I've got Jake's number on speed dial. Lock the door and stay in the car until I get back."

"Let's call him together. You can't go running after whoever is out there by yourself."

"Why not? It won't be the first time I've gone running after something lurking in the darkness."

"I didn't realize that was part of a pastor's job description." Chloe wanted to grab Ben's hand and keep him from leaving.

"It isn't. Good thing I haven't always been a pastor." He brushed the bangs from her eyes and smiled, his teeth flashing white in the darkness. "Now, stop worrying and stay put."

With that he shut the door and started across the yard toward the lake.

Chloe watched him go, sure that at any moment someone would swoop down on him. Instead, he seemed to disappear, blending into the shadows and fading into the night. Chloe found the cell phone, scrolling through the contact numbers until she found Jake's.

He picked up quickly, his gruff voice filling her with relief. "Reed here."

"It's Chloe. Davidson."

"Calling from Ben's cell phone. Is he okay?"

"I don't know," she explained quickly, her words rushing out so that she wasn't sure Jake would be able to make any sense of them.

"You're at your place?"

"Yes."

"Stay where you are. I'll be there in ten."

Ten minutes. Six hundred seconds. Plenty of time for a shot to be fired, a knife to be buried deep in a chest. A man to die.

Images filled Chloe's head. Black night. Fire. A shadowy figure. Danger. Pain.

Fear.

She wanted to sink down in the seat, hide her head until help arrived. Wanted to embrace the weak-willed, wimpy woman she'd become and let Ben and Jake handle the problem.

Wanted to, but couldn't.

Adam had died because of her investigation into the death of Ana Benedict, had died because of what that investigation had uncovered about The Strangers. She had no intention of letting the same thing happen to Ben. Fear or no fear, she was getting out of the car and she was going to face whatever was hiding in the darkness.

Hands shaking, she shoved open the car door and took a gulping breath of cool air. The yard was silent and still, waiting for whatever would come. Chloe waited, too, breathless and watching, hoping to see Ben return before she actually had to go after him. Finally, she couldn't put it off any longer and she stepped away from the car, leaves and grass crunching under her feet, releasing the heavy scent of earth and decay.

Up ahead, the dark water of the lake washed over rocks and wood, lapping against the shore in rhythmic waves that should have been soothing but weren't.

I could really use some help right about now, Lord.

The prayer chanted through her mind as she skirted a thick grove of trees and approached the lake. The shoreline was empty, tall reeds and thick grasses heavy and overgrown, tangled in bunches near the water's edge. A boat bobbed on the surface of the lake, the rickety dock it was tied to barely keeping it from floating away.

"Ben?" She whispered his name as she moved toward the dock, peering into the shadows afraid of what she might find there.

"I thought you were staying in the car."

He spoke from behind her, his voice so unexpected,

Chloe bit back a scream, whirling to face him, her heart in her throat. "I didn't want you to be out here by yourself."

"So you decided to come out by *yourself?*" The moon was behind him, casting shadows across his face, making his expression impossible to read.

"It seemed like a good idea at the time."

"It wasn't." He cupped her elbow, tugging her back toward the house.

"Did you see someone?"

"No, but that doesn't mean someone wasn't here."

"What do we do now?"

"We go back to the car and you get in it and lock the door. I walk around the house and see if there's any evidence that someone has been hanging around. Maybe talk to the downstairs tenant, see if he's heard anything. Once Jake gets here and checks things out, we'll head over to the veterinary clinic."

"It's getting a little late for that."

"It's not late at all." His hand rested on her back, the warmth of it seeping through her jacket and warming her chilled skin. "I hear sirens. Jake is on the way. Stay in the car this time, okay?"

"Okay."

The door shut again and this time Chloe stayed where she was, watching Ben move around the perimeter of the house as the sound of sirens drifted into the car and her rapidly beating heart subsided.

Chapter Eleven

By the time Jake and Ben finished searching the property, Chloe had come up with several excuses to return to her apartment and lock herself in for the night. Her head ached. Her leg throbbed. She really didn't think a puppy was a good idea.

All of them fled her mind as Ben pulled open the car door and slid in, a woodsy, masculine scent floating into the car with him. "We're all set."

"Did you find anything?"

"Nothing but a few smudged footprints near the window under your apartment. They could be from anyone and could have been there for a few days." He started the engine. "Someone was out there tonight, though. I'm sure of it."

"You saw someone?"

"Felt someone. Whether or not that someone has anything to do with what's been happening to you, I can't say."

"How could it not? It's exactly what's been happening to me for months."

"It started after the accident?"

Had it? It seemed that what had happened after the accident was crystal clear, the threat she felt like a waking nightmare she couldn't escape from. What had come before was less clear and Chloe couldn't say for sure that she hadn't felt the same way. She couldn't say she had, either. "I don't know."

"The man who was convicted of murder—"

"Matthew Jackson." His pale face and coal-black eyes were tattooed into her memory, his skeletal frame standing outside the burning car, something she would never forget.

"According to the news reports I heard, Jackson never admitted to sabotaging your car. It's possible he didn't."

"He was there, Ben. Standing outside the car while it burned around us. He had a gun." The police speculated that he'd been planning to kill Chloe if she got out of the car. The fire that had scarred her, had saved her life. The bent metal that had held her inside the burning wreck had kept her from certain death.

The thought made her shudder and she wrapped her arms around her waist. "Jackson wanted me dead. He was at the scene of the accident. It seems pretty obvious he had something to do with it."

"Maybe he did, but maybe the accident has nothing to do with what's happening now." Ben turned into the parking lot of a well-lit building and turned to face her. "What if the D.C. police were heading in the wrong direction? What if they couldn't find evidence that you were being stalked because they were looking for a connection to Jackson and couldn't find it?"

She rubbed the ache in her thigh, wincing a little as bunched muscles contracted even more. "They looked in every direction. My old caseload, my personal relationships. They investigated thoroughly but couldn't find anyone else who had a grudge against me."

"Did you?"

"Did I what?"

"Investigate." His eyes were liquid fire in the dim light, his face carved from stone, but his hand was gentle as it wrapped around hers, his fingers skimming across her palm and settling there. "It's what you do. It would seem natural for you to check things out yourself."

"I was too sick at first. By the time I was healthy enough to think about investigating, Jackson was in jail and it seemed the police had covered all the bases."

"If it were my life on the line, I don't think I'd rely solely on the police to investigate." His hand dropped away from hers and he opened his door. "This is it. Tori's clinic. Let's head in and see what those puppies are like."

Chloe grabbed his arm before he could get out, scowling as he turned to face her. "You're good, Ben Avery. Really good. But I know exactly what you're up to and…" She planned on saying it wasn't going to work, that she had no intention of digging into her old caseloads, no intention of searching for someone who might want her dead. But he'd planted a seed and it was already growing in the fallow soil of her heart.

"And what?" His gaze touched her hair, her cheeks, her lips, lingering there for a second before he met her eyes.

Her skin heated, but she ignored it and the wild beating of her heart. "And it's working. But I use computer forensics to investigate crime. If someone is really coming after me, that won't be hidden in a computer file or found in a deleted e-mail."

"But his reason might be."

He had a good point and Chloe mulled it over as she got out of the car. "I'll have to look through my open cases. Maybe I'll find something there."

"If you do, go to Jake with it. Don't try to confront the person yourself."

"I'm not *that* crazy. One near-death experience in a lifetime is more than enough."

He chuckled and pressed a hand to Chloe's lower spine. "Come on. Tori is probably pacing the floor wondering what's taking so long."

"Maybe she's left." Which might be a good thing.

"Maybe, but it's doubtful. She's got to find homes for these puppies before her grandfather finds another litter."

"Her grandfather brought her the puppies?"

"Yeah. That was this week. Last week, he found an abandoned potbellied pig. The week before he found a goat."

"What's he do? Ride around looking for strays?"

"When he's not riding around looking for Opal."

"Opal?"

"Yeah. Sam's got a thing for her. You probably remember meeting him the night of the wedding. Tall, gray hair, smitten look on his face."

"I remember. I tried to find out what's going on with them, but Opal is keeping mum."

"That's probably for the best."

"Why's that?"

"It'll give you an excuse to keep mum about what's going on with us." He shouldered open the clinic door, gesturing for Chloe to precede him into the brightly lit reception area.

"Nothing is going on with us."

"I'm not so sure you're right about that, Chloe." He smiled, the gentle curve of his lips spearing into Chloe's heart.

She blinked, took a step back, denying what she was feeling. Refusing it. She didn't need to add a man to her already complicated life. She *wouldn't* add a man to it. "Ben—"

"You're finally here. I was beginning to wonder if you were coming at all." A woman strode toward them, her movements brisk despite what looked like an advanced pregnancy. Tall and striking with bright red hair and green eyes, she exuded confidence and warmth as she offered a hand to Chloe. "You must be Chloe. I'm Tori Stone. You met my grandfather the other night."

"I remember."

"Yeah, well, Sam is hard to forget. The puppies are this way. I've only got two left. This litter has been pretty easy to place. The last one…" She paused, shuddered. "Not so much."

"Was something wrong with them?"

"Wrong? No. They were just homely. Poor little guys. Eventually we found some people who were willing to overlook that." She smiled, led them to a closed door. "Here we are. I've got a few patients to check on. I'll let you two take a look. Then come back in a few minutes to see what you think."

She pushed open the door and motioned for Chloe to go in. "Feel free to take them out of the crate, but close the door if you do or they'll be down the hall and into trouble before you know it. See you in a few."

Chloe stepped into the room. It housed an exam table, cabinets, a counter. The crate sat on the floor near the far wall, the wiggling, squirming balls of fur inside it looking more like overgrown dust bunnies than dogs.

"Those are puppies? They look more like miniature mops or giant dust bunnies to me." Ben's comment neatly mimicked what Chloe was thinking, and she smiled.

"Except for the tails."

"There is that." Ben knelt down. "Which do you want to see? The fuzzy one or the fuzzier one."

"Either."

Ben reached in and pulled out a handful of wiggling cream-colored puppy. "Try this one."

She lifted it to her chest, stroking silky fur and feeling the vibrating excitement of the puppy surge through her. It strained against her hold, licking her hands and neck and rolling sideways for a belly rub. "It's awfully cute."

"So's this one." Ben lifted out the second pup and set it on the floor. Its paws were black, its torso dark brown, its tail wagging so fast, Chloe thought it might knock itself over.

"If I *were* to decide to bring one home I wouldn't know which to choose." Chloe set the one she was holding down, and watched as it scampered across the floor, rushing from wall to wall, skidding on the tile floor and slamming into the door.

Chloe laughed, kneeling down, her bad leg protesting the move. She ignored it, picking up the brown puppy and holding it up so she could look in its eyes. "This one is quieter."

"Definitely."

She put it back down, smiling as it climbed up her legs and settled down for a nap. "I don't know, Ben.

They're both adorable, but I'm not sure I'm ready for a pet."

"Ever have one before?"

"Not even a fish. The closest I came to it was Speedy."

"The stuffed turtle."

"Exactly."

Ben lifted the cream-colored puppy and rubbed it under its chin as he settled down beside Chloe. "Like I said before, there's a first time for everything."

"I'm just not sure now is the right time for this particular first."

"It's your decision to make." He placed the puppy down on the floor, watching as it raced away. "But it might be fun to have a quirky little guy like that racing around the apartment."

A soft knock sounded on the door and Tori strode in. "I see you've met Cain and Abel."

She knelt down next to Chloe, smoothing the fur on the dark puppy's back. "They're brothers, but the similarity ends there. Cain is full of energy and life. Lovable but constantly in trouble."

"Then this one must be Abel." Chloe stroked the puppy's head.

"Yes. Sweet as pie. Cute as a button. Smart as a whip." She grinned. "But lazy."

"They're both sweet as pie."

"You're right about that, Chloe, but their personalities are very different. If you decide you want to take one, you need to think about which will fit better with your lifestyle."

Chloe nodded, watching Cain as he chased his tail. His energy level high, his exuberance appealing. A year or two ago, he would have been her choice. Now, though, she wasn't sure she could keep up with the wiggling ball of energy. The quieter puppy, on the other hand, was more her speed, his slow movements as he finally roused himself to join his brother's play made her smile.

"You don't have to make up your mind tonight, of course. I can hold them both for a few days while you decide." Tori started to rise and Ben hurried to offer a hand up. "Thanks, Ben. Why don't I give you a couple more minutes with the puppies? Then we'll call it a night."

The door closed behind Tori's retreating figure.

"What do you think?" Ben lifted Cain and rubbed his belly.

"I think you should take that one home with you."

"We didn't come here to pick a puppy for me. We came for you. You need some company, remember?"

"And you don't?"

"My life is busy. I don't have time for a puppy."

"Mine is, too, and neither do I."

"So, I guess we leave them here."

"I guess we do." She lifted the brown puppy who'd come to sit in her lap again, surprised by the disappointment she felt. "Sorry, guy."

"Of course, there's another option." Ben knelt down in front of Chloe, lifting Abel from her arms and setting him on the floor.

"What's that?"

"We could *make* time for them." He grabbed Chloe's hand and tugged her to her feet, his hands wrapping around her waist to hold her steady.

"Come on, Chloe. You know you want to." His grin was just the right side of wicked, his eyes flashing with amusement and a challenge Chloe knew she should ignore, but couldn't.

"So you're saying if I take Abel, you'll take Cain?"

"I'm saying if you take one I'll take the other. Which one of us gets the hyperactive guy is up for debate."

"Debate? I think it's pretty obvious that the more active puppy should go to the more able-bodied person. My bum leg won't let me chase after anything much faster than Abel."

"You may have a point. One way or another, we'll have to work out visitation. A couple of walks a week. Maybe a playdate or two." He leaned a shoulder against the wall. "Just because you and I aren't together, doesn't mean the boys shouldn't be able to spend time with each other."

He looked serious, his face set in somber lines, sandy hair falling over his forehead, but laughter danced in his eyes.

Chloe's own laughter bubbled out, spilling into the room, the feeling of it new and fresh. Life, hope, joy. So many things she'd thought she'd never have again, but that suddenly seemed possible. Here, in the brightly lit room, two puppies scampering near her feet, Ben's amused eyes staring into hers, she could almost forget the darkness that waited outside, the shadows that seemed determined to follow her wherever she went.

Almost.

"Don't stop." He brushed strands of hair from Chloe's cheeks, his fingers lingering for a moment before dropping away.

"Stop what?"

"Laughing. It's good for the soul."

"I guess I need to find more things to laugh about, then."

"You will. Sorrow fades in time."

"Sorrow I can handle. It's the guilt that's eating me alive."

"You've got nothing to feel guilty about."

"Don't I?" She leaned down and scooped Abel into her arms, the fuzzy warmth of the puppy comforting. "My investigation caused Adam's death."

"The person who sabotaged your car caused his death."

"No matter which way you try to paint the picture, it'll always be the same. I found information that I passed on to the FBI. Because of that The Strangers dismantled. Because of *that,* Matthew Jackson tried to kill me and killed Adam instead."

"It seems to me you're taking a lot of responsibility for something you couldn't know would happen."

"I'm not taking responsibility. I'm just…"

"What?"

"Wishing I'd made different choices. Wishing that Adam hadn't died in my place."

Ben's hands framed her face, the rough calluses on his palms rasping against her skin. "He didn't die in your place, Chloe. He was killed in a tragic accident that had nothing to do with you and everything to do with someone else's sin."

"The words sound good, Ben, but they don't feel like the truth."

"Then it's good that how we feel doesn't actually determine the facts." His hands slid to her neck, his thumbs brushing against the tender flesh under her jaw and spreading warmth in their wake.

Chloe's heart jumped, and she stepped back, refusing to put a name to what she'd promised herself she'd never feel again. "We should find Tori and tell her we've decided to take the puppies."

For a moment, she didn't think Ben was going to acknowledge her comment. His vivid eyes stared into hers, secrets and shadows hidden in their depth.

Finally, he nodded. "Let me corral Cain first."

Chloe waited at the door, Abel sleeping in her arms, his fuzzy head pressed into the crook of her elbow, her heartbeat slowing, the places where Ben's hands had rested cooling. She shouldn't be letting him affect her so much, shouldn't be having this kind of reaction to him.

Shouldn't be, but it didn't seem she had much of a choice. No matter how much she might want to tell herself differently, Ben was becoming a fixture in her life. She wasn't sure she liked it and was even less sure she could change it. All she *could* do was pray that Ben wouldn't eventually suffer for being her friend and that she wouldn't eventually be left heartbroken again.

Chapter Twelve

Having a puppy in the apartment proved to be as much of a distraction as Ben had said it would be. The cozy rooms Chloe loved so much were even more inviting with a ball of fur keeping her company in them.

And company was definitely something she needed at three in the morning when nightmares woke her and fear kept her from returning to sleep.

She shifted in the easy chair, hoping a change in position would alleviate the ache in her leg. Abel whined, moving into a more comfortable spot, his body heat seeping through the flannel pajamas Chloe wore and easing the knotted muscles of her thigh.

"You're a living heating pad, puppy." His tail thumped, his eyes opened briefly before he went back to sleep again.

Chloe wished she could do the same, but the dream she'd woken from refused to release its hold and her heart hammered in response, the quick, sickening thud enough to convince her she was having a heart attack. She wasn't. Despite the pressure in her chest, the too-rapid throb of her pulse and the cold sweat that beaded her brow, she knew she was suffering from nothing more than panic.

She wanted to get up and move, pace the floor, run a mile, talk to someone. She lifted the phone, realized what she was doing and set it down again. She couldn't call Opal at this time of the morning. Not when Opal was already so worried about Chloe's mental health. She wouldn't call Ben. All she could do was sit and wait while seconds became minutes and minutes hours.

Or she could use the time to do what Ben had suggested. She could pull her laptop from the closet where she'd shoved it when she'd moved in and revisit the cases she'd been working on around the time of the accident. As much as she wanted to believe that Matthew Jackson had been convicted of a crime he *had* committed, Ben had planted a seed of doubt and Chloe couldn't ignore it no matter how much she wanted to.

And the fact was, she really didn't want to.

It was a surprising change to the head-in-the-sand attitude she'd taken for so long; Chloe's mood lifted as a small spark of the person she'd once been took hold, urging her to face the situation, sort out the facts and find out for herself what was what, who was who and just how she could keep herself alive.

Maybe coming to Lakeview had given her back some of her old confidence and enthusiasm. Maybe talking to Ben had. Or maybe as her physical health and strength returned, her will to survive was kicking in stronger than ever. Whatever the case, Chloe was an investigator. She'd spent almost a decade of her life seeking evidence and answers. She'd found them for the FBI, for private investigators, for the police. Now she was going to find them for herself.

"Sorry, pup, you're going to have to move." She stood, setting Abel down on the ground and moving to her bedroom. The puppy scampered after her, waddling into the closet when she opened the door, pawing at the box she pulled out.

"This is mine, Abel. Tomorrow we'll get you some fun toys to play with."

Abel tilted his head to one side as if he were actually listening. Chloe smiled. "It's good to know I won't be talking to myself anymore. Come on. We've got work to do."

She grabbed her laptop from the box and carried it to the kitchen. Her hands were shaking as she set it up on the tiny table there. It wasn't fear that made them tremble. Excitement, anticipation, the drive to succeed—all the things that had made her good at computer forensics—those were what had her hands shaking and her heart racing.

Her elbow hit the Bible she'd set on the edge of the table and she shoved it away, then paused, pulling it back toward her, the yearning she'd felt since she'd come to Lakeview as real and as tangible as anything she might find stored on the computer.

After Adam's betrayal, she'd prayed for understanding, prayed that she could accept what had happened and move on. In those dark moments, she'd felt sure that God was listening, that He understood and cried with her. Then Adam had been killed and that certainty had been ripped away, a gaping hole all that remained of her fragile faith.

But maybe faith couldn't disappear or fade away. Maybe it couldn't be ripped from a life. Maybe, like the information she pulled from computer systems, it was only hidden from sight, waiting for a little effort, a little attention, to bring it back into view again.

She pushed the laptop toward the center of the table, opened her Bible to the first chapter of John and started reading.

"You've caught the biggest fish again, friend." Ben eyed Jake's cooler full of fish and his own empty one.

"Again? If I remember correctly, you've brought in the biggest catch three times running."

"You may be right, but that doesn't make my loss this time any less painful." He stepped out onto the dock, tied the boat. "I guess I'll be heading to the grocery store before I cook dinner for Chloe. Preparing store-bought fish after a fishing trip isn't a very manly thing to do, but I'll swallow my pride and do it."

"Your pitiful act is falling on deaf ears."

"Anyone ever tell you you're coldhearted?"

"Not coldhearted. Practical. The way I see it, if you want a couple of my fish, you'll have to trade for them."

"A trade or a trip to the grocery store? I don't even need time to think about it. What do you want?"

"A babysitter. Tiffany's birthday is next week and I want to take her out. Unfortunately, her parents are going out of town and she doesn't trust just anyone to watch the kids."

"And you think she'll let me do it?"

"I *know* she will. I asked."

"You've got to be pretty desperate to be asking me, Jake. You do know I haven't changed a diaper in years? I'll probably end up putting it on backward or upside down."

"Desperation has nothing to do with it. You're the

closest thing to a brother I've ever had. I trust you. Besides, Isaac is four weeks old. He won't care what way his diaper goes on."

"Since you put it that way, I guess I'll do it. No fish necessary."

"Thanks." Jake slapped him on the back and handed over the cooler filled with fish. "And just so we're clear, I would have given you these anyway."

"You say that *after* I've already committed to hours of diaper duty and baby-doll play." Which he had to admit he'd probably enjoy. *If* Isaac and his sister, Honor, didn't spend the entire time crying for their parents.

"Amazing how that worked out, isn't it?" Jake grinned and started toward his car. "Is six-thirty Friday okay with you?"

"I'll be there."

"Great. And now we'd both better get moving. I don't want to miss Honor's bath and I'm sure you don't want to be late for your date."

"Whoa! Hold up there. I'm cooking dinner for Chloe. That's not the same as a date."

"Then what *is* it the same as?"

"Cooking dinner for you and Tiffany or for my sister and Shane."

"Really? Because the way I see it, when you cook dinner for me and Tiffany or Raven and Shane, you're cooking for family. Chloe isn't family. So you cooking dinner for her doesn't seem like the same thing at all."

"She needs a friend. I'm being one."

"You just keep telling yourself that." Jake grinned and got into his car, his face sobering as he ran a hand over his hair. "I hate to even ask, but did you ask Chloe about the suicide attempt?"

"She denied it."

"Do you believe her?"

"Yeah, I do."

"Then so do I. Which means we're dealing with a second murder attempt. We just have to find a way to prove it."

"Did the police in D.C. collect evidence?"

"It seemed like a cut-and-dry suicide attempt. They weren't looking for evidence of murder. When they went back in afterward, the place had been cleaned by some friends who were getting it ready for her return from the hospital."

"Convenient for the murderer. Do we know who those friends were?"

"You'll have to ask Chloe when you're there tonight. Or I'll give her a ring tomorrow."

"I'll ask."

"And I'll keep searching for answers. If Chloe's in danger, I plan to figure out where it's coming from."

"That makes two of us."

"You just be careful, friend. I'm a cop. You're not."

"I can handle myself." He might have left the military years ago, but he hadn't forgotten what he learned there.

Jake nodded, but the concern in his eyes didn't fade. "There's something going on here I don't like. Chloe's brought trouble into town. Big trouble. The fact that you're involved with her—"

"I'm not *involved* with anyone."

"You're cooking her dinner. You went and picked out puppies with her. You're involved, Ben, and that makes things all the more complicated." He scowled. "Like I said, be careful."

The car door shut before Ben could respond. That

was probably for the best. There wasn't much left to say. Denying that he was involved with Chloe wouldn't convince Jake. The truth was, Ben wasn't all that convinced, either. Much as he might tell himself he wasn't interested in Chloe beyond wanting to help her adjust to her life in Lakeview, the truth seemed much more complex. He was intrigued, compelled, drawn into the sadness he saw in her eyes, the laughter that must have come much more frequently before the tragedy.

Despite what she'd been through, she was strong, determined and dedicated to creating a better life for herself. Ben understood that. He'd lived it. Even her struggles with faith and trust were familiar to him. He understood Chloe and that wasn't something he could say about many of the women he'd met.

Whether or not that meant anything, whether or not he *wanted* it to mean anything remained to be seen. For right now, he'd enjoy spending a few hours with an interesting woman and not worry about what would come next. God had everything under control.

Ben just wasn't sure *he* did.

He sighed, hefted the cooler containing the fish and strode toward his car. Like Jake, he had a bad feeling about Chloe's situation. Her story was like a puzzle with missing pieces. Until the last one was found the picture would remain unclear. And until it *was* clear Ben wouldn't rest easy. Danger lurked around Chloe. He felt it every time he was near her. He couldn't see it and didn't know what direction it was coming from, but he knew it was there and that if they weren't careful it would destroy Chloe and anyone who stood in the way.

Fortunately, Ben planned to be careful. Really careful. He might not know what role Chloe was going to play in his life, but he knew exactly what role he planned to play in hers. He was going to keep her safe. A little caution and a lot of prayer would go a long way toward that. Dinner and puppy choosing were extra.

Speaking of which, he had some trout to cook and a dog to walk.

And a very attractive woman to spend the evening with.

Despite his concerns, Ben couldn't help smiling as he got in his car and headed home.

Chapter Thirteen

Abel's soft whine commanded Chloe's attention and she glanced up from the file she was searching through. The puppy sat by the door, his head cocked to one side, his ears perked.

"You want to go out?"

Abel barked and scratched a paw against the door, his pint-size body vibrating with excitement.

"Sorry, buddy, you're going to have to wait. I took you out a half-hour ago and I don't plan to do the stairs again for a while."

Abel barked again. Chloe ignored him, choosing instead to stand and stretch tight, tense muscles. Her leg throbbed, her neck ached and she was sure she'd soon regret so many hours spent in one position, but right now all she felt was relief. She'd managed to search through sixteen files. All of them were cases that she'd been working on before the accident. Of those, four had caught and held her attention. Two were high-profile divorces, one involved tracing laundered funds and the last had required searching for evidence against a teacher who'd been accused of having a relationship with one of his students. In each case, Chloe'd been asked to retrieve information from the suspects' computers. Deleted e-mails, deleted files, things that most people assumed were gone could often still be found if one knew how to look. And Chloe definitely knew how to look.

She downed some cold coffee and limped back to her seat. Of the sixteen cases she'd been investigating, the ones that intrigued her were those she'd done the least amount of work on before the accident. Each of the four suspects had a lot to lose. A politician, a doctor, a respected business owner, a teacher with a wife and children. Any of them might have been desperate to keep his secrets hidden, but had one been desperate enough to commit murder? And if he had, what would cause him to keep coming after Chloe even after she'd dropped her investigation?

She didn't have answers to the questions, but at least she finally had questions. Until now, she'd been sliding closer and closer to believing she really was going crazy. Hopefully asking questions and seeking answers was the beginning of healing.

Abel barked again, jumping up against the door in what seemed like a desperate bid for escape.

"Am I that bad of company?"

A soft tap sounded on the wood and Abel tumbled backward, barking furiously and running for cover behind Chloe's legs.

"Some watchdog you are." Chloe scooped him up and strode toward the door. "Who's there?"

"Ben."

Ben? He wasn't supposed to be over until six. She glanced at the clock, realized that it *was* six and pulled open the door.

He looked as good as he had the night before, his sandy hair curling near his collar, his eyes blazing against his deeply tanned face. When he smiled, Chloe's heart melted into a puddle of yearning that she absolutely refused to acknowledge.

"Hi."

"Hi, yourself." He stepped into the living room, a cooler and brown paper bag in his arms, Cain nipping at the leash and tumbling along behind.

Ben glanced around the room, his gaze settling on the coffee table and the computer that sat there. Chloe had a notebook and pen lying next to it. A few crumbled sheets of paper were scattered on the table. One or two had dropped onto the floor. "Looks like you were working. Want to reschedule for another time?"

It would probably be for the best. Send Ben and his puppy on their way. Spend a few more hours doing research. Heat up a frozen meal and spend the rest of the evening alone. Those were safe and reasonable things to do. Unfortunately, Chloe didn't feel like being safe or reasonable. She felt like enjoying a couple of hours in the company of a man who demanded nothing more from her than conversation. "And miss out on a home-cooked meal? I don't think so."

"You don't usually do home cooked?"

"Only if heating things up in the microwave counts as home cooking."

Ben shook his head and smiled. "Not quite."

"I didn't think so. Opal says I'm culinary challenged. The fact is, I'm lazy. It seems like too much effort to cook a fancy meal for one."

"I'm with you on that. Cooking is much more fun when you're doing it for someone other than yourself."

He stepped toward the kitchen, his tall, broad frame filling the room and stealing Chloe's breath.

She didn't understand it, didn't like it and was absolutely sure it could only mean trouble, but there was definitely something about Ben that drew her to him. His steadiness, his confidence, his faith, they were like blazing lights in what had become an ever-darkening world. When he was around, Chloe's anxiety and fear seemed to melt away; when he spoke, she could almost believe that everything was going to be okay.

It had been a long time since Chloe had felt that way around someone. Even before the accident she'd been self-reliant, depending on herself for the stability she craved. As much as she'd loved Adam, being with him had been more exciting than comforting, more stormy ocean than placid lake. They'd brought out the best in each other only when they weren't bringing out each others' worst. After he'd confessed to seeing another woman, Chloe finally acknowledged what she'd known all along—marrying him would send her right back into the chaotic life she'd worked so hard to escape.

"Are you okay?" Ben had moved back across the room and was standing in front of her, solid and warm. More real than nightmares or memories. More steady than Chloe's own rioting emotions.

"Fine. Just…" Confused? Scared? Guilty? All fit, but she wouldn't give them voice. "Sluggish. Sitting in front of the computer for too long does that to me."

He didn't believe her and she was sure he'd ask more questions, push for answers she wasn't sure she could give. Instead, he brushed her hair back from her face, hooking it behind her ears, his hands lingering on her shoulders, his thumbs resting against her collarbone. "I guess we'll have to do something about that."

To Chloe's horror an image flashed through her mind. Ben leaning close, his breath warm against her lips just before…

She shoved the thought away, her pulse accelerating, her cheeks heating as she stepped back. "What did you have in mind?"

"Nothing so horrible. Just a walk by the lake. I think the boys would enjoy it. I know I would."

A walk. She could do that. And she could do it without letting her mind wander back to very dangerous territory. "That sounds good. I've been cooped up inside most of the day. Besides quick trips outside for Abel, I've pretty much stayed put."

"Good. That's what Jake and I both want you to do."

"Did you two enjoy your fishing trip today?" *Did you talk about me? Does Jake think I'm as crazy as the D.C. police seem to think I am?* Those were the questions she wanted to ask, but didn't.

"It could have been better." Ben strode back into the kitchen, pulled open the drawer beneath Chloe's oven and grabbed a large frying pan.

"How so?"

"I could have caught a few edible fish." He pulled several plastic containers from the bag he'd carried in.

"You had to buy our dinner?"

"Worse." He opened the cooler and pulled out two large fish. "I had to trade for it."

"Trade?"

"Yeah. My babysitting services for Jake's fish."

"Babysitting for Jake's kids. Doesn't he have a baby and a toddler?" She was sure that was what Tiffany had said, but couldn't imagine Ben doing diaper duty.

"Yep. And unless Honor has been potty trained sometime in the past two days, they're both still in diapers." He pulled open a drawer, frowned, pulled open another one. "Knives?"

"To your right."

"Thanks. Here's the problem. I'm good at a few things. Cooking. Martial arts. Rock climbing. I'm even pretty decent at corralling teenagers. I'm not so good at others things. Like burping and changing babies, or playing baby doll with a two-year-old. I'm pretty confident I can handle one of the kids at a time, but double-duty might be beyond me."

"I'm sure you'll do just fine."

"I'm sure I'd do even better if I had another adult there with me."

"Very subtle, Ben."

"Subtlety is my middle name." He grinned, finished prepping the first fish and started on the second.

"And caution is mine. I might be willing to offer my help if I knew anything at all about kids, but I don't. Besides babysitting when I was a teenager, I haven't had much contact with the younger crowd."

"No little brothers or sisters in your life?"

"I was my mother's first and only mistake." The words slipped out and heat rose in Chloe's cheeks. Again.

"Sounds like your mother and mine were a lot alike."

"You said you had a sister."

"I do. My mother was too caught up in drugs and alcohol to keep her first mistake from repeating itself. Raven is younger than me. She and her husband live outside of town."

"I've always wanted a sister." Someone to share the aloneness with. Someone who would be the family connection Chloe had craved as a child and still sometimes yearned for.

"It was great. When she was little I actually did diaper duty, gave her baths, made sure she was fed."

"You were a lot older than her?"

"There's six years difference."

"That's…" Crazy. Sad. Horrifying.

"It is what it is. I took care of her the best I could until social services stepped in." He finished the second fish, opened up a shallow container and dipped both into a mixture of spices. "After that, we were separated. It took me years to find her again. And, actually, she was the one who found me. Just showed up at the church one day. I've barely let her out of my sight since."

"That's a great story."

"It is." He grinned. "I never get tired of telling it. So, what do you say?"

"About?"

"Giving me a hand with Jake's kids."

"I doubt Jake would want me over at his place."

"Why wouldn't he?"

"I'm a walking danger zone."

"And his house is like Fort Knox. Locks. Alarms. You name it, he's got it."

"His wife—"

"You've met Tiffany. She's as laid-back as Jake is intense. She'll probably feel a lot more comfortable if there are two of us with the kids."

"She did seem pretty easygoing when I met her." But that didn't mean Chloe wanted to spend the evening watching her kids. Not when doing so meant she'd be spending another evening with Ben. Ben whose vivid gaze compelled her and whose laughter warmed the

cold, hard knot of pain she'd been carrying around for
months. Ben who could easily fill the empty place in
her heart and who could just as easily break it.

"She is, but she's also a mama bear when it comes
to her kids. I doubt she'll be able to enjoy her birthday
dinner if she's worrying about whether or not I'll be
able to handle Honor and Isaac on my own."

"Jake is taking her out for her birthday?"

"Yes. Does that make a difference?"

"Every woman deserves to be treated special on her
birthday." Chloe's own birthdays were less than memorable. Her mother and grandmother hadn't wanted to
acknowledge the infamous date of her birth. Most of
her boyfriends had been too caught up in themselves to
mark the day. Even Adam hadn't made much of it,
his quick phone calls and hasty dinner arrangements
making her feel more second-thought than special.
Opal had sent cards and gifts, but she was the only
one who'd ever cared enough to do so.

"Does that mean you'll help?" Ben laid the fish in
the sizzling hot pain and a spicy aroma filled the air.

Chloe's stomach rumbled, reminding her that she
hadn't eaten since breakfast and that her mind might
be fuzzy from lack of food. Now was not a good time
to make decisions. She knew it, but couldn't find the
wherewithal to care. "I'll help if you get Jake and Tiffany's consent first."

"That goes without saying." He nodded toward the
containers he'd set on the counter. "There's corn-bread
batter in the yellow container. I'll get the oven pre-
heated. If you oil a pan and pour the batter into it,
we can get it started. I don't know about you, but I'm
starving."

"I could definitely eat." A horse. A house. Anything large and filling.

Chloe followed Ben's instructions, then handed him the pan, her mouth watering as he slid it into the oven, a feeling of companionship and camaraderie washing over her. She and Adam had spent a lot of time together, but not all of it had been easy and comfortable. As a matter of fact, too much of that time had been spent arguing about his relationships with other women and Chloe's unwillingness to accept those friendships. She'd felt sure that innocent lunches and dinner would eventually turn into something less innocent. He'd insisted he loved her too much to be tempted by anyone else. In the end, Chloe's opinion regarding the matter had been proven accurate. That was cold comfort in the wake of all that had happened.

She ran her hand over already mussed hair and pulled plates out of the cupboard, hoping to distract herself from thoughts of what had been. "Is there anything else I can do to help?"

"Grab the ice cream out of the bag and throw it in the freezer. I almost forgot about it."

"Forgot about ice cream? Is that even possible?"

"Chalk it up to last-minute changes in the menu and an ornery puppy who decided he didn't want to leave the house."

"Last-minute menu changes?"

"Opal called to ask me why I'd talked you into getting a puppy."

"I haven't spoken to her since yesterday afternoon. How could she possibly know about Abel?"

"The same way anyone in Lakeview knows anything. Rumor mill. Although I'm not sure if that's an accurate description since it was your landlady who called Opal with the information."

"I had a feeling I wouldn't get much privacy living in a house owned by Opal's friend." Chloe pulled forks, knives and spoons out of a drawer, grabbed napkins from the counter and finished setting the table. "So what did Opal's lecture about Abel have to do with last-minute menu plans?"

"I haven't figured that one out yet. One minute we were talking about dogs taking over Blooming Baskets and the next she was asking me what I planned to serve tonight." He grinned, flipping the fish and opening another plastic container. "I'd been planning to have fresh fruit for dessert, but Opal told me that wouldn't do. Apparently, you need chocolate and ice cream and lots of it."

"I guess I'll have to give her a call after you leave and tell her to stop meddling."

"Do you *want* her to stop meddling?" He opened the oven, peeked at the corn bread and closed it again, leaning a hip against the counter, his eyes meeting Chloe's and capturing her gaze.

"The truth? No. Every time Opal sticks her nose into my business, I realize how much she cares."

"I feel the same about my foster parents. Mom calls every Monday. Dad checks in by e-mail a couple times a week. It's good to know they're there even if their hints about marriage and children are getting old."

"They want you to get married again?"

"They want me to be happy. I think that's what all good parents want for their children." He pulled the bread out of the oven, turned off the burner and grabbed a plate. "Ready to eat?"

"It smells delicious."

"Hopefully it will be. Of course, if it's not, I'll just blame Jake for catching bad fish."

"You two are good friends."

"He moved here from D.C. a few years back. We've been like brothers ever since." He placed spice-crusted fish on her plate, spooned what looked like a three-bean salad from a container he pulled from the bag.

"He met Tiffany here?"

"Met her. Married her. Had a couple of kids."

"I'm surprised you haven't followed in his footsteps." The words slipped out and Chloe pressed her lips together. "Sorry, it's none of my business."

He shrugged, placed a plate in front of her. "I think a lot of people are surprised I haven't remarried, but what I had with Theresa was pretty special."

"What was she like?"

"Sweet. Soft-spoken. A little shy. Strong faith. Strong spirit. Really into homey things. Sewing. Cooking."

"She would have made a perfect pastor's wife."

"She would have, but that's not why I loved her." He sat down across from Chloe. "Unfortunately it's what just about every woman I've dated has been trying to be. I guess they all have the same idea about what it takes to be a pastor's wife."

"What's your idea?"

"My idea is that a pastor's wife should be whatever God calls her to be. Whether that means sewing, cooking, serving in church ministries, teaching. Computer forensics." He grinned, the humor in his eyes making the comment a joke rather than a promise. "We'd better eat before the puppies get restless. Do you mind if I ask the blessing?"

"Not at all."

Ben wrapped a hand around hers, his grip firm and strong as he offered a simple prayer of thanks.

This was what home should be. Not four walls and furniture, but companionship, friendship. Faith shared and expressed. The intimacy of the moment wrapped around Chloe's heart, holding it tight and promising something she shouldn't want, but did—more dinners, more quiet conversations, more Ben.

And that wasn't good at all.

As soon as Ben finished speaking, she tugged away from his hold, avoiding his deep blue gaze as she bit into the aromatic fish he'd prepared.

Ben's easy charm was nice, but there was no way she planned to fall for it. Her life was too complicated, her worries too real to waste energy and emotion on a relationship that was destined to fail the same way her other relationships had.

But what if it wasn't?

The question whispered through her mind, tempting her to believe in impossibilities, happily-ever-afters and a hundred dreams she'd buried with Adam and his betrayal.

But happily-ever-afters and dreams were for people who hadn't been deceived, people who still believed in love and all that it meant.

Chloe wasn't one of them.

Chapter Fourteen

They went for a walk after dinner, the two puppies tumbling along on leashes, the soft rustle of grass and the gentle lap of water against the shore filling the night. The waning moon cast a silvery glow across the dry grass, giving the world an ethereal beauty Chloe tried hard to appreciate. Tried. Despite Ben's presence, she didn't like being out after dark, the open space, the hulking trees and shadowy bushes taking on forms and faces that she was half convinced were real.

"Cold?"

She hadn't realized she was shivering until Ben spoke. At his words, she pulled her jacket closed, knowing it was fear and not the cold that had her shaking. "Maybe a little."

"Here." He shrugged off his jacket, draped it over her shoulders, the masculine outdoorsy scent of it surrounding Chloe.

"Now *you're* going to be cold."

"Not even close. My foster parents loved camping. They used to take us kids into the mountains every fall. *That* was cold. Compared to it, tonight is downright balmy." He wrapped a hand around her elbow, leading her along a sparsely covered patch of lawn, the rocks and soil treacherous under Chloe's unsteady gait.

"I've never been camping."

"Our church sponsors a youth camping trip every spring. You can sign up as chaperone and see what it's like."

"It sounds like fun, but spring is months away. Anything could happen before then."

"You think you'll move back to D.C.?"

"No, but I may not be able to stay here much longer."

"I know you're not asking for my opinion."

"But you'll give it anyway?"

He chuckled, the sound filling the night. "Something like that."

"Then I guess I'll ask. What's your opinion?"

"Trouble has a way of following us no matter how far we run from it. If we're going to have to face it anyway, we may as well face it with people who care about us."

"Maybe, but the trouble that's following me is dangerous. Not just to me, but to everyone around me. I couldn't live with myself if something happened to Opal because of me. I'd feel the same way if something happened to you, Tiffany or Jake."

"You're making our welfare your responsibility, but we can all take care of ourselves."

"That's what I thought about Adam and look what happened to him." An image filled her mind—fire, hot metal, Adam, blood seeping from his head and dripping onto the white shirt he wore.

"What happened to Adam had nothing to do with whether or not he could take care of himself. What Jackson did was unexpected. Something no one could have known to be prepared for. We're in a completely different situation now. We know there's potential danger and we're prepared for it."

"Forewarned is forearmed?"

"Exactly."

"It's not good enough, Ben. Until we find the person who's been stalking me, no one will be safe."

"Jake is working hard to find the answers we need." He turned her back toward the house. "I saw that you were working on your computer when I arrived. Dig anything up?"

"Not as much as I would have liked. I decided to look back over the cases I was working on before the accident. It's possible I've got information that I don't know I have. Something that a person might be willing to commit murder over to keep quiet."

"Maybe."

"But?"

"Someone has spent an awful lot of time trying to make it look like you're having a breakdown. I wonder why."

"Revenge?"

"That's the obvious reason, but usually acts of revenge are brutal and quick. This seems more like slow, malicious torture."

"I can't think of anyone who'd want to torture me. My clients and business acquaintances don't know me well enough to care. My friends have only been friends since I moved to D.C."

"How long ago was that?"

"Six years."

"Where were you before?"

"Chicago. I've got a few friends there that I still

keep in touch with, but I can't imagine any of them wanting to harm me."

"Maybe not, but the way I see it, what's going on is really personal, more personal than just wanting to keep you out of an investigation. Maybe even more personal than wanting to pay you back for a perceived wrong. If that's true, someone you know is doing this to you."

"If someone in my life hated me that much, wouldn't I know it?"

"Not necessarily." They'd reached the porch and Ben gestured to the swing. "Want to sit for a minute?"

"If I sit, I might not be able to get back up. My leg's been giving me trouble today." Not to mention the fact that she'd had about all she could take of the darkness. Having Ben around might offer some sense of security, but a warning was crawling up her spine. Outside was not where she should be and the quicker she got back into the apartment the happier she'd be.

"Too bad, but it's probably for the best. I've got to get home. I've got a sermon to deliver in the morning. I'll walk you up to your apartment and then head out." He lifted Cain, who was racing back and forth across the porch, and pushed open the front door.

"What's your sermon about?"

"If I told you that, you'd have no reason to come hear it."

"Who said I was thinking about coming?"

"You probably weren't, but I bet you are now."

Chloe laughed. "As a matter of fact, I am."

"Good. Keep thinking about it and I'll be looking for you tomorrow." He laced his fingers through hers and led her up the stairs, waiting while she closed and locked the door.

She could hear his retreating footsteps as she collapsed into the easy chair. Hanging out with Ben had been fun, almost exhilarating, but it had done nothing to solve her problems. What it *had* done was give her something to think about. For the past few months she'd waffled between believing a member of The Strangers was after her and believing she was coming unhinged. It hadn't occurred to her that something completely different might be going on. Her injuries, her grief, her surgeries had consumed her life and left no room for much more than reaction to the circumstances she'd found herself in.

It was time to change that. To act instead of react. To start using her skills to find the answers she needed—who? Why?

She grabbed her laptop, pulled the comforter off her bed and settled back into the chair, flicking on the television and letting background noise fade as she began searching through her files once again. This time, though, she also reread e-mails from friends and co-workers, searching for something that would point her in the right direction and praying that she'd know it if she saw it.

Fire. Heat. The screaming sound of sirens. Her own frantic cries for help choking and gasping out as she reached for Adam's hand. Get out. We need to get out! *The words shrieked through her mind, but she couldn't get the door open, couldn't find her way out of the smoke and flames. She banged her fist against the window and saw the shadow, leaning close, staring in at her, eyes glowing like the flames—red and filled with hate. She screamed, turning toward Adam, wanting desperately to wake him, to get them both out alive. But Adam wasn't there. Instead, she saw sandy hair,* broad shoulders, a strong face covered with blood. Blue eyes wide and lifeless.

Ben.

Chloe screamed again, lunging up, fighting against the seat belt and her pain. No. Not a seat belt. A blanket. Not a car. An easy chair. Not the past. The present.

She took a deep, steadying breath and lifted Abel, who sat whining on the floor. He felt warm and solid, his furry body comforting as Chloe stood and paced across the room. Seeing Ben in the nightmare had made it that much more terrifying, the new twist on the old dream filling her with dread.

"I need this to be over. Not tomorrow. Not the next day. Now. Before anyone else is hurt." The words were a prayer and a plea. One Chloe could only hope God heard and would answer. Anything else didn't bear thinking about.

She glanced at the clock. Four a.m. Too early to leave the house. Too late to try to get more sleep. She scratched the puppy under his chin and set him down on the floor. "How about a snack? Then we can do some more work on the computer."

Not that the hours she'd spent the previous night had revealed much. As far as she was concerned, she'd hit a dead end. She'd have to either find a way around it or take a different path.

"One that isn't as clearly connected to me. Maybe not a friend or a co-worker of mine. Maybe someone who…" What? Chloe shook her head, uncovered the plastic container of brownies Ben had left the previous night.

"I don't know who's after me, Abel, but I can tell you this—Ben's brownies are almost good enough to make me forget my worries for a while."

Almost, but not quite.

Chloe bit into the thick chocolate, poured a glass of milk, and sat down at her computer desk. Instead of logging on, she grabbed a pencil and piece of paper. Ben had given her a new possibility to consider. Were there others? Jackson was in jail, The Strangers weren't after her, she couldn't find any evidence that one of her friends or co-workers had an axe to grind with her. What else was there? Who else was there?

Adam's friends? His co-workers?

He'd been acting odd in the month before they broke up. After he'd confessed to seeing someone else, Chloe had chalked his behavior up to guilt and stress. Could something else have caused it?

She jotted a note down on the paper, wishing she could pick up the phone and call Ben, discuss the idea with him.

"Scratch that thought. I don't need to call Ben. I don't need to discuss my idea with him. I've got you to talk to, buddy." She bent down to stroke Abel's soft fur. "And a plate of brownies to devour."

But brownies were a poor substitute for human company and conversation, and Chloe figured she'd trade a brownie or two for someone willing to listen to her at this time of the morning.

She sighed, pacing across the floor, pulling back the curtains on the balcony door. The darkness beyond the window was complete, the moon already set, the stars hidden behind thick clouds. Soon it would be dawn, but until then, Chloe was alone, waiting for the darkness to disappear and for the bright light of day to pull her completely out of the nightmare.

Chapter Fifteen

It had been weeks since Chloe had been to church and she almost decided to skip it again, her throbbing head and aching leg protesting the hours spent in front of the computer. Only the thought of having to explain her absence to Opal got her in the shower, dressed and out the door. The church parking lot was nearly full when she arrived, the sanctuary buzzing with people as she moved down the aisle and found a seat near the back. Maybe if she was lucky, she'd go unnoticed, though based on the number of people who were looking her way, she doubted it.

"I *thought* that was your beat-up old Mustang in the parking lot. You should have called me. We could have ridden here together." Opal slid into the pew beside Chloe, hair bouncing around her square face, her dark gaze shrewd. "Everything go okay last night? You look a little pale."

"It was fine."

"Fine? You spent the evening with one of Lakeview's most eligible bachelors and all you can manage to say is that it was fine?"

"The food was wonderful."

"And the company?"

"Wonderful, too."

"I knew it."

"Knew what?"

"That you and Ben would hit it off. Now, tell me why you're so pale."

"I didn't sleep well."

"Because?"

"My leg's been bothering me." That was as much of the truth as she was prepared to give.

"You've got an appointment with the doctor this week, right?"

"Yes."

"Well, make sure you tell him how much trouble you're having. I don't like the way you've been limping around."

"I fractured my femur and crushed my knee, Opal. The pain from that isn't going to go away."

"I know, but I still don't like it." She sighed, her flowery perfume nearly choking Chloe as she leaned close and patted her hand. "I'm glad you're here this morning. I didn't think any of my children would settle close to home. I'm glad one finally had the good sense to move back."

"Really? One of the girls is planning to move here?" Chloe couldn't help hoping that Opal's third daughter Anna was the one who would be returning. Five years older than Chloe, she'd been a good role model and friend when they were kids.

"I'm talking about you." Opal huffed the words, her disgust obvious. "That you didn't realize that wounds me deeply, Chloe."

"Wounds you deeply? I think we're heading for a guilt trip. Which means you want something from me."

Opal chuckled, her hand wrapping around Chloe's, the skin, once smooth and pale, now wrinkled and spotted with age. Still, her grip was firm, her eyes bright. "You know me too well, my dear. I do have a favor to ask."

"Do you need me to open the store for you tomorrow?"

"No, nothing like that. I've decided to go…" she glanced around, her broad, strong face flushing pink "…on the senior singles trip."

"Senior singles trip?"

"To Richmond for a few days of shopping and fun. Our Sunday school has been planning the trip for a while. I figure since I had to cut my visit with Elizabeth short when Jenna went into labor, I deserve a few days off."

"It sounds like fun."

"It will be, but I'll be gone Thursday through Sunday. Mary Alice is going to work full time those days. Between you, her and Laura we should be okay."

"So what do you need me to do?"

"Can you bring my mail in the house and check on Checkers?"

"Checkers does not need to be checked on. He can fend for himself just fine."

"Checkers is a sweet cat once you get to know him. He just needs a lot of love."

"And a pound of flesh." Chloe had been to Opal's house one time since her return to Lakeview and during the visit she'd been attacked by a very fat, very grumpy black-and-white cat.

"He barely touched you, Chloe. I'd think a young

woman whose rearing I had a hand in would be too tough to complain about a tiny little scratch." Opal turned her attention to the pulpit and the choir that was filling the loft.

"It was more than a scratch, but I'll take care of Checkers anyway."

"Maybe I did raise you right after all." Opal smiled. "Just remember, Checkers is sweet, but he's finicky. He likes his dinner served at six o'clock on the dot. No sooner. No later."

Six o'clock in November meant being out past sundown. The thought filled Chloe with trepidation and she wiped a damp palm against her black skirt. "It might be better if I feed him in the afternoon. Maybe during my lunch break."

"The last time I went away Anna was in town. She put Checkers's food in the bowl in the morning and he refused to touch it. I'd hate to think of him going hungry for four days."

Chloe sighed. "All right. I'll feed him at six. Was there something else you needed me to do?"

"I need to go shopping and I need a fashion expert to come with me."

"Fashion expert? For a trip to Richmond?"

"I've got a date Friday night." Opal's cheeks went pink again and Chloe couldn't help smiling.

"A date with Sam?"

"If it's any of your business, yes."

"Good for you, Opal."

"So you'll come shopping?"

"I'm not a fashion expert."

"You're the closest thing I've got. What do you say? It'll only be for a few hours tomorrow night."

"What time?"

"As soon as we close the store."

"Sounds good." It would sound better if they were going during the day, but Chloe didn't have the heart to say no.

"Wonderful. We'll have dinner, spend a few hours clothes shopping, and—" Before she could complete the thought the call to worship began and the before-church chatter ceased.

That worked for Chloe.

The noisy prattle of the sanctuary had done nothing to ease her pounding headache or offer her relief from the tension she'd been feeling all morning. She'd come hoping to find some small sense of peace. All she'd found were more worries. The thought of taking care of Checkers, of driving to Opal's house at night, filled her with a sick dread. Going shopping after dark didn't make her any happier. The fact that either bothered her only made Chloe even more conscious of just how much her life had changed in the past eleven months.

The music faded and Ben strode to the pulpit, his long legs and broad shoulders showcased to perfection in a dark suit and light blue shirt. His words were strong, but not dramatic as he welcomed the congregation, prayed, then stepped aside so that the music minister could lead the first song. Chloe knew her attention should be on the man leading the music, but instead it was drawn to Ben again and again. His smile seemed to encompass the room, his eyes even more vivid in the bright light that streamed in through tall windows.

He scanned the sanctuary, his gaze traveling the room. There was no way he could see Chloe in the midst of the crowd, but somehow he found her, his eyes meeting hers, his lips quirking in a half smile that made her treacherous heart dance a jig.

"Are you going to sing, or just stand there gawking at Ben?" Opal elbowed Chloe in the side, her quiet hiss forcing Chloe's attention away from the man who'd been taking up too many of her thoughts during the past few days.

"I wasn't gawking." She'd been looking. Maybe even staring. But she hadn't been gawking.

"Good to know. Now sing before someone notices that you're not. I don't want to spend the entire ride to Richmond answering questions about your disinterest in music."

"No one's noticing, Opal."

"*Everyone's* noticing. Now, sing."

Chloe managed to do as Opal suggested without glancing at Ben again. By the time he stood up to deliver the sermon, the tension and anxiety that had accompanied her through the long predawn hours had finally eased, the familiar hymns and sweet sounds of voices joining in praise accomplishing what no amount of alone-time could.

When Ben finally spoke, his words about faith in the midst of crisis spoke to her soul, the message echoing the quiet yearning that had brought her back to her Bible again and again over the past few days. She might not understand God's plan or His will, but she had to trust that He would work His best in her life.

The sermon ended and Chloe stood for the final hymn, the quick movement making her lightheaded. She grabbed the front of the pew, holding herself steady as she tried to blink the darkness from the edges of her vision.

"Are you okay? You've gone white as a sheet." Opal touched her arm, true concern etching lines around her eyes and mouth.

"Fine. I just stood up too quickly."

Opal's lips tightened and she shook her head. "A little dizzy? Sit down. Put your head between your knees."

"That won't be necessary. I'm completely recovered."

"Are you sure? Maybe I should drive you home."

"And then have to come pick me up for work tomorrow? I don't think so."

"Chloe—"

"Opal, I'm fine. I promise."

Opal looked like she wanted to argue, but raising four kids must have taught her when to fight and when to let go. "All right, but if you get out to your car and change your mind let me know."

"I will."

"I'll call you this evening to finalize plans for my trip to Richmond."

"To check up on me, you mean."

"That, too. Now, I'd better go see if I can find Sam so I can let him know I'm definitely going on the trip." She leaned over and kissed Chloe's cheek. "Be good, my dear. And be careful."

"I will be."

Opal merged into the crowd that was exiting the sanctuary while Chloe held back, waiting until the room emptied and just a few clusters of people remained. When she was sure her limping progress wouldn't block anyone's exit, she stepped out into the aisle and headed to door.

"Chloe, I was hoping I'd see you here." Brian McMath stepped up beside her, his slim, runner's frame dressed to perfection in a dark suit and staid tie.

"Brian. It's good to see you again." And would

remain good as long as he didn't mention her scars again.

"I'm glad you feel that way. I've been thinking about the conversation we had the other day and I wanted to apologize if I came on too strong. I hope my interest in your scars and the medical treatment of them didn't make you uncomfortable." Coming from another doctor, the words might have sounded sincere. Coming from Brian McMath, they sounded phony and well-practiced.

"I appreciate your apology."

"Good. Then maybe you'll let me make things up to you. How about having lunch with me?" They stepped out of the sanctuary and headed toward the exit.

"I'm sorry, I can't."

"You have plans?"

"Yes." She planned to take Abel for a walk. Maybe take a nap.

"With Opal?"

Obviously, Brian wasn't going to give up. Chloe was about to tell him exactly what she had planned and why she wasn't going to disrupt those plans for him, when they stepped out into watery light and she saw Ben.

He looked great standing on the church steps, his hair curling around his collar, his relaxed confidence appealing. He must have sensed her gaze because he looked up, his half smile becoming a full-out grin as she approached.

"I thought I saw you sitting beside Opal. I'm glad you came." His hand was warm as he clasped it around hers, pulling her a step closer, his gaze settling on Brian. "I'm glad you're here, too, Brian. I hear things were hectic at the hospital this weekend. I thought maybe you'd be caught up in a case there."

"I don't believe in working on Sunday, pastor. I'm sure you know me well enough to know that."

"I'm sure I do." Ben smiled again, but Chloe had the distinct impression he didn't really care for the doctor or his comments.

Brian nodded, then turned to Chloe. "Since we're not going to be able to have lunch today, I'm going to take off. Maybe I'll see you at the quilting circle this Wednesday." He strode away before Chloe could comment and she wasn't sorry to see him leave.

"You're smiling. I guess that means you're glad to see him go."

"He's a little overwhelming."

"Good choice of words. So, maybe since you're not having lunch with Brian, you'd like to come over to my place and have lunch with me."

"Abel won't be happy if I leave him home alone much longer."

"You can bring him over."

"I don't want to put you out." She also didn't want to say no. No matter how much she knew she should.

"I've got beef stew and homemade rolls already made. More than enough for two people."

She really *should* refuse. Chloe knew it. But even as she was telling herself that she should stay away from Ben she was opening her mouth to agree. "Beef stew and rolls sound good. I can bring what's left of the brownies over for dessert."

"Sounds good. I'll meet you over at my place in fifteen minutes or so."

"See you then." Chloe limped down the steps and got in her car, sure that she was making a mistake. Allowing Ben into her life was dangerous for both of them. Chloe had already had her heart broken once, she had no intention of letting it happen again. But what bothered her more than thoughts of heartbreak was the dream—the image of Ben broken and lifeless in the front seat of a burning car.

Just thinking about it made her shudder. Sure Ben could take care of himself. Sure he was capable and strong, but Adam had been, too, and despite what Ben had said the previous night, Chloe couldn't help worrying.

She stepped out of the car and started up the porch steps, a flash of movement to the left catching her attention. She turned, her pulse leaping, her heart racing. She wasn't sure what she expected to see, but the small ball of fluff that was rushing toward her wasn't it. "Abel?"

She scooped the puppy up into her arms, fear burning a path down her throat and settling deep in her stomach. "How'd you get out here?"

She asked, but she really didn't want to know, didn't want to imagine someone opening her apartment door while she was gone, didn't want to think that someone might still be there. Instead, she stumbled back toward her car, locked herself inside, hesitating with her hand on the phone. She hadn't crated Abel before she'd left. Was it possible he'd snuck out the door while she was leaving? Slipped down the stairs and out the door without her notice?

Maybe.

Or maybe someone had broken into her apartment and inadvertently let him out. She could call the police. She could go see if her apartment door was open.

She could sit here all day trying to decide what to do.

She rubbed the puppy's fur, wishing she didn't have

so much doubt in her ability to know real danger from imagined. She didn't want to call the police and look like a fool. She didn't want to not call if something was really going on. Abel growled a deep warning that made the hair on the back of Chloe's neck stand on end. She scanned the driveway, the yard, the trees. The porch.

She froze, watching in horror as the door she'd left closed slowly began to open.

Chapter Sixteen

Ben hadn't planned on inviting Chloe to lunch. Then again, he hadn't planned on seeing her at church. When he'd glanced around the sanctuary and caught sight of her, the jolt of awareness he'd felt was an unexpected surprise.

"I don't know what your plans are, Lord, but I sure would like to. Chloe's not the kind of woman I can be just friends with. If that's all You've got planned for us, I'm not sure I'm up for the task."

Cain barked, his feet slipping on tile as he raced through the kitchen and parked himself in front of the front door.

"Are they here?" Ben strode across the room and nudged Cain out of the way as a soft tap sounded on the wood. "Hi..."

The greeting died on his lips as he caught sight of Chloe, her face white, the few freckles that dusted the bridge of her nose standing out in sharp contrast.

He pulled her into the house, his hands skimming down thin arms and coming to rest on her waist. She was shaking, her breath coming in short, quick gasps. "Hey, are you okay?"

"Yes. No." A tear rolled down her cheek, and she swiped it away, the gesture abrupt and filled with irritation.

"What's wrong?"

"Everything." She sniffed back more tears, pacing across the room, her limp pronounced, her posture stiff.

"That covers a lot of bases, Chloe."

"It does, doesn't it?"

"What happened?" He urged her around to face him. Her eyes were deep emerald and filled with stark emotion. Anger. Frustration. Not the fear or sadness he'd expected to see.

"Just one more piece of evidence proving that I'm as unhinged as the D.C. police think."

"No one thinks you're unhinged."

"No, they just believe my imagination is working overtime. The worst part is, they're right."

"You've got a reason for saying that. Why don't you tell me?"

"Abel was outside when I got home from church. I hadn't left him out there."

Ben's hand tightened on Chloe's shoulder and he had to force his grip to ease. "Did you call Jake?"

"I was going to. I got in my car and grabbed the phone, but my downstairs neighbor came out before I made the call. I guess Abel was hanging out in the foyer. Connor thought he was a stray and put him outside. He was very apologetic."

She paused, a smile chasing away some of her irritation. "The fact that I was having a panic attack when he came outside sent him into fits of remorse. He wanted to call an ambulance, but I told him I'd be fine once I stopped hyperventilating."

She was making light of the situation, but Ben knew it had bothered her a lot more than she was saying. "I'm sure he'll get over the trauma eventually. Did you ever call Jake?"

"So he could come and tell me that Abel slipped out of the house while I was leaving?" She raked a hand through her hair and shook her head. "No way. I've been through that kind of embarrassment one too many times."

"I think it's better to be a little embarrassed than a lot dead." The words were harsher than he'd meant them and Chloe stiffened, the color that had slowly returned to her face gone again.

"Connor went up to the apartment with me. It was locked up tight. No sign that anyone had been there. Nothing out of the ordinary."

"That's how your apartment was when we found the photos on your digital camera and how it was when you overdosed on pain medication you've said you didn't take." His words were hard, ground out through gritted teeth and frustration. Chloe was an intelligent, strong woman. The fact that she seemed to *want* to believe that she was imagining things was something he couldn't understand.

"But this time nothing happened. No weird photos. No missing medicine."

"How do you know, Chloe? Did you check every container in your refrigerator? Make sure the furnace hadn't been tampered with? We need to call Jake and let him do what he does best—look for evidence."

"And when he finds nothing, I'll be right back where

I started—struggling to figure out what's going on while everyone around me insists that nothing is."

"You'll never be back where you started." He smoothed the bangs out of her eyes, silky strands of hair catching on his rough palms. "You have people here who believe in you. That's not going to change."

"Won't it? What if this stuff goes on for a month? Two months? Don't you think Jake is going to get a little tired of running to my rescue when there's nothing to rescue me from?"

"There's something to rescue you from, Chloe. Just because we don't know what that is yet, doesn't mean it isn't real. Jake knows that. I know that. Neither of us are going to give up until we find the person responsible for everything that's happened to you."

She smiled, moving away from his touch, her hair sliding over his knuckles, the dark strands falling over her shoulders and covering the scars on her neck. What she'd been through couldn't be hidden, though. It lived in her eyes and her voice. "I think I know that, but I still don't want to go through the same thing I went through in D.C., feeling sure something terrible was going to happen only to have the police prove me wrong every time."

"They didn't prove you wrong. They just never proved you right. That's what we're going to do and the first step is letting Jake take a look at your apartment."

"He can look, but you're the one who's going to take responsibility if he decides it was a big waste of his time."

"Jake's philosophy is better safe than sorry. I feel the same." Ben picked up the phone and dialed Jake's home number, antsy to get things moving. No way did he believe Chloe had let Abel out of the apartment without realizing it. If she hadn't let the puppy out, someone else had. The sooner they discovered what that person had been doing in her apartment, the better Ben would feel.

"Reed here."

"Jake, it's Ben."

"What's up?"

"We've got a situation. I thought you might like to check it out."

"Tell me."

Ben gave Jake the details, knowing his friend would be as anxious to find out what was going on as he was.

"I'll be at your house in fifteen minutes. If Chloe gives me the key, I can go back to her apartment and check things out."

"Thanks."

"What did he say?" Chloe leaned against the wall, her posture deceptively relaxed, the anxiety she'd managed to harness showing only in her white-knuckled fists.

"He'll be here in fifteen minutes to get your keys. He wants to check things out."

"There won't be any evidence to lead him in the right direction. There never is."

"This time might be different."

"Or it might be the same as every other time." She smiled, but the frustration in her eyes was unmistakable. "I'm ready for the nightmare to be over, but no matter how hard I look, I can't see any ending to it."

"There's an ending to it. It may take time, but we'll find it." Ben pulled her forward, wrapping his arms around her waist. She leaned her head against his chest, her hair tickling his chin, a subtle floral scent drifting on the air. He wanted to inhale deeply, take it into his lungs and savor it. Memorize it so that in five years, ten, twenty, he'd remember standing in his house with Chloe, staring out over the parsonage yard, realizing…

What?

That it felt right, good, *permanent*. That there was going to be much more to their relationship than either of them expected or even wanted.

He shoved aside the thought, but didn't move away from Chloe. Partly because holding her *did* feel right, partly because she seemed to need his support.

Her hands rested on his waist, her body not stiff, but not relaxed, either. As if she didn't want to allow herself to get too close. And maybe she didn't. She'd been through a lot with Adam. Keeping her distance might be the only way she felt she could keep her heart intact.

"You're right about it taking time to find the answers, Ben." She spoke quietly, lifting her head so that she could meet his gaze, her eyes the color of spring's promise, but filled with the starkness of winter. "That's exactly what I'm worried about. Time. I think it's running out."

He wished he could tell her she was wrong, but he felt the same way. Time wasn't on their side and the longer it took for them to track down Chloe's stalker, the more likely it was that that person would act again. Maybe next time with more serious results. "God is in control, *not* the person who's stalking you. It's His timing, His will that's going to be done. We can take comfort in that."

"Maybe so, but right now it seems like a cold comfort." She frowned, stepped out of his arms. "I've been a Christian since I was fifteen. I *know* God will work things out in His time and His way. I just wish I knew what that meant for my life."

"I think that's the hardest thing about faith, Chloe. Trusting the driver even when we can't clearly see the road He's taking us on."

"Oh, I can see the road all right. It's covered with ice and has a hundred-foot drop on either side."

Ben chuckled, smoothing his hands over Chloe's silky hair, framing her face with his palms. "If God's the driver, you don't have to worry about going over the edge."

"Maybe that's the problem. Maybe I've been doing most of the driving these past few years."

"If that's the case, you'd better take it slow and drive carefully."

"You're not going to tell me I should get out of the driver's seat?" She raised a dark eyebrow, the smile that curved her lips softening the sharp line of her jaw.

"I didn't think you'd want to hear me say something you already know."

"I do know it, but doing it isn't always as easy as it should be. I like plans. I like purpose. I like to know where I'm headed." She turned to stare out the window, her gaze fixed on some distant point. A thought. A memory. Something sad and ugly from the look in her eyes.

He wrapped an arm around her waist, tugging her back against his chest, wanting to offer comfort, but not sure that words could touch the hurt that Chloe tried so hard to hide. "There is a plan, you know. And a purpose. Whether you see it or not."

She nodded, her hair brushing against his chin, the silky strands reminding him of long-ago days, of femininity and softness, sweet smiles and gentle laughter. It had been a long time since he'd had any of those things in his life. Today, with Chloe in his arms and the gray-gold beauty of autumn outside the window, he missed them more than he had since the first days following Theresa's death.

That meant something and he couldn't ignore it. If there was one thing he'd learned from watching Theresa live, watching her die, it was that life was too short to waste time, to make excuses, to turn away from what God willed and wanted. His wife had embraced every challenge, every problem with open arms and an open heart. She hadn't let fear stop her, hadn't let her disease keep her from the things she felt called to do. Her example had set the course for much of Ben's life in the years since he'd buried her.

And it would set his course now.

If this was what God had planned for his life, if *Chloe* was, he wouldn't turn his back on it.

His arm tightened a fraction on her waist and he pulled her a little closer. One way or another, he had a feeling that with Chloe things were going to get a whole lot worse before they got better.

Chapter Seventeen

Jake arrived less than fifteen minutes after Ben called him, his face set in hard lines, his long legs eating up the ground as he paced Ben's living room. He didn't look happy and Chloe figured that could only mean bad news.

"I just got a call from a friend on the Arlington police force. He heard I was checking into your case and thought I might be interested in knowing that your fiancé had filed a crime report a few months before he was killed. Did you know that?"

"Yes. It didn't seem like a big deal at the time. Someone broke into his apartment, took a watch, a tie and cuff links. A few dollar bills he'd left lying on his dresser."

"It didn't seem like a big deal at the time, but now it does?"

"I was thinking about things last night. Ben had asked me if I'd felt stalked before the accident. The weeks leading up to it are blurry, but I don't recall anything strange happening. To me."

"But things *were* happening to Adam?" Jake pulled

his notebook out, started writing. "What besides the break-in?"

"What are you thinking, Jake?" Ben lounged near the door, his shoulder against the wall, his thick hair mussed.

"I'm thinking there may be a connection between the break-in and the accident. I'm thinking that maybe Adam is that connection. That he was the intended victim, not Chloe."

"I wondered that, too, but why try to kill Adam by sabotaging *my* car?"

"Good question. I don't have an answer yet, but I plan to find one." Jake paced back across the room, paused in front of Chloe, his dark blue eyes staring into hers. "Do you have any ideas? Anything that didn't seem important at the time, but that seems like it might be connected now."

"Yes."

"You answered pretty quickly."

"Like I said, I was thinking about it last night. I planned to call you tomorrow."

"You should have called me this morning."

"What's done is done, Jake. Let's move on from here." Ben seemed completely at ease, but Chloe sensed a tension in him that belied his relaxed posture.

"Good point." Jake's sharp gaze was still on Chloe "So, tell me what you thought of last night."

"Not much, just some little things that didn't seem related when I looked at them separately. Once I started connecting the dots, they seemed to make a cohesive picture."

"Go ahead."

"A week or so before we broke up, Adam had his

cell phone and home phone number changed. He said he was getting too many crank calls."

"Did you ask him what he meant?"

"Yes. He didn't give me a lot of details. Just said he was getting a lot of hang ups during the day and in the middle of the night. Once he had the number changed everything seemed fine."

She hesitated, then continued. "After I found out he'd been seeing someone else, I figured the calls had been from his girlfriend and put the issue out of my mind."

"Anything else?"

"Nothing definitive. Just a sense I had that something was wrong. In the months before we broke up, even in the weeks after, Adam didn't seem himself."

"He was seeing another woman and hiding it from you. Once you did find out, you broke up with him. I think that's a good reason to not be himself."

"That's what I thought, but Adam didn't believe in dwelling on things. Whether it was his mistake or someone else's, he was always quick to forgive and move on. Maybe I'm wrong, but when I think back, it seems like he was worried. Maybe even scared. And that wasn't like Adam at all."

"Looking backward at something doesn't often give us a clear picture." But as he spoke, Jake was scribbling in his notebook.

"Maybe not, but I've struggled to think of a reason someone would want to hurt me. If the stalker is after me because of The Strangers case, why the slow torture? Why not just do what Jackson did and get it over with quickly? If he's trying to keep me from discovering information hidden in one of the computers I was working on before the accident, he succeeded. I quit my job. Moved away. Why keep coming after me and risk being found out?"

"You're making good points."

"They're Ben's not mine, but they make sense."

"They do and they're leading in the direction I've been thinking this case was going—if we're going to find your stalker we need to start looking at people who knew your fiancé, who were close to him, who might have had something to gain from his death and yours."

"Everyone loved Adam. I can't imagine someone wanting to hurt him."

"Someone did hurt him. It's time to find out who. When I get back to the office, I'm going to call and see if any evidence was collected from Adam's apartment after the break-in, and I'm going to see if I can get copies of phone records for his two old numbers. Maybe we'll find a pattern of calls, match a number and name to it. You make a list of Adam's friends and co-workers. And see if you can track down the name of the woman he was seeing."

"His business partner might be able to tell me. James and Adam went to high school together. They were like brothers."

"Then that's where you should start. I'm going to head over to your apartment and do the preliminary walk-through. You can meet me there in a half hour and we'll go through the place together."

He stepped out the door and drove away, leaving Chloe alone with Ben again. She wasn't sure how she felt about that. In the moments before Jake had arrived, she'd stood with Ben's arm wrapped around her waist, his breath ruffling her hair, the comfort of his presence making her want to lean back against his chest, accept his support. His strength.

She hadn't, but that was more a matter of timing than willpower. If Jake hadn't arrived and broken the silence that seemed filled with dreams and hopes, Chloe might have caved in to temptation, allowed herself to lean on Ben for a just a little while.

And that would have been a disaster. A little while with Ben could never be enough.

"Did you love him?" Ben's question pulled Chloe from her thoughts and she met his eyes, saw sympathy and concern in his gaze.

Had she loved Adam?

For a while she'd thought so, his attentiveness, humor and gregarious personality a perfect foil for her own more serious nature. Things had changed though, the excitement of new love fading. Or maybe the relationship hadn't changed as much as Chloe's perception of it had. She'd wanted to be first, not second, a necessity rather than an extra, a vital part of Adam's life rather than one more person to spend time with. She wanted so much more than what Adam wanted to give.

"I thought I did, but I don't think I knew what love really was."

"And you do now?"

"Now I know what it isn't."

"What's that?"

"Physical attraction, a sudden thrill of emotion when you see the person walk into the room." She shrugged. "In the end, I wanted more than that. Loyalty. Friendship. Shared goals and dreams. Maybe I wanted too much."

"I don't think you wanted any more than what you

deserve." Ben was standing so close Chloe could see the flecks of silver in his eyes, could smell the woodsy fragrance that clung to him, feel the heat of his body warming the air around her.

She stepped back, swallowing past her suddenly dry throat. Everything she'd wanted from Adam, everything he couldn't give, she could see in Ben's eyes.

That wasn't good. At all.

She started toward the front door, wanting to put distance between them. "It must be time to go over to my house now."

"Why? Am I making you uncomfortable?"

"Not at all."

He grinned, a slow deliberate curving of his lips, his eyes flashing with humor. "Could have fooled me. But you're right, we'd better get going. Grab your pup. I'll grab mine and we'll head out."

"You don't have to come."

"Is that the same as, 'I don't want you to come'?"

She wanted to say yes, but couldn't get the word past her lips. How could it be that in just over a week of knowing the man, he'd become such a big part of her life? She shook her head, lifting Abel and carrying him toward the door. "No. It's the same as 'You don't have to come.'"

He smiled, looped an arm through hers. "In that case, I think I'll tag along."

Ben's cell phone rang before they could walk out the door. "Give me a minute to get this. It might be an emergency."

He lifted the phone, frowning as he glanced at the caller ID. "It's Jake. He must have found something."

Chloe tensed, not sure what Jake was going to say, but pretty certain it wouldn't be good.

"Hello? Yeah, we're still at my place." He met Chloe's eyes, the heat of his gaze spearing through Chloe.

She paced across the room, her heart beating a hard, fast rhythm. She told herself it was from fear, that worry over what Jake had to say was causing her pulse to race, but she knew that was only part of the truth.

"I'll ask her. Chloe?"

She turned to face Ben again, steeling herself against the force of his gaze and for whatever he had to say. "Yes?"

"Whose photo was on your dresser?"

"No one's. I've got photographs hanging on my wall, but nothing on my dresser."

Ben relayed the information to Jake, listened for a moment, then nodded. "We'll be there in ten."

He hung up the phone and pulled open the door, gesturing for Chloe to step outside. "Jake found a photograph on your dresser. A picture of a man and woman. Both their heads have been cut out of the photo. You didn't see it when you got home this afternoon?"

"I didn't walk through the apartment. I just grabbed Abel's leash and the brownies and left. Since the door was locked, I assumed no one had been there."

"Someone was. Who has the key besides you?"

"My landlady. Opal. That's it."

"Who would have had access to it?"

"No one."

"Then whoever it was got in some other way. Let's get over to your place and see what Jake is thinking."

Chloe stepped outside, the cool overcast day doing nothing to reassure her as she hurried to her car and pulled open the door. Ben stopped her before she got in, his hand on her arm, his expression grim. "When we get to your place, Jake is going to ask a lot of questions. He comes off as gruff, but he means well."

"I get that about him."

"Good, because if you've got any idea who might be behind this, you need to tell him. No matter how unlikely you think it is. Any clue. Any detail you remember that might seem insignificant. He needs to know it all if he's going to be able to help you."

"If I had any idea who was behind what's been going on, I would have told the D.C. police." She shoved her bangs out of her eyes, disgusted to realize her hand was shaking. "But I'll answer his questions the best way I can. I'm as anxious as he is to get this all over with."

"It'll be over soon." Ben pulled her into a brief hug before he started toward his car. "I'll follow you to your place."

Chloe climbed into the Mustang and pulled out onto the road, her stomach churning with nerves. When she was in D.C. she'd been desperate for someone to believe in her. Now she had two people standing beside her, doing everything they could to help her. Three if she counted Opal. That should have made her feel better. Instead, it increased her worry.

"But I'm not going to worry. I'm going to act. The answers are somewhere. I just have to find them." She muttered the words and Abel barked, as though agreeing.

She absently patted his head, her mind racing ahead. To the apartment. To the conversation she was about to have with Jake. To what needed to be done to find out who might have wanted to hurt Adam. Who was still trying to hurt Chloe.

"Lord, I'm going to need your help on this in a big

way. The path I'm on is treacherous, but I know you can steer me to safety."

The prayer whispered through her mind as Chloe pulled up in front of the Victorian and stepped out of the car, waiting for Ben to do the same.

Chapter Eighteen

Jake was waiting in her apartment, a silver frame held in gloved hands. She knew the picture even before she got close enough to see it. The old-fashioned silver frame was one she'd bought from an antique dealer in Georgetown, the Victorian scrolling and fine details easily recognizable.

"I found this on your dresser. Is it yours?" As Ben had predicted, Jake's words were as gruff as ever, his gaze hard.

"Yes. It's our engagement picture. We had it taken a few weeks after Adam proposed. I couldn't make myself throw it away. I gave it to Adam's parents before I moved." She leaned close, blanching as she caught sight of the photograph.

Adam's face had been cut out, leaving a neat oval where his head had been. Chloe's image had fared even worse. It looked like someone had taken a razor blade and sliced through that side of the photo over and over again.

"Call them. See what they did with it."

It wasn't a request and Chloe didn't even consider

arguing. Her heart was pounding as she lifted the phone and dialed the familiar number.

"Hello?" The once vibrant voice of Karen Mitchell sounded weak and quiet, as if losing her only son had sapped some of her own life.

"Karen? It's Chloe."

"Chloe! How are you feeling, dear?"

"Fine. I just—"

"Then you're over your cold? I'm glad. You've been through so much this past year. Did the picture arrive in one piece?"

"Picture?" Chloe's hand tightened around the phone, her heart racing so fast she was sure she it would jump out of her chest.

"Your engagement photo. That is what you wanted me to send, isn't it?"

"Karen, I didn't ask you send the engagement picture. I didn't ask you to send anything."

"Dear, you called me last week and asked me to send it to you."

"No, I—"

Jake shook his head, a sharp, quick gesture that stalled the words in Chloe's throat. "Ask her where she sent it."

"Karen, listen, can you give me the address you sent the photo to?"

"So it didn't arrive? What a shame. I know how much the picture means to you."

"Do you have the address I gave you?"

"Of course. It's right in my address book." Papers rustled, Karen's words carrying over the sound and the throbbing pulse of Chloe's terror. "Here it is." She rattled off the address, a PO box that Chloe didn't recognize.

She wrote it down, her hand trembling, the letters and numbers wobbly and unclear. "Okay. Thanks."

"Is everything all right, dear? You don't seem yourself."

"Everything is fine. Listen, I was wondering if you still had Adam's laptop."

Jake raised an eyebrow at the question, but kept silent as she continued the conversation.

"Not his laptop. Jordyn said it belonged to the business. I do have his other computer, though. It's in the spare room with his other things. I haven't had the heart to go through everything."

"I understand. And I hate to even bring this up, but I'd really like to take a look at the computer. Can I send you the money to have it shipped here?"

Karen was silent for a moment. When she spoke, her voice was stronger than it had been. "Is something going on, Chloe?"

"I'm not sure. I'm hoping that Adam's computer might help me figure it out."

"I'll send it to you then. Shall I ship it to the same address?"

"No. Send it to this one." Chloe rattled off her address and phone number, then hung up, her pulse racing with anticipation and with fear.

"Asking for the computer was good thinking. If Adam was having trouble with someone, there may be evidence of that on his computer." Ben was holding Abel, his strong hand smoothing the puppy's long fur.

"That's what I'm hoping."

"What *I'm* hoping," Jake interrupted their conversation. "Is that our perpetrator's mistake will be to our benefit."

"Mistake?" In Chloe's estimation, her stalker had made far too few of those.

"The PO box. He had to have known how easily he could be traced through it."

"Maybe he didn't care." Ben sat on the couch, stretching his long legs, looking as if he belonged there.

"Or she." Jake leaned a shoulder against the wall, his brow creasing. "Someone was impersonating Chloe. It would be hard for a man to sound like a woman."

"A woman." Chloe rolled the words across her tongue, testing them out. "That would make sense."

"Hell hath no fury like a woman scorned." Jake muttered the words, his gaze on the photo. "And based on the way you've been carved out of this photo, I'm thinking someone definitely felt scorned."

"All we need to do is find out who." Chloe glanced at the photo again.

"Any ideas?"

"No, but the answer may lie in Adam's computers. Karen's going to send me his PC. I'll see if I can get James's permission to take a look at his laptop. E-mails. Old files. There may be a name there somewhere. If there is, I'll find it."

"Good. While you do that, I'll check into phone records and get information on our PO box owner."

"How long will that take?" Ben asked the question that was foremost in Chloe's mind.

"A few days, but getting the information is no guarantee we'll find our stalker. It's unlikely our perp is using a real name. In the long run, that won't matter. We're going to find our quarry. It's only a matter of time." Jake placed the framed photo in an evidence bag, sealed it closed. "I've already dusted for prints and checked to see if the locks on the balcony or front door were jimmied."

"Were they?" Chloe would rather think someone had jimmied her door than spend hours worrying that someone had her key.

"Not that I could see, but it wouldn't take much to open your front door. A credit card would probably do it."

"I thought that was only in the movies."

"No. It's a pretty simple thing to do once you know how. It's probably a good idea if you get new locks and bolts installed."

"I can call someone tomorrow."

"Or we can take care of it today." Ben stood and strode to the balcony door. "This one needs a bolt, too."

"I'm on the second floor."

"And your neighbors are gone more than they're home. It wouldn't be hard for someone to use a ladder to gain access to your apartment."

"Ben's right. It doesn't make sense to take chances. I'm going to get back to the office and run the prints I've found. Make a few phone calls. I'll be sending patrol cars down this way every hour or so until we get this case solved."

"I appreciate it."

"Just be careful and watch your back." Jake strode out the door and Ben started after him.

"I'm going to run to the hardware store and go home for some tools. Then I'll be back. Keep the door bolted until then."

"I've got tools."

"What kind?"

"What do you need?" Chloe hurried to her room and

pulled a small toolbox from her closet, setting it on the bed and opening it.

"That looks pretty complete. I don't suppose you have spare locks in there."

"Spare locks aren't on the list of things a single woman needs to keep in her house."

"But pink hammers are?" He lifted the tool, smiling a little as he hefted the weight in his hand.

"Just because it's pink doesn't mean it's not functional."

"I'm sure it's functional. I'm just surprised."

"That it's functional? Or that I have a pink hammer?"

"That you'd choose something so frivolous. You told me the day we met that you weren't into frivolous things."

"The hammer isn't frivolous. It's functional and cute. And if you keep making fun of it, you might just end up with one for Christmas."

"We're going to exchange Christmas gifts?" He raised a brow, a smile hovering at the corner of his lips.

"Maybe. If I live that long." She meant it as a joke, but the words fell flat, the worry behind them seeping through. "Forget I said that."

"You know I can't." His hand cupped her jaw, his fingers caressing the tender flesh near her ear. "And you know I'm going to tell you everything will be okay. That Christmas will come and you'll be here to see it."

"I wish I were as confident of that as you are."

"I'll be confident for both of us." His gaze drifted from her eyes to her mouth, his fingers smoothing a trail from her jaw to her neck as he leaned toward her. "I shouldn't do this."

"No, you shouldn't."

"So tell me to stop."

She should, she really should. But she didn't. And as he leaned toward her, she leaned forward. Just a fraction of an inch, but it was enough. His lips brushed hers, the contact shivering through her.

She jerked back, nearly falling into the closet.

"Whoa!" Ben grabbed her arm, pulling her up before she landed in a heap on top of her shoes. "Careful."

"Sorry." Her cheeks were on fire, her heart skipping. This was definitely not good.

So why did she feel so happy about it?

"Don't apologize." Ben seemed completely unperturbed. "I'm not planning to."

He strode out of the room and out the front door, leaving Chloe alone with the two puppies. Curled up on the kitchen floor, neither bothered to rouse as she grabbed aspirin from the counter and swallowed two.

Ben had kissed her.

Or maybe she'd kissed Ben.

She wasn't sure which was more the truth and was pretty sure it didn't matter. After almost a year of saying that she would never, ever, *ever* get involved with another man, she'd just allowed herself to do exactly that.

"This isn't good, boys. It isn't good at all."

Neither of the puppies responded and Chloe dropped down into a chair, wincing as her leg protested the movement. "I think I need to go back to sleep and start this day all over again."

But she couldn't.

So the best thing she could do was get busy, take her mind off her terror and her confusing feelings for Ben.

Confusing?

Not hardly.

She knew exactly what she was feeling. That was the problem.

"Enough of this. I've got plenty to do besides mooning over a man."

She logged onto her computer, pulled up her address book and dialed James Kelly's home number. Adam's business partner and fellow private investigator, James had been the one who'd first contacted Chloe, bringing her in on an investigation he and Adam were working together. He'd been thrilled when she and Adam began dating, devastated when they'd broken up. In the months following Adam's death, shared grief had made Chloe's friendship with James even stronger.

Still, talking to him about Adam's betrayal, trying to get information about the woman he'd been seeing, wasn't something Chloe had ever planned to do.

"Hello?"

"James? It's Chloe."

"Finally. My wife's been telling me not to call and check in on you, but I was getting close to ignoring her suggestion and giving you a ring."

"Were you really going to call to see how I was doing or were you going to call and ask me to take on a few cases?"

"Maybe a little of both."

Chloe smiled, imagining James's round face and balding head. A year older than his friend, James had always been more settled, more staid, maybe a little more boring than Adam. His generous spirit and calm nature had drawn others to him and had been the backbone of the private investigation service he'd co-owned with Adam. "Then I'll answer both. I'm doing fine. I don't freelance anymore."

"That's too bad. I haven't been able to find anyone as good as you."

"Or as reasonably priced?"

"That, too." There was a smile in his voice and Chloe felt some of the tension of the day easing.

"Keep looking. Eventually you will."

"If you'd agree to do a few simple jobs for me, I wouldn't have to go to all that effort."

"Few and simple? I doubt it."

James chuckled. "True. So, if you didn't call to tell me you were going back to work, what did you call about?"

"I have a favor to ask."

"Go ahead."

"Do you still have Adam's work laptop?"

"In my office. It hasn't been used since…he passed away."

"Do you mind if I take a look at it?"

"Take a look at it as in dig inside and see what you find?"

"Yes."

"Should I ask why?"

"It's complicated."

"I don't like the sound of that. Is everything okay?"

"It'll be better after I get the laptop." She hoped.

"I'll have Jordyn send it to you first thing tomorrow morning. Do we have your new address on file?"

"I gave it to Jordyn before I left."

"Then you can expect to get the laptop by the end of the week. And I'll be expecting to hear just exactly what you were searching for once you find it."

"It's a deal, James. Thanks a lot." She hesitated, not wanting to ask the next question no matter how much she knew it needed asking. "Listen, there's one more thing."

"What's that?"

"I've been wondering about the months before the accident. Adam didn't seem like himself in the weeks before it happened."

"You two had broken up. It was a pretty rough time for him."

"You know why we broke up, right?" She hadn't told him, but she was sure Adam had.

He was silent for a moment, then spoke quietly, his voice more subdued. "Yes. I was surprised and disappointed when Adam told me he was the cause. You two were the perfect match. I told him I couldn't understand why he'd mess that up."

Chloe ignored the last comment, not wanting to discuss her own disappointments, her own sense of failure. "You said you were surprised. You didn't know he was seeing someone?"

"Not until after the breakup. Even then he probably wouldn't have told me. If…"

"What?"

"I was being a little hard on you. I thought you'd just decided to call things off. He didn't want you taking the rap, so he told me what'd happened."

"Did he tell you who the other woman was?"

"No."

"Would you tell me if he had?"

"Chloe, Adam is gone. I don't have to keep his secrets anymore." The sadness in his voice was unmistakable and Chloe could feel her own grief welling up.

"Do you think there's anyone who does know?"

"You know how he was. A different lunch da— companion every day. Too many friends to count. He had more on his social calendar for a week than I usually have all month, but I doubt there was anyone who knew him better than we did. If neither us knew who she was. No one did." He sighed.

"You're right, but if you think of anything—or anyone—"

"I'll let you know." He sighed. "I've got to get going. My wife is waiting for me to take her to dinner. Jordyn will send you the laptop. Let me know if you need anything else. And if you decide to go back to freelancing, I want to be the first client on your list."

"I'll keep that in mind."

"He really did love you, Chloe. You know that don't you?"

"No." She swallowed back sadness and regret. "I don't, but thanks for saying it. I'll be in touch."

She hung up the phone before he could say more, unwilling to discuss what she mostly refused to even think about. Maybe he was right, maybe Adam *had* loved her in his own way. But in the end that hadn't been enough for either of them.

Chloe forced her sadness away, forced herself to brew a pot of coffee, to feed the puppies, to get her mind off the past and into the present. Ben would be back soon. They'd put new locks and bolts on the doors, but Chloe wasn't foolish enough to think that would keep her safe. Only one thing could do that— finding the person stalking her. In a couple days, she'd have both of Adam's computers. If there was information on them, some hint about what had been going on in the months before his death, she'd find it.

Chapter Nineteen

Monday morning came too early, the alarm sounding an insistent beep that pulled Chloe from restless sleep and into the new day. She groaned and yanked the covers over her head, wishing she could ignore the sound and go back to sleep.

Unfortunately, even if she'd been willing to face Opal's wrath—which she wasn't—she couldn't ignore Abel's muffled cries. Obviously he was as ready to be out of his bed as Chloe was to stay in hers.

"I'm coming."

She felt sluggish and off balance as she stumbled to the shower wishing she'd gotten into bed at a much earlier hour. Especially since she'd done absolutely nothing constructive during the hours she'd been awake. After she and Ben put bolts on the front and balcony doors, he'd left for home, rushing to get ready for the evening service. A service Chloe might have attended if she hadn't been worried about what might happen in her apartment during her absence.

And if she hadn't wanted to put some distance between herself and Ben.

Working together in the apartment had felt comfortable, their movements in sync, their conversations easy; Chloe had found herself thinking about spending time with him next week, next month, next year. That worried her almost as much as the kiss.

So, instead of enjoying fellowship and fun, she'd locked herself in the apartment and spent most of the night pacing the floor, checking the locks, listening for footfalls on the stairs, imagining the doorknob slowly turning.

"Good choice, Chloe." She scowled at her reflection in the mirror as she scraped still-wet hair into a ponytail. Her skin was pallid, the freckles on her nose and cheeks standing out in stark relief, the hollows under her cheeks shadowed. The day had barely begun and she was already tired and out of sorts. The worst part was, she'd left the container of brownies at Ben's house the previous day and couldn't find a drop of chocolate in the house.

"Opal better have some at the shop, Abel, or I'm going to leave you with her and go hunt some down." She lifted the puppy, attached his leash and started toward the front door.

As tired as she felt, she was glad to be going to work. At least when she was at Blooming Baskets she wouldn't be alone. Opal would be there, customers would drop by, Jenna would probably stop in for a few hours with the baby. There'd be plenty to keep Chloe's mind off her nightmares.

And off Ben.

And the kiss.

And the way her heart melted when she looked into his eyes.

"Stop it! He's a man. Just like any other man you know."

Liar.

Maybe. But she wasn't going to admit it. Nor would she spend any more time thinking about a man who seemed too good to be true and probably was.

"Too good to be true is always bad news, right, pup?"

Abel barked his agreement and Chloe stepped out of the apartment and started down the stairs. The house was quiet. The retired couple across the hall were probably still asleep, but downstairs soft music drifted from beneath the door that led to Connor's apartment. For a split second, Chloe considered knocking on his door and asking for an escort to her car, but she had mace in her pocket, a panic button on her key chain. An escort seemed like overkill, though it definitely would have gone a long way in making her want to walk out the door.

Outside, clouds boiled up from the horizon, the steel gray of the sky doing nothing to lift Chloe's mood. The silvery sheen of the lake, the gray-brown bark of the trees, the fall-brown grass, sapped the world of color and life, creating a place of silence. Of death.

"Forget going to Blooming Baskets and *hoping* for chocolate. I'm going to make sure I get some." She muttered the words as she put Abel in the back seat of the car and slammed the door shut.

Twenty minutes later, she strode into Blooming Baskets, a paper bag in one hand, Abel's leash and a drink carrier in the other. Coffee for Opal. Hot chocolate for herself.

Opal stepped out of the back room, a small white basket in her hands and a scowl on her face. "It's about time you got here. I was worried sick wondering what had happened to you."

"I'm not due in for five minutes."

"Chloe Davidson, every day for the past two weeks, you've been here at 7:45. It is now 7:55. You've aged me ten years for every minute. Do you realize how many years that makes me?"

"A hundred and sixty-four?" Chloe tried not to laugh as she set the bag on the front counter.

"Exactly."

"Sorry. I didn't realize you'd be worried."

"Didn't you? Just wait. One day you'll have kids. Then you'll know what it is to wait for someone to call and let you know they're okay."

"I don't think kids are in my future, Opal."

"You'd make a great mother."

"That won't be an issue since I'm not planning on getting married." She passed Opal the cup of coffee, telling herself that what she was saying was absolutely the truth. She was not interested in men. And she was not interested in Ben.

"You brought me coffee?"

"Consider it a peace offering. I really am sorry I worried you, but every once in a while a girl's just got to have chocolate."

"Is that what you've got in the bag?"

"Yep. Two chocolate cake doughnuts. Each."

"Are they glazed?"

"Are there any other kind?"

"Not in my mind." Opal smiled, pulled a doughnut out of the bag and handed it to Chloe.

"Eat. You're looking pale again."

"I didn't sleep well last night."

"Probably the puppy keeping you awake."

"Probably. What's on the schedule for today?"

"Plenty. Four baskets for the missionary luncheon at Grace Christian. Prep for the Costello wedding shower this Saturday. Two arrangements for the hospital. One that needs to be delivered to a retirement village outside of town. Two to private residents."

"Are you delivering or am I?"

"I am. It'll take me less time."

"Because you're a lead foot."

"Because I know where I'm going. Besides, you do look exhausted. It's probably for the best that you not spend the day driving around. And I think we'll skip tonight, too. I can't drag you out shopping when you're so exhausted."

"You weren't going to be dragging me, Opal. I was happy to go with you."

"Be that as it may, you're not going to go. Betsy Reynolds has decided to go to Richmond, too. She called me last night and was begging me to go shopping with her. I'll just call and tell her I can do it after all."

"So I'm being replaced," Chloe teased, biting into the rich chocolate doughnut, happy to be out of the apartment and away from her worries for a while. She had made plenty of mistakes in her life, but coming to Lakeview wasn't one of them. Maybe she hadn't quite gotten the hang of floral design, but at least she had some measure of stability in her life again. She also had Opal and that was worth its weight in gold.

"Not yet, but if you keep talking instead of working, I just might have to." Opal's amused words were enough to get Chloe moving, and she lifted Abel and brought him to the back room.

It didn't take long to ease into the flow of the day.

By noon, Opal was out in the van making her deliveries and Chloe was cleaning up petals and stems from the work area in the back of the shop. She tried to work quickly, but the sluggish feeling she'd woken with hadn't left despite hot chocolate, two cups of coffee and a sugar-laden doughnut.

Doughnuts. She'd managed to eat both of hers.

The bell over the front door rang and she stepped out into the front of the shop, pasting a smile on her face and hoping she looked more lively than she felt.

"Hi, can I help…?" The question died on her lips as she caught sight of Ben, his jaw shadowed by a beard, his eyes blazing brilliant blue, a smile curving his lips. Dark jeans. A soft flannel shirt layered over a black T-shirt that hugged well-defined muscles. He looked good, really good.

Chloe resisted the urge to smooth the strands of hair that had fallen from her ponytail and were straggling around her face. "Ben, what are you doing here?"

"I was driving by and thought I'd stop in to see how you were doing."

"Driving by?"

"Driving by on my way here to see how you're doing."

Laughter bubbled up and spilled out, filling the room and chasing away the anxiety that had plagued Chloe all morning. "Thanks."

"For what?" He stepped closer, reaching for her hand and tugging her out from behind the display case, his gaze taking in her black pants and pink shirt, her scraggly hair and makeup-free face.

"For stopping in to see how I was doing. And for making me laugh."

"You're welcome." He did what she hadn't, reaching

out and smoothing strands of hair from her cheeks, his fingers blazing trails of warmth that made her heart race.

She stepped back, her face heating, her mind shouting that if she didn't watch it she'd be in big trouble. That she was already *in* big trouble.

"So how *are* you doing?"

"I'm doing great."

"Liar."

"I'm doing okay."

"Try again."

"I feel lousy. Happy now?"

"Not even close." He ran a hand over his jaw. "I won't be happy until we find the person who's after you."

"*If* we find the person." *Before he finishes what he started.*

She didn't say the rest, but it was what she'd been thinking during the darkest hours of the night and what she was still thinking in the cold gray light of the November day.

"We'll find him. Jake's heading in the right direction with the investigation. I feel strongly about that. So does he."

"You spoke to him today?"

"I stopped by his office before I came here."

"I wish you hadn't."

"Because you think I'm getting too involved?" He crossed his arms over his chest, his stance relaxed, but alert, his gaze just a little hard.

"Because I don't want you involved at all." At least her head didn't. Her heart was another matter entirely.

"Funny, I don't think that's the truth, either."

"The truth is simple. Getting involved with me is

dangerous. Anyone in his right mind would see that and go running in the other direction." Chloe shoved her bangs out of her eyes, grabbed a small white basket from behind the counter, then stalked across the room to pull white and pink roses from the cooler.

"I'm not just anyone. And I'm not running." The hint of steel in his voice surprised Chloe and she met his eyes, saw the hard determination there.

"Ben—"

"Maybe you're used to people abandoning you when things get tough, but that's not my style. Whatever happens in the next days, weeks or months, I plan to be part of it."

"Why? We've known each other a week—"

"Ten days." He grinned, but the steel was still there.

"My point is, you don't have a commitment to me. There's no reason for you to get more involved in my problems than you already are."

"Whether or not I have a commitment to you has nothing to do with it."

"It has everything to do with it." She placed a square of floral foam in the bottom of the basket and jabbed a rose into it. "We barely know each other and you're letting yourself get caught up in my mess. You could be off doing a hundred other things that would be a lot less dangerous to your health."

"And yet here I am." He grabbed her hand before she could mash another rose into the arrangement. "Don't you think there's a reason for that, Chloe? A reason God brought us into each other's lives at exactly this time?"

"I stopped thinking I understood God's ways months ago." She slid her hand away from his, using less force to place the next flower.

"You don't have to understand, you just have to trust."

She looked up and into the vibrant blue depths of his eyes, felt herself drawn into them and into his certainty. "Trust isn't easy for me."

"It's not easy for anyone when things get tough. We doubt. We question. In the end, we either choose to believe God is still working His will through our lives or we end up turning away from our faith. I don't think you're the kind to turn away."

"You're right. I'm not." But there had been times before she'd come to Lakeview that she'd wondered if she might, if maybe everything she'd believed, everything she'd trusted in was a lie.

She pulled baby's breath from the cooler, shoving a few stems in between the roses.

"Then have faith that God put me into your life for a reason and stop worrying so much about what that might mean." Ben pulled baby's breath from the pile she'd set on the counter and pressed the stem into the foam, his knuckles brushing against hers, the simple act of working together sealing the connection that shouldn't be between them, but was.

"You're wrong, Ben. I do have to worry about what that might mean."

"Because you're afraid of what might happen to anyone who gets close to you?"

"Because I've *lived* what might happen to anyone who gets close to me and I don't want to live it again."

"You're not going to."

"You can't know that."

"No, I can't." His knuckles brushed against hers again, but this time he turned his hand and captured her fingers, his thumb caressing the tender flesh on the underside of her wrist. "But I do know this—there's nothing in the world that can keep God's will and plan from being worked out and His plan is always for our best. Whatever happens, it'll be okay."

He tugged her forward so that she was leaning over the glass display case, just inches from Ben and the strength he offered. For a moment she was sure he would kiss her again. She thought about moving forward, thought about pulling back, hadn't quite decided between the two when he brushed a hand over her hair.

A pink petal fluttered down and settled in the floral arrangement she was designing.

"Were you fighting with roses when I got here?"

"I was fighting with Abel who was fighting with pink hydrangea. Opal will not be pleased."

"I bet not. Will she be back soon?"

"Probably within the hour."

"And you're here alone until then?"

"Yes."

"I'm not sure that's such a good idea."

"Good idea or not, it is what it is." Chloe shoved more baby's breath into the sea of white and pink roses and frowned. "This isn't exactly going the way I planned."

"What'd you plan?"

"Something that looked a lot better."

He eyed the floral arrangement and Chloe expected him to say what most people would—it looks great. Instead, he pulled a few roses from the middle of the basket, spaced them closer to the edge of the foam. "Maybe a little more of the filler would help."

"A pastor, a chef *and* a floral designer. Is there anything you can't do?"

"I can't leave you alone here by yourself."

"Sure you can. Just walk out the door."

"Not until Opal gets here. So, what do you say we finish this and order a pizza? I don't know about you, but I'm ready for lunch."

"Ben—"

"It's just lunch."

"It's just you babysitting me."

"It doesn't feel anything at all like babysitting to me." The words were warm and filled with promise.

"I don't think this is a good idea."

"Good idea or not, it is what it is." He smiled, his eyes flashing with amusement.

And suddenly having him around didn't seem like such a bad thing. Despite her worry, despite her fear, for just a while, Chloe decided to believe what Ben had said—that God had put him in her life for a reason, that a divine plan was being worked out and that in the end everything would be okay.

Chapter Twenty

There were two messages on Chloe's machine when she got home. The first from Karen telling her that Adam's hard drive was on the way. The second was from Adam's former receptionist, Jordyn Winslow. She'd mailed the laptop and wanted to know if Chloe needed anything else.

Chloe glanced at the clock as she stripped off her jacket. Jordyn had her ear to the ground when it came to matters that involved anything to do with Adam and James's business or their personal lives. She prided herself on knowing their schedules during work and away from it. If there was anyone besides James who might have an idea of who Adam had been seeing, it was Jordyn.

It was just past five when Chloe picked up the phone, almost hoping that the receptionist had left for the day. It would be much easier to leave a message than to ask what needed asking in person.

Her hopes were dashed when Jordyn's chipper voice filled the line.

"Kelly and Hill Investigative Services. Can I help

you?" The greeting was the same, but different. Adam's name no longer a part of it. Grief speared Chloe's heart, making her mute for a moment too long.

"*Hello?* Can I help you?" Jordyn's tone had lost some of its peppiness.

"Jordyn, it's Chloe."

"Hi, Chloe. It's good to hear from you. James said you're settling in down there. Is it as peaceful as you were hoping?"

"Yes. The lake is beautiful and the area is much quieter than D.C."

"I bet. Personally, I'm not sure I could do what you've done. Move out to the country. Too many years of suburban life have spoiled me. I like the convenience of having everything close by. I don't know how you're keeping your sanity." Was the comment about sanity a subtle jab? Chloe could never be sure with Jordyn. They'd known each other for the three years Chloe had been freelancing for the company, but they'd never been friends.

"Rural life isn't for everyone, but it's definitely for me."

"To each her own, I suppose. Though I'm not sure what the point of giving up a lucrative business to become a florist was. You'd done well for yourself, Chloe. It's a shame to waste all those years of work." Jordyn's words were patronizing, but Chloe didn't let them bother her. A fixture at Adam and James's office since they'd partnered as private investigators ten years before, Jordyn had an opinion about most things and wasn't afraid to share them.

"Like you said, to each her own. My decision might not make sense to you, but I haven't regretted it." Chloe set fresh water and food down for Abel and limped to the balcony, unbolting the French doors and stepping out in the crisp evening air.

"Yes, well, we'll see how you feel in a month. Did you get my message?"

"Yes, thanks for sending the laptop out."

"James said you needed it ASAP. I wasn't sure there was quite as much hurry as he made it out to be, but humored him anyway. You know how men can be."

Not really, but she didn't plan to admit that to Jordyn whose blond-haired beauty attracted more men than Chloe had ever been able to keep track of. "They're interesting, that's for sure."

"*Interesting?* Frustrating is more the word I was thinking. Anyway, the laptop is on the way. You should receive it by the end of the week. James didn't say what you needed it for."

Chloe decided the nonquestion needed no response, and she ignored it. "I appreciate you getting it out so quickly, Jordyn. I know how busy you are."

"Not as busy anymore. Adam kept things hopping around here. Without him, things just aren't the same."

"Adam did love his job." *Go ahead, bring it up. Ask her before you chicken out.* "Jordyn, you asked if I needed anything else, and I was wondering…"

If she knew who Adam had cheated with? If she'd watched him leave for lunch with his girlfriend and silently applauded Chloe's downfall.

"What?"

"Adam was seeing someone besides me. I wondered if you knew who it was." There, it was out, and a lot less painful to say than she'd thought it would be.

"I'd heard rumors that's why the two of you broke up, but I didn't want to believe it was true. Adam seemed like such a loyal type of guy."

"Yeah, he did. I guess you don't know who he was seeing?"

"I'm afraid not."

"All right. Thanks anyway."

"No problem. Do me a favor and call me when the laptop arrives, okay? I've got it insured and want to make sure it gets there in one piece."

"Sure."

"Great. I'll talk to you soon, then." The phone line went dead, and Chloe set the receiver down. James didn't know who Adam had been seeing. Jordyn didn't. Chloe certainly didn't.

But the computers might. One e-mail, that's all it would take. One note that spoke of more than friendship. Deleted or not, they'd be there, buried in the computer, waiting to be found.

Chloe just wasn't sure she was ready to find the information. A nameless, faceless woman was much easier to deal with than a real identity. A name. Maybe a face. Maybe the knowledge that it was someone Chloe knew, had maybe even liked.

Not that it mattered now. Adam was gone, his betrayal minuscule in comparison to his death. All they'd shared—laughter, joy, tears and pain—fading to bittersweet memory.

Hot tears filled Chloe's eyes and she blinked them back, rubbing at the band of scars on her hand, the cool air from the still-opened French doors bathing her heated face. She wanted so badly to go back to the night of the accident, rewind the clock, change the outcome. But the past couldn't be changed. All she could do was move forward into the unknown.

As if he sensed her distress, Abel whined, rolling over on his back and begging for attention. She knelt down and scratched him under the chin. "You're a good puppy. Even if you did destroy the hydrangea and chew the leg of Opal's desk."

His tail thumped the floor, his tongue lolled out, the sight comical and cute. If she'd had her cameras she'd have taken a picture, but Jake hadn't returned them and had made no mention of how long they'd be in his custody. Instead, she straightened, limping into the kitchen and eyeing the contents of her refrigerator. There wasn't much. Some fruit. A bag of baby carrots. A nearly empty half-gallon of milk. Apple juice. Why hadn't she stopped at the store on the way home and picked up groceries?

She dug into the cupboard, found a box of Pop-Tarts, and ripped open the wrapper. They weren't chocolate, but they were better than nothing.

Abel barked, tumbling toward the door, just as a soft rap sounded against the wood.

"Who is it?"

"It's Mrs. Anderson, dear. I've got a package for you."

"A package?" Chloe pulled open the door and smiled at her neighbor, a spry woman of eighty-nine who spent her days volunteering at the community center and her evenings enjoying the company of her husband of sixty years.

"Yes. Charles said it was on the front porch when he came home. I guess it couldn't fit in your mailbox." She held out what looked like a wrapped shoe box. "He thought it best to bring it inside. No sense leaving it outside for thieves to get."

"Thank you for bringing it over, Mrs. Anderson. And please tell your husband I appreciate him bringing it inside."

"It was no problem at all, dear. Now, I've got to run. It's senior night at the movie theater and Charles and I are going to meet some friends there."

"Have fun."

"You, too."

Chloe waited until the elderly woman was back inside her apartment, then closed the door and bolted it. The package was light and wrapped in brown packing paper, her name and address printed in broad, firm letters on one side. She turned the package over, saw no sign of a return address, nothing to indicate where it had come from.

A warning shivered along her spine, the box like a coiled serpent ready to strike. Anything could be inside. Pictures. Letters. Poison. Body parts.

"Okay. You're really losing it, Chloe. Knock it off before you convince yourself there are explosives inside and call the bomb squad to rescue you."

She set the box on the kitchen table, took a steak knife and slit through tape and paper. There was more paper beneath, bright yellow wrapping paper that she made quick work of. The white box inside looked innocuous enough, but there was no card or note. There also weren't any blood stains or awful odors, but that didn't mean there wasn't something awful inside.

Finally, Chloe couldn't put off the inevitable any longer. She braced herself and lifted the lid, nearly laughing out loud when she saw what was inside. A brown and green turtle was shoved into the small space, one golden eye staring up at her.

She pulled it out, smiling as she saw the dog tag hanging from a string around its neck. Speedy Too.

Ben.

How he'd managed to find a floppy stuffed turtle,

Chloe didn't know. Why he'd taken the time to buy it and send it to her was something she wasn't sure she *wanted* to know. Everything else aside—all the danger, all the fear, all the nightmares—she wasn't ready to get involved in a relationship. She wasn't sure she'd ever be ready for that.

But if she were, someone like Ben would be perfect....

Don't even go there, Chloe. Don't even think about it. Ben is a charming guy with a congregation of single women standing in line hoping to get his attention. Let them. You're not interested.

Aren't you?

She ran her hand over the turtle's shell, imagining Ben buying it and the dog tag, wrapping them in the box, going to the post office. He'd gone through a lot of trouble and that wasn't something many people had done for her in the past.

She grabbed the phone, found Ben's number and dialed.

"Hello?" His voice rumbled across the line, comfortably familiar and much too welcome.

"Hi, Ben. It's Chloe."

"Hey. Everything okay?" His voice deepened, warmed, pulled her in.

"Fine." She smoothed her hand over the turtle again, her throat tight for reasons she refused to name. "I got a package in the mail today."

"Did you?"

"No return address. No note. At first I thought it might be an unpleasant surprise."

"More mutilated pictures?"

"I was thinking something explosive. I got pretty close to calling the bomb squad."

"That would have made interesting news for the gossip mill."

"Fortunately, it didn't come to that."

"No?"

"It seems someone has a thing for turtles. Speedy ones."

"You don't say."

"I do. And I also say that that someone shouldn't have gone to so much trouble."

"Who said it was any trouble? Maybe that someone happened to be shopping for a birthday present for his niece and saw the turtle and thought of you."

"And just happened to find a pet tag with the perfect name written on it?"

"Something like that." He laughed, the sound rumbling across the phone line.

"You could have just brought it over. It would have saved you the effort and the cost of postage."

"And have you give me a hundred reasons why you couldn't accept it?"

"I wouldn't have given you a hundred reasons."

"Sure you would have. And then I would have felt obligated to list a hundred reasons why you *could* accept it. That seemed like a lot more effort than putting it in the box and mailing it."

Chloe smiled, setting Speedy Too down on the counter and crossing to the balcony. The night was clear, the stars bright in the indigo sky. "You're probably right. I would have argued, but in the end you would have convinced me. Speedy Too is the most thoughtful gift I've ever received."

"Then I'm glad I followed my gut and bought it."

"Ben, I'm not sure what you want from me, but—"

"I don't want anything from you, but friendship."

"A kiss is a little more than friendship."

"Let's chalk that up to a momentary lapse of judgment and forget it happened."

"I don't think that's possible."

"And *I* think I'm flattered."

Chloe's cheeks heated, and she was glad Ben wasn't there to see it. "You know what I mean. A kiss changes everything. It takes nothing and makes it into something."

"What's between us could never be nothing. Kiss or no kiss."

"That's just the thing. I don't want there to be something between us."

"There already is." He sighed, and she could picture him standing in his kitchen, maybe a cup of coffee in his hands, his hair falling across his forehead.

"I—"

"Let's be friends for a while, Chloe. We can worry about what comes next later."

"Nothing is going to come next."

"You just keep telling yourself that."

"I will. And now I've really got to go. Abel needs some attention."

Chloe could hear Ben's laughter as she hung up the phone and she couldn't stop her answering smile. He was right. There was something between them. From the moment she'd met him she'd felt the connection, a living thing that seemed to be growing with every moment they spent together.

Friendship.

She liked the sound of that.

The silence of the night wrapped around her, the bright stars and crescent moon hanging over the dark lake, the distant mountains rising up to touch the sky.

God's creation. His design. Ready for His purpose. His will. Whatever that might be.

Maybe one day Chloe would know. For now, she could barely see the beauty for the shadows. She shuddered, stepping back into the apartment and closing the door against the darkness.

Abel tumbled near her feet as she sat down in front of her laptop and pulled up work files. Maybe she'd missed something in her previous searches. Maybe there was something there still waiting to be discovered.

She could only pray that if there was, she'd find it soon because no matter how confident Ben and Jake were, Chloe had a feeling that all her fears were about to come true and that the nightmare she'd been running from for months would soon overtake her.

Twenty-One

Three nights and eighteen hours of searching computer files revealed no secrets that seemed worth killing to keep hidden. Jake's investigation seemed to be turning up just as few leads. When he stopped by the shop Thursday to tell her there'd been no fingerprints on the frame or photo and that a man they'd identified as the owner of the PO box had gone to ground and couldn't be located, Chloe was ready to lock up the shop and go home.

If it hadn't been just a little past nine in the morning, she might have.

The day seemed to stretch on for an eternity, and by the time she was ready to close Blooming Baskets for the evening, Chloe wanted nothing more than a hot bath to sooth her aching leg and a warm bed to hide in. That's exactly what she planned to have. *After* she did the exercises the orthopedic specialist had recommended during Chloe's appointment the previous day and *after* she fed Opal's demon cat and checked her mail.

Unfortunately, doing the last meant making the fifteen-minute drive to Opal's house in the dark, getting out of the Mustang in the dark, walking into a dark house in the dark.

"I've got to stop this kind of negative thinking, Abel. Dark, dark, dark, dark. Obsessing on it is only making me more nervous. I need to refocus my thoughts. Try to look at the bright side of things." Chloe stopped at the head of Opal's driveway, reaching out her window to pull mail out of the box, then following the winding path toward the ranch-style house her friend owned. Built in the seventies, the house wasn't nearly as fancy as some of its neighbors, but the three-acre lakefront lot was a premium and Opal loved it.

Chloe loved it, too. Her fondest childhood memories centered around Opal and her family, their house, the lake and the small cottage next door where Chloe had spent seven summers of her life.

She pulled up in front of the house and turned off the engine, the headlights dying and leaving the area shadowed and foreboding.

As fond as her memories of the place were, Chloe wasn't sure she wanted to get out of the car and go into the house. It looked different at night, the windows gaping wounds that bled darkness, the front door an ebony slash against the pale siding. Abandoned. Lonely. The kind of place where bad things might happen and probably would.

"But it's just a house, right? There's no one lurking in the shadows, waiting for me to get out of the car."

Abel snored in response, his head resting on his paws as he snoozed on the back seat. "You know you're supposed to be a companion, a watchdog, a fierce defender of your human, don't you?"

Abel opened one eye and closed it again.

"Obviously, I'm on my own on this one. Which is okay, because I can handle it." She took a deep breath, pulled Opal's keys from her purse and started to open the car door. Headlights shone in the rearview mirror, the unexpected brightness nearly blinding Chloe. She jumped, jamming her car keys back into the ignition, fear squeezing the breath from her lungs. No one should be coming down the driveway while Opal was away. She needed to put the car in reverse and drive away while she still could, but the oncoming car blocked her retreat, the blue spruce that lined the driveway prevented her from pulling around it.

She was trapped.

No. Not trapped. All she had to do was use her cell phone and call for help. Of course, by the time help arrived it might be too late. She'd be lying dead on the pavement.

Get out of the car. Go in the house. Call for help.

She grabbed her purse, Opal's keys still in her hand, and jumped from the car, racing toward the house, headlights pinning her against the gray-black night.

An easy target to see.

An easy one to take out with a gun.

Or to ram with a car.

There were a million ways Chloe could be killed here in the dark in front of Opal's house, but not if she could get inside the house first.

A door slammed, someone shouted, but Chloe's focus was on the door and safety. She shoved the keys into the lock, opened the door, jerked it closed again.

The doorbell rang before she could even turn the lock, the sound so jarring Chloe stumbled forward, knocking into the door, her cell phone tumbling from her hand. She landed hard on her knees, her pulse echoing hollowly in her ears as the doorbell chimed again and the door swung open.

A dark figure loomed in the threshold, then crouched beside her, the scent of pine and man enveloping Chloe as he leaned close. "You run pretty fast for a woman with one bad leg."

Ben.

She didn't know whether to hug him or hit him and settled for accepting the hand he offered and allowing herself to be pulled to her feet. "I wasn't expecting company."

"Neither was I. Are you okay?"

"Besides my wounded pride, I'm fine. I need to go out and get Abel, though. He might not be doing as well out alone in a strange place."

"He's fine. I grabbed him and put him back in your car before he could get too far."

"Thanks. Should I ask why you're here?"

"Opal called me this morning and asked me to stop by to feed her cat. Apparently he likes to be fed at six o'clock on the dot."

"Not a minute sooner."

"Or later."

"It sounds like she told you the exact same thing she told me."

"That her cat is finicky and refuses to eat if the food is put in his bowl at any other time of the day and that when Opal's daughter took care of Checkers he didn't eat the entire time, because she fed him in the morning."

"Verbatim." Chloe raked a hand through her hair and shook her head. Amused. Irritated. Happy that Ben was there with her, but not sure she was happy to be feeling that way.

"You know she's matchmaking, right?" Ben flicked on the light, spreading a warm glow through the small living room and illuminating his tan face and sandy hair, his vivid eyes, the hard angle of his jaw and the soft curve of his lips.

"Yeah, and I cannot believe that the same woman who told her kids to keep their noses out of other people's business is sticking hers into ours."

"She probably figured she was killing two birds with one stone. She gets us together for a few minutes and makes sure you're safe."

"You're probably right. What happened Sunday really shook her. I think she was hoping I'd be safer here than I'd been in D.C."

"You will be soon."

"I hope you're right, but to be honest, I'm not so sure. I've been researching my old case files for the past three nights and I can't find anything even remotely suspicious."

"Have you heard from Jake?"

"Yeah, he's coming up empty, too. The biggest lead he has is the PO box, but the owner has disappeared."

"How about the phone records?"

"Jake hasn't mentioned them, probably for fear of embarrassing me. No doubt there were thousands of calls, most of them from women."

"That's Adam's embarrassment, not yours."

"Is it? Because it doesn't feel that way." She moved through the house, not wanting to continue the conversation.

The living room opened into a modern kitchen, the white cupboards, tile floor and granite counters much different than the dark wood and linoleum of past years. Despite the changes, the room had the same homey feel as it had when Chloe was a girl, the taupe walls, white wainscoting, and deep blue chair rail inviting all who visited to stay awhile.

Checkers, however, wasn't as welcoming.

He stood in one corner of the room, guarding two porcelain bowls, his tubby black-and-white body stiff with irritation.

"All right, cat. We can do this the hard way, or the easy way."

"I take it you've had run-ins with him before?" Ben moved into the kitchen, his hand wrapping around her arm as he moved between her and the cat.

"Yes. At our very first meeting. The one and only time I've been here since I've been back in Lakeview."

"Bite or scratch?"

"Scratch."

"Then he doesn't completely despise you. Last time I was here, he nearly chewed through my thumb."

"Then I guess you'd better keep your distance. Your congregation won't be happy with me if you show up Sunday with a digit missing."

"Are you kidding me? I consider this a personal challenge. Do you know where Opal keeps the cat food?"

"In the cupboard under the sink."

"Okay. So, here's the plan. I'll distract him. You grab the food and pour it into the bowl."

Chloe pulled a plastic container filled with cat food out from under the cupboard and turned toward Checkers.

He hissed, his tail fluffing, his golden eyes glittering.

"Is there a plan B?"

"I'm afraid not." Ben smiled and grabbed a dish

towel that hung from the refrigerator door handle. "Ready?"

"As I'll ever be."

He stepped forward, trailing the towel on the floor in front of the cat. "Come on, kitty, out of the way."

Checkers leaped past him, yowling wildly as he raced from the room.

"I thought maybe he'd play, but I guess scare tactics work just as well."

"He'll be back." Chloe poured the food and refilled the water dish. "But our mission is accomplished."

"With no casualties." Ben took the food container from her hand and returned it. "We make a good team."

They did. That was the problem. They seemed to complement each other almost too much, fitting into each other's lives with almost frightening ease, as if they'd known each other years rather than days. If the circumstances had been different, if *Chloe* were different, her heart would probably flutter with anticipation every time she saw him, her mind jumping forward weeks and months and imagining the relationship lasting far into the future.

Who was she kidding? Her mind already did.

"Hey." His hands framed her face, forcing her to look up and into his eyes before they smoothed back into the loose strands of her hair. "Whatever you're worrying about, don't."

"I'm not worrying." She spoke lightly and leaned away from his touch, but he didn't release his hold, his hands dropping to her shoulders, his thumbs caressing the skin over her collarbones.

"You *are* worrying. Maybe about the case. Maybe about us."

Us. He spoke the word with confidence. As if they weren't just a team, but a couple. "Ben—"

"But you don't need to worry, Chloe. Between you, me and Jake, we'll find the person who's after you." He paused. "As for us, we're friends. There's nothing to worry about there."

Friends? He'd claimed that twice now and she hadn't believed him either time. As much as she didn't want it, the truth was in her mind, in her heart. What was between them now might be friendship, but it was something more, too. "You keep saying we're friends, Ben, but I get the feeling you might be interested in something more."

His eyes blazed into hers. Then, as if he'd banked whatever fire was inside, they cooled. "What I'm interested in is entirely up to you. Come on, we need to finish up here. I've got a business meeting at the church in half an hour. And you need to get home and rest up for tomorrow night when we tackle the Reed kids together."

The end to the conversation was purposeful and Chloe didn't see any reason to try to continue it. What would she say? What could she say? If things were up to her, she'd…

What?

Be content with friendship?

Try for something more?

She didn't know. Couldn't know until after all the other problems in her life were solved. If they were ever solved. And right now, she wasn't sure they would be.

Twenty-Two

Friday night came much more quickly than Chloe was happy with. It wasn't that she didn't want to babysit for Tiffany and Jake's kids, it was simply that she hadn't done any babysitting in years. The closest she'd been to a child under five was at church, and even then she hadn't been hands-on, preferring to stay away from nursery duty in favor of working with teens.

The tiny infant Tiffany placed in her arms was nothing like the teenagers Chloe had worked with. As a matter of fact, he looked way too delicate for her peace of mind. She glanced at the clock over the Reeds' fireplace mantel. Six-oh-five.

Ben had better hurry up. There was no way she wanted to be left alone with two kids under the age of three.

"Did Ben say how long he'd be?" Jake's voice was gruff.

"Actually, he promised to be here before you left. I'm sure he'll be here soon." She hoped. He'd left as soon as they'd finished feeding Checkers, handing her scribbled directions to Jake's house and telling Chloe there was an emergency he had to deal with before meeting her there.

That was forty minutes ago.

Not that she was counting.

"Maybe we should stick around until he gets here." Tiffany touched her son's downy cheek, smiling a little as the baby turned toward her hand.

"We've got reservations, hon. If we're late, we might not get a table."

"Then we'll make new reservations for another night."

"Not on your birthday." He met Chloe's eyes. "Will it be a problem if we leave?"

"No, go ahead. I wouldn't want you to lose your table."

"Isaac's already been fed. Just lay him down in his bassinet and he should drop right off to sleep." Tiffany smoothed a hand over her son's dark hair, the softness in her face, the love in her eyes so obvious it almost hurt to look at.

Chloe glanced down at the baby's smooth skin and deep blue eyes. He looked like his father. The little red-headed girl standing close to Jake, a pint-size version of her mother. "Will I need to feed him again before you get back?"

"Nope. We should be home before his next feeding. Right, honey?"

"Three hours tops." Jake speared Chloe with a look that left no doubt about what he was thinking. "You have done this before haven't you?"

"I used to babysit all the time."

"Infants?"

"Yes."

"Toddlers?"

"Yes."

"Then you know how quickly a kid Honor's age can get into trouble."

"I do." She just hoped she was still up to the task of keeping them out of it.

"She needs to be watched at all times. Don't—"

"Honey." Tiffany placed a hand on Jake's arms. "You just said you didn't want to be late. Shouldn't we be going?"

"Right. We won't be far. Just at the clubhouse. If anything happens call me on my cell."

"I will."

Tiffany leaned down to kiss her daughter. "Be good for Ms. Chloe." She straightened and turned back to Chloe. "She can stay up for another half hour. Then she needs to get in bed. Though she might not be as easy to get settled as Isaac."

"I'll do my best. I'm sure everything will be fine."

"It better be." Jake grumbled the words as he leaned over to kiss his daughter, waiting until his wife opened the front door and stepped outside before he speared Chloe with a dark look. "An off-duty friend of mine is going to be here in five minutes. He'll be doing stakeout until Ben shows up. If anything happens, just flick the lights. He'll come in and help until we get back."

"That isn't—" The hard look in his eyes kept her from finishing the thought. "Okay. Great. Have fun."

"You, too." He stepped outside and shut the door, leaving Chloe with a sleepy infant, a bouncy toddler and absolutely no idea what she was going to do with either.

Ben's cell phone rang as he pulled up in front of Jake's house. Forty minutes late. He grimaced, grabbing the phone as he stepped out of the car. "Ben Avery."

"You done with that emergency, yet?" Jake's voice was gritty and soft. Obviously, he'd snuck away from his wife to make the call.

"I just pulled up in front of your house."

"Martin's still there?"

Ben glanced at the small blue pickup parked on the street in front of the house and waved at the off-duty deputy. "Yeah. He's here."

"Good. Do me a favor and tell him he's free to go home, but if he mentions a word of this to my wife, he's fired."

Ben laughed, striding toward the vehicle. "You didn't tell her?"

"And have her lecture me all night about my lack of faith in humankind? I don't think so."

"She's right. You don't have much faith in people."

"Sure I do. It just depends on the people." He paused. "I've got to get back to the table before Tiffany catches on to what I'm doing. Take care of my kids."

"You know I will."

"See you."

Ben sent Martin home and strode toward the restored Queen Ann that Jake and Tiffany lived in. Hopefully, Chloe hadn't had it too hard while he was MIA.

He knocked on the door, bracing himself for utter chaos.

"Who's there?" Chloe's voice sounded through the door, muted, but firm and calm. Maybe things inside the house weren't quite as bad as he'd expected.

"Ben."

"And I should let you in why?"

"Because you can't manage without me?"

"Try again."

"Because I realize the error of my ways and want to apologize?"

"Still not working."

"Because I've got half a dozen chocolate chip cookies in my hand?"

"That'll work." She swung the door open, stepping back to let him in. The brightly lit foyer with its colorful quilts hanging from the hall was as familiar as Ben's own home.

Chloe was familiar, too. Like an old friend he'd reconnected with rather than someone he'd only recently met. Tonight, she'd left her black hair hanging loose, the bangs falling into her eyes and hiding her expression as they so often did.

"You said you had cookies?"

"Right here." He handed her the bag that Ella had packed for him, smiling when Chloe dug in, pulling out a cookie and biting into it.

"Delicious. So good I think I'll have another." She pulled a second from the bag. "You weren't baking cookies while I was babysitting, were you?"

"I don't think that would get me too many points with you or the Reeds." He shrugged out of his jacket, dropped it onto the couch. "I had a big problem to deal with. It took a little longer than I expected."

"A *little* longer? You said you'd be here before Jake and Tiffany left."

"I tried, but I got held up."

"Is everything okay?"

"I'm happy to report that Mammoth is doing fine."

"Mammoth?" Chloe moved through the foyer and into the kitchen. Ben followed, noting the subtle hitch to her stride and the gingerly way she moved as she bent to pick a stuffed bear from the floor. "Should I ask?"

"He's a pig. His owner lives a few miles outside of town. She collects animals that no one else wants."

"And Mammoth is one of them?"

"Yes. And he lives up to his name. He's huge. When he gets out of his pen, he isn't always easy to corral again."

"Did you manage it?"

"Yeah, but my clothes didn't survive to tell the story. I had to go home and change. How about you? It looks like you managed to settle the troops."

"Nearly. Honor isn't quite asleep yet."

"Maybe I should go peek in on her."

"I don't think you're going to have to." Chloe cocked her head and smiled. "I think I hear the pitter-patter of little feet."

Seconds later, Honor appeared, her chubby cheeks rosy, her smile wide as she raced toward him.

He swooped down to grab her, tickling her belly as he lifted her into his arms. "Hey, little bit, aren't you supposed to be in bed?"

She giggled and wriggled in his arms as he started back toward the hall and the stairs that led to her room. "Want to come?"

Chloe shook her head, a half smile softening her face as she watched. "I think I'll let you settle her down this time."

It didn't take long to tuck Honor back in bed. Convincing her to stay there took a few more minutes. By the time Ben made it back downstairs, Chloe was seated in a chair, a cup of coffee in her hand. "Want some?"

"I think I will. And a couple of those cookies if you saved me any."

"I might have. Sit down. I'll get you the bag and some coffee." She started to rise, but Ben pressed her back down into her seat, not liking the pale cast to her skin or the dark circles beneath her eyes. "I'll get it."

He'd been hoping there'd be swift resolution to Chloe's troubles, that Jake's investigation would quickly lead to a suspect and an arrest. Unfortunately, evidence was elusive, the leads going nowhere.

He had a feeling that the answers they needed were right at their fingertips. More precisely, at Chloe's fingertips. Her investigative skills would lead them to the person they were seeking. It was just a matter of time.

"You're quiet."

Chloe's words pulled him from his thoughts and he carried his coffee and the cookies to the table, taking a seat opposite her. "Just thinking."

"About?"

"You."

Her cheeks heated, the subtle color making her eyes seem even more green, her skin even more silky. "I'm not sure that's a good idea."

"I'm not sure there's anything either of us can do about it." Whether Chloe liked it or not, they'd been brought together for a reason and Ben had every intention of seeing things through to the end. No matter what that might be. "Have you received the laptop and hard drive you were waiting for?"

"Not yet. I'm hoping they'll both be there when I get home. I'm anxious to get started. I think if there are any clues to what's going on, they'll be on one of Adam's computers."

"I was thinking the same."

"If we're right, the case could be solved in days. If we're wrong…" She fiddled with her coffee cup, her long fingers and sturdy hands more capable looking than graceful.

"What?"

"I don't know. That's the scary part. What will happen if we're wrong and I don't find something? What direction can we go except back where we were? Jackson and The Strangers or me going insane."

"The second isn't even a possibility. The first is doubtful."

"And everything else is a mystery?"

"For now, but hopefully not for much longer."

"Hopefully not." She stood and stretched, her slim figure encased in her work uniform of black slacks and a fitted pink sweater, her hair a dark waterfall that slid across her cheek as she leaned over the sink and rinsed her coffee cup.

Ben imagined her doing that in the morning, bright sunlight reflecting off her blue-black hair, her eyes still dark from sleep.

And decided it might be best to force his mind in another direction. "Were the kiddos good for you?"

"Isaac's been asleep the whole time. Honor is a little firecracker, but we had fun."

"You like kids?"

"I guess I do." She leaned against the counter. "I hadn't thought about it much before tonight."

"Too busy?"

"Too sure I'd never have them."

"Adam didn't want kids?"

"He did. I just couldn't imagine ever being a mother. Mine was lousy at it. I figured I probably would be, too."

"And now?"

"I still think I'd be lousy at it, but at least I know I like kids." She grinned and snagged the cookie bag from Ben's hand. "You've had three. The last one is mine."

"I fought a pig for those cookies."

"And I wrangled a two-year-old into bed."

"Good point. The cookie is all yours."

"Thanks. Of course, I planned on eating it anyway." She pulled the cookie from the bag. "I'd better go check on Isaac and Honor."

He caught her hand before she could walk way, feeling the delicate bones beneath her skin, the subtleness of her flesh. "Just so you know. I think you're wrong."

"About?"

"Being a mother. Personally, I think you'd make a great one."

She stared at him for just a moment, her eyes wide. Then her lips curved in a half smile. "Opal was saying the same thing to me a few days ago."

"Yeah?"

"Yeah. And I told her the same thing I'm going to tell you. Whether or not I'll be a good mother isn't an issue since I don't plan to ever get married."

"That's a shame." He stood, lifted a lock of her hair, let it slide through his fingers. "Because I think you'd make a good wife, too."

Her cheeks turned cherry red and she backed away. "I suppose I should say I'm glad you think so."

"But you're not going to?"

"Good guess. Now, I really do need to check on the kids." She hurried away and this time Ben let her go.

He probably shouldn't have mentioned Chloe having kids or getting married. Probably shouldn't have, but he didn't regret it. She was a woman who understood the value of family and relationships, and no matter how hard he tried, he couldn't imagine her living her life alone. What that meant as far as he was concerned, he didn't know.

Or maybe he did.

Maybe he just wasn't ready to accept it.

Eventually, though, he'd have to face the facts. His life had changed since he'd met Chloe, and unless he missed his guess, it was going to continue to change. God's plan was being worked out, the tide of events that had brought Chloe into his life was leading them ever closer to a conclusion that hadn't yet been made clear.

Time.

That's all they needed.

Ben could only pray they'd get it.

Twenty-Three

Ben insisted on following Chloe home and, no matter her misgiving about their relationship, Chloe was happy for his company as she hurried across the yard. The new moon steeped the night in blackness and the silence seemed filled with danger, every soft sound amplified, every shadow sinister. She tried to ignore the fear that coursed through her as she stepped into the house and up the stairs, but it was like a living thing, wrapping around her lungs and stealing her breath.

If Ben noticed her anxiety, he didn't comment, just followed her up the stairs to her apartment. A package sat next to her door, and Chloe recognized it immediately. "Adam's hard drive. I was hoping it would come today."

She started to lift it, but Ben took it from her hands. "I'll get this. You get the door. It'll be easier that way."

"Thanks." She pushed the door open and flicked on the light, Abel's happy yips greeting her. "I'm coming, little guy—"

Ben pulled her to a stop before she could cross the

room. "Why don't you wait here? I'll get the pup. He's in your room?"

"Yes. In his crate."

"Wait here." He didn't give her time to argue, and she didn't bother asking why he was walking through the small living room, pulling open the coat closet door, then stepping into the bathroom, ignoring Abel's unhappy cries.

She didn't have to ask. She knew why.

He was checking things out, making sure there wasn't anything or anyone unexpected waiting behind a closed door.

Just the thought of someone lurking behind the shower curtain or in a closet made her skin crawl. She stayed put as Ben stepped into her room and released Abel who bounded out to dance around her feet.

She lifted him and stepped across the living room and into her bedroom, watching as Ben pulled open the closet door. "I guess it's a good thing I've got a small place. It cuts down on the number of places someone can hide."

"I'm not too worried about someone hiding here, but it's always better to be sure."

He moved back out into the living room, pushed the curtains away from the balcony doors. They were still bolted shut against the darkness outside.

"It looks like everything is just as it should be."

He lifted the hard drive from the floor where it he'd set it. "Where do you want this?"

"Over next to my computer, but I'll do it once I take the packaging off."

"Tell you what. While you do that, I'll bring Abel out."

"That's not necessary, Ben."

"Actually, it is." There was a hint of a smile in his eyes, but Chloe had no doubt he that he intended to do exactly what he suggested whether she protested or not.

He pulled the house keys from her hand, grabbed the leash that was hanging from the knob and pushed open the door. "I'll be back in a few."

The door closed, the lock slid home, Chloe shook her head.

"Infuriating, exasperating man."

Strong, dependable man.

Attractive, loyal, intelligent man.

"You are *not* going to spend the next fifteen minutes listing all Ben's attributes. Do something constructive instead."

She tore the packaging from the hard drive, pulled the machine from the box. She'd helped Adam choose his PC more than a year ago when he'd upgraded from an outdated slower model. They'd purposely chosen a system that was compatible with Chloe's, thinking they'd be merging their lives. Now Adam was gone, but maybe some of who he'd been was left behind, easy to find in his e-mail accounts or perhaps hidden deep in the bowels of the hard drive. Whatever was there, Chloe would find it and she prayed that when she did, the shadowy stranger who haunted her dreams would be pulled into the light, that the nightmare she was living would be over.

But even that wouldn't bring Adam back.

Tears burned her eyes, but she ignored them, forcing herself to move instead, to focus her attention on the hard drive, on connecting it to her own system, typing in the password she'd created out of random letters and numbers. She only meant to make sure everything was working, but each keystroke brought her closer to solving the mystery and she was drawn deeper and deeper into the investigation.

Adam's e-mail account had been canceled a few months after his death. It didn't matter. The computer system hadn't been cleaned and anything that had been there was still there, begging to be found. She started typing, the sound of the front door opening and closing barely registering as she began her search.

"Coffee?" Ben's voice pulled her from the trail she'd been following and Chloe struggled to make sense of his question.

"What?"

"Want a cup of coffee? I've just brewed a pot."

Groggy and fuzzy-headed, Chloe stood, wincing as stiff muscles protested. "Maybe I will have some."

"Are you making any progress?"

"I've retrieved e-mails from the months before the accident and printed them out so I can read them more carefully. Right now, I'm not seeing anything unusual."

"What would be unusual?"

"Maybe if I knew it I'd find it." She accepted the cup Ben held out for her, rubbing a hand against the crick in her neck. "Computer forensics is a lot like searching for needles in haystacks. Lots and lots of stuff you don't want to find and only one thing you're really looking for."

"You love it, though."

She took a sip of coffee and met his eyes. "I do."

"But you're not doing it anymore. Why?"

"The accident made me reassess my life. I decided to move back to a place I loved and try something new for a living." Something that didn't remind her of the past and all its horrors.

"Maybe."

"Maybe what?"

"Maybe that's what you're telling yourself, but I'm not sure it's the truth." He stared at her through hooded eyes, his expression hidden.

"Then what do *you* think the truth is?"

"I think you're doing penance. Denying yourself a job you love because you think Adam's death is your fault."

"I don't need to be psychoanalyzed, Ben."

"That's good, because I don't know the first thing about doing it." He placed his coffee cup in the sink, shrugged on the jacket he must have taken off when he came back inside. "What I do know is that God has a purpose and plan for each of us. When we're living that, we find contentment and reason. When we're denying it, we can never be satisfied with what we accomplish."

"Are you saying you think I'm supposed to work with computers, not flowers?"

"I'm saying I've watched you do both and it's obvious to me which one you should be doing. I'm just not sure why it's not obvious to you. It's late. I'm going to head out." He pulled open the door and stepped out into the hall. "You know, you've got a skill not many people possess, Chloe. A tenacity and drive that allows you to search for answers relentlessly. It's a gift. One you're wasting in Opal's shop."

"It's not a gift. It's a job. One I've chosen not to do anymore."

"Too bad. There are a lot of people you could help, a lot of good you could do. Lock the door. I'll see you tomorrow at six." He strode away, and Chloe closed the door, shoving the bolt into place.

"He's wrong, Abel." She picked up the puppy, rubbed his head. "Just because I mutilated one flower arrangement doesn't mean I'm not cut out to be a florist. And just because I spent a few minutes—" she glanced at the clock "—an hour and a half in front of the computer without budging doesn't mean that's what I should spend my life doing."

Did it?

When she'd left D.C. she'd been running. From the nightmare, from her terror and memories. From her guilt. She'd thought leaving her old life behind would free her from those things. And maybe, as Ben had suggested, she'd thought denying herself the career she'd loved would serve as payment for the fact that she'd survived while Adam perished.

Penance.

It wasn't something she'd ever thought about, wasn't something she'd consciously sought to give, but maybe Ben was right. Maybe she *was* punishing herself, denying herself the career she'd worked so hard for, the skill she'd spent years honing because she couldn't bear the thought that her life stretched out before her while Adam's had been cut short.

Maybe.

But that wasn't the only reason she'd left her old life behind. When Ben had spoken of God's purpose and plan, the words had dug talons into her soul that closed tight and weren't letting go. Before the accident, she hadn't wondered what God thought of her career, her marriage plans, her day-to-day activities. She'd prayed, gone to church, tried to live her life with integrity. She just wasn't sure she'd lived it with purpose.

When she'd left D.C., that's what she'd been looking for. A chance to step back, take a clearer look at where she'd been, where she was going and how those things fit into God's will and plan. Slowly, it seemed she was finding the answers here in this quiet rural town with its tight-knit community and beautiful landscape. The longer she stayed in Lakeview the more she felt the truth. There *was* a correct path to take, a clear direction He had set for her. All she had to do was trust that it was for the best, that wherever it led, He'd be there.

And that was the hard part.

Faith. Believing in what couldn't be seen, trusting in something that could only sometimes be felt. Hoping in a future that sometimes seemed uncertain. "But I want to believe, Lord. I want to trust. I want to have faith that wherever You lead, I can go. That whatever happens, You're in control of it, working it out for the best. For *my* best."

A sense of peace filled her as she placed Abel on the floor and poured herself another cup of coffee. She might not know what the future would bring, she might not even know what tomorrow would bring, but she knew that it was all in God's hands. For now, that would have to be enough.

"Come on, Abel. We've got more files to discover."

A killer to uncover.

A job to do. A new life to create. One that might have more to do with computers than flowers. More to do with faith than work. More to do with trust than doubt.

More to do with God than self.

And that, Chloe thought, was going to be the biggest change of all.

Twenty-Four

She found it at just past three in the morning. A deleted e-mail that chased fatigue from her body and brought her straight up in her seat, her heart thrumming with excitement. She printed it out, scanned the content one more time. Just three lines. Innocuous out of context, but in light of what had happened, a red flag.

You'll regret what you've done. Maybe not today or tomorrow, but eventually. Once you see the error of your ways, we'll talk. J.

J.?

Chloe could think of at least five of Adam's friends who had that name. Probably more. The message had been e-mailed from a free online account and contained no clue as to who the sender was. Chloe printed out the contents of Adam's address book, searching for the e-mail address and finding it. There was no contact information and no name listed. Chloe would have to give Jake the address and see if he could have the user information released from the e-mail provider.

An hour later, she was still at the computer, but hadn't found any more e-mails from the same account. That seemed odd. Of course, everything seemed odd in the wee hours of the morning. Finally, she gave up, crawling into bed and staring up at the ceiling, praying for sleep that didn't want to come. When it did, Chloe's dreams were filled with troubling images. Not the nightmare. More a mishmash of faces and voices, identities and words that were just out of reach.

She woke more tired than when she'd gone to bed, grabbed a quick cup of coffee, then called Jake. He took down the e-mail address and promised to look into it immediately, but even that didn't seem fast enough. Like the images in her dreams, the answers they needed to find the stalker were just out of reach.

She glanced at the clock. Nine o'clock was early for anyone to be in Adam's old office, but she dialed the number anyway. James and Jordyn were both in for a few hours on Saturday. Hopefully, one of them would get back to her.

To her surprise, Jordyn answered the phone, her upbeat tone a little too bright after so few hours of sleep. "Kelly and Hill Investigations, how can I help you?"

"Jordyn, it's Chloe."

"You're calling early."

"I'm doing some research and need to get more information from you."

"Well, you're lucky you reached me. James is testifying on Monday. We're working on his testimony. Otherwise I wouldn't be in for several more hours."

"I'm glad things worked out."

"So, what do you need?"

"You've got a list of company contacts, right?"

"Yes, but that information is confidential."

"I don't need the whole list. I've got an e-mail address and I thought it might belong to one of Adam's clients. I was hoping you could check the list and see if the address matches anyone on the list."

"I don't know, Chloe. I'm not sure I'm allowed to do that. Why don't you give me the address and I'll check with James?"

"That's fine." Chloe rattled it off. "Can you please tell James this is really important?"

"I'll tell him, but I can't promise we'll be back to you with this before Monday."

"That's all right." Though it seemed like a long time to wait when she was so close to finding the information she'd been seeking.

"Good. By the way, did you get Adam's laptop yet?"

"No, but hopefully it will come in today and I'll find some more e-mails from the address I just gave you."

"Good luck with that. Adam wasn't much for keeping old e-mails. He was always losing communications from clients and then having me call to have them resend the information. It used to drive me to distraction."

"Deleted e-mails are no problem, Jordyn. The information is still in the computer's memory, it's just hidden."

"Yes, well, you're the expert in those things. Not me. Good luck on your search and I'll get back to you once I speak to James."

Chloe hung up the phone and paced across the room. She had a lead, but nowhere to run with it. She'd have to wait until the laptop arrived, wait until Jordyn got back to her, wait until Jake was able to get the contact information from the e-mail account.

Wait.

"But I'm not so good at waiting, pup." She grabbed the leash from the door. "Let's take a quick walk. Then maybe we should get out for a while. Run to the pet store. Get some groceries. Hopefully, when we get back I'll have some more ideas about tracing the person who's using that address."

A few hours of shopping hadn't given Chloe any clearer insight into the problem. It *had* filled her cupboards, though, and when the phone rang at a little past noon, she was putting together a grilled cheese sandwich and a salad.

"Hello?"

"Chloe, it's Ben."

Chloe's heart leaped at his voice. "Hi. What's up?"

"Cain. He's racing around the house like a sugar-hyped kid. I thought maybe it was time for that play-date."

"I don't know."

"You're busy?"

"Having lunch."

"Maybe I could join you."

"You're inviting yourself for lunch?"

"It's easier than waiting for an invitation."

Chloe laughed. "I'm not a fancy cook. Grilled cheese and salad."

"I'll bring dessert. See you in ten."

He made it in seven, the cool, crisp scent of autumn drifting into the apartment as he strode through the door, a brown paper bag in one hand, Cain dancing around his feet. "You look tired."

"Is that the way you greet every woman you have lunch with or am I just special?"

"You're definitely special." He smiled, but there was a hint of truth in his words and in the somber gaze he swept over her. "How long did you stay up last night?"

"Long enough to find what I was looking for." She grabbed the printed e-mail and handed it to Ben. "Tell me what you think while I grill the sandwiches."

He read it quickly, his expression darkening. "Did you call Jake?"

"First thing this morning. He's going to try and get the e-mail provider to release the account holder's contact information."

"Which may or may not be useful."

"True, but I'm hoping I'll find a few more e-mails on Adam's laptop. Maybe contact information in his address book. That will definitely be useful."

"And that'll be here when?"

"Probably today or Monday. I'm hoping for today."

"Me, too. The sooner we get this solved, the better I'll feel." He frowned, staring down at the e-mail as if he could find the sender's identity hidden in the message. "This could be about anything business or personal."

"And it might not have anything to do with the accident or the break-in or the phone calls Adam received, but look at the date on it. That's just a couple of days after Adam and I broke up. I think that's significant."

"It's a start, anyway."

"Yeah. Hopefully of something big." Chloe placed grilled cheese sandwiches on a platter, salad in a bowl and set both on the table. "I'm ready for all this to be over."

"Have you decided what you're going to do when it is?"

"I can't think past today. When everything is settled, I'll plan for more."

Ben nodded, not asking the questions Chloe could see in his eyes. "We'd better eat and get these dogs outside. Cain needs to run off some energy."

The walk was pleasant, though Chloe was sure Ben was as distracted as she was, conversation that had always seemed to flow so easily when she was with him, felt stilted and strange.

"Is something wrong?" She asked the question as they moved back up the stairs to her apartment. "You're quiet today."

He met her gaze, his eyes the vivid blue of the sky in spring. "I'm worried. We've got bits and pieces of the puzzle, but not enough to see the picture clearly. Whoever is after you must realize how close we're getting."

"I don't think he cares."

"Which worries me even more." He raked a hand through his hair and frowned. "Maybe you should leave town for a while."

"Where would I go? My friends are all in D.C. I haven't heard from my mother or grandmother in years."

"Anywhere where you can stay hidden until this is over. My parents. One of my foster siblings. They'd be willing to take you in."

"But I'm not willing to go. I've been running for almost a year. I won't run anymore." She meant it. Despite the fear, despite the nightmare, she couldn't keep running. Not if she ever wanted to have the life she dreamed of, the peace she longed for.

The muscle in Ben's jaw tightened, but he nodded. "I can understand that. I even respect it. But I don't like it."

"I'll be careful, Ben. I'm not planning to make myself any more vulnerable than I already am." She hesitated, then wrapped her arms around his waist, hugging him close for just a moment before she stepped away.

"What was that for?"

"For caring. There haven't been that many people in my life who have."

"I care, Chloe." He leaned forward, brushed his lips against hers. "And when you're ready, maybe we'll discuss just how much. I've got to go. We've got a prayer meeting at the church. Then I've got to run to the hospital to visit a sick friend. How about I come by and pick you up and we go to Opal's together?"

"Sure."

He smiled. "I think this is the first time I've offered to help that you haven't argued. We're making progress. I'll see you."

The apartment was silent in the wake of his departure, Chloe's heart beating just a little faster than normal. She pressed a finger against her lips, sure she could still feel his warmth there.

She'd come to Lakeview hoping to find peace and safety, but it seemed she'd found a lot more—community, friendship, contentment. Ben. Faith, first budding, then blooming, filling her heart, telling her that no matter what happened, everything would be okay.

Twenty-Five

The mail carrier knocked on her door at three, the short quick rap against the wood startling Chloe from the half-sleep she'd fallen into.

Excitement, anticipation and fear coursed through her as she tore open the box and set the laptop up on her kitchen table.

As Jordyn had said, most of Adam's e-mails had been deleted. Chloe checked the address book, found it empty, and frowned. Adam might have deleted e-mails, but would he have deleted the contents of his address book?

She didn't think so.

But someone else might have. Someone who had something to hide. James? Jordyn? Had one of them been embezzling funds? Or doing something else illegal that Adam had uncovered? If so, why sabotage Chloe's car? Why come after her?

She didn't have the answers, but Chloe hoped she'd find them. *Prayed* she'd find them.

First, she grabbed the phone, called Jake again, this time leaving a message on his voice mail. She knew her thoughts were rambling and unclear, her words unfocused, but her mind was already racing forward, following paths and trails through the computer files, hurrying toward the key to everything that had happened.

She searched for two hours, printing out copies of deleted e-mails, scanning through them, coming up blank time and time again.

"It's in here. I know it is." She stood and stretched, her thigh screaming in protest, her muscles cramped from too many hours spent in front of the computer, frustration thrumming through her. Whatever was imbedded in the computer was going to have to remain there for another hour or so. She had Checkers to feed, Opal's mail to check.

The thought of calling Ben and asking him to do both by himself flitted through her mind, but she pushed it aside. An hour away from the computer would do her good, clear her mind. So would talking to Ben. Maybe he could come in afterward, read through the files she'd already printed, see if anything struck him as off.

"Good excuse for inviting him over, Chloe." She mumbled the words, then lifted Abel. "Sorry, guy. You're going to have to stay home this time. But I'll take you out for a little while now to make up for it." She grabbed her purse and keys and headed outside.

Evening had come, painting the sky deep purple, the trees and grass gray. Chloe shivered from the chill and from the fear that she could never quite leave behind. She wouldn't let it beat her though, wouldn't go back inside and lock herself into the apartment, hide her head under the pillows.

But maybe she should have.

As she moved down the steps and out into the yard, Abel barked, darting toward a shadow that was separating from the trees. A woman. Above average height. Blond hair. Very familiar.

And suddenly very frightening, the wild look in her blue eyes telling Chloe all she needed to know about Adam's receptionist.

She forced down fear and panic, took a step back toward the house. "Jordyn. What are you doing here?"

"I'm sure you already know."

"You got the information from James and brought it for me?" Chloe took another step back as she spoke, moving away from the tree line and toward the house, her hand sliding toward her pocket and the pepper spray she carried there.

"Don't play stupid, Chloe. It's an insult to Adam and his taste in women." She pulled something from her pocket and pointed it at Chloe. The tiny gun looked more like a toy than a weapon. "And while you're at it, stop trying to get back to your apartment. That older couple who's always coming and going might not look so cute with bullets in their heads."

Chloe blanched at the words, but did as Jordyn commanded, stopping short, her heart hammering a frantic rhythm. One swift movement and she'd have the pepper spray in her hand, but first she needed to be close enough to use it.

The panic button!

Her hand slid over the zipper of her purse. Why had she put the keys in it when she'd locked the door?

"Drop the purse, Chloe. Now."

Die now or stay alive and hope for escape?

There was no choice, and Chloe dropped the purse. Jordyn smiled, the cold wildness in her eyes making

Chloe shiver. "That's better. Now, keep your hand out of your pocket. I'm sure you're still carrying around pepper spray. You would have been smart to get something a little more deadly." She waved the gun. "It's too late now, though, isn't it?"

"What's going on, Jordyn?"

"What do you *think* is going on? I've come for a visit to see how you're holding up. Losing Adam must have been so devastating for you. Of course, since he was never really yours, I guess you can't complain."

"What do you want?"

"Revenge."

"For what?"

"For what you did to Adam, of course. What he and I had was special. You ruined it. Then you killed him."

"I didn't kill him."

"Of course you did." She spit the words out, moving a step closer.

Come on. Keep coming.

Just a few steps closer and Chloe would take a chance and go for the pepper spray.

"If you hadn't brought that information to the FBI, Adam would still be alive."

"Then it wasn't you who sabotaged my car?" Keep her talking. Keep her moving forward.

"Maybe you really *are* stupid. Matthew Jackson wanted you dead. It would have made me very happy for you to end up that way. But I didn't do anything to your car. I have more subtle ways of getting rid of people who stand in my way." She smiled, her teeth flashing white in the fading light. "Take the pepper spray out of your pocket. Throw it into the trees."

Chloe hesitated.

"Now, Chloe, or those sweet old people will be vulture food."

Chloe did as she was told, her muscles tight and ready for action. If only she knew what action to take.

"By the way, I wanted to tell you when we chatted just how much I love your place. Very cute. Very quaint. Very you. Now, come on. We have to go before the newest man in your life shows up and makes me go to more effort than I already have."

"Go where?"

"To finish what I started in D.C. I thought dissolving those pills in that bit of orange juice you had in your fridge would take care of things, but you managed to survive. Too bad. Overdosing wouldn't have been such a bad way to die."

"Look, Jordyn—"

"You look, Chloe. I played second fiddle to you for years, knowing that eventually Adam would come back to me. He did. Just as he was supposed to. Then you ruined everything. I'm sure guilt is eating you alive. It's time to put an end to your misery. And mine."

"Whatever you're planning won't work. I already told the police that I thought you or James might be responsible for everything that's been happening."

"But you're crazy, Chloe. Everyone in D.C. knows it. Since Adam's death, it's obvious the trauma was too much for you to deal with. All those night terrors in the hospital, your insistence that someone was after you. It was only a matter of time before you cracked."

"Things are different here."

"Are they? You think that because you've got some good-looking pastor hanging around and a sheriff who seems to be taking you seriously that no one will believe it when your suicide note is found? I've got news for you, Chloe, people believe whatever is easiest. Get in the car."

"There'll be an investigation, Jordyn, and you'll be one of the top suspects."

"I doubt it, but even if I am, they won't be able to prove anything. They'll have your suicide note, but no body. No evidence to link the two of us together. Nothing that a prosecutor would be willing to bring to trial, anyway. Do you know how many killers are free because there's simply no evidence to link them to the crime? Now get in the car. We've got places to go."

No way. Gun or no gun, Chloe wasn't getting in the car, she pivoted, the sharp movement sending pain shooting up her thigh. Her leg collapsed out from under her and she stumbled, tried to right herself. Something slammed into her head, stars burst in front of her eyes and she was falling into darkness and into the nightmare.

Chloe wasn't answering the door and she hadn't answered her phone. It was possible she was in the apartment, caught up in the investigation and oblivious to the world. Ben had seen her in action, watched her fingers fly across the keyboard. Doing so had been a surprise and revelation, had told him a lot more than Chloe's words just how much she needed to be back at her work.

Maybe she was working now, bent over the computer, intent, focused. Maybe. But he didn't think so. What he thought was that Chloe was gone. The fact that her car was still parked in the driveway could only mean one thing—trouble.

He dialed Jake's number as he strode back outside,

praying that he was wrong, knowing that he was right and hoping that he and Jake would be able to find Chloe in time.

Chloe woke to icy terror and throbbing pain, water filling her nose and throat. The urge to gasp for breath, to suck in liquid in hopes of finding air nearly overwhelmed her. Darkness beneath, darkness above, something tied to her legs and pulling her down. She fought against it, pushing upward, out of the water, gasping for air, sucking in huge heaving breaths, the sickening pain in her head worsening with the movement.

She blinked, trying to clear her vision, caught a glimpse of wood, an oar. Saw Jordyn staring down at her, watching through glassy eyes.

"You just won't die will you?" She lifted the oar, swinging hard.

Chloe ducked back under the water, the weight on her legs dragging her down farther than she expected. She tried to keep her buoyancy, but sank deep, the darkness of the water profound, her lungs screaming in protest.

More fighting, more struggling, until finally she broke the surface of the water again. The boat was farther away now, the quiet slap of the oar hitting the water the only sound Chloe could hear. It was near dark, the hazy purple of dusk deepening to blue-black, the crisp day turning frigid with night. Chloe shivered, sank back under the water again, choking. Gasping. Sliding into darkness. She flailed, the cold and the weight on her legs sapping her energy, stealing her strength. She struggled back up again, tried to swim toward shore and sank again.

If you want to live, you'd better stop panicking and think, Chloe.

The thought pierced through her terror. Think or die. It was as simple as that.

She let herself sink into the water, reaching down to feel whatever it was that was dragging her down. Thick rope wrapped her ankles together, pulled taut by something. What? A weight? An anchor? She pulled hard on the rope, yanking the object up until she was holding what felt like a cinder block. Then she pushed to the surface again, just managing to suck in a breath of air before she sank beneath the water again. Her vision swam, her stomach heaved and she almost lost her grip on the weight and on consciousness. She bit the inside of her cheek, the pain clearing her head as she struggled back out of the water again.

Where was the shore? Where was safety?

In the dim light the shore looked too far away, the house in the distance tiny and insubstantial. To the left, the lake stretched as far as Chloe could see. To the right, trees shot up at the shoreline, distant and unreachable. Still, if her legs were free, she could swim to safety easily enough.

If.

Jake hopped out of his car and strode toward Ben, his stride long and stiff, his face grim. "Any sign of her?"

"No, but I found her puppy hiding under her car."

"Not good." The sympathy and worry in Jake's gaze was obvious. "When was the last time you spoke to her?"

"Around noon." Ben ran a hand over his jaw, forcing himself to think clearly, to stay focused. "I've already walked the perimeter of the house twice. The earth's too dry to hold prints."

"Did you talk to her neighbors?"

"I tried. They weren't home." Ben surveyed the area, urgency pounding through him, demanding action. "Something's happened to her."

"I've called in all my off-duty officers. We'll work a grid from here to the lake and the road. If she's here, we'll find her."

"And if she's not?"

"We'll contact media, get her picture out there. Pray that somebody's seen her."

"I've been doing that. Now I want to act."

"Understood, but we go traipsing around without a plan and we'll waste time, maybe destroy evidence." Jake's phone rang and he answered, his jaw tight, his words terse. "Reed, here. Yeah. I'll check it out. Thanks."

"What's up?"

"Guy a half a mile from here was walking his dog and found a boat washed up in the reeds near his house. He said there's some stuff inside of it. A purse. Flowers. It seemed strange so he called it in."

"Let's go."

"Maybe I should take this one myself."

"Maybe not. Let's go." Ben strode toward the cruiser, fear a hard knot in his chest. Chloe was somewhere nearby. He felt that as surely as he felt that she was in danger. They had to find her. Soon.

They took the cruiser, racing the half mile to a long tree-lined driveway and a two-story home that looked out over the lake. The man who met them seemed shaken as he led them down to the water. There was no dock, just thick weed-choked grass and slick rocks. A boat bobbed in the water, white lilies on its waterlogged bottom, a purse lying on its side, the contents spilling out.

"When did you first notice this?" Jake spoke as he moved toward the boat.

"Just a few minutes ago. I saw it when I let the dog out. It wasn't here when I got home an hour ago."

"And did you see anyone out here? Hear anything?"

"Nothing. It's just been a regular day." The man ran a hand over sparse hair. "I might not have thought that much about the boat, but the flowers and purse worried me."

"They worry me, too. I'm glad you called." Jake pulled on gloves, grabbed the bow of the boat and dragged it up over the rocks and onto shore. "There's a paper here. Looks like a note." He picked it up, holding it gingerly, his face hardening as he read. "We've got a problem."

"We already had one."

"It's just gotten worse." He gestured Ben over, holding the note out for him to see. The words were smudged but easy to read.

"A suicide note."

"*Chloe's* suicide note."

"Written by someone else." Ben shoved the boat back toward the water.

"We need to get other transportation. That boat could contain evidence."

"We don't have time to find another boat." Ben gritted his teeth and stared his friend down. He was going out on the lake, with or without Jake. With or without his approval.

Finally, Jake nodded. "Let's go."

A few minutes of swimming with the cinder block in her arm convinced Chloe that she'd be better off expending her energy in another way. First she tried feeling for the ends of the rope, hoping she might be able to untie it, but each time she stopped paddling with her free arm, she dipped under the water.

"That's not going to work, Chloe. Come up with something else." She spoke out loud, the words sputtering and gasping into air and water, her teeth chattering. "Lord, if there's some way out of this, I hope you'll show me quickly because I don't know how much longer I can do this."

But there didn't seem to be a way out, just one painful stroke after another toward a way-too-distant shore. Chloe's head throbbed with each movement, her body telling her to quit while her mind screamed for her to keep going. She slipped under the water, choking and gagging as she surfaced again, the rope wrapping around her wrist and sliding over her skin.

Sliding over her skin.

The thought worked its way past her pain and fatigue, and she reached down, tried to shove the rope past her jeans. It moved. Not much, but enough to give her hope. One handed wasn't going to work though. She'd have to let go of the cinder block. Use both hands to shove the rope down. Once she did that, she'd be pulled back down toward the bottom of the lake. If she failed, she didn't know if she'd be able to fight her way back up again.

Unfortunately, her choices were limited and so was her time.

"Lord, I trust You. Whatever happens, I know You're with me." With that, she let go of the cement block, grabbed the rope that was wrapped around her legs and started to push it down as she sank deeper into the water. The rope pulled tight, so tight she couldn't get her fingers between it and her legs. Panic speared through her, but she forced it back, trying again, feeling fingernails bend and skin tear as she finally made room between rope and denim. Pull. Tug. Push. Yank. Muscles quivering. Head pounding. Fear like she'd only ever known once before. The nightmare, but different. Not fire and hot metal. Water and burning lungs. Blackness outside and inside. Alone.

But not alone.

God had not abandoned her. Would not abandon her.

The rope moved, inching down toward her ankles, scraping past her jeans. She yanked the fabric up with one hand, shoving the rope down, feeling it give. Then she was free, floating up toward the surface, her lungs ready to explode, the desperate need for oxygen making her want to gasp and breathe and hope for the best.

She broke the surface of the lake, coughing and gasping, her body trembling with fatigue and with cold. She had to swim, but her movements were clumsy, her efforts weak.

She wasn't going to give up, though. She wasn't going to quit. She was going to get out of the lake and she was going to make sure Jordyn was arrested for her crimes.

Her energy and attention were focused on the goal—a distant light that she was sure must be home. What she wasn't sure about was whether or not she was actually getting any closer to it.

Suddenly the light disappeared, a dark shape appearing in front of Chloe. For a moment, her muddled thoughts conjured a monster rising up from the depth of the lake. Then the truth of what she was seeing registered—a boat.

Jordyn. She was sure it was the same boat. Sure that Jordyn would lean over the edge, raise the oar, slam it down into the water. Or worse. Take out the gun and shoot her.

She turned, trying to swim away, her arms flailing, her muscles giving out. She sank. Surfaced. Sank again.

"Chloe!" The shout carried over the splash and gasp of her frantic attempt to escape.

An arm hooked around her waist and she was pulled back against a hard chest. "Stop struggling, Chloe. I've got you."

Ben.

His voice rumbled in her ear, his body warming her, but doing nothing to ease the shivers that racked her body.

"Are you okay?"

She nodded, but her teeth were chattering too hard to get the words out.

"Here she comes, Jake."

Before Chloe knew what was happening, she was out of Ben's arms and in a boat, a leather jacket draped around her shoulders, Jake Reed flashing a light in her face. "You hurt anywhere?"

"My head." The words rasped out as Ben pulled himself into the boat. "Jordyn hit me with something. Maybe her gun."

"Jordyn Winslow? That's one of the names you gave me earlier."

"Yes, Adam's receptionist." She was still shivering, her muscles so tight with cold she wasn't sure she'd ever be warm again.

Ben pulled her toward him, rubbed her arms briskly,

the heat he generated speeding through her body. "Better?"

"Yes." But not because she was warmer. Because he was there, warm, solid, steady.

He ran a hand over the back of her head, probing the tender flesh there. "You're bleeding. Can you call for an ambulance, Jake?"

"There's no—"

"There's no sense arguing. You're going to the hospital."

"I'm not much for hospitals. My experiences there haven't been pleasant."

"Maybe not in the past, but this time will be different. This time I'll be with you." Ben's words were a warm caress against her ear and Chloe relaxed back into his arms, allowing herself to believe what she hadn't in a very long time—that she was safe and that everything was going to be all right.

Twenty-Six

"Fifteen stitches does not make me an invalid, Opal." Chloe smiled as she spoke, accepting the bowl of chicken noodle soup Opal handed her.

"Fifteen stitches *and* a concussion. The doctor said you should take it easy."

"And I have been."

"How does starting back up in computer forensics constitute resting?"

"I haven't done any work. I've just been contacting old clients and letting them know I will be."

"Yes, well, I still have to decide if I forgive you for that. You were doing so well at Blooming Baskets."

Chloe would have laughed if she wasn't sure it would send pain shooting through her head. "Opal, I have as much artistic vision as a rock and you know it."

"Okay, so flowers weren't the perfect fit for you."

"But computers are."

"Apparently so. And you know that I'm happy if you are. If computers are what you're meant to do, far be it from me to try to keep you from them." Opal leaned forward and kissed her cheek. "Now, I've really got to get home. Checkers is still angry about not being fed on time Saturday night."

"Maybe if you explained that I was fighting for my life and kind of distracted, he'll forgive me."

"Doubtful. Call me if you need something."

"I will." Chloe started to rise, but froze when Opal sent a searing look in her direction.

"Do not get up from there. At all."

Before Chloe could respond, a soft knock sounded on the door. "Good. Now I really can leave." Opal hurried to the door and pulled it open. "You're late."

"Two minutes. And I had good reason." Ben stepped into the room, a white paper bag in his hand. "Apple pie and ice cream from Becky's."

"I suppose that's acceptable. I'll be back in an hour or so. Thanks for taking over for me."

"Opal, please tell me you didn't ask Ben to come babysit me."

"I did not ask him to babysit you. I asked him to lend a hand. I'll see you in a bit." She walked out the door before Chloe could tell her exactly what she thought of her meddling ways.

"Feeling better?" Ben sat on the couch beside her, his gaze taking in everything about her appearance.

Unfortunately, that included scraggly hair, pale skin, swollen hands and, of course, plenty of stitches.

"Now that Jordyn is in custody, I feel better than I have in almost a year. I still can't believe she went home and was acting like nothing happened. I was sure she'd take off and go into hiding."

"From what Jake says, she'd convinced herself that no one would suspect her. In her mind, she'd committed the perfect crime."

"Except I didn't die."

"Thank the Lord for that." Ben ran a hand over his jaw, his eyes shadowed. "I was sure we'd lost you when I saw that suicide note."

"I guess I'm tougher than you think."

"I've always thought you were tough. I was just afraid whoever had you was tougher."

"Jordyn did pack a pretty mean punch." Chloe fingered the bandage at the back of her head. "She really was crazy, Ben. I found e-mails in Adam's laptop—"

"What were you doing working when you're supposed to be resting?"

"I just took a quick peek."

"How long of a quick peek?"

"A couple of hours."

"That's what I thought." Ben chuckled, his hand resting on her shoulder, his finger warm against her neck. "So, what did you find?"

"That Jordyn thought she and Adam were going to be together forever. She's been in love with him for years."

"Was she the other woman?"

"I think so. From what I gathered, they went out a few times years ago. Then seemed to reconnect for a while, during the months before Adam died. She proclaimed her love for him over and over again in her e-mails."

"And scared him away?"

"Knowing Adam, yes." She shrugged. "The most recent e-mails, the ones she sent right before he died, were mostly hateful rantings. She threatened me a few times. Told him that if he got back together with me, we'd both be sorry."

"Did you show Jake?"

"Yeah, he's already come by for the e-mails and taken the laptop in as evidence. He mentioned something that surprised me."

"What's that?"

"He thinks there might be a connection between Jordyn and Matthew Jackson. I was freelancing for James when I worked on The Strangers case. There's a good possibility Jordyn somehow made contact with one of the group's members, maybe hoping she'd find someone who wanted to get me out of the way. There's no proof that's what happened, but it makes sense."

"If he's right that might have been enough to send her over the edge. If she thought she'd get rid of you, but it backfired and Adam was killed—"

"She would have gone a little crazy. Guilt can be a terrible thing."

"I'm not sure she was capable of guilt, but she did corner the market on hate."

"I wish…" Chloe's voice trailed off and she shook her head, not sure what she wished, what she wanted.

"That you could have known?"

"Yes, but even that wouldn't have saved Adam."

Ben pulled her into his arms, his hands smoothing down her back and resting at her waist. "No, it wouldn't have, but you can't spend your life thinking about that, Chloe."

"I know." She blinked hard, trying to force back tears. They refused to be stopped and slid down her cheeks, dripping onto Ben's shirt.

He brushed away the moisture, his palm warm against her skin. "Are you crying for Adam?"

"He never even had a chance."

"But you do. A chance at life. At friendship. At love. Adam wouldn't want you to pass that up."

At love?

Chloe looked up into his eyes, felt herself pulled in again. Into his confidence. His strength. Into all the things she'd wanted for so long, but was sure she'd never have.

"You're right. He wouldn't. And I don't want to pass those things up, either."

His lips curved, the slow, easy smile tugging at Chloe's heart. "That makes two of us."

He leaned forward, kissing her with passion and with promise, chasing the nightmare away and replacing it with a dream of the future spent with a man who shared her faith, her goals, her heart. A man put into her life by God. A gift that Chloe would always be thankful for.

Epilogue

The dark night pressed in around her, the sound of laughter and music a backdrop to the wild beating of her heart. Chloe shoved a box of floral decorations out of the way and reached for her suitcase and the small bag of clothes sitting beside it, the heady aroma of hyacinth drifting on the air and filling her with longing and with joy. This was it, then. A new beginning. A new dream. A new life.

She was ready for it.

"Need a hand?" The words were warm and filled with humor, the dark figure that stepped from the shadows stealing her breath.

"Maybe more than one. I thought I'd put the suitcase into your car, but Tiffany and Opal helped me pack and I'm not sure I can handle it while I'm wearing heels."

"Then let me handle it for you." Ben's arms slipped around her waist, pulling her backward. She turned, staring up into his face, wanting to memorize this moment, the way she felt standing in his arms.

He smiled, caressing her shoulder, his fingers gliding over her skin, trailing heat with every touch. "Have I told you how beautiful you look today?"

"A hundred times."

"Then this will be a hundred and one. You're beautiful, Chloe. So beautiful you take my breath away." He trailed kisses up her neck, his hand cupping the back of her head, his body warm against hers.

"I was just thinking the same about you."

"That I'm beautiful?" His laughter rumbled near her ear.

"That you take my breath away." Chloe sank into his embrace, her love for Ben strong and sure and undeniable. "And that if we keep this up we may not make our flight."

"I'm not sure that would be such a bad thing."

"Me, neither." She tilted her head as his lips caressed the sensitive flesh beneath her jaw.

"So maybe we should go to my place and forget the airport." His eyes gleamed in the moonlight, dark and filled with promise.

"There you are." Opal bustled across the parking lot, salt and pepper curls bouncing with each step. "I thought you were changing into your traveling suit and coming right back to the reception."

"I got sidetracked."

"So I see, but if you two plan on making that flight to Thailand, you'd better get moving."

Ben met Chloe's gaze, the joy, the hope that she felt reflected in his eyes. "I'll get the suitcase into the car."

"I'll get changed."

"And I'll have everybody ready and waiting to say goodbye and throw rose petals. Five minutes. And don't make me come looking for you again."

Chloe smiled, following Opal back into the church

and closing herself into Ben's office, her *husband's* office. She'd lived through so much heartache, so many tears, but those were in the past. Today was for new beginnings, fresh starts. Laughter. Joy. Peace.

A soft knock sounded at the door, and Chloe opened it, her heart skipping a beat as she caught sight of Ben. He'd changed into jeans and a polo shirt, his sandy hair falling over his forehead, his eyes gleaming brilliant blue. "Ready?"

"Absolutely."

"Then let's get started on the rest of our lives." He wrapped an arm around her waist, led her into the reception hall. His foster parents were there, standing beside the door with a dozen or more of his foster siblings. His sister Raven and her husband, Shane, were there, too. Opal. Sam. Tiffany and Jake. Hawke and Miranda.

So many people, so much happiness.

Chloe's heart welled with it, her eyes filling as white rose petals fell like gentle spring rain, washing over her, washing through her as Ben swept her into his arms and carried her into the future.

* * * * *

Dear Reader,

Faith isn't always easy. Often we wonder how things can be going so badly when we're trying so hard to trust God, serve Him and seek His will. The answer is as simple as it is complicated. God never promised that our lives would be free of pain and troubles. He only promised that whatever we're going through, He'll be with us through it. That's a lesson Chloe Davidson must learn as she begins a new life in Lakeview, Virginia, and faces some of the most difficult times of her life.

I hope you enjoy reading her story, and I pray that whatever troubles you may be going through, you'll have peace that can only come from the One who truly understands.

I love to hear from readers. You can contact me at Shirlee@shirleemccoy.com, or 1121 Annapolis Road, PMB 244, Odenton, Maryland, 21113-1633.

Blessings,

Shirlee McCoy

Questions for Discussion

1. Chloe leaves her old life in Washington, D.C., to begin a new one in Lakeview. Why? What is she running from? Have you ever run from an uncomfortable situation?

2. As she settles into a new routine, Chloe can't help but be drawn into the lives of the people who live in Lakeview. How does she feel about belonging to a new community?

3. Chloe has a lot of fears that stem from the night her ex-fiancé, Adam, died. She seems to feel that her terror makes her weak. Do you think that is true? What are her strengths and weaknesses?

4. Ben is drawn to Chloe immediately. How does his view of her differ from Chloe's view of herself? How does his confidence in Chloe help her regain confidence in herself?

5. Ben is a widower who loved his late wife. When he meets Chloe, he's not looking for a relationship. What is it about Chloe that makes him change his mind?

6. Chloe and Ben are attracted to each other immediately, but that isn't what draws them closer. What makes them a good match? In what way does this reflect God's plan for every relationship?

7. Struggles are part of life. During those struggles we can grow closer to God, or further away from

Him. What happened to Chloe after the accident? What happened to Ben after his wife died?

8. Chloe makes an effort to get to know some of the townspeople by attending the church's quilting group. Have you ever taken that first step and been happy with the result? Unhappy? Why?

9. God has a plan for each of our lives. Sometimes that plan is easy to see. Sometimes it's not. How does Chloe find the strength to trust in God's plan when she doesn't understand it?

10. What struggles are you going through? How can you lean more fully on God's grace as you face these trials?

celebrating
15
YEARS

Love Inspired

CLASSICS

Four sweet, heartfelt stories from fan-favorite
Love Inspired® Books authors!

The McKaslin clan returns with love and hope in

SWEET BLESSINGS and BLESSED VOWS

by Jillian Hart

And discover
another wonderful, heartfelt story of reconnection in

**A SEASON FOR GRACE
and THE HEART OF GRACE**

by Linda Goodnight

Get two happily-ever-afters for the price of one!

Available in July 2012 wherever books are sold.

www.LoveInspiredBooks.com

LIC65155

REQUEST YOUR FREE BOOKS!

2 FREE INSPIRATIONAL NOVELS
PLUS 2
FREE
MYSTERY GIFTS

YES! Please send me 2 FREE Love Inspired® novels and my 2 FREE mystery gifts (gifts are worth about $10). After receiving them, if I don't wish to receive any more books, I can return the shipping statement marked "cancel." If I don't cancel, I will receive 6 brand-new novels every month and be billed just $4.49 per book in the U.S. or $4.99 per book in Canada. That's a saving of at least 22% off the cover price. It's quite a bargain! Shipping and handling is just 50¢ per book in the U.S. and 75¢ per book in Canada.* I understand that accepting the 2 free books and gifts places me under no obligation to buy anything. I can always return a shipment and cancel at any time. Even if I never buy another book, the two free books and gifts are mine to keep forever.

105/305 IDN FEGR

Name	(PLEASE PRINT)	

Address		Apt. #

City	State/Prov.	Zip/Postal Code

Signature (if under 18, a parent or guardian must sign)

Mail to the **Reader Service:**
IN U.S.A.: P.O. Box 1867, Buffalo, NY 14240-1867
IN CANADA: P.O. Box 609, Fort Erie, Ontario L2A 5X3

Not valid for current subscribers to Love Inspired books.

**Are you a subscriber to Love Inspired books
and want to receive the larger-print edition?
Call 1-800-873-8635 or visit www.ReaderService.com.**

* Terms and prices subject to change without notice. Prices do not include applicable taxes. Sales tax applicable in N.Y. Canadian residents will be charged applicable taxes. Offer not valid in Quebec. This offer is limited to one order per household. All orders subject to credit approval. Credit or debit balances in a customer's account(s) may be offset by any other outstanding balance owed by or to the customer. Please allow 4 to 6 weeks for delivery. Offer available while quantities last.

Your Privacy—The Reader Service is committed to protecting your privacy. Our Privacy Policy is available online at www.ReaderService.com or upon request from the Reader Service.

We make a portion of our mailing list available to reputable third parties that offer products we believe may interest you. If you prefer that we not exchange your name with third parties, or if you wish to clarify or modify your communication preferences, please visit us at www.ReaderService.com/consumerschoice or write to us at Reader Service Preference Service, P.O. Box 9062, Buffalo, NY 14269. Include your complete name and address.

For a sneak peek at Valerie Hansen's
heart-stopping inspirational romantic suspense
THREAT OF DARKNESS, read on!

If Samantha Rochard hadn't already been so keyed up that she could barely think straight, she might have shrieked when she saw the cop's face. Her jaw did drop and she was pretty sure her gasp was audible. His light brown hair and eyes and his broad shoulders were all too familiar. It couldn't be him, of course. It simply couldn't be. She hadn't had one of these déjà vu moments for months. Maybe years.

Her pulse leaped as reality replaced imagination. She couldn't catch her breath. This was not another bad dream. John Waltham, the man who'd broken her heart so badly she'd wondered if she'd ever recover, was standing right in front of her, big as life.

Before she could decide how to greet him, he set the mood of their reunion. His "What did you think you were *doing?*" was delivered with such force it was practically a growl.

That attitude stiffened her spine and made it easy to answer, "My job."

"You're a nurse, not a cop."

"Oh, so I'm supposed to just stand there while you and your buddies waltz in here and start shooting?"

"If necessary, yes."

"Don't be silly. I knew Bobby Joe wasn't going to hurt me," she insisted, wishing she fully believed her own assertion. When an addict was under the influence, there was no way to predict what he or she might do.

Handling the pistol expertly, John unloaded it and passed

it to one of his fellow officers to bag as evidence before turning back to Samantha.

She noticed that his expression had softened some, but it was too little too late. "What are you doing back in town?" She eyed him from head to toe. "And why are you dressed like a member of our police force?"

"Because that's what I am. I've come home," he said flatly.

Samantha couldn't believe her ears. After all he'd put her through, all the tears she'd shed after he'd left her high and dry, he had the unmitigated gall to return and go back to work as if nothing had changed. How *dare* he!

Pick up THREAT OF DARKNESS
for the rest of Samantha and John's exciting, suspenseful
love story, available in June 2012, only from
Love Inspired® Suspense.

Love Inspired
SUSPENSE
RIVETING INSPIRATIONAL ROMANCE

FITZGERALD BAY

Law-enforcement siblings fight for justice and family.

Follow the men and women of Fitzgerald Bay as they unravel the mystery of their small town and find love in the process, with:

THE LAWMAN'S LEGACY by Shirlee McCoy
January 2012

THE ROOKIE'S ASSIGNMENT by Valerie Hansen
February 2012

THE DETECTIVE'S SECRET DAUGHTER
by Rachelle McCalla
March 2012

THE WIDOW'S PROTECTOR by Stephanie Newton
April 2012

THE BLACK SHEEP'S REDEMPTION by Lynette Eason
May 2012

THE DEPUTY'S DUTY by Terri Reed
June 2012

*Available wherever
books are sold.*

www.LoveInspiredBooks.com

LISCONT12